INTERNATION
PG LENG

A Bounty of Bone

From the U.S:

"A jaw-dropping suspense thriller unlike anything you've ever read . . .Unputdownable . . . in the tradition of Conrad's *Heart of Darkness*, author PG Lengsfelder creates a journey that takes [his heroine] into truly dangerous geographic, physical, and psychological territory. . . Lengsfelder walks the blurry line between magic and reality in a number of hair-raising situations that may keep readers up long past their bedtime."

— *BestThrillers.com*

))))

From the U.K:

". . . So begins a whirlwind . . . cross-African adventure to uncover the truth about [a young woman's] whereabouts. . . A great mix of thriller, magic, superstition, and adventure with the beautiful backdrop of Africa. Eunis is a tenacious character who doesn't give up, even when told to by everyone around her. There is a chorus of fantastic, colourful characters. A real page-turner of a book."

— *LoveReading.co.uk*

))))

From India:

"There are moments when reading a book makes you feel like you're right there with the characters . . . *A BOUNTY OF BONE* . . . is one of one of those. . . a story of fate, of faith, and of friendship, and how all of these things make us who we are, not how we look. . . It runs the gamut of emotions; tender and terrifying, heart-breaking, and hopeful. . . [with] important themes, including acceptance, loss, and loneliness. PG Lengsfelder delivers a vivid, descriptive, story with unforgettable characters . . . [A] heart-wrenching, fast-paced thriller . . . with an ending totally satisfying and shocking. . . A beautiful book that can be finished in a short amount of time and manages to tap into every emotion. . . very different from your normal read.

— *The BookishElf.com*

OTHER BOOKS BY PG LENGSFELDER

FICTION

Beautiful to the Bone

(The Eunis Trilogy Book One)

Our Song, Memento Mori

NONFICTION

Filthy Rich and Other Non-Profit Fantasies (co-author)

Non-Profit Piggy Goes to Market

A Bounty Of Bone

The Eunis Trilogy – Book Two

A novel inspired by real events

PG LENGSFELDER

Woodsmoke Publishing
Boulder, Colorado

Woodsmoke Publishing
Colorado, United States

www.WoodsmokePublishing.com

Cover design by BookDesigners.com

A Bounty of Bone/ PG Lengsfelder. – 1st edition
ISBN 978-0-9972513-5-7 (Paperback edition)
ISBN 978-0-9972513-6-4 (eBook edition)

For Brooke, Yuri, and Lakota,
a beautiful soul and my eternal sidekick.

Table of Contents

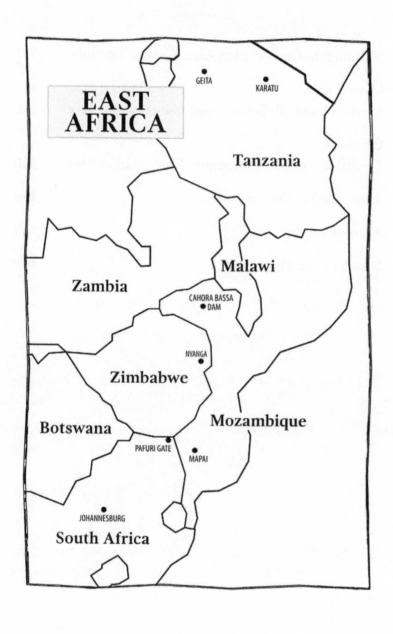

Chapter 1

Bemidji, Minnesota - New York City - Great Falls, Montana

Kingdom Lake had grown cool, cooler than even I could handle. The walleye and Green Heron didn't seem to mind, but the afternoon wind on my shoulder reminded me, winter soon. *Another season. Where you gonna swim now?*

I'd slipped out of the lake and dried off, the Jack Pines beginning to sway. I'd been thinking about Momma and me and the farmhouse, how—even after I'd finished the rehab of the house—the three of us were incompatible. And how it was almost Halloween and I'd toughed out the masquerade for another year, as if it brought me safety. Safety in sour familiarity.

Loved the house, of course, and my wetlands. But Momma—*holy crap*—she stung at everything I did like a wasp; she called *me* ungrateful, useless, and a serpent. Every day alone gnawed on my heart, betraying something.

As the temperature dropped over the lake and woods, the moisture in me, around me—around everything—started firing my body frequencies. When it came in waves like this, as it had since I was a child, I expected rain or wind or *something*.

But the blue sky still held enough saffron to light the lake in a false warm glow. So, I waited. Then, as if by decree, purple clouds gathered in the west, coming quickly and soon all around and over me. A Presence. The clouds twisted, overrun by fast moving roots.

The orange fingers of the western sun spread across the sky, until I was alone, the sky sealed in exquisite flame. And I thought, *how can I ever leave Minnesota?*

A howl of air sucked at the cloud cover; flames parting, a theatre curtain or portal opening, introducing a perfect circle allowing the hidden blue sky an eye on me, while all else was a dome of Indian Paintbrush. A hole in the sky inviting me to leave.

)))

"A Cavum or Fallstreak Hole." My old high school friend Gordon Mingle, a meteorologist, trying to make scientific sense of my phone call and what I'd seen. "Very rare yet glimpsed all over the world."

I cradled the phone like an anchor. "It was if . . ."

"What?"

"As if it was holding me, telling me . . . I don't know what."

"Yes, you do. Your intuition again," Gordon said. "Follow it."

"No, it's just science."

"Sure, both things can be true," he said. "Tiny water droplets *colder* than freezing but they haven't yet frozen. It's like they're waiting for a reason to freeze and then something—maybe an airplane or a large flock of birds or some other force—wanders through and turns the droplets to ice crystals. And when they grow and fall, they open a hole in the sky."

"That's what I saw?"

"And the hole expands as the neighboring droplets freeze. You are very lucky. And this is not your first time with such phenomena. I wonder if you'd join me in New York?"

)))

Even with Gordon running interference for me, his TV channel boss, a guy named Charlie Grissom, probably wasn't prepared to meet a disfigured thirty-nine-year-old albino woman, a hideous brown birthmark staining my left cheek from eye to chin. Momma's "Mark of the devil."

Grissom sat back, more skepticism than fear. "Gordon tells me you have an aptitude for weather and that he'd like you on his team." Hundreds of Lucite-embedded butterflies studded Grissom's wall.

Apparently, Gordon had mentioned nothing about my—how-shall-we-say—divination approach to weather forecasting: I smell rain before a cloud appears. I hear thunder before the sky strikes white. I feel wind before it cossets a tree. Where and why this instinct resides in me, I don't know. When it will imbue me is still a riddle.

I tugged at my hair. Gordon smiled and nodded at me. *Play along.* "Well," I said, "I've always had a feel for weather, even as a child." Gordon frowned. *Don't go there.*

I regrouped. "You see my background is as a researcher. . ."

"Genetics." Grissom with a bitter taste in his mouth.

"Yes. DNA and cellular research, but I also understand weather patterns; they're not so different." *They're not at all the same.*

"She's very good." Gordon tossed his head, somehow younger, making it casual and inevitable, but still without merit.

Grissom scrunched his face. "But Eunis, you're not a meteorologist."

"No, but I . . . detect weather patterns." *Under the right circumstances, whatever they might be.*

Grissom started to say something but stopped, tapped his desk, and began to stand up, end of interview.

Gordon saw it slipping away. "Charlie, let me try her for a month. You won't be disappointed. You know I need help."

Grissom shook his head. "I just don't see . . ."

"I'll pay her out of my own salary," said Gordon.

I looked at Gordon like he was crazy. "No."

Charlie Grissom exhaled. "If I didn't know you, Gordon Mingle, I'd say . . ."

"What?" Gordon shared a sideways smile with Grissom.

"Nothing, never mind." Grissom waved us both off.

A step out of the office, Gordon turned to me. "See."

"You're an optimist," I said, "and that's what worries me."

"You'll make your mark on the battlefield," Gordon said.

"It's also where I'll most likely die."

Nevertheless, I was hired at Weather One TV.

☽☽☽

In June 1805, Lewis and Clark portaged around the mammoth waterfalls of Great Falls, Montana. The ordeal took them three weeks and eighteen harrowing miles. It almost killed Meriwether Lewis. Seems crazy taking on an odyssey like that.

More than 100 years later, in 1912, the falls were dammed— eighty-seven feet high.

When I arrived with the Weather One TV crew in early January, those colossal falls towered above us and spread out like the top half of a diamond, glutted left and right with icy fingers, like those of a skeleton, trying to break over it. The rocks below were blue-white ice-capped islands around which small pools of frigid water crept or stalled. A mass of stone and ice.

Sheila, our bulldog on-air celebrity, insisted that we shoot below the center of the spill, which her producer Rick Kaplan pointed out meant we had to traverse several hundred or more yards of massive rock and glacial footing *without* metal-clawed boots. I put the van keys in my pocket and zipped them up, already so out of my element; me on a TV crew.

The frozen chutes of Great Falls dwarfed Sheila. The combative wind buried most sound, but Kaplan yelled at Sheila anyway. "We can frame you and the falls better from back there." Len the cameraman gave a small twitch of resignation; he'd been through this before. *Sheila gets what she wants.* Sheila just waved and continued climbing the ice outcroppings.

Len watched them both climb and when Kaplan looked back, Len ran his fingers up and down his upper chest. "Don't forget to switch on her mike."

Kaplan couldn't hear him. He probably said *what*, but all we saw was his mouth move and his questioning expression. Before Kaplan could grab it, his Mets cap flew off and tumbled through the air above the ice floes and dark water then disappeared into it.

"You'd better go down there," Len said to me. "It's fucking freezing and with this wind, who knows. We can't afford a bunch of botched standups. You understand what I'm sayin'?" *Hurricane Sheila might be worse than the cold.*

"Got it." I'd checked: the temperature hovered around zero, *without* the wind chill. *Thank you, Minnesota, for toughening me up.*

I climbed down the embankment and shuffled across a small bridge of ice that first Sheila then Kaplan had traversed as they made their way up the tables of rock and ice to the base of the dam. Three football fields across and they were about a third of the way. As I moved through a large cavern of ice, Kaplan had his back to me waving at Sheila to do precisely that, *turn on your mike*. She raised a hand in acknowledgement, slipped off a glove and reached behind her and under her parka to flip on the wireless.

Then in my ears, as strong as the wind, and around my heart: frequencies shifted. Pressure built on my chest. Electrons bounced. *Oh shit, what am I supposed to tell them now?* I stepped into the clear and yelled at Kaplan. "We've got to get out of here!"

He didn't hear me, and I thought to shut up; I needed this job. He started moving back toward me, fighting the wind, not because of my admonition, but because Sheila was taking her place below the dam, signaling Kaplan to scoot out of the shot and for Len to prepare to roll camera.

I had to do something. "Get her out of there!" I screamed.

Kaplan couldn't hear, so I closed in on him, falling once and cracking my knee on protruding rock. That made him move faster. "You okay?" He lifted me up.

"We've got to get out of here. She's gotta come down now."

"Hey," he said smiling, "you don't know Sheila. She'll—"

"Now!" And I started climbing to her. *Geez, what the hell am I doing?*

"Are you nuts?" he yelled.

I yelled back, "Temperature's changing."

"A little colder isn't gonna change—"

"This ain't New Haven," I said. But I doubted he could hear me anymore, the wind ratcheting twofold.

He tried reaching for me, then tagged raggedly behind as I slipped and fell toward her. He did the same, until she noticed, waving me away. I could barely make out her words against the warming gale. But she was clearly ticked off. "Get out of here," she hollered. Bulldog turned pit bull.

I got within five yards of her and motioned for her to come down. That's when Kaplan caught up with me and grabbed my parka. "You're gonna get fired for this."

"Tell her to come down, *now!*" I shouted.

That's when the first loud crack swept across the 300-yard mouth of the falls. "It's warming. It's warming *fast.*"

He'd heard the crack. Sheila looked over her shoulder. He tried to reason with me. "We'll get the shot and then—"

I shoved him, probably a little too hard because he fell backward onto a slab of ice and started sliding away from us. Just as well. I moved within a couple yards of her. "Come on, take my hand."

"Who the fuck—?" She readied to bite.

The second crack ripped through the canyon—a monstrous whip shaking the canyon and beyond. Shelia turned almost as pale as I. I brushed sweat off my cheek. It was already *above* freezing. All around us the wind howled, and hot like an immense hair drier had been flipped on upstream. Sheets of steam began twisting off the cornices.

"Can we get one shot before—?" she asked.

I grabbed her hand. "We're gonna slide if we have to, to get down. You understand?" The ground began to rumble. She nodded.

The icy tentacles that had held the water frozen above the dam were now spreading, and the rocks around us began appearing. The small icy pools no longer listless but rising, streaming forward and past us to the awakening Missouri.

A mass of ice cleaved off the base of the dam and sliced toward us. I wrapped my arms around Sheila and pushed her toward shore—we slid tearing our faces on ice and rock, first one plateau then another (a drop of six-eight feet crushing my right side), until we landed at Kaplan's boots. "Shit."

"Jesus!" Sheila rubbed her back, tried to stand. "Damn it!"

"We gotta go," I said reaching for Sheila.

"Just wait a goddamn minute, okay. Give me a chance."

"I'm sorry." I grabbed her arm, I lifted her up.

"Jesus, fuck, lady."

"Go, please!" I yelled. "Please!" The Missouri now turbulent.

She looked at me and saw that I was freaked. She glowered. She jumped to a boulder, hit her head, and slid back down. A swath of skin scraped away from the right side of her face. Crimson trickled to her eye. I pushed her from behind.

"Sonovabitch." She slapped at my hand.

"I'm so sorry, I'm so sorry," I said. "Don't stop."

I lunged behind her, up the embankment to Len's camera perch. Chunks of remaining glacier thundered down the cascades to the pool, disappearing beneath the surface like drunken trucks, only to reemerge several yards downstream, dangerous to anything or anyone in their path; then continued their journey bobbing away, along the swiftly rising Missouri. I was shit sure out of my new job.

))))

"Let's see." Sheila held an ice pack against her grated cheek and forehead. She took coffee from Kaplan. She wouldn't look at me. We gathered around the small monitor in Len's room. At first, Len had been so cold and stunned by the first boom he'd done nothing. But being a pro and having already framed the shot, he'd begun to roll camera about the time I'd reached Sheila. He had pulled back, framing wide to see the hot wind ripping slabs of ice off the falls' cornice, as the heat severed the crust along a jagged fracture line, and as we stumbled and slid down the slope narrowly ahead of the supernatural torrent.

"Holy shit," said Sheila, "this footage is fucking awesome!"

Kaplan slapped Len on the back. "I buy dinner tonight."

Len smiled. "Already per diem. You think Charlie will be pleased?"

Kaplan hugged Len. "Ya think! Geez, you gotta upload this to the station immediately."

Then the three of them looked at me.

"What?" I asked, ready for my pink slip.

Sheila pulled the ice pack from her cheek, put down the coffee and felt the ridges along her face. "What happened out there?" she said. "I've been doing this a long time and I've never seen anything like it. Beginner's luck?"

I shrugged. "Warm Chinook wind."

"No shit," she said. "But no warning, nothing in the weather models? And so spontaneously?"

Kaplan slid open the door to the small balcony and retrieved the thermometer he'd placed there and held it in his palm. "It's fifty-freakin'-degrees; an enormous swing. In the opposite direction. In minutes. Historical."

"So?" Sheila eyed me, as much anticipation as demand. "How'd you know?"

"I didn't. I wouldn't have let any of us go out there if I had," I said.

Kaplan closed the balcony door. "But you knew instantly that the wind was heating up—even before any of us felt it."

"Not exactly." They weren't buying it. "Okay." I stepped over to Len's bed and knelt by his open laptop.

"Hey!" Len tried to intercept me as his screen came awake. A naked man and woman in eager exploration flashed by. Len looked at me, eyes pleading. When I made no mention to the others, he thanked me with downcast eyes.

I hesitated above his keyboard. I typed in the GFS (Global Forecast System): the purple, pink, green and yellow isobars replacing the porn. "Here," I said. Len stepped away, relieved. Sheila took front row and Kaplan perched over her.

"Jet streams," she said staring at the screen, "so what? I know what weather forecasts look like."

Why did I think this job would be different? I couldn't tell them the truth, so I told them what they *could* believe. "You remember that I was a geneticist."

"Okay," she said. *So what?*

"So just like certain DNA patterns indicate genetic switches, these isobars tell you things to expect, like when they get closer together you can expect greater winds, colder temperatures. Or as they spread out, warmer temperatures."

"Like hell I need *you* of all people to tell me how to read weather patterns," Sheila said.

Please don't sack me. "But the bars . . ."

"Yeah?" She still couldn't see the connection.

Appeal to her scientific mind. "Well, I have a scientific instinct with these models. Call it a kind of . . ." I bent the words carefully, still addicted to pleasing but scooching closer to the truth. ". . . intuition. They resonate with me."

"Resonate?"

Kaplan cleared his throat; I was, once again, approaching Sheila's edge.

"That's the only way I can explain it," I said. "I see things in the patterns that others don't."

Sheila closed one eye in resistance, but she thought about it. "Well," she said, "I guess; better than images of Jesus appearing in grapefruit, totemic shrouds materializing in toilet paper, and . . ." she said with a deep messianic voice, 'He thunders, He brings the wind from His storehouses and measures out the waters.'

The crew let free a nervous laugh.

"I'm still a scientist by training," I reassured her, also seeing that, at least on some things, we were in agreement. I really needed that job.

"So, you're saying that you saw the models and assimilating them you had some sense of how things could turn around?"

Kaplan wasn't a believer. "Turn more than fifty degrees *warmer*, in less than ten minutes, in Montana, in Arctic January?"

"Like I said, it's an instinct." I closed out the website and pulled down the laptop cover. "Based on scientific parameters."

Would they buy it?

"Shit," Len said in amazement.

At least I had one believer.

ⅅⅅⅅ

That evening after dinner, I stepped out onto the small balcony overlooking the Missouri. The Montana night clear, the sky big, bigger than any sky I'd seen before, even in Minnesota. After a few minutes I came in and sat on the edge of my bed. I still had a job. Len *did* upload the footage and it went viral. I watched Anderson Cooper narrate the sequence. In it I caught a glimpse of the ice cavern in which, without warning, my ears had filled with sound and the frequencies around my heart had been altered. For the first time since I was a child, I began to consider that my freakish and unaccountable intuition in highly charged spaces might, in fact, be a gift. Or as Roddy had put it, 'Your lucky charm.' Roddy was another story, a desire, for which I had no answers. But I'd quickly learned that to love—a human, a pet, a place—eventually brings sorrow.

Kaplan knocked on my door. "Deluxe, eh?" he said referring to our unassuming but ostensibly hygienic motel rooms by the river. "Mind if I come in?" Kaplan could have been a wrestler or a butterball turkey, but I wouldn't have expected him to be a Yale graduate. "Summa cum laude," Sheila had said. "Very smart. Maybe you'll learn something."

"Sure." I said to Kaplan. I sat on the end of the bed; he sat at the desk. I wondered how many people had sat on that same bedspread naked. I wondered how often the motel washed the bedspreads. I wondered what Roddy would say if he knew I was living in New York and hadn't called him.

Kaplan's eyes wandered across the river to the rambling railyard on the other side "That view's a real cowcatcher, don't ya think?" He slapped his thigh. As far from Yale as he could get.

Straight-faced, I replied, "Hard for me to keep track."

"Good," he bobbed. "I thought so. You follow my twisted mind." He pulled two pint bottles from his jacket. "I stopped by the liquor store. You looked like you could use a drink; calm you down. Gin or tequila?" He held one in each hand.

I pointed to the tequila.

"Good," he said, "I drink gin." He pulled the paper covering off two plastic bathroom cups and poured us each a drink.

"Why're we here?" I asked. Nobody bothered to tell me anything.

"You obviously noticed how windy it was when we landed." He passed me the cup and lifted his. "Cheers."

"Cheers." The first swallow reassuring.

He winced at the first sting of gin then went on. "Great Falls is one of the windiest cities in the country. Average daily wind speed of almost thirteen miles per hour."

"That was the story we came for?"

"Yup. But hey, we don't have to think about anything else till morning. Everything we shoot in Great Falls from now on will just be fodder after what you gave us."

"I didn't do anything." My involuntary attributes still best suited for a carnival sideshow.

"Maybe an Emmy," he said.

"Cowcatcher stuff."

"Yeah," Kaplan said. "Sure. Accept the kudos."

It had been over eight months since Roddy had held me, since I'd basically told him to go away, since anyone had touched me. I'd never understood much about my mother or her sinister narratives, and I'd never known who my father was. But one thing I was sure about—despite my mother's so-called allegiance to The Bible—she and my dad were both hedonists. Maybe he still is. Which is probably how I was conceived. And in that way, I am their spawn. Anyway, I was skin hungry.

I slept with Kaplan.

Chapter 2

New York City

The Weather One channel was the talk of meteorologists worldwide, and the public watched and re-watched the footage for a week. Luckily, Sheila was the star, Kaplan the subtext. I hardly visible and referred to off-handedly as an associate producer. That officially made me a member of the team.

The looks I got when I returned to the station covered the gamut: appreciative smiles and pats on the back to undisguised revulsion. While sitting in a ladies room stall, two women came in. "She's a fucking monster. You see her face?"

"And now she's a damn Associate Producer. She just friggin' got here. Dumb luck. I've been waiting almost a year."

"She's got no experience, no freakin' credentials. Who the fuck is she, anyway?"

"I'll tell you what she is, she's bad luck. You'll see."

Momma blamed my brother's death on me. She blamed my husband's death on me. She blamed my lover's death on me. She even blamed my sweet dog's death on me. "Just look at your face,"

*shed say. "What use are you ever gonna be to anyone? Except to
bring bad luck and death." A superstitious, backwoods woman,
my Momma. But over the years, premature deaths struck down so
many of the people I'd touched, even loved, that I wondered . . .*

☽ ☽ ☽

Those first few weeks returning to New York I'd moved back in
with Ruthie Bluestone and her extended family. They'd adopted
me on my first stay in New York a year earlier, and without
them and their generosity I doubt I would have survived the
city or the dire situations I got myself into. I loved each and
every one of them, and they loved me back.

They lived above Ruthie's Jamaican deli, fabric store and
psychic parlor: Ruthie's Roti. I imagined I could run all the
way home to Ruthie's, beating all the local subway stops, that's
how excited I was to have a real job. An Associate Producer,
in television! Given the nightly swimming which I'd resumed
in New York, maybe I could have beaten the subway. Instead,
I measured out my enthusiasm, occasionally looking up and
smiling at people in the metro. My gargoyle face drew the usual
response—eyes averted.

Out of the subway, a hunched street vendor offered scarves,
ties, and headbands off her folding table, her eyes inert.
Whatever her history, her breakdown weighed on my heart. I
stopped to say a word, maybe buy something. Only with effort
she looked up, desolate. Hard to hold those eyes. I went back
to perusing her wares. A young man, a goat patch goatee and
heavily tattooed, slipped between a line of parked cars and
behind her to the woman's cigar box, lifted the lid and grabbed
a bunch of bills from it.

"Hey!" I said.

He patted the shank on his hip. "Watcha gonna do about it, Beastie?"

Me? I was frozen.

He stuffed the bills in his jacket. He gave me the finger. He ran across the street. He laughed. "Fuck you, Beastie." A cab almost hit him; he banged its hood; he continued away from us.

The woman vendor, probably not much older than I when I looked closer, showed no emotion. "Your money, keep it closer next time, okay?" I tapped the box. I moved it toward her. Her face hung empty. "I'm sorry," I said. I moved on.

☽☽☽

Ruthie's storefront was taped up and down with butcher paper scribbled with the day's dishes. But the constant sign propped in her window supplied the best résumé of what Ruthie meant to the neighborhood:

Spiritual Readings & Conjure
Miss Ruthie Bluestone

Help in all matters of life, love, health & reuniting with loved ones.

- Remove evil influences
- Improve financial status
- Interpret dreams
- Read bone

To me, she meant so much more; the loving mother I never had. And the only other person I knew with albinism.

The storefront curtain was down, and the deli already closed; odd since it commonly stayed open till 10 PM, even on weeknights. I let myself in with my key, ready to share my good news. The storefront was empty although the chafing dishes still steamed. A wail came from the kitchen in the rear, so chilling it spread like voltage up my arms. I ran through the beaded curtain and found Ruthie at the table surrounded by her family—Vinnette, Simone and Anthony—all with tragedy in their eyes. *Something had happened to Anthony Junior!*

"My god, what's happened?" I asked.

Ruthie didn't look up; she released another shrill scream.

"It's Kyra," said Vinnette.

Anthony saw I had no idea. "Ruthie's niece, our youngest cousin."

Ruthie howled. I squirmed, immobilized.

"What's wrong with people?" Vinnette went to the sink and got her mother a glass of water. She returned quickly; Ruthie waved it away.

"Mom," said Vinnette, "please drink."

Simone put her hands over her mouth and lay a hand on Ruthie's shoulder. Another earsplitting shriek. Something so terrible I was afraid to ask and knowing whatever it was I wouldn't be able to temper their pain.

Anthony directed me out of the kitchen, into the storefront. "Kyra, Ruthie's youngest sister's daughter . . ." His eyes began to well up. He wiped them and sniffled. "There are ten siblings . . . Anyway, her youngest sister's daughter, Kyra . . . she's only just twenty and, oh god . . ." Anthony, always the cool man of the house, came unglued. I waited. He gathered himself again. "In Jamaica, Kyra's the first of her family to go to college. Mico University. Kingston. Wanted to teach. Fascinated by everything. Wanted to learn about her roots. Thought it would make her a better teacher. Told her mom, *I'm going go to Africa.* And she got a scholarship. That's the way she was. Smart. Directed. Tanzania." He hung his head, he started to suffer again. He hugged himself. His body jerked. He pulled a handkerchief from his back pocket; blew his nose. "Sorry."

"No, no." I wasn't sure putting my hand on his arm would solve anything. But I did.

"She was there three months." He squeezed his eyes closed. Ruthie still sobbing in the kitchen.

I waited. He couldn't regroup. She must have died. Gingerly, I asked, "She died?"

He trembled and looked at me. "Worse. They cut off her hands."

☽ ☽ ☽

Vinnette put Ruthie to bed. Simone went to hold Junior. After an hour or so, having heard it all from Vinnette and Anthony, I went upstairs to my room. I didn't bother to take off my clothes. I just turned off the light. I laid there, chilled and damp, New York's streets a low rumble. The solitary light from the apartment above, in the building across the alley, cloaked my room in a pale urine-colored brume.

It went like this: Ruthie's niece had been abducted one evening on her way home from school. She was found four days later propped up against an alley wall, barely alive, both hands hacked off. She'd been taken to a doctor's home; then transferred. No one knew where. Ruthie's sister in Jamaica hadn't heard anything for days. No numbers; no leads. No money to fly to Africa. No way to know if the young woman was safe, if she was getting proper care or if she was still alive. And one last thing: Kyra Nafasi was albino. Like me.

))))

A few days passed and Ruthie's wailings became deafening silence. Her anguish constricted the apartment walls. The family shuffled around the shop as if carrying weights. When I finally mentioned my new TV job to Ruthie and Vinnette, Ruthie flickered with life. "You can find Kyra!"

"Ruthie, I'm in television weather. I have no power; I follow orders."

"But you said *global*," Vinnette rubbed her mother's shoulders, encouraging. "You must have connections."

"I just got the job."

"But you would try?" Ruthie took my hands in hers. "I know you would try. You are our only hope."

))))

Gordon pulled me into his office early the next morning. He looked unhappy, too.

"What's the matter?" I asked.

"The New Turn is happening. The investor is in. We're going big, worldwide."

"That's great, isn't it?"

"Well, yes," he said. "Your adventure in Great Falls couldn't have come at a better time; it probably moved launch up a month, or three. We're hot right now." He flit his hands up and down. "No pun intended."

"None taken. So, what's the problem?" Then I thought, *I've been sacked.*

"They're taking you away from me. You're not on my team anymore." He picked a pencil from his desk.

"But you're short a person," I said.

"I was, but so was Sheila. She wants you."

"And?" I said.

"And Charlie Grissom said *yes* to her." Gordon tossed the pencil down.

I put a hand on his shoulder. He'd been a support since my days in Bemidji. "That's easy, I'll just say no."

He turned to me; his face recovered to its usual kindness. "You shouldn't do that Eunis, this is a major coup for you. And for the station. You're everything I'd hoped."

"I'm just a driver, really. What can they do if I say no?"

Gordon blew a long low breath. "Don't. Don't piss off Charlie. Or Sheila. I'll be fine. And they're giving me a full-time producer. And I don't have to pay your salary anymore. Even though you're a heckuva driver."

I walked over to Gordon, one of the few men I knew I could hug without sexual atoms being exercised. I'd come looking for a new life . . . one I wouldn't need to explain, and he'd given it to me. I gave him a squeeze. "Thank you."

"Just be careful," he said, eyes uneasy. "Don't let the past slow you down."

))))

In the elevator, I met Chaz Keyes, one of the station's on-air weathermen. Fiftyish with hazel eyes and a Q rating off the charts, especially with women. "You're here early," I said, lassitude dragging my words. I'd ridden that elevator at least twice a day for almost a month, but it seemed to have lost its welcoming familiarity. Everything had. But even at that ungodly hour his eyes were clear and determined. Salubrious. If I'd been more upbeat I'd say he looked edible. Or maybe it was the look he gave me.

"Today's meeting is a big deal, you understand?" Chaz said. "Charlie's going to dole out destinations for the New Turn launch."

I nodded, not nearly as excited as I'd been when I'd left the station the night before. All I could think of was Ruthie's niece. How powerless we all were.

"I know where you're headed," Chaz said.

"You do?"

"Hmm. Charlie gave me a peek last night. I think you and I should have a drink—before we go, I mean. Get to know each other. We might work together sometime." He was trying to be casual. But he was studying my body, and as I say, he wasn't the first. I'd say *men*, except that it seemed to go beyond just men. Anyhow, I was finally getting used to being looked at, and with a face like mine I needed all the help I could get.

"How about now? Buy me a cup of coffee?" I said.

Chaz was no fool. "You want to know where you're headed, right? Sure, Charlie's going to tell everyone in a couple hours anyway. Just so you don't say anything to anyone until the meeting. Act surprised, okay? My secretary's probably got a cup of Sumatran Dark already brewing in my office. Might even be a brioche or a bear claw in there too."

As I said, Chaz's Q Score was justifiably high. He also scored high as one of Charlie Grissom's preferred meteorologists. "Great." I said, perhaps looking for a distraction.

He closed the door behind us, poured us each a mug and sat across from me. "I'm glad I get a chance to know you, even if we only have a few more days. That Montana shoot, you've already got a reputation."

"A reputation?" *What was that gonna be?*

"And the one in upstate New York your second week, when you predicted the temps would warm there too. Two otherworldly predictions in just four weeks. I'd say that's hot." He raised his coffee mug in salute.

"Yes, but—"

"My producer, Carmen, thought you had some weird inside information. She couldn't figure how you knew there'd be such dramatic shifts in weather. I mean, you were spot on. Well, not exactly. Temperature only climbed to about sixty-nine degrees upstate, but still."

None of it felt very important.

He went on, "And the Great Falls heat wave; it looks like that beat the seven-minute forty-seven degree rise in 1980. You set the new North American record."

"I didn't set any record." I stared into my mug of Sumatran.

"Well, everyone here at the station is thankful for it." He tipped his cup to me again and sipped from it. "It means we travel first class throughout the world. Unless, of course, you get Trenton."

"Our country's first capital," I said, my melancholy unshakeable.

He pulled back. "Really? I didn't know that."

"Hmm."

"You were a history major in college?"

"Genetics," I said. "But I like to pick at lots of things."

"Interesting. So, want to know our destinations?"

"Sure." Maybe coffee and the impending trip would divert my lethargy.

"South Africa and Brazil. Not bad, huh? We did good." He crossed his legs, satisfied with himself.

He'd been purposely unclear, as if teasing me to ask who was going where. A small opening, but maybe in South Africa, being on the continent, I could make calls for Ruthie and her family; have better success than they'd had. I said, "You're so lucky." *Could I steer his desires?* "Everything I hear about Brazil and Rio de Janeiro is extraordinary: the weather, the food, the. . . the beautiful women. It will be amazing this time of year. All expenses. Better than South Africa, I'll bet. I'll get nighttime temperatures dropping below freezing in some places. Mosquitos in others. And then, naturally, the accommodations; we won't be sitting around any pools drinking mojitos . . ."

His hazel eyes lost focus, the way, I suppose, one might look at a lottery ticket and see that you've come up one number short.

Had I set the hook? I barreled on. "Do we have any idea what the stories will be about?"

"Ah, no, not yet" he said, diverted. He put down his coffee. "Listen Eunis, I just remembered something I have to do before the meeting. Maybe I could take you to dinner in the next night or so."

"I'd like that," I said.

"You'll excuse me?"

"Of course."

》》》

Chaz followed Charlie Grissom out of his office. The consternation on Charlie's face and the look of relief on Chaz's told me I had a ray of hope. My dodgy maneuver might have worked. Charlie could hardly afford a revolt now. Perhaps he'd given Chaz Keyes what *Chaz* wanted: Brazil. Had I gotten what I wanted?

"Thank you all for being here," said Charlie as the last of the crews slipped into their seats.

"I'm here cause I'm hopin' you're gonna send me with Chaz," said the office manager; she eyed Chaz lasciviously. Everyone chuckled. Except Sheila who appeared cranky.

Charlie looked up from his prepared agenda and over his glasses. "Someone's got to hold down the fort, Sheri. But I think we could send you downtown for some Chinese food."

A smattering of cheers.

"Balls!" she said followed by a loud pop of gum.

"As you're all aware by now," continued Charlie, "thanks to some excellent PR . . ." He looked my way and the group applauded, though a few kept their arms crossed against their chests, ". . . the launch has been moved up, and I have the destinations here." He raised a sheet of paper. "But before I read them to you, I want you all to know how much we value *all* your contributions, from graphic artists to editors to field crews, and needless to say our on-air staff. We're taking on a giant competitor, a smart and well-financed giant. But our investors think we've got a solid plan. The feature stories we deliver along with our excellent weather forecasting, will make us a powerful force in global television. The world is already a smaller place and what all of us do out there, and here in the studio, will have a profound effect on people of all nations everywhere."

"And all I get is Chinatown?" said the office manager. A chorus of *aaaaws*.

"For now," he said to her, "just for now." He returned to the greater audience. "There will be some shuffling of crews . . ."

A few groans.

". . . but it in no way reflects on the work you've been doing; it's strictly logistical. Everyone will get a chance to travel, even if you're not in the initial wave." Charlie began reading the first series of crew trips: "Gordon and Glenn will be joined by Ben. They'll be headed to . . ." Charlie milking this like the Academy Awards. ". . . China."

A palpable rush of excitement gushed from the group.

"Andy Pogue, you're getting a new producer from CNN. You and your crew . . . you'll be flying to . . . Norway."

"Get out your *trollveggen*," yelled Denni, a Scandinavian blonde and gorgeous. Another on-air face with a high Q Score.

"Wait Denni, you're next," said Charlie. "You, John P. and Sam, your assignment is in South America."

My heart dropped; Chaz Keyes hadn't taken the bait;

apparently, he was still headed to Africa. And I to Brazil. As if that was hard labor. The group applauded. "Way to go Denni!"

"Denni, your exact destination will be determined in the next couple of days. Also going to South America, Brazil in fact, will be Chaz Keyes and his crew." The group buzzed.

Chaz got a happy squeeze from his producer, Carmen.

"And finally, Sheila . . . You knew you'd be in the first wave, didn't you? Well, you and Kaplan and Eunis are going to South Africa."

Chapter 3

New York City

"**A**frica!" screamed Ruthie and gave me a huge hug. "Vinnette! Anthony!"

"But Ruthie, listen . . ." I said, trying to limit her expectations.

"Africa!" she yelled again and did a little dance.

Vinnette ran in. "What?"

All the support and shelter Ruthie and her family had given me in the past had been incalculable. "It's South Africa. Africa's a big place," I said.

"You would try," Ruthie repeated, and tightened around my hands until they hurt.

"I could make calls, sure," I said very *un*sure. "I could try. But I'll only be in South Africa."

Ruthie let go my hands. "I'm gonna call my sistah in Jamaica. You give us hope."

"Ruthie, wait!" I tugged at her arm. "I'm told communication between the countries is spotty and in Tanzania it's worse. It's very rural and fragmented." I thought about the promises I'd made in the past, promises that hadn't worked out. "I can't promise anything," I said, my jaw tight.

Undeterred, Ruthie continued, "You be my sistah too, Eunis. I keep my hand on Bible, I find an Obeah man, bring you luck, protect you from duppy spirit. I know you'll find someting."

$$\mathbb{D}\,\mathbb{D}\,\mathbb{D}$$

When I arrived at work the next morning, Charlie Grissom intercepted me at the elevator. "We've got a problem."

Chaz had changed his mind. "What kind of problem?"

"Legal reminded me: you haven't been here even five weeks, not on staff, not even officially on payroll."

"And some of the others are pissed that I'm going to Africa," I said, feeling my assignment slipping away.

"No, no, it's not that. Under the CPA South African rules, you can't legally get a work visa yet or passport clearance. I'll have to assign someone else."

"No, you can't do that!"

"Excuse me!" His face flushed. "Don't get ahead of yourself! You've done lots moving us forward but—"

"Give me a few days," I said.

"What good will that do? Rules are rules."

"I know someone who might help. Will you just hold off three-four days? Please?"

He looked skeptical. "No, I don't think so."

"Please." I went to touch his arm; he recoiled.

Some staff watched from afar. "Only because you're Gordon's friend," Charlie said. "Okay. Forty-eight hours, that's it. Otherwise, I'm moving someone else to Sheila. You can join a local team."

"Three days, please." I gave him my best waifish look.

"Itineraries are being set. Most of the producers have family to think about. Forty-eight hours. You're wasting all of our time."

$$))\,)$$

At lunch, I made my way through thick sleet. From the Canal Street stop, it's about thirty minutes through the Holland Tunnel by train to 18th Street in Jersey City, then south to Hudson Street in the cover of the Goldman Sachs Tower, a pretty toney neighborhood for a small-time employment lawyer.

All the way I'd wrestled with the idea of calling Roddy in advance, but I wasn't sure he'd see me after I'd given him no hope of romance and had shut down all communication for almost a year. "It's a tragedy when we can't grow old with the people we love," he said at the time. It was unconscionable that I should ask him a favor, that I should just show up and use whatever wiles I held over him. But I had no one else to turn to. Seeing him frightened me.

Despite my umbrella, by the time I found the address, an older five-story building that had somehow withstood the urban renewal, I was dank and irritated with the situation and with him. If we'd just been friends—which I'd repeatedly suggested—none of this would have been an issue.

Jerrod P. Bloomfield
Attorney at Law
Employment, Labor, Immigration

"Damn it." Instead of taking the elevator to the fifth floor, I stomped up the stairs hoping my prickliness would be worn smooth. Instead, by the time I reached his office door, an old-fashioned stenciled-glass entry, I fumed.

I knocked on the door. No reply. I knocked again, louder. This time an attractive woman about my age, opened the door and said, "It's open." She returned to her seat in the small waiting area and resumed reading a People magazine, which always reminds me of my mother, and always irritates me because it does. "No open umbrellas inside," she said without looking up. "Bad luck." I closed it.

The front room had rationed furnishings: three mildly discomforting waiting room chairs (circa 1960), a stern secretary's desk (fit for the Wisconsin Synod), and a couple of watercolors. Portugal, I think. Which made sense given what Roddy had told me about his background. No one sat at the front desk. I'd never seen his workspace before, only the apartment he had once shared with my friend Elizabeth and Sydney, their daughter. I hadn't known what to expect. I heard muffled intermittent voices coming from his inner office. "Is he in?" I asked the woman sitting alongside me. Hard to hide my impatience. She had thick dark eyebrows and full lips. She might have been Hispanic. Striking. Some people have all the luck.

She looked up from her magazine. "He's in with a client. Do you have an appointment?"

"No." I moderated my tone. It wasn't the woman's fault. "No."

"Well, he's supposed to take a lunch break after this consultation." She looked at the wall clock. "Another five minutes or so. You might want to come back in a couple hours."

"I'll just wait. I have to get back to work soon." I considered leaving.

She gave me a funny look; my hostility meter rose again. I picked up an old copy of The New Yorker; then, finding it in my hands and not knowing what to do with it, put it down. "Do you have an appointment?" I asked.

Once more she lifted her head from the magazine, this time with a bit more pique. "Oh yes. I always have an appointment." She smiled, like a Cheshire.

"I see. Well, how long do you expect your appointment to last?" As if my butting in line wasn't already bad enough.

She raised an eyebrow. "As long as it takes."

The door to Roddy's office opened. An elderly Chinese man shuffled out leaving the door slightly ajar. The Chinaman made his way across the waiting area and when he saw my face, he picked up his pace; then proceeded out.

"Renee, sweetheart, you out there?" Roddy's voice. *Was he gonna look as good as before?*

The attractive woman rose and with a slight turn to catch my eye, sashayed into his office. Roddy came to the door as she arrived at it. She threw her arms around his neck and pulled him to her, a meld that he readily accepted. He wasn't a tall man, but with her twined around him like that he looked, I don't know, bigger. Strong. I knew those arms.

After several grinding interplays during which I considered retreat and/or clearing my throat, he looked up and over her. "Eunis?" Like my name was beyond reason.

"It's me." I lowered my head.

He untangled from Renee. "What!" she said.

He held her hands. "She's an old friend."

Renee looked at me, offended. "She can wait till we've had our . . . our *lunch* date."

He turned to me. His skin still had the warmth of well-creamed coffee, and he still wore his forty-something-year scars confidently. "I thought you were in Minnesota."

"I was," I said, unable to look at Renee.

"Let's go." Renee tugged at him. "She can come back after."

"I can't, I only have a few minutes and it's an emergency," I said.

He looked concerned. "Emergency?"

"I wouldn't be bothering you if it weren't." *What was I even doing there?*

"Renee, sweetheart," he said, "how bout we make it dinner tonight?"

"I thought we were doing that too." A pout.

"It sounds like I've got to help my friend. You can appreciate that." He released her hands, a moment when I thought, *he still wants me.*

Renee took an inventory of me: my long stringy wet hair and dripping coat, my colorless skin, my oversized nose, the birthmark. She rose up, placed her hands on his chest and kissed him on the mouth. A little extra tongue. "Well, I guess," she said. "Where shall we go?"

"I'll call you later, okay," he said.

"You be good." She paraded to the door, gave us both one last look, and left, closing the door rather gently, as if she had no concerns.

I stood up. "I'm sorry to barge in like this."

"Take off your coat." He blushed; I'm sure he blushed. "Coffee, tea?" he asked, steeling himself.

"Sure, whatever's easiest. I won't take much of your time."

He ushered me into his inner office, an agreeable smell, rich in leather—leather-bound books to the ceiling behind him on the shelf. Meticulously organized. He either used those books daily as a resource or he never looked at them. The smell was worth it.

Beyond his pedestal desk, a puffy old swivel chair; worn leather. Cozy. So unlike the outer office. His desk showed its age, one of those dark mahogany leather tops, maybe four feet across, spacious but not grandiose. He seated me in one of two sumptuous leather chairs that faced his desk, handed me a cup of orange ginger tea; then surprised me by going around and sitting behind his desk. *What did I expect?*

"Those watercolors in your front office, those are Portugal?" I trusted the warmth of the tea to ground me.

"You remember . . ."

"I do," I said. "How's Sydney? Your mother, is she . . .?"

"Syd's great, eight and a half now. Can't believe I've got an eight-and-a-half-year-old daughter. Third grade. My mother, she passed away about eight months ago, a little bit after I last saw you."

He explored my face, a tenderness that made me lower my eyes and sip at my tea. "Sorry," I said, lamenting everything.

"Well," he realigned in his chair. "Thanks, she had a tough life."

He would have called me if I'd been a better friend, if I hadn't cut him off. "I hope she'll be peaceful," I said. Meaningless words when true comfort would have been to be there for him.

"Yes." He reached for and took a sip from the mug that sat next to the phone. The cup embellished with Johnny Cash's famous middle-finger salute, just like the one my brother Lyle drank from every morning. Roddy tapped the mug. "You know he gave it to me?"

"Lyle?"

He nodded. "The day of the concert."

My brother had died the morning after. *Impossible to love without hurting.* The damage of that memory must have shown on my face. Roddy swiveled to his library and, not unlike my deceased husband, Harold, he followed his finger to a book and pulled it out. He flipped through a few pages and then back a couple. He read:

> *"Perhaps the whole root of our trouble, the human trouble, is that we will sacrifice all the beauty of our lives, will imprison ourselves in totems, taboos, crosses, blood sacrifices, steeples, mosques, races, armies, flags, nations, in order to deny the fact of death, the only fact we have. It seems to me that one ought to rejoice in the fact of death--ought to decide, indeed, to earn one's death by confronting with passion the conundrum of life."*

"Wow. Who wrote that?" I asked.

"James Baldwin." He looked me over in a courteous but practiced way. "What is your conundrum?"

I'd strayed from my mission. I sat up and explained my employment/travel issues. I left out the part about Kyra and

Tanzania. When he heard that I'd been in the city almost a month he said, "Elizabeth would've liked to have heard from you. Give her a call."

"I will, I'm sorry." I hoped he knew that my apology was to be shared but I was too embarrassed to single him out.

He rubbed his brow. "Do you have a valid passport?"

"Aah, no."

"Oh boy." Rather than leveling me with the scorn I deserved, his words fell gently. "And when are you supposed to leave?"

"Six days. But I need clearance in the next forty-eight hours."

He made a low whistling sound. "How important is it for you to be in South Africa?"

I met his eyes, still cerulean with a hint of green, still kind. "Very important."

))))

When I returned to the station, I kept a lookout for Charlie Grissom; I wanted to keep well off his radar for as long as possible. In my cubicle, taped to the middle monitor, a note: "x 351."

I dialed it. Chaz Keyes picked up. "This is Chaz."

"It's Eunis."

"Dinner tonight?" he asked.

I thought about Renee wrapped around Roddy. "Sure."

Chaz considered it preferable to meet at least a few blocks from work, and I could see his point. I've always been a kind of detective, so I think like that too. Discretion. Stay low. But just before leaving to meet him around seven o'clock, his producer Carmen came by my desk, a wad of papers in hand. "I want to apologize," she said.

"For what?"

"For digging around your desk." She had an ingenuous face, clean, freckled, a natural sandy blonde. Didn't look like a Carmen at all. She chose clothes that I found stylish yet almost suggestive, as if innocent of her choices; clothes I liked very much. She was athletic, like me, but trimmer. We could never share clothes.

"You dug around my desk?" I said.

Her head dipped.

"You could've just asked," I said, straightening my files.

"Sheila's one of my best buds," Carmen said, the total of her *mea culpa*. "You obviously have an instinct for weather. And, hey, we're all appreciative."

"It's over, done. I'm good." I reassured her.

She relaxed. "Thanks." She seemed younger than her years, as unlike Sheila as anyone in the office, except maybe me. Or maybe that was another of my blind spots.

"Can I ask you," I said, seeing a natural opening, "what's the tension between Sheila and Chaz Keyes?"

She blushed. She swept hair from her forehead. "Personal stuff."

"I got that."

"It didn't go well." At this she looked particularly repentant.

"What?" I said acknowledging her look.

"Wow, you are creepy perceptive. Oh, geez, sorry, that didn't come out right. I just meant . . ."

"It's okay," I said. "But since I'll be traveling with Sheila . . ."

"It's just . . . Chaz is such an enigma. That's what some of us call him."

"Chaz, an enigma?"

"Maybe *challenge* is more accurate." Then, like someone with firsthand experience, she said, "He knows what he's doing."

I wagged my head and squinted. "I don't understand?"

"In bed; the guy knows what he's doing. He's as good as he looks."

"Oooh." I nodded. "Why didn't he and Sheila stick?"

She fiddled with the papers in her hand.

"Carmen, I'm sorry, I shouldn't be asking—"

"Me," she said. Bluntly.

"Huh?"

"I took a swing with him," Carmen admitted. "I'm not proud of it; well, maybe I am. Sheila's forgiven me. Rebecca in accounting, too."

"Oh," I said realizing what I'd stepped into. "I see."

"Not that I ever even made it to his apartment; it was always my place. None of us did. Like I said, it's okay. We all knew what we were getting in to. It's not like he's married or anything."

"Sure. Of course not."

"Well," she rattled the papers at me, "if I don't talk to you before I leave, enjoy Africa. And don't worry about Sheila. She can be an ass, but she can also be a saint."

"Not many of those around," I said.

"No."

"Enjoy Brazil."

And she was off.

Chapter 4

New York City

Two blocks from the Weather One studios, steam billowed from the street subway grates. Chaz Keyes stepped from a cloud of it, held his hand out to me and smiled. Discreet, as we'd agreed. Even in the subdued light of the building lobby, his eyes cut through the night. A man of uncommon good looks and wayward enough to spark hunger for the experience. "You made it." He gave me a gentle hug. "What sounds good? Italian, French, a burger?"

"I'm good with anything, as long as it's not chicken," I said.

"You even hungry? Maybe a drink to whet your appette?"

There were many ways to interpret that. "I could, sure."

He hailed a cab and took me to lower Manhattan to a dimly lit bar with snuggly chairs set in alcoves for two. "What'll it be?" he asked when the waiter arrived.

"Don Julio *anejo* and a slice of lime," I said to the waiter, who cringed at my features.

"Ooh, that sounds tasty." Chaz rubbed his hands together. "Makes your clothes fall off."

"What?" *Was I dinning into trouble?*

"A bad joke. Sorry," said Chaz.

"You sir?" asked the waiter, a rangy kid too young to be working in the place.

"Ginger ale, two cubes of ice, also a slice of lime. Oh, and that *magyu* you guys do so well."

"Excellent choice," said the waiter and loped off. Chaz wasted no time refocusing on me.

"You're not going to join me?" I asked.

"I don't drink."

After all I'd heard it struck me as funny.

He grinned. "You should smile more often; you have great dimples; like crescents."

"So I've been told."

He angled closer. "Very lucky, the symbol of Paradise. According to Islam." He reached for my cheek.

I pulled away in surprise. "I'm not superstitious and I'm not religious."

He withdrew his hand. "Didn't mean to scare you."

"I'm not scared. I just like my space. I don't believe in black cats, stepping on cracks or Friday the Thirteenth either." I started to fold my hands across my chest, but after a moment's hesitation they landed in my lap, annoyed.

He cocked his head. "But there's some history there."

"*That* obvious?"

"Your tone," he said. "I'm right, aren't I?"

"Hmm."

He waited for me to extrapolate. When I didn't, he said, "The Japanese have these ceramic bowls, *Kintsugi*, and when they break, they put them back to together with gold, making them more perfect than they were originally."

"Ah, I understand," I sniffed, "a parable."

"Okay, well anyway . . ." he rubbed his head. "Just be careful with Sheila." The waiter arrived with our drinks and the appetizer.

There, the first salvo. *Sheila.*

"Your wagyu," said the waiter setting the plate between us. "God's butter."

"Dig in," Chaz said pointing to the large bone split in half and the smoke-grey pulp inside.

"What's that?" I asked.

"Roasted bone marrow. The femur. Delicious. Cheers." He lifted his ginger ale.

"You don't think you'll be taken down by the Cow Spirit?"

"So, you are superstitious."

I laughed. "Definitely not." I hoisted my tequila.

"You've probably heard all the stories by now. Me. Sheila. You know." He clinked my glass. He dove into the wagyu.

"Stories?" I felt transparent. I took a generous swig of the Don Julio.

"Eunis," he tossed his head, "it's a close community."

I feigned ignorance.

"Okay, anyway, you'll get to like Sheila," he said.

"But?"

"No buts." He stroked his glass, wistful. "She's got edges, like the rest of us."

I leaned closer. "Yes, but there's something more." Raising my eyes, he could see my resolve.

After a moment, he admitted, "She's a little bit . . . superstitious."

"What does that mean?"

"She believes in things we can't see."

I nodded. "Seems . . . reasonable."

"Yes, absolutely. But she has this thing about . . . The Eye."

"The what?"

He hesitated. "The Evil Eye."

I laughed. "The Evil Eye?" I couldn't believe we were having this conversation—Chaz Keyes and me. "Is she drawn to it or frightened of it?"

"Both," he said.

"So . . . what are you suggesting?"

"That you be sensitive to that in her; just be careful." He folded his hands and put station politics quickly behind. From there our conversation sped along all night, surprising and deep, and not the least bit pretentious. Nor full of gossip. He talked about his ex-wife. Hard miles. He'd been a professional baseball player in Nebraska or Kansas . . . somewhere. Messed up his ankle. Was a "butt double" for Robert Downey Jr.

"What does that mean?" I asked.

"A photo shoot," he said. "I was an assistant, free-lancing for a photographer. Downey had to leave, another appointment. I guess I was a good match." *Probably something I shouldn't question Sheila about.*

He fell into weather forecasting in a small town in Texas. He'd caught someone's eye, which lead to his current high profile at Weather One. He liked the city but always thought he'd be "on earth" a lot sooner; surprised that he wasn't already there. "I'll be out of this business in a year, at peace, in a cabin, Montana probably. Nature around me, not green screens." He spoke of his grown daughter who he adored. "She's the best thing that's ever happened to me. As soon as I get back from this assignment, we'll spend a few weeks together in Kauai. Catch up."

I told him about swimming in the waterways and lakes of Bemidji. I didn't mention my childhood fascination with mermaids, or about *Freyja*, the Norse goddess and my mother's ideal of beauty. I told him that I'd become certain I wanted to live in New York City, though I didn't tell him why: how I wanted to learn to live around and with people. I also left out details of my first experience in New York. The ghosts. The sex. The murder.

"There was," I hesitated, "something very personal about the event in Great Falls, the melting ice."

"How do you mean?"

"Saying it sounds weird."

"So?"

"Can't explain it. That heatwave: it almost felt like I drew it in. I know, I know, that's Sheila woo-woo ridiculous. *But something.*"

He shrugged as if to say, *who's to say?* All in all, he was a gentleman, and smart with an offhand sense of humor. I did not see his apartment. I did not sleep with him. I wanted to see him again.

Meanwhile, according to Chaz, Sheila wrestled with spirits and the unseen. I found myself resistant to the coming assignment. I represented *both*—the quantifiable scientific and the nebulous intuitive—to Sheila. Why the hell was she taking me on this trip?

I slept fitfully that night. The recurring dream: I return to Minnesota, to the farmhouse I grew up in. I descend into my room, the dank root cellar where Momma kept me out of sight. The cellar is a catacomb of lamps, candelabras, candle sticks, an old chandelier. All layered in cobwebs and a cocoon of dust, my unlit potential.

))))

I gave Roddy half the day before I called him. I knew I shouldn't push him, but if I could just make it to South Africa maybe I could ease Ruthie's pain. Or at least give her closure. "So?" I asked.

"Nothing yet," he said. "Have you gotten your passport photos?"

"Got 'em." *He wasn't saying no or that it was impossible.*

"Well then proceed to the next counter. In the meantime, what do you call yourself?"

"Usually, it's *self*." I pretended to be loose while time ticked loudly away.

Roddy remained matter of fact. "Producer, Associate Producer . . . ?"

"Associate Producer."

". . . Technician."

"No, "I said. "Associate Producer."

"A Technician," he said. "A Technician, a Technician. You're a Technician . . . *aren't you?*"

"Why yes, I'm a Technician; I'm sure that's what they'd call me."

"If someone phoned," he continued, "—I'm not saying it's going to happen—if someone called the station, there's someone there who will vouch for you as a Technician? Maybe even in writing?"

Gordon. "Yes."

"You're sure?" His tone autocratic.

"Yes." I made a point of giving Roddy Gordon's number and vice versa.

"Then carry on." He hung up the phone before I could ask him what my chances looked like.

))))

Calling the South African Consulate in New York started a treadmill of frustration. First, their voicemail was down, then their line constantly busy. After trying for most of the day to schedule my required in-person meeting, I finally decided to go down there and talk to Roddy's contact, a man named Stewart Wilson. "Meet only with Mr. Wilson," Roddy said. "He knows you're coming. Remind him of our conversation."

When I arrived the man at the barren reception desk told me Mr. Wilson was on vacation.

"This is urgent," I said.

"Well, I'm sorry miss. Maybe Mr. Biobaku can help."

"Fine," I said.

I waited more than two hours for Mr. Biobaku. I could imagine Charlie Grissom or Sheila crossing me off the list as I waited, absent as I was from my ongoing station responsibilities.

"Where is Mr. Biobaku?" I'd tried to be patient.

The receptionist looked up at me with the same unsettled

look he'd had when I'd first arrived two hours earlier. A prim man dressed in prim clothing. "I'm sure he'll be out soon."

I checked my watch. He saw my exasperation. He looked away.

"Please tell him it's urgent. You'll be closing soon, and I can't wait until tomorrow."

"Well, we're closed tomorrow. Maybe Monday."

At this I raised my voice. My echo carried. "Please call Mr. Biobaku."

"I can't leave the desk." Unmoved by my rising wind, he returned to his magazine.

"Call him." I pointed to the phone.

He didn't raise his head from his reading. "The phone is broken; all of them."

"Then how does he know I'm here?!" My voice rang through the empty lobby.

"I'm sorry miss."

I hadn't even gotten past 33rd Street and the South African bureaucracy already had me rubbing my temples and searching for ibuprofen.

I walked over to the only door I saw and pulled on it. It was locked.

"You can't go in there," he said, his eyes still scanning the magazine. He turned the page.

From behind me, a door opened and a tall black African man in his overcoat came out on his way to the front door. He saw me tugging on the door. "Can I help?" the man said.

"Mr. Biobaku?" I asked.

"No, I'm Mr. Wilson."

)))

"Please sit." Stewart Wilson, thin but stately, offered me a seat in his spartan office. "I have but a moment, and I've already turned off the coffee. But perhaps you'd like a kiwi. From my country." He raised a bowl of the fruit.

I deferred. "Did Roddy—Mr. Bloomfield—explain my situation?" I sat.

"Only that I should do what I could. You're on a tight deadline."

"Five days," I said, before glancing at the clock above his head. 5:30PM. I'd lost another day. "Actually, four before I leave. But I need clearance by tomorrow."

"Well then, I'm sorry there's nothing I can do for you." He began to rise.

"I have to go!" I said.

"Give me a month and I can probably arrange it since you're a friend of Mr. Bloomfield." He looked at his watch. "I have a train to catch."

"I've got a wonderful job, but I'll lose it if I can't go with my colleagues. It's a once in a lifetime opportunity."

"You just waited too long to see me." He motioned to the door.

I didn't move. "Mr. Wilson, do you have daughters?"

He gave me a callous look. "That's really none of your business."

Too late to retreat. "Well, if you do, I'm sure they're more attractive than I. And I'll bet if they're of working age, that they have many more opportunities than I do. I would guess they are smart and quite successful." I waited to see his response; his face thawed, just enough for me to go on. "But as a father, I assume that you're a compassionate man, and you're thankful that your daughters don't look like me."

"Miss Cloonis, I would never—"

"Without question," I assured him. "I can see that in your face. What I'm asking . . . it's a once in a lifetime chance to see the world. These kiwis," I pointed to the bowl, "they're from The Land of the Silver Mist, right?"

Surprise lit his eyes, a kind of wonder, as if I'd taken him homeward somehow. "Yes, a beautiful region."

"Lush, I'm told."

"Yes," he said. "Emerald. With mountains and stone."

"That's where I'm supposed to go with my colleagues," I said.

He thought for a moment. "I am a father. I would not want my daughters to do what you are doing."

"Would you stop me? I mean, if I were your daughter?"

"You're not my daughter."

"No, I'm not. But you are the person—in this case a man, a father—who determines if I go on. Do you hold me back?"

"What you're asking is impossible. Clearance by tomorrow. Mick Jagger doesn't get that kind of service."

"Yeah. I'm one young inconsequential woman. Check my records. You need anything—paperwork, references, fees—let me know and I'll be sure you get it. I just need to leave for South Africa in four days."

He huffed, but I sensed resignation. "You're just lucky I didn't leave *after* closing hours," he said. "I often do. Where would you be then?" He ushered me out the door. I thanked him, hoping I hadn't misread his eyes.

Mr. Stewart Wilson waved at me. "Send my best to Mr. Bloomfield."

☽☽☽

"So, you got your Yellow Fever vaccination, and your Section Eleven-Two visa. Excellent." Roddy tipped back in his chair. "You're good for ninety days."

"We'll be returning in two weeks," I said, thinking that maybe he—and I—would reconsider the obstinance I'd thrown in his way since the day I'd met him. "Thank you, as usual. You're a good friend."

He bent forward. "Always will be."

Then Elizabeth, my friend, Roddy's ex-wife, popped into my head, leveling me with accusatory eyes. . . and Renee, Roddy's current flame, teeth showing, watching too.

Roddy went on. "I did very little. It's still more about your lucky charm." He said it without that eager look he used to give me, and I guessed that I was as lucky as I had any right to be, that he was still my friend.

Chapter 5

Johannesburg, South Africa

"Listen to this," I said to Kaplan after our plane leveled off and I'd stopped strangling the armrest and wrenching at my hair. "'Fever, rash, jaundice, diarrhea; dark colored urine; damage to vital organs, interruption of blood supply to the brain; severe headache leading to shock, hemorrhaging bowels, paralysis, coma and death.'"

"What are you talking about?" Kaplan put down his book, *The Body Keeps the Score*.

"I'm not finished," I said, and continued. "'Severe joint pain, vomiting, kidney damage, liver failure; inflammation of spinal cord and brain; worms reproducing in liver, kidneys and intestines.'"

Kaplan said, "I thought it was over at *death*."

"Kaplan," I said, "we're going into a bacterial incubator."

"Excuse me." The man across the aisle canted in our direction, ebony skin, curly gray hair, a neatly trimmed beard. He reminded me of Stewart Wilson's refinement. "I couldn't help overhearing you," he said. "That last one, it's *only*

Schistosomiasis, it's caused by a parasite that penetrates your skin; just don't swim in contaminated water. Bladder cancer likely but mortality is low."

"Reassuring," I said. I'd already crammed down books on spiders, snakes, and flora. Only *nyoka marsh*—marsh snakes— appealed to me.

"No problem." The man smiled and went back to reading his Daily Sun.

Kaplan seemed amused. I looked behind us. Sheila out cold asleep. "She's so relaxed," I said.

"She took a sedative."

))))

When we landed—8,000 miles and seventeen hours later, with the refueling stop in Dakar—we were met by our cameraman, Marius and his soundman, Trig. The imposing Johannesburg airport, all concrete and glass, bustling with travelers. Flights appeared to be taking off and landing continuously. I had nothing but Kennedy Airport to compare it to, but Tambo was modern, even antiseptic. Perhaps I'd overreacted.

"Breakfast or your hotel?" asked Marius. He shook Sheila's hand then Kaplan's and after a quick double-take, waved a hand at me and grabbed Sheila's luggage.

"Hotel." Sheila left no doubt.

As we walked toward their van, Trig came up beside me. "What do you do?" He volunteered to take my luggage.

"I'm the Associate Producer."

"Oh." And fell silent.

We all piled into the van, Marius driving and Trig shotgun.

Marius glanced at me and said something to Trig that sounded facetious, "*Sy sal nogal 'n skouspel wees.*" Trig snuck a self-conscious smile at me and quickly turned again to the road.

I don't know if it was what Marius said or the van itself, but a frequency mobilized around my heart. I asked Sheila to roll down the window. I took deep breaths and tried to concentrate on the perfect blue sky and 70° weather. Sheila closely monitored me.

〉〉〉

From crisply manicured green lawns and the paved slatestone driveway, panels of blue glass rose to the equally blue sky. The hotel and the room elegant by my standards, lots of light and a panoramic view of the pool and the airport. Johannesburg forty minutes to our west, a mere twenty-three miles, and we never saw it.

First thing in the room, I opened my luggage and found my hand sanitizer. I'd packed all the prerequisite rugged clothing. I double-checked the safari shirts, pants, hat, boots. Always prepared. I took a shower and then, stretching out on the king-sized bed, pulled the photo of Kyra Nafasi, and the phone number Ruthie had written down for me. Kyra smiled back at me, hopeful, excited, ready; a bright-eyed girl with white corn hair like mine—not long like mine, but cut in a pageboy that framed her innocent, joyful face. If not for her pale violet eyes and substantial lips, she could have been Asian. I dialed the number. The phone rang several times. Just before I hung up a woman answered. "Yes?"

"Is this Dr. Allen's office?"

"Who's calling?" Her voice coarse and distrustful.

"I'm looking for a young woman, Kyra Nafasi. The doctor—" The line disconnected. I'd heard phone lines could be spotty. I dialed again. This time the phone rang for several minutes with no answer.

I'd promised I'd call Ruthie when I got to South Africa, and with our team leaving first thing the next morning, I rang her. She was already up.

"You found her?"

"Ruthie, I just arrived a few hours ago," I said. "I'm in South Africa, not Tanzania, remember?"

"You be militantly."

I squinted. "What?"

"No back down," she said.

"No, no, no back down," I said. "But please don't get your hopes up."

"My sistah in bad way." Ruthie took a breath. "They took her to hospital. She gone crazy with worry. You gotta do someting."

I looked at Kyra's photo again. "I'll do everything I can, but I may not call you for a few days; we're going on our shoot. I don't know about the cell service. Tanzania is far from here. I don't want you to get your hopes up," I repeated.

"You do everting?"

"I will. I'll make calls."

"You bona fide," Ruthie said. "We thank you."

I hung up, more unsure of my promises than ever.

)))

At dinner we met with Marius and Trig in the hotel's restaurant to go over our plan. An early dinner. Sheila demanded it; I'd hardly had time to swim my laps. Kaplan sat to my left, Sheila to my right; the two sunburned South Africans across. Marius probably thirty, a chiseled, razor-clean face and a cool demeanor. He seldom looked at me, and never met my eyes. Trig was probably a bit older gauging by his receding hairline. A bit more ruffled, dressed in torn khakis even for dinner, but he appeared more relaxed than his buddy, if they were in fact friends. Hard to tell.

Sheila drummed her fingers on the table as we waited for our waiter. "So," she said stretching her neck, "four hours to Tzaneen and Iron Crown Mountain?"

Trig looked to Marius to take the lead, which he did. "Indeed. Four hundred kilometers, perhaps a bit longer. If you want to grab standups in the mist, we'd better get an early start."

She snuck a look at me. "Let's go tonight."

Kaplan leaned forward. "Sheila, we all could use a good night's sleep."

She shared a look with Marius. "No, tonight. We'll have our dinner, pack up and drive. Eunis, you make arrangements at Silver Mist; tell them we're coming in a night early."

Trig leaned in. "We won't be there till eleven, maybe midnight."

Sheila, unruffled, said, "Just as well."

When the waiter arrived, the table had fallen tense and silent. He looked us over then left. It was another fifteen minutes before a waitress showed up and took our order.

)))

Kaplan and Sheila slept next to me in the rear of the vehicle, heads bobbing. I'd seen Sheila snap a pill just as we got going, perhaps another sedative. In the darkness I heard Trig ask Marius, "What'd you say to her?"

"Sheila?"

"Yeah," Trig said.

"Nothing."

"*Dopkass.*" Trig's intonation asserted *bullshit.*

Marius wanted to be rid of the topic. "I told her we could have a problem. That's all."

Trig looked into the dark backseat; I'd closed my eyes pretending to sleep. He lowered his voice. "She's fine."

"Maybe," whispered Marius. "But you saw the reaction of the waiter, and that's in Joburg. Better that we get in late at night."

Trig just shook his head.

After that I had trouble sleeping. About two hours into the trip, Trig had taken over the driving and Marius was sound asleep, snoring. I inclined close to Trig's ear and gently touched him on the shoulder; he jumped. "Sorry." I spoke quietly. "I'm trying to reach a doctor in Tanzania."

"A doctor?"

"For a friend of mine. A Dr. Allen."

He didn't move except to say, "Where?"

"In the north, probably Simiyu."

"That's pretty rural. And Allen, that's a very common name. Is it e-n or a-n?"

"Don't know," I said.

"One L or two?"

"Don't know," I admitted.

Trig chuckled. "Are you sure it's his last name?"

"I don't know," I admitted again.

"And you are asking me *what?*"

"How would you find him?" I said.

"You sure it's a man not a woman?"

"Pretty sure," I said.

He chuckled again "I'd say don't bother."

"I have to."

"Look, I'm not trying to be *stroppy*—difficult—but unless you can call him, or her, directly, good freakin' luck."

I sat watching the outline of my reflection against the rolling blackness. All my life my face had been an issue, but I'd forever had a grand image of how I could be useful in the world. At least for my dear friends, how could I look away now?

☽☽☽

We arrived after midnight and by sunrise, quarter to six that morning, we'd already four-wheeled twelve windy dust-blown miles. The South Africans would not let me drive, a relief because despite my lack of sleep, I relished watching the otherworldly countryside, even with the dust and the jarring potholes. I'm not sure Kaplan and Sheila shared my enchantment. Plush scrub vegetation occasionally peeked through the mist as if I was watching a mercurial, drug-induced diorama.

Sheila turned to me. "Where should we set up?"

Even Kaplan seemed surprised she was asking me.

"You want me to choose?" I said.

"I'm talking to you, aren't I?"

"Uh, well, how bout up there?" I pointed. "It appears to be the highest peak. Probably the best views."

Sheila motioned to Marius, and he took the fork in the road to the summit, some 7,000 feet. By the time we'd reached the top and set up for Sheila's first on-camera report on moisture, we knew we had a problem.

The area around the villages of Tzaneen and Haenertsburg is known as The Wolkberg, and the Land of the Silver Mist. The idea was for Sheila to begin her standup *in* the mist and then reveal herself as she walked into a clearing. Kinda like what Chaz Keyes looked like stepping out of the New York City steam vents. The snag to Sheila's plan: the mist, truly epic and thick, offered no clearing.

So, while Sheila paced furiously, making everyone nervous, the heat and humidity steadily rose. Kaplan had Marius shoot copious close up tracking "b" roll of the pink, lilac and verdant vegetation over which Sheila could later add narrative when we returned home.

Next, Kaplan had us shoot a couple of extreme close-ups with her, to settle her down. Rivulets of sweat kept rolling across her forehead and cheeks, even though the temperature hovered around 75°. I kept patting her down with pancake makeup. Marius maintained a stricken look, as if I were spreading battery acid on her face. "Not okay?" I asked.

"No, it looks fine." He turned from me.

When Sheila finished her standups and she'd stepped away from the camera, I handed her a bottle of water. "Is there something I can do?" I asked.

She took a swig, sweating again. "Not unless you can turn the clocks forward." She went to her backpack. I trailed.

"Huh?" I said.

"You of all people," she said. "Of all people."

I didn't understand what she was driving at.

"It's Friday, Friday the thirteenth." She pulled a small leather pouch from the backpack, and from it something that she held firmly in her fist.

I said, "I think we're in good hands." I nodded to Kaplan as the mist crept over him; Marius and Trig already enveloped in it and invisible though only a few yards away.

She held her closed fist to her lips. "I don't like not seeing what's around me."

I pointed to her clenched fist. "What's that?"

She opened her hand. "An alligator tooth. It's good luck. What does your sixth sense tell you?"

"About what?"

"About this, this place." Her body contracted as if the swirling fog would consume her.

"Nothing," I said. "It's beautiful and magical." I wanted to console her with a touch, but she wouldn't have appreciated that. She fairly crackled with static.

"Do you sense any hyenas?" She twisted around several times, as if beasts just outside the curtain of mist were about to lunge at her. "They hunt at twilight and first light."

I glossed over it. "Hyenas? I wouldn't know."

"But you'd tell me if you did?" She kept turning, taking stock of the tight perimeter.

"If I hear of one, absolutely. But it doesn't seem likely. What do I know?"

I got her to wait in the van.

In the late afternoon it cleared for a short time exposing hundred-mile vistas. We were surrounded in fynbos vegetation, somewhat reminiscent of the flora throughout the Minnesota waterways around and in which I grew up, though here we were in high chaparral. I recognized sorrel, milkwort and iris and a few others. Despite its generally brushwood appearance, when I looked closely, the thickets gifted soft swatches of red, orange, and purple. An inordinate number of butterflies fluttered around us, a few landing on my shoulders. Given the free time, Kaplan danced around taking photographs of them. Later I found out they were the rare Wolkberg Zulu (largely white with brown clusters and small touches of orange). Also, there was the Wolkberg Widow (with wings like smoldering embers), and the Wolkberg Sandman (a sooty brown with orange shoulders and two piercing "eyes" on its wing). It started to make sense: Charlie Grissom had picked this location in part for his butterfly collection; Kaplan probably tasked with bringing back the goods.

Then the fog started rolling in again. We'd been given— at most—ten, fifteen minutes surrounded in breathtaking splendor. But, like magic, the fog began reclaiming it.

"Let's get started," Kaplan clapped, "while we've got light. Eunis, hold up the Flexfill. Sheila, sweetheart, you're not chewing on an over-cooked steak." Only Kaplan could talk to her like that. Sheila regrouped and dropped *half* of her attack dog demeanor. Kaplan yelled "Roll camera." Sheila straightened up. The mist gathered around her.

"Three, two, one," she said and began her lines. "Why is it that as fog rolls in we feel a sense of magic and the supernatural?

Well, here on Iron Crown Mountain in South Africa, it's the beginning of summer, and that feeling is visceral, prompted by high humidity and the cooler ground. The rapidly changing envelope of air seeks a space around which its water content can condense. Like it's looking for a host. Condensation replaces evaporation."

"And cut," said Kaplan. "Sheila, I like it, but that line about *the host*, maybe that's a bit too over the top."

She fired back. "Charlie said 'give it balls.'"

"Well, let's try one without *the host*. We can decide which one to use when we cut it together because," and this was where Kaplan was so masterful with Sheila, "you look great walking out of the brush like that. I don't want to cut away from you until you've finished your lines."

She began again, the haze growing thicker. No sooner had she concluded her lines than the fog completely enveloped her.

"Cut. Excellent," said Kaplan nodding to Marius and looking to Trig for his okay that the sound was free of problems.

Explosively, sheet lightning illuminated everything shrouding us. The area surrounding Sheila even brighter, a chaotic light—up, down, and all around—the size of a ten-foot ball or a giant NBC peacock, followed immediately by an explosion so loud it forced me to the ground and Trig to rip off his headphones in pain. "Shit!" he said, rubbing his ears.

"What the fuck!" cried Kaplan.

Marius held tight to his camera and shivered.

"Sheila?" I was maybe thirty feet away, already headed in her direction. But she was no longer visible. Kaplan followed. Two more explosions rocked the mountaintop. I'm sure they could hear the sound miles away as it echoed for more than a minute.

I almost tripped over her. "Sheila!" I knelt next to her. She groaned, struggling to push herself off the ground. "Are you okay?" I asked.

"It came up through my feet." Dazed, she talked to the ground. "It left through the top of my head." I let her speak. "Huge, it was huge. Clear. Inside . . . three shades of white. Dazzling." She was in shock, the alchemy of the land still prickling all of us.

She turned to me as Kaplan, then Trig, appeared above us. She pointed at me. "It was you. You've brought the bad luck, the *buda*; you've got the wicked eye."

Chapter 6

The Silver Mist, Haenertsburg, South Africa

The remaining lightning and rolls of thunder lasted less than three minutes. It moved quickly to the horizon with a wind that also cleared the mist and left parts of the brush polished and dripping. No one knew what to say, least of all me. But I saw the dread in Sheila's eyes as she composed herself in the Land Rover. The rest of us packed up. Marius smoked a cigarette, which I'd never seen him do before. Kaplan, despite going to each of us, and making sure he made physical contact, couldn't mediate the tension. It hung over us like the departed mist. As the storm traveled southward, the sky around us revealed distant silhouetted peaks, and above them the pale blue, yellow and orange layers of descending dusk. Only I seemed to register its beauty.

Before we got in the Land Rover, Kaplan pulled me aside. "Keep a low profile, even at the lodge. It'll blow over; she gets skitty like this sometimes. And on this one, who can blame her? I think it's what they call 'ball lightning.' Very rare."

"I just hope she's fine," I said. "What can that feel like?"

"She'll be okay. She says her legs are burning. She wants to sleep. We have a doctor waiting at the lodge just in case." He eased for a moment, no longer the Organized Force. He pressed his lips. "Let me handle this, I'm sorry."

"Not to worry," I said.

I dined in my room. I researched "ball lightning." According to Wikipedia, it's an unexplained atmospheric phenomenon. The scientific websites were a bit more specific: negative ions collect in the air and hot plasma gas forms. The victim's DNA is shuffled; blood type can change. I fell asleep trying to reach a phone number in Tanzania, some 2,000 miles away—a number that may or may not have been Dr. Allen's, with an e-n or a-n.

)))

At 6AM, a knock on my door. I threw on a t-shirt and some shorts; I opened the door. Helplessness was written large over Kaplan's face, a look I'd never seen before. "She wants you to stay behind."

I stood speechless, as helpless as he looked.

"We'll go to Kruger National Park," Kaplan said, "and then into Mozambique; probably six days, maybe ten total. By then she'll come to reason."

"How is she?" I asked.

"Physically, she's shaken but fine according to the doctor. He wants to check her out again when we return. Emotionally, she's rattled and not thinking clearly. But she's tough, she'll be fine."

"She's not sending me back?"

"Too expensive," Kaplan confessed. "Anyway, I talked her out it."

"You know I'm not responsible for this."

"I know, I know."

"And it's Marius too, isn't it?" I said. "He's spooked."

His eyes admitted as much. "Old superstitions die hard."

"You're going to be okay without the extra hands?" I asked.

"I don't have much choice, do I?" He turned to go. He said, "I think of you sometimes."

"Well," I conceded, "neither of us need *that* complication now, do we?"

"Definitely not."

"Thank you," I said.

"For what?"

"For coming here rather than leaving a note. And for trying."

He patted my arm. "You'd do the same."

$$\text{)))}$$

I propped the photo of Kyra Nafasi on the bureau. I sat on the end of the bed staring at it, wondering how she could survive that kind of brutality . . . If in fact she'd survived. I called hospital after hospital in Tanzania's northern region. Phones promptly disconnected. Phones rang unanswered. Those that picked up could barely hear me or splintered in my ear like shattering crystalware. *Never heard of her. Don't know a Dr. Allen.* And a few languages they, nor I, had any way to translate.

Then I got a text from Roddy. "Hope your shoot is going well. May the force be with you. It's your time to shine—R."

Shine? Beautiful Kyra shone down on me, young, eyes bright, face gentle and confident. *You mean shine like that?* Not idling in that dusty outpost, counting down the days I had a job. After all that Gordon, Roddy, and Stewart Wilson at the consulate had done for me. All that Ruthie and her family had done for me. Shine how? Where? Nowhere, except in dust, to sit for the next ten days till the crew got back. Nowhere to swim. I walked around that calloused little lodge three or four times, its wooden sides compacted, stripped by wind so tough that moisture could no longer seep in. It would be there till the wind chipped it down—pellet by pellet—or it burned. Sturdy but immobile, waiting for its fate. My legs restless.

I checked what it might take to get me to Tanzania (or at least closer to it) and back in time to meet up with Kaplan and the crew, as if I'd never left. Railroad routes had been discontinued. As for flights, first I'd have to find a ride back to the Johannesburg airport, *away* from my destination; then fly to Ethiopia, then to Dar es-Salaam, Tanzania and then to Dodoma, Tanzania; *if* I could find a seat and *if* they'd take an almost-maxed-out credit card for the $1800 round trip. Over sixty hours of flight time alone, while I could travel by road from my current location in the Land of the Silver Mist to Dodoma in under forty.

After several calls, including one where the airline representative told me, "It's a shame because if there *were* direct flights, you could be there in three and a half hours," it was clear that the circuitous flights that did exist were full, and I had one option. The only question: could I chance it?

꒰꒰꒰

The large African woman at the lodge's front desk warned, "You cannot go through Zimbabwe, you realize that." I nodded. But it wasn't until I stood along the caked road with my backpack, in my t-shirt, shorts and brimmed bucket hat, watching heat vapors rise from the earth, waiting for the mini-bus east into Mozambique, that I realized how ill-equipped I was for *any* journey. *What the hell.*

Guija, Mozambique was more than eight hours away, assuming the bus was on time and there were no issues at border customs. The scheduled time came and went.

"There is no bus," said a young British camper and his buddy when I flagged them down an hour later, only an incidental reaction to my face. Fine talc settled on the hood of their vehicle and my arms. "The only way in is by four by four," one of them said. I'm sure I looked dejected. "We've got room if you don't mind squeezing in."

Kinda squirrely, Eunis; several ways your body could be found. But with these guys? So fresh faced? "Sure," I said.

They introduced themselves as Lewis and Freddie, on holiday from the university. I couldn't remember who was who. It didn't help that their scruffy blondeness merged, which made the three of us unusually white cargo in their chalky white Land Cruiser.

They chatted away and broke out a joint (which I declined). Besides the usual tug of testosterone I felt from them, I was content to watch the hilly countryside give way to the flat scrub and distant hills. As the day heated up, the cruiser's jerky rocking created a small breeze cooling my face and driving off the mosquitos. From time to time, the road powder clouded my sunglasses. I removed and wiped them clean, an occasion for whomever of the boys wasn't driving to make concerted eye contact with me.

As we headed to Kruger National Park, I expected to see lots of wildlife. I used that unspoken motivation to keep my eyes on the tall grasses and bramble, and away from theirs. Curiously, there were times it looked and felt like I was at the bottom of a dry sea.

By midday we had crossed the Letaba River having seen only one family of elephants off in the distance, a porcupine, and a water buffalo. We arrived at the Mozambique border post of Giriyondo—nothing more than a large, thatched shack— with twenty or so cars backed up from the gate.

"Want something cool to drink?" Freddie, I think, reaching into the cooler.

"Put that away," said Lewis.

"A beer?" Freddie smiled self-consciously at me.

"Remember the last time?" Lewis said.

"Oh right."

"What?" I asked, letting down my hair to shake out the grit.

"Brilliant hair!" said Lewis. "Like corn silk, so white."

"Effervescent," said Freddie, as if correcting Lewis or upstaging him. Their sparring made me uncomfortable. He moved the beers to the cooler, and laid a tent on top of it, synching it down.

"They don't allow alcohol?" I asked.

"Oh, they *do*, and soon it will be theirs if we're not careful. They're bent as a nine-bob note." Lewis gave Freddie a reprimanding look.

"You should wear your hair down." Freddie said.

"A bit too hot for that." I fanned my neck and pulled my hair back up.

The boys were polite enough not to stare, but in a t-shirt and shorts, which is the only way a born-and-bred Minnesota girl could handle that heat, well . . . I just had to be alert. Probably, I flattered myself. At any rate, the sun got hotter, and my skin can't handle sun, so I slipped on a long-sleeved camping shirt.

By the time we'd moved to the front of the line, Lewis or Freddie pointed about 100 yards away, reminding me that this was only the first of the two customs we had to pass through. I pulled out my passport and visa.

Lewis turned to Freddie. "DA three-forty-one?"

"Check," said Freddie.

"A duplicate?" Lewis said, keeping his eyes straight ahead.

"No, why?" asked Freddie.

"We will need one for Mozambique too."

Freddie smiled at me. "Forms and more forms."

The South African border guard approached us. "Papers please." He wore sage army fatigues, a baseball style cap, a thick woven mesh belt with eyelets, and boots. He sported a clean very white t-shirt under his fatigues. He gave me a sullen look as I handed him my papers. "You!" he said to Freddie. "You take those from her." Which Freddie did and the guard waved him to hand them to him. "You are American?" he said to me after glancing at my passport, disbelieving. "Where's your reservation?"

"Reservation?" I asked.

"Tonight's reservation papers. You have to sleep somewhere in the park to come through this border. Even you, crockadillapig, can't sleep out in the bush with the snakes." A booming laugh. I caught Freddie and Lewis sharing a pained look.

"I don't have a reservation," I said.

"You boys want to go in without her?" He looked at the new line that had formed behind our Toyota.

Both frozen, Freddie finally said, "We have beer."

"Good," said the guard and Lewis looked disgusted. Freddie led him to the back of the Land Cruiser and pulled out a beer. "How many do you have in there?" asked the guard craning to see.

"A sixer."

"Give them here," the guard said.

Which Freddie did, reluctantly.

"Now get out of here and return with the proper papers, the three of you."

Chapter 7

The Pafuri Gate,
South Africa/Mozambique

We piled back into the 4x4. I didn't know what to say.
I didn't have to: Freddie—or at least the one I called
Freddie (it felt too late to ask who was who)—said, "Well, I
guess we're heading north." Lewis didn't look overjoyed but
didn't argue.

"This is very nice of you," I said. "But won't we have the
same problem at the next border crossing?" I'd already begun
feeling dehydrated.

"Possibly, but with any luck we should make it in time,
before they close the border, and it's a little more . . . rustic."

"What he means," said Lewis, "is that we have a better
chance of bribing the guards up there. More remote."

"Oh," I said. The six-pack of beer must have been nothing
more than a goodwill gesture.

As he slid in, Lewis tapped the steering wheel, tempering
too much enthusiasm. "Of course," he said, "there's always two
kinds of luck."

"You're sure you want to do this for me?" I began to worry about strings that might be attached.

Freddie opened the door for me. "Why not, it's an adventure."

Sure is. Kyra out there, somewhere. My luck had held out so far. If Lewis and Freddie were kind enough to support my undertaking, how could I not take my chances?

Heading north along the boundary of the park, the road was hard pounded, except when it was mud. Occasional cloudbursts and the high humidity slowed the heat from dispersing all the rainwater. The mosquitos got larger and, dry or wet, the road was a mire, slowing us. Posted at forty kilometers (twenty-four mph) tops, but we couldn't even sustain that. Any manicured areas and agriculture were long gone, replaced by a desiccated landscape of tall grass, scrub mopane and taller mopane trees that belied the mugginess. From time to time we'd see deer— *impala*, Lewis corrected me—or water buffalo. Occasionally we'd come upon a large pond or lake, and in it a couple of hippos, or around it a zebra or a giraffe. If the mosquitos weren't immediately upon us, we'd get out and on one occasion I picked up a mopane leaf and inside was a strange earlike pod. When I broke it, it smelled like turpentine.

"No protein yet," said Freddie, a Food Science major it turned out.

"Eunis would like them." Lewis a clever look, testing me. "All plump; that pretty black, gray and yellow."

"What does that mean?" I ran my finger over the pod.

"Later in the season there are swarms of fat worms that feed on these leaves."

"Yeah," said Lewis indicating we should get back on the road, "dry or roasted, people eat them."

I winced. "The worms?"

"Some make a stew. You know, soak them; add garlic and ginger."

A few miles west of the Pafuri Gate, the country changed dramatically. The hard-bitten shrub and mopane gave way to some small hills and lush green woodlands. "We're lucky the rainy season hasn't begun in earnest quite yet." Lewis stopped the car, turned it off and re-settled into his seat. "Plains normally flood around here, often serious floods. That river there, what's it called Lew?" (I'd had a 50-50 chance and had guessed incorrectly. Freddie was Lewis; Lewis was Freddie.)

Lewis checked the map. "Luvuvhu."

"Yeah," said Freddie. "Too much water. I'm told it rages. Over the bridge, over everything. People and cars swept downstream. Very sudden. Aah, but we're charmed." He winked at me, and then as proof, he scoped out the untroubled landscape. "You wonder why forecasters aren't ready for such things."

I thought better of opening *that* topic. "How far are we?"

"Not far." The real Lewis slapped a mosquito from his neck, pushed Freddie to the passenger seat, and turned on the ignition. "Four kilometers."

The sun began to set as we reached the South African side of the Pafuri Gate, a long, counterweighted bar blocking the road. Three male guards, arms kneaded dogmatically against their chests, apparently unhappy at our last-minute arrival. One tossed aside a cigarette.

"Here we go," said Freddie.

Each man dressed differently. One in camouflage jacket and ash-colored slacks. The second in a knee-length black trench coat and olive fatigue pants. The last, the chunkier of the three, wore a blue Adidas t-shirt, long shorts, and sneakers. They all wore black berets.

"Which one do you think is the leader?" Freddie smiled at the oncoming trio. "I'm taking bets."

"Too easy. First one to speak," said Lewis. He looked at me. "Better that *you* don't speak." He turned to the approaching guards. "Good afternoon, gentlemen." He leaned out the window.

"Passports, three-forty-ones, insurance papers. Please step out of the vehicle." The man in the camouflage jacket started to open Lewis' door. The man nodded to his compatriots, and they moved to the rear of our vehicle. "Let's be quick. You have another fifteen minutes, no ten, before we close and they're already closing up." He pointed the fifty yards to the Mozambique border; a woman on foot in traditional African garb, talking to those guards.

When I stepped out, the big man in shorts passed by, and almost fell over avoiding me. "Bladdy hell!"

"What is this you bring with you?" The leader in camouflage took the documents in his fist and slapped them against his leg. "You boys crazy." The big man scampered to the back of the Land Cruiser.

"She's our friend, she's American." Freddie got out the passenger side and moved to the front near me.

The leader held up his arm to stop him. "You boys go

in there and fill out the Embark/Disembark card for your passports, including hers. And don't forget your food receipts. Any salt or sugar?"

"No," said Lewis.

"Go on then." The leader didn't take his eyes off me. He said to the other two guards, "Go in with them and keep them moving." He pointed to a small, newly painted guardhouse, so tiny I wasn't sure four men could fit in it.

"What a G!" said the chunky guard, still keeping his distance. His disparaging tone clear.

"Go on." The leader waved them to the guardhouse. They began crowding in; Lewis looked back to me. The big one shoved him in.

"You are American?" asked the leader. He had a fierce, weather face, with pores that stood open against his sable skin.

"I am."

"I don't know what your friends have told you, but I strongly suggest you all turn around." Before I could open my mouth, he continued. "You are different, and where you are going people are going to be fearful of you."

"I'll be fine," I said.

"Those boys won't be able to protect you. No vacation can be so important."

"It's not a vacation." *But what is it?*

His jaw moved back and forth. He reached into the breast pocket of his jacket, and with broad hands pulled out what appeared to be a spider larger than his hand could contain. In one motion, he crushed it, setting the remaining body of the spider in his pocket and the other in his mouth. He began chewing on it. Later, when I asked, Lewis opined that it might have been Devil's Claw, a traditional anti-inflammatory. Said to be good for back pain. "Can cause diarrhea, too. But," he added, "it *could* have been a spider; there are all sorts of hoary superstitions still practiced here."

The guard scoffed. "What kind of business can you have in Limpopo Park?"

"No, not business exactly," I said. "I'm going on through the park."

"I should turn you around, for your own sake."

"No please, I'm trying to find a young girl."

He kept chewing and staring at me. "I should turn you around," he repeated. I stayed silent after that. Finally, with a deep sigh, he said, "You have boom?" Just then Lewis and Freddie and the other two guards came out of the small shack. "Howzit?" called the leader.

"Okay," said trench coat with a wave.

The leader spit spider juice to the dirt, turned to me. "Boom? You have it or not?" He pantomimed rolling a joint and sucking on it.

"You'll let us through?" asked Lewis.

The guard held out his thick, scarred palm and I went to the back seat. I tugged on Freddie's backpack where I'd seen him pull his small bag of stash. Lewis gave me a panicky glance, but when Freddie began to look too, Lewis turned him back to the guards.

I drew the bag out and gave it to the guard. "Can we go?" I asked.

He opened it, smelled it. "They can go." He waved to the

heavy one to open the gate. Freddie hung his head, closed his eyes, and swore under his breath. "Shite!"

I jumped into the backseat. Lewis got behind the wheel. Freddie glared at me as he slid in. The heavy guard put his weight on the barrier, and it began to rise. As we passed, he looked at me then turned away—fear he apparently wanted to control but couldn't.

〉〉〉

Fifty yards later, we were at the Mozambique border. It consisted of little more than chain link fence and a large round thatched roof hut. Hanging above the hut, the Mozambican flag, an AK-47 Kalashnikov rifle prominent on it. Not a family destination.

Two large, muscled guards walked slowly to us, dressed in identical military camouflage, dark blue berets, and yellow tinted sunglasses.

"You're cutting it close," said the bigger of the two, broad faced, mutilated lips, a gun on her hip.

"You, *Mzungu,*" she looked at me in the backseat, "hand those to me."

"What?"

"Your glasses," she said with impatience.

"These?" I held up my sunglasses.

"Yes," she said. "Give them to me."

Which I did. She examined them and waved us through.

〉〉〉

Around the campfire that evening, we traded college stories (theirs raunchy, mine benign) and cell phone numbers I was sure we'd never use. We drank the other six-pack Lewis had hidden plus a small pint of already dented vodka. Night sounds rose up around us. The fire snapped. The liquor crawled up on me. "I'm going to Tanzania."

"Tanzania!" Freddie stepped into the flickering light; Lewis handed him a joint. "Hitchhiking?"

"Smoke this," Lewis said through tight lips before exhaling. "They didn't get the good stuff. Let's celebrate our victories."

Yes, victories. I bowed to Lewis ever so slightly. We sat quietly nodding at the flames. Then Freddie asked again, "What's Tanzania about? And *you know* we won't be going there."

"I know." *Where to begin?* Buoyed by the ease with which I'd crossed two borders (three if I counted The States), I felt encouraged. Probably the vodka and pot. "I gave a friend hope, never thinking I could actually help. And here I am."

"Now another thirty-five hundred kilometers?" Freddie jousting with me.

"Two thousand miles," underscored Lewis.

"The closer I get," I shrugged, "the better chance of finding out what happened to a young woman. It's the least I can do. And it costs me nothing but time, which I have."

With those words, I invited something in, something vengeful. Smelled it even before it started snorting. It stampeded toward us, bulky, coming fast thru the tall brush. Untamed. "What's that?" I said, my neck ice. Lewis cocked his head.

Freddie caught and stifled his next word. "Baboon?" he whispered.

"Bigger," guessed Lewis, voice tight. "Hyena, maybe."

Whatever it was, could we make it to the Land Cruiser?

Lewis caught my eye. We both turned to Fred. Before any of us could get to our feet, it stopped. Suddenly nimble. Voiceless. It couldn't have been more than a few yards from us. Yet nothing whispered its existence.

I was on my feet, energy plowing through my body. Death ready to spring on me, calf muscles and Achilles' saying *hold your ground*. It's coming . . .

We held our breath, not sure if we should move. Not sure if one step or gulp of air would unleash it. By the look on their faces, Lewis and Freddie had no more idea than I. Even all three of us probably couldn't take it. Maybe survive. But . . . they were both willing to fight. *And here I am, totally unprepared.*

The Land Cruiser shimmied at the firelight's boundaries; perhaps twenty yards away, and out of reach. No outrunning the darkness. *What* was I ready to fight? The darkness invented stories. In each of them I asked myself—*if I survive this, and if I don't lose two more friends, is this a smart way to use my time? Why am I here?*

We waited another ten minutes scanning the periphery in total silence, the crackling fire breathing for us, until each of us could breathe on our own.

I asked, "Hyena are out here?"

A hushed unison, "Of course."

Far off in the almost deserted campground, someone turned on music—African by the sound of it—though it seemed a disservice to the setting and its primal energy. The music quickly became part of the air, deluding us that we were once again safe. Lewis motioned us back to the fire.

"Tanzania?" Freddie reprised his questioning. He motioned Lew to relight the joint.

"Right," I sighed. "Well . . ." I launched into my story about the station work (but not my intuitive episodes). I told them about Kyra.

"You're sure she's still alive?" asked Lewis.

"I'm not," I said.

After an awkward silence, Lewis spoke up. "Don't go. Way too dangerous."

Freddie said, "Stay with us our last few nights. I'd like to get to know you better."

Lewis ignored Freddie's maneuver. "We can't go with you, you must know that," he said.

"I do," I said. "I do." I had no idea what I was doing but so far so good.

Chapter 8

Parque de Nacional de Limpopo, Mozambique

That night the three of us slept in the tent, a tent big enough for two. I'd argued that I could sleep outside in my sleeping bag; they wouldn't hear of it. The lack of humidity made breathing more challenging for me. Yet sounds of the bush breathed everywhere, signals and warnings. Climbing into a smaller enclosure seemed counterintuitive. Yet inside, I was grateful; as if the canvas had the power to protect me, from *what* I couldn't be sure; I sensed restlessness in the bush. The cackles, the shrills, the sudden exorcizing of all sound—didn't keep me from sleep, if anything it lulled me. The testosterone in the tent tempted me to find relaxation—but I did not.

Well after the boys fell asleep, another force woke me: soundless, or should I say, it squeezed sound from the landscape, steadily, till there was none. I tried going back to sleep. But I could *feel* something taking its place. Breathing came easier. Then late—perhaps around midnight, possibly later (exhausted, having lost all sense of time)—there came a tapping on the tent. The boys oblivious. Freddie snoring. One of them farting.

It tapped again. The canvas roof. I held my breath; I didn't want to wake the boys. Probably nothing. It came, again and again. I waited. *Rain.* Quite a bit if I could count on my senses. Like a friend, comforting me. I fell asleep to its refrain.

))))

"Shite!" Freddie peered out of the tent. "Shite!"

Lewis stirred.

"What?" I asked.

"It's bloody bucketing!"

"Okay?" To me, a little rain, liquid dreams.

Freddie panted. "The plan was to take the bloody back road. Shorter." He looked to the floor for some sort of confirmation then above, as thrumming increased. The tent rippled with wind, swelled with small rumbles of thunder. "It was kind of on the map," he continued, spooked. "Kind of. An offshoot of Route Four-Two-Three. We'd drop you off at the Limpopo before we head to the airport."

"That's sweet of you, but why don't we take one of the more common—?"

"It isn't dust anymore, it's *clag!*" Freddie lowered his voice, a growl not markedly above the downpour. "Shite!"

"That bad?" I said. "We can take more established roads."

"Come here." He waved me to the tent flap and opened it. He held his hand out, and when I didn't, he pulled mine out with his, palms up. "Open your hand." He flicked his finger hard against my upper arm.

"Hey!" I readied to punch him back. In seconds, water overflowed my outstretched palm.

"All the roads are turning to shit."

I dumped the water and patted my hand dry, soaking my cutoffs. "You don't know that." The rain had cooled the heat; it wasn't so bad, though my instinct told me the shower wasn't about to stop.

"If we take the short cut, the one I planned," said Fred, "it'd be about an hour and a half. . . depending on the road—one I've never been on before. Call it three hours in this weather. Likely more. I don't know my way around here anymore than you do."

"Then maybe the traditional roads?" I suggested again.

"Dirt!" He lashed out. "*Dirt* roads. In clear conditions, probably twelve hours. But in this . . ." He pulled his hand inside the tent and shook off the water, spraying Lewis, ". . . double it; maybe even triple it."

"Thirty-six hours?" I said.

"What's thirty-six hours?" Lewis sat up, his sleeping bag slipped open, revealing his happiness with the morning. He pulled the sleeping bag around his waist and looked guilty.

"It's raining," I said.

"It's chucking down, hard!" Freddie closed the flap.

"We'll wait it out." Lewis began wrestling with the bag, pulling his shorts on.

"Can't do that." Freddie motioned for both of us to get moving.

"Why not?" Lew just wanted to get into his shorts.

Freddie pointed. A steady stream rolled into our tent, across the powdered earth and out the other side of the tent.

"Allowing for the lay of the land, I'm surprised we're not sitting in the middle of a shallow pond. We need to get out. And if this really is bad, you and I, Mister Clarke, need to head in the other direction—without delay."

"The plane tickets," Lew said.

Freddie wasn't pleased; he made it clear with a pained look. "Exactly."

Without further discussion the three of us packed, hunched over, bumping butts, and wrestling for space. I stuffed my sleeping bag like I was wrestling a gorilla, gambit by gambit as if the pounding sky challenged me to meet it with equal intensity. But it really wasn't the overwrought rain that was the problem. It was Fred.

"It's just rain," I said. Was going back even an option anymore? Especially with my mouth yappin', making statements I shouldn't have been making. Certainly not to Ruthie. And after what I'd just told the guys?

I hadn't been used to hearing myself speak for so many years, then when I did, I'd gotten to like it—maybe a little too much. Thinking I could find Kyra? Hubris. What did I really think I could do—with no language but my own, one shitty map, no knowledge of Mozambique or Tanzania; thousands of Dr. Allens avoiding me, almost no money, all for a young girl I'd never met, didn't know, who could be . . . by now . . . dead. To the locals I was a nosey *mzungu* and not a very bright one, at that. Oh, and the first impression I made with my face, enough to terrify a witch doctor.

Lewis joined us hovered around the tent opening. "What about the tent?" He turned and looked at the peak. A large dark mass had accumulated. Water began filtering through the canvas to the ground, turning it to mud. The tent whipped with the steady sound of a shooting arcade. "To hell with it." Freddie flung the hood over his head. "It's a beat-up piece of rental turd; we'll leave it here. I'll pay for it."

Lew's head wavered; he hadn't heard properly. "What?"

"Let's go." Freddie didn't wait. He disappeared into the pewter light. I bolted after him through a steady sheet of water, through an inch or two of gunk, maybe more, sucking at my shoes, to the Land Cruiser. I threw my shit into the backseat, Lewis went for shotgun, and Freddie and I collided at the driver door.

"Go round." Freddie pointed to the other side of the vehicle.

"I could drive, you know." I swallowed rain.

"It's bleeding wet out here. Go on, it's my bloody name on the rental."

I went to the other side and got in the back. Fred cranked the engine. It didn't take. A bandolier of liquid bullets sheared across the windshield. "Just rain?!" quarreled Fred, though he never looked my way. He dropped open his hood, shook off his parka. "Johannesburg, right? We're turning around. We're all agreed?"

Lewis nodded acknowledging, "Seems right to me—at least heading back in the right direction. We can't miss that flight."

They both turned to me.

I massaged my head. "There's a part of me . . ."

"You can't be serious." Lewis, not Freddie, nonplussed.

"Start the car, Fred. She's mad crazy, not in her right blooming head."

Freddie turned the key again; the Cruiser gave off a gruff but solid hum.

"C'mon guys, it's just a little rain," I said, "not locusts. I'll be fine. Don't worry about me."

"A *little* rain?"

"Even our tent wasn't that bad," I said. "I think you're making more of this—" A pain jumped through my chest. It must have shown.

Lewis reached for me. "You alright?"

I drew away as if touching might create an electrical arc. A warning? I felt Ruthie take my hand. Her whole family hovered over me, imploring me. *Kyra!*

I gathered my backpack. "I'm supposed to go forward. I'll be fine. Along the road someone will give me a ride, probably someone leaving the campsite."

"No, no, no. Sit back down, sister. You can't go out in this." Freddie reached over and grabbed for my pack.

"I've got to go." I tugged back. "You said three hours. I have the time."

"It was a guess, by car and not in this slop." He wouldn't let go of my pack.

I wrestled for it. "You said three hours in this weather."

He held tight to it. "A torrential blitzkrieg. . . And not on an unnamed road. On foot."

I let go. "You said it was on the map."

"Kind of."

"Okay," I said. "It'll stop raining. Really, I don't mind getting wet. I've been wet all my life. It agrees with me." Wetlands, lakes: the best of my Bemidji childhood purled over me. "I think I'll kind of enjoy it."

"Can't let you go," said Freddie.

"Stop," injected Lew. "Listen. If we drive her to Mapai, she can cross the Limpopo River there; someone will give her a lift. She'd be a fifth of the way up Mozambique. And we could make it back."

"In this . . .? Tight," Freddie said. "Very tight. I don't think any of this makes sense—for us or for Eunis. Come on, let's head back."

"No, I'm going." I grabbed again for my gear.

"Mulish!" Freddie hit the accelerator; I fell backward. We were off. He switched the wipers to high.

Lewis apprehensive. "Where are you going?"

Freddie leaned into the windshield. "Like you said, Limpopo."

"You shouldn't do this," I said. "It's not fair. Let me off. You guys have plans."

"I know." Fred peered into the abyss, the 4x4 hurling us off the seats and against the frame as we drove forward, Freddie's own manic energy wrestling with it.

"Fred!" Lew grabbed the handle over the door. It came off in his hand. "Shit!"

"Just eighty-five kilos," Fred yelled back.

"What's that?" I asked above the roar of rain. "Fifty miles?"

"About. Just keep your eyes open." Freddie flipped on the headlights. "Shit!" They made visibility worse; he turned them off.

Lew seized Fred's arm. "Sod's Law. What do you think you're doing? Let her go if she's that crazy."

Freddie cast him off. "It was your idea."

"Just a thought, really."

"Just keep us on the fuckin' road, okay?" said Freddie. "It should be mostly flat, pretty open, mostly mopane scrub and trees around here."

"And ironwoods." Lewis reminding us of what could meet us head on.

It had no effect. "Probably." Freddie patted the Cruiser's dusty dashboard, inviting its participation, then raised his chalky fingertips and, alert to the deluge around him, laughed. In a dropped voice he continued, "Just keep your eyes open."

The first forty-five minutes (after Lewis and I hounded him to slow down), Freddie kept a constant twenty miles an hour. Lewis and I pointed out bloated shapes as they appeared left or right. Sporadically, the Cruiser *skated* left *and* right. We slogged through deep ruts and puddles, spraying the windows so thick with mud we had to crank them open to wipe them off, further smearing the scuz and blurring our visibility.

The rain lightened up here and there, once even ceasing altogether (the sun striking through the clouds and twisting the landscape into a combo of colors I've never seen before: a belt of steel gray sky, and below it a band of rose and orange dust. Above the gray, white gold. But only for about five minutes before the harness of metal gray absorbed the others, and the rain started up again).

Three or four times we rammed or slid off a bush, but no crunching impact. After a while we all got into the rhythm of our jobs. We all relaxed, *a little*. An adventure.

"See," said Freddie. "Half-way there. Piece of piss."

Lewis stared ahead, still watchful. "How do you know that?"

"Chicualacuala, we just passed it."

"What?" Lew rubbed the window to see.

"Chicualacuala, almost the halfway point, more or less. Somewhere off on our left, across the river."

Lewis rocked forward. "A real town!"

Freddie pointed to his left. "Across the river, behind us a bit."

In a blink, the air and rain shifted, containing violence. Goosebumps ran up my arms. "I don't think we—" The Toyota lurched forward and began sliding down a slope.

"Shit!" Freddie wrestled with the wheel, tapped the brake. It merely turned us parallel to the slope. The 4x4 slid faster, and worse, backward. Freddie grabbed the hand brake; practically tore it off the floor. We slowed a bit.

Then we went under.

In seconds, the river flowed over the open windows and worked its way up Lewis' hip.

"Sack-it, everybody out!" Freddie lifted his hands off the wheel to show us he had zero control. He leapt for the window, but the 4x4—now in the river's current—took on more water and traveled downstream.

My first instinct was to get free of the vehicle. I expected they'd do the same. But Lewis hesitated. I reached over the seat and, with the rising water assisting me, pulled him into the back. "Hey, what!?"

What the hell was I doing?! I shoved him out the backseat window. In a flash, he trailed the slab of metal. I yelled to Lew, "Feet in front, go with the flow. Get away from the car as soon as you can. It'll suck you down."

Freddie was halfway out his window.

"Shit no, Freddie," I yelled. "The Cruiser's gonna pull you under or pin you. Get out this side, *behind* it."

But he was already out the window into the river, flapping arms trying to get right, spiraling. The Toyota rolled into him, pressing him downstream, a metal leviathan taking control of how he would end.

I dove out my window. The 4x4 took on more water but stayed afloat. "Freddie! Freddie can you hear me?"

"Yes." He began coughing.

I yelled, "Can you move left or right?"

"No, Cruiser's got me pinned."

This is your fault, Eunis. "Can you slip over the top?" *Under too dangerous.*

"Maybe," he spluttered.

"Come."

Freddie tried to propel himself atop the Cruiser. He slipped off. I heard the 4x4 bash part of his body, a terrible hallow wallop like a melon split open. "Freddie? Freddie, you okay?" I heard voices through the rain. But not his. "Freddie?"

A groan.

"Shit." I took a lungful and dove under the 4x4, the water churned and muddy. I could barely make out a tire. The river wanted to twirl me around, but I headed for that tire, the only visible constant in the bedlam of brown grit. When I came up—still on the north side trailing the vehicle—Freddie thrashed about on the other side. "Freddie?"

He hacked. "I guess I bodged this."

"Shut up. Stay where you are. I'm coming to get you."

"No!"

I dove again, swimming with the unshakeable current, blinded by the silt, pounded by boles and debris. The right side of my head slammed against the under carriage of the 4x4. Light plowed through my skull and hammered it with pain. I'd opened a gash and the river's gravel peppered it. Unless I outswam the current, I'd stayed pinned, almost out of air. Then *Freyja*, my childhood hero, inhabited me, her mermaid hair flowing over my shoulders. I surged forward and surfaced an arm's length from Freddie. I gasped for air.

His eyelids fluttered open. "You're an arsehole." He coughed river. Clearly weakening, his arm flailed at the Toyota's roof.

"Shut up. You listen," I said. The voices on the shore louder. "I'm a good swimmer."

"I'll bet you're a regular Melusine," he said. "But you're also an arsehole. Why kill us both? Get to shore."

"No one's dying here, not today anyhow." A protest rather than a statement.

The 4x4 started to tumble forward on us. I grabbed him around the waist. "Don't pull me under like the typical drowning victim."

"Who says I'm drowning?"

"Okay," I managed to say, "you're waving unconvincingly. Take a deep breath and swim with me, don't fight me. I'll guide you."

"Up stream, no fucking way." He flayed at the roiling river.

"Oh yes!" I slapped him hard once to the left of his chin. His eyes bugged out like a cartoon wolf. "Take the fucking breath," I screamed. And he did.

I pulled him under with me, a couple of extra feet deeper to avoid the tires and wheels. He dragged, like the guy in Bemidji who tried to rape me in Kingdom Lake. I'd had to hit him too; knocked him out. But Freddie, still conscious, stayed with me. We drifted upwards. He tried to paddle with his free hand. Of little use. Our backs scrapped along the 4x4's undercarriage. He trilled bubbles, losing more air. He swallowed redundant river. He began convulsing. He bucked. I strained. The river slowed. *Widening out?* My arms burned. *You're not going to die this way. This is* your *domain.* The water churned. I propelled through; I held him tight to my body. *Avoid drag.* I commanded myself one, two and a third last thrust. A moment of light-headedness, the end near, *my last flash of consciousness before eternity?* We emerged above the surface, still bobbing and reeling. The rain had stopped.

"There!" I heard Lew's voice. "Eunis, here. Over here!"

Freddie spluttered, coughed; threw up. He clung to me. We drifted to the far shore. The flooded river spread wider, the current decelerating. Once again, I'd put someone near to me close to death. Not this time, thank goodness; this time Lewis and Freddie were alive, and I'd made it, inelegantly, to Mozambique.

Chapter 9

Mapai, Mozambique

A small group of brightly clothed Bantu men and women, and their mud-caked oxen, watched from the riverbank as the Toyota drifted past them and struck with a thud against a crudely made barge of recycled wood, worn tires and Styrofoam. They cheered and clapped.

I lugged Freddie to the shore and pried his fingers off my arm. "You rest."

He threw his head back, rubbed his throat and coughed several times.

Lewis ran up to us. "You two alright?"

I lay spread-eagled on the mud, watching threaded clouds clear to blue. My eyes hurt. "He drank the river," I said. "Watch him."

My view eclipsed; a very dark-skinned man in casual western clothes leaned over me, blocking the sky. "Limpopo flowed not past but through you, eh?" He wore dark glasses but not the wide, foreboding reflector kind so in vogue, but rather hexagonal 1960's-style "granny" glasses, the type I suppose

John Lennon or Gloria Steinem might have worn. His clean white shirt and brown trousers suggested a man of some polish. He removed his glasses. His head somewhat egg-shaped. "Your John Muir said so, no?" A cryptic, tight-lipped smile. Despite his thin frame, his rolled-up sleeves left no doubt that he was well toned, even muscular.

"American? English?" he asked, his eyes persistent. "Not Mozambican?" Sheen defined his high cheekbones, yet his clean-shaven cheeks, taught and concave, showed little perspiration. A man loose in his body. Nor did he appear to be surprised by my albinism or my distorted features.

"British," said Lewis.

"The three of you?" asked the African, not taking his eyes off me.

"My friend and I," said Lewis. He pointed to Freddie wheezing on the sand. "She's American."

The man lifted his head and acknowledged Lew. "Your vehicle?" He pointed to the Toyota. When he did, no longer blocking the sun, I had to squint. I missed my sunglasses.

"Yes," Lewis said.

"Where do you go next?" he inquired.

"Johannesburg, we have to catch a flight."

He seemed disappointed. "I can help you get the Toyota back across. It will cost, of course." He raised his hands in explanation. "Not me. But those men," he gestured at the locals along the shore. "They must get paid. Do you have money?"

The Bantu had gathered around the Toyota, chattering among themselves. Lewis assured the African. "We have *some* money . . ."

Freddie groaned.

". . . Not much," Lew added.

The African called to Freddie. "You are okay?"

Fred waved. "Knackered, but fine." He hacked anew.

The African turned to me and reached out. "I will help you up."

I hesitated.

"*Sitiyenera kusokoneza ndi Limpopo*," he said. "You should not fool with river." He wiggled his fingers for me to take his hand. I took it. He lifted me off the wet sand and silt. He held my hand until I pushed his away. "Thank you," I said. I began separating the soaked t-shirt from my skin and brushing the clumps of mud off me.

Freddie rose unsteadily and stumbled into me, giving me a hug. "You are something, sister."

The African's eyes widened, a raven quality that went beyond their onyx cast. "She is your sister?"

"No," said Freddie, "that's just a phrase. She's our friend. We've been traveling with her for a few days. She's trying to get to Tanzania. We have to go back home."

The African slipped his dark glasses back on. "*Mwayi.*" He translated. "How fortunate. Perhaps I can help. Let me introduce myself. I'm Erevu Ngowa. I am Tanzanian."

Lewis seemed relieved. "You can help her?"

"I can try." His English excellent, even formal, with very little accent.

I became immediately resistant. "I'll be fine." *Maybe I should return with Lew and Fred.*

"Eunis," Freddie injected, finally steadying, "the man is

trying to help you. And we really must get going. Unless you'll reconsider coming with us."

"'Once you carry your own water,'" quoted Mr. Ngowa, "'you'll remember every drop.' An African proverb. You will never forget Tanzania."

"Eunis?" said Lew.

"You go," I said to the boys, "you've already done too much, I'll be fine."

Lewis gave it a second thought. "Mr. Ngowa, how is it that you can help our friend?"

"I said *I will try*," the man said. "My business here is almost done, and I will be flying home soon."

"Thank you, sir," I said having no idea what my next steps would be, "but I don't have airfare."

"Hmm, no airfare. Perhaps that won't be an issue," he said, very off handed.

Freddie started tugging on Lewis' sleeve. Lewis brushed back his hair, assuming a fatherly role, though I've never had the experience of one to compare. "What kind of business are you in, sir?"

Freddie leaned into Lewis *sotto voce*. "You can see he's no spiv."

The African gave no indication that he'd heard Freddie or cared. He looked to the horizon which had now cleared. "Troposcatter." Then back to us, knowing full well we had no idea what he was talking about. He produced that strained, ambiguous smile again. *Who did he remind me of?* "This land," Mr. Ngowa continued, "with its terrain, allows us to transmit microwave signals almost two hundred miles, using the troposphere. We scout and build tropospheric scatter antennas."

"You mean beyond line of sight?" I asked.

He looked surprised. "Why, yes. Do you know about such things?"

"A little. I'm learning."

"Well then, perhaps I can show you one, if we have time."

"Well, *we* don't have time," Freddie interjected. "And if you could negotiate a price we can afford," he looked to the Toyota, "we would be very appreciative. Wouldn't we, Lew?"

Lewis checked with me. I nodded. "You better go."

Lewis studied Ngowa one last time. "You'll take care of her?"

"I will do my best," said the Tanzanian.

Lewis still the worried dad, placed his hand on my arm. "You call us when you get to Tanzania, okay?"

"Okay."

"Lew!" Freddie gave me a peck on the cheek, embraced me and started toward the beached Toyota.

Lewis hugged me. "You be safe. And you call us."

The boys scurried to the Toyota, Mr. Ngowa hustling after them. I thought, *I should be thankful for Ngowa's offer.* Yet I was diffident. *Why was he open to helping me?* My childhood aversion to trusting anyone. People could be generous; I'd been the recipient of some, the victim of others. So, when Freddie came running back with my water-logged backpack, I seriously considered re-joining them to Johannesburg. Freddie said nothing but again kissed me on the cheek before sprinting to the Toyota as the Bantu loaded it on to the makeshift barge.

Quite a few of the locals had spread along either side of the flooded river, watching captain-less skiffs, chunks of natural debris and the carcasses of rats, mongoose, dogs, baboons, and a bloated blue wildebeest drift swiftly by.

Above the hum of the river and the babble of the people, came the clonk and clank of an engine. Across the river a familiar van pulled to the bank. Out of it came Marius and Sheila with the rest of the Weather One crew close behind. They began to set up to shoot footage. I caught a glimpse of Kaplan; I wanted to wave but . . .

A wooden rowboat overflowing with sand had lodged on the bank twenty or so yards from me. In that split second, I decided to hide from the crew. I moved to it, a fugitive, head low. I laid down behind it. If Sheila caught me there, I'd certainly be fired, sent home immediately and Gordon would be dealing with the fallout for years. *I'd never find answers for Ruthie and her family.* Hiding behind the doomed skiff, I questioned how warped my choices had become.

My backpack! All I had. It sat in the sand, alone, a temptation to anyone walking along my side of the river. If I were to retrieve it, Marius, who had affixed the camera to the tripod and was looking through the eyepiece framing the shot, could easily identify me. I breathed heavily. I peeked above the dinghy. Sheila and Kaplan stood alongside Marius and Trig, all surveying the swollen river.

Directly across from me, several yards from where I lay, Kaplan spotted a fat beige crocodile paddling with the current. He began pointing for Marius to grab footage of it. I ducked my head.

Only a minute later voices erupted, Sheila's the loudest among them. *Had they seen me?* I snuck a look above the rowboat. All eyes tracked a young steenbok or impala as it thrashed desperately away from the closing crocodile. It never made it to shore. The croc pulled the helpless animal under, then whipped it viciously side-to-side like a ragdoll. Blood circled the beast and its predator before the near lifeless antelope and the croc disappeared below the surface.

"You are a bit squeamish? That is the word, yes?" Mr. Ngowa stood above me, holding my backpack. "This is yours, yes?"

"Yes," I said above a whisper, unable to move. "Thank you." A sigh of relief.

"Perhaps you would be more comfortable if we moved on," he said.

"Well," I searched for an explanation, "I just need to ground myself after, you know . . ."

He nodded, tucked the backpack next to me, and sat down on the edge of the sand-logged boat. "Very well." And there he sat for thirty or forty minutes as the Weather One crew videotaped b-roll and a couple of standups with Sheila. All the while, he watched the TV crew and the rolling river, and never said another word to me. If he made the connection between the crew and me, I didn't know. I shut my eyes to the sun's glare and nested in the sand. When I heard the Weather One 4x4 start up and drive off, I had mixed feelings. What, exactly, was I doing?

Lew and Fred and the Toyota were gone. Mr. Ngowa loomed above me watching the river. "I really don't want to take advantage of your generosity," I said looking into his sunglasses. "Why would you want to help me?"

"Do you know what *buda* is?"

I sat up and looked again to make sure that the van and Sheila's crew were gone. "Superstition," I said. Caked sand trickled from my chest and arms. *Buda.* Sheila had mentioned it. Freddie, too.

"It means," he continued, 'the one with the evil eye.' In Swahili, *jicho baya*. The one that shape-shifts and is given strength by the evil spirit. Many years ago, when I was in your country, in Los Angeles, a man I met through business dealings, turned on me. He pointed at me and accused me '*buda!*' Like that."

Ngowa placed his index finger gently on my throat. His eyes—hidden behind his shades—steady on me. His voice restrained. "He was not African. He was a white man, from New Jersey, I think. He was trying to manipulate my emotions. *Kuphwanya.* He wanted to pillage me." Ngowa's energy rushed into and through me. I couldn't speak. He lifted his hand off my throat. He *looked* at it. "Do you know what I did with the white man?"

I could hardly move my head.

He continued. "The *buda* curses are rooted in envy. So, I turned on him, this evil spirit, like hyena, so he knew I could attack, but also to offer him this thought . . ." Ngowa rolled out another African saying, then translated. "Between imitation and envy, imitation is better.' And the Los Angeles white man, this *buda* himself, became my business partner. You see, you never know when you meet people if they are light or dark. I am open to all, why limit my options?" He bent his head as if to say *at your service*.

I managed to speak. "I don't understand."

"I think you do," he said. "But let us not quibble. Perhaps we will not be friends, but perhaps allies, eh?"

He didn't wait for me to repeat my straight-forward question. *How could I help him?*

"Naturally, "Mr. Ngowa went on, "I serve someone too, and he wants what he wants. He pays me well for it, and if we do not take off this afternoon, he will be displeased."

I reminded him. "I have almost no money."

"In U.S. dollars or Tanzanian shillings?"

"Dollars, but not many."

"You will not need them for our flight. But once you land you shouldn't have U.S. currency on your person."

"Why not?" I asked.

He thought for a moment. "It will bring bad luck."

Chapter 10

Guija, Mozambique

Despite the torrential rain, dust had already begun again to sweep across the road, a cloak of tiny grains pelting the windshield and occasionally my face. "I don't understand how I can help you," I said to Mr. Ngowa. I rubbed my eyes.

"We will see. Do not worry." He kept his attention on the road. At the same time, he opened the glove compartment and fished out an old pair of sunglasses. "Our sun, it hurts your eyes," he said. "Here." He handed them to me, an odd pair with bold yellow striated frames, like those of a tiger.

"Thank you, that's kind."

He identified with my mirthful reaction to them and chuckled. "They were given to me by a colleague's wife; she designs such things." He set aside their absurdity. "Better to stumble with toe than tongue. A gift is a gift." I thanked him again; what more could I say, he being so charitable?

Out of Mapai, and shortly after we passed a row of slaughtered carcasses hanging from a roadside butchery, Ngowa turned his rattle-trap Jeep south for another thirty minutes to a low concrete block building, surrounded entirely by sand. It sat apart from the few other structures. No shrubs, no trees. No visible indication or signage what it was.

He told me to go inside and that he would come in separately, and stand within earshot, which he did. The building possessed a sour, locked in odor. It clattered despite the few bodies and the marginal activity in it. A bank of some sort.

A very small Chinese woman, only with difficulty able to see over the counter, came to the teller's window. She took one look at me, turned her back on me and walked away, Mr. Ngowa only a short distance behind. Somehow, I knew he'd disapprove if I asked for his help, so I never turned to him. Nor did he offer assistance.

I called out. "Can someone help me here, please. *Chonde*." Two women joined the tiny woman under a doorjamb leading to another office. *Chonde!* I repeated.

A fourth, rather hefty woman, also Chinese, came from behind and pushed the others aside, coming forward.

"I can help you," she said.

I explained that I wanted to change my dollars into Tanzanian shillings. She pointed to a sign indicating some sort of additional Mozambican fee for changing directly into Tanzanian currency, and I acknowledged it.

She took my passport and money, counted it slowly, snapping the crisper ones, and laying the bills into a drawer below her. She counted out the equivalent in Tanzanian shillings, slipped them across the counter and began to walk away.

"No, no!" I heard Mr. Ngowa say. "That will not do."

The teller turned to him. Ngowa motioned her forward. He pointed to me. "Put the money back on the counter." This was where I was going to lose my last $150.

"Miss?" he said to the woman.

"Zhou." She lifted her chin, ready to brawl.

"Miss Zhou, I believe you shorted this woman." Ngowa tapped the counter.

She looked at him and dismissed him. "*Pitani mukamuvutitse wopusa wina.*"

"Shall I call Mr. Hsu?" Ngowa leveled her with a stare.

She froze. "You know Hsu?"

"Shall I call him?" Ngowa asked again.

"No," she moved forward. "Pehaps you are right. Perhaps I made a small error."

"I am sure you would want to correct it," said Mr. Ngowa.

"Yes, I would want to correct it," she said opening the drawer.

And so I walked out fully paid.

"Thank you," I said to Mr. Ngowa.

"Allies," he said holding open the passenger door for me. Then didn't say another word till we reached gargantuan antennas, another half hour away. At their base, nothing but a badly windswept wooden shack. Unmanned.

The two antennas sat side by side, like giant convex drive-in movie screens or billboards, 200 to 300 feet tall, with wingspans half as wide.

"This is a tropospheric relay station," Mr. Ngowa explained. "They are spread throughout parts of Africa, the world, and your own country. The transmitting site sends the signal to the horizon, and when it hits its peak at the bottom of the stratosphere, it reradiates or scatters the transmission in a forward direction to a receiving site. Basically UHF, ultrahigh frequency microwaves above three hundred megahertz—in our system, usually higher. Do you gauge what I am saying?"

"A little bit. I studied scientific patterns in college. When you say, 'its peak,' you mean the highest curve of the earth between sites?"

"Correct. Its value being that it can go beyond line of sight by bouncing the signal with very low maintenance."

"But weather patterns can mess with this system?" I said.

"Very perceptive," he said. "They can, but there are ways to improve the tropo reliability. It's quite technical and not my area of expertise."

"Are you familiar with the Schumann Frequency, the earth's resonance?" I said. "The way lightning affects it and all of us?"

"Yes." He assessed me, a moment in which I sensed I delighted him. "The earth's heartbeat. Frequencies affect all of us. It's particularly strong in Africa." He looked at his watch. "We will need to move on. The plane is ready. I cannot be late."

))))

A man in a claret burnoose opened the car door for Mr. Ngowa and shook his hand. Ngowa said something to him and waved at me to climbed out of the Jeep. We were ringed by small clumps of damp and powdered dirt, in every direction. A small shrub hare darted out of the underbrush. The man in the burnoose recoiled at the sight of me (not unusual), but then proceeded to avoid meeting my eyes or even recognize my existence. I grabbed my backpack and began rooting through it for my passport. On first search it wasn't there. I flushed. *Oh please, no.*

"Something wrong?" Ngowa headed for the cockpit of the small, fixed-wing plane.

"Can't find my passport," I said. Blood rushed to my head. *Fuck!*

"I'm sure it is there, and you will not need it here," he assured me.

Not need it to leave? "But when I get to Tanzania . . .?"

"Did you remove it from your backpack?" He strapped a thin worn leather pouch over his back.

"Yes, at the bank."

"I saw her return it to you," he said.

I relaxed. "She did?"

"So, you will find it during our flight, I am sure. Please hurry, we must be on our way."

The man in the burnoose handed Mr. Ngowa an envelope or a thin book. Ngowa slipped it into his leather pouch, while the man in the burnoose took Ngowa's small suitcase and stored it astern of the pilot's seat. He looked at Ngowa for further directions, but Ngowa signaled him to step away. As Ngowa climbed into the cockpit and took his place at the dashboard, he opened his palm, unfurled some sort of simple-stringed necklace, and draped it around his neck. Looking closely, a small wooden disc dangled from it, resembling an eye.

The single-prop plane had seen better days. Painted white, it had begun shedding its newer, sooty skin, revealing an undercoat of flecked red stripes along its fuselage and wings.

Neither the plane nor the Jeep mirrored the refinement I'd envisaged for Ngowa, nor had I ever supposed him as the pilot. Why this disturbed me, I can't say. Once again, I questioned my good luck in finding him.

He signaled for me to get in the cockpit with him. Once in, we almost brushed shoulders nor was it big enough to leave my backpack at my feet. I dropped it over the seat and surveyed the stripped-down interior. It had an almost aquatic motif—a Byzantine panel of levers, switches, buttons, gauges, and straggly wires. A collection of controls where I had none. It raised my flying anxiety to a new level. I yanked at my hair.

He turned the key, engaged the propeller, and told me to strap myself in.

"I've only flown six times," I said looking at the joystick—not even a steering wheel. The tin metal junker began to reverberate. It rattled through my feet, up my legs and body. I banded my arms around myself.

He laughed. "Six times—you are sure of the number, I can see."

"I am," I said, the memory of each previous flight starting to roll distressfully across my chest. But the rattle of the plane so loud that I sat back.

"You still need to strap yourself in." He stared straight ahead at the caked earth beneath our wheels. "We carry precious cargo."

"We do?"

"Yes, you." A microscopic curve crooked his lips, leaving a mildly rigid smile.

I returned an anemic one of my own and harnessed myself in.

"You do not like flying?" he said. He brought the howl of the engine louder.

"I told you, this is only my sixth time."

"*Értóng.* This is not The Flying Dutchman." He released the brake. The propeller circled so fast, it stood still. "We will make it to the ground if you let us," he said, his eye pinned on the dirt and dust ahead of us.

A nervous chuckle. "Me? I'm trusting *you.*"

"Well, yes, as you see, we are allies." He fingered the amulet he'd placed around his neck. He pushed the joystick forward and the plane bumped along the earth, humming and clanging with shrill cries from the wheels.

"What was that?" I said. The cockpit so loud he didn't hear me. Or gave no indication that he had. We gained speed. I closed my eyes. We left the ground. My stomach rolled. The plane tilted. I opened my eyes.

"Is it true," he asked, "that *buda* is unhappy in small enclosures? That they don't like to fly in manmade machines?"

"What?"

"You seem like a fish out of water," he said. A peculiar delight rolled off his words.

I gave him an incredulous look. "Yes, I'm uncomfortable. I told you, I don't like to fly."

"No, I see that. Well, it is not a long flight, and you can watch the land below. But remember that I am the one piloting, and you will thank me." He had a strange way of seeing himself.

"Without question, I will." I took a breath.

"Yes," he said above the engine's bellow. "We go west then north. Over Parque Nacional de Banhine, over Parque Nacional de Zinave. Five hours to Nyanga, where we'll refuel."

Five hours! "I thought a couple hours. Five hours, holy sh—
. . . Nyanga, where's that?"

"Zimbabwe," he said. No emotion on his face, but I'd swear
he was prodding me. "You can see this is no jet. But it will get
us there."

I took in a breath, I looked below; the land flat and baked,
studded with captive trees far to the horizon, fighting to hold
their moisture. So unlike Minnesota with its autonomous
hydration. He motioned to my lap. "You are crossing your
fingers. You think that helps?" Once more, that dismissive
smirk of his.

Sure enough, I hadn't realized I'd crossed them. "No, I-I
don't know what I was thinking." I unlaced them.

"You do not think I would hurt myself, do you?" he asked.

"What?" I tried to measure his face, but his concentration
was on piloting. I appreciated that. Something swiftly came
over me, out of my mouth, "What are you wearing around
your neck?"

"I think you know." Ngowa tapped hard on a dial that
didn't meet his favor.

My jaw constricted. "I wouldn't ask if I did." *That sounded
rude.*

He murmured under his breath—in Swahili, I think.
"Maswali yako yatajibiwa hivi karibuni." He continued to tend
to his dials, feigning that he hadn't heard me, or that he wasn't
going to respond.

I reached out and clutched his arm. "I didn't mean—"

He yelped and let loose the air stick; the plane lurched and
began to dive. "What are you doing?!" he screamed.

I freed his arm, surprised I'd even touched him.

The plane began to roll. His eyes too. He fumbled with the stick, struggling against the spin. "We are allies, stop this!" he yelled.

My stomach dropped away; words knocked from me. I gripped the seat.

The plane shuddered, rotated, stalled, the engine spluttering. We began to leave the blue. The earth and sky pulled at me, both with force; we plummeted. Ngowa set his feet hard against the dented metal floor and pulled urgently on the stick. "*Buda!*" He rotated the stick; he planted his feet again and grimaced against the gravitational pull. The plane banked, he pulled up on the stick, he retook control.

We stabilized. He wouldn't look at me.

I trembled. "I'm sorry, I didn't mean to—"

"I can leave you in Nyanga." He stared straight ahead.

"Why didn't you leave me in Mapai?" I sounded ungrateful.

"I was doing you a good deed. Is that not what you call it?" He finally looked at me. "I know who you are. Why cannot we work together?" A measure of fear, for the first time, in his eyes.

I huffed, still trying to catch my breath. "I don't know what you mean."

"I should have left you in Chicualacuala."

"The village *before* Mapai?" I said. "You met me after that."

He appeared to rethink his comment. "Of course." He leaned, more relaxed, into his seat. "So, do you want to get to Tanzania?"

"I do, and I'm sorry; I'm not sure what spooked me."

He took hold of the amulet hanging from his neck. "I can even quote *your* scripture, if that appeases you."

"No thanks, I got plenty of that at home."

Mr. Ngowa went ahead anyhow, parroting The Bible, "'Your path led through the sea, your way through the mighty waters, though your footprints were not seen.'"

"Huh? Who do you think I am?" I asked.

He gripped the joystick more firmly. "Let me get us to Nyanga. You can depart there."

Chapter 11

Nyanga, Zimbabwe

We flew inland, to the dry western side of a mountain range, and too close to it. Even though we stayed low, I didn't see more than twelve or fifteen people below during the entire flight. I attempted to make conversation with Mr. Ngowa, to ask about the local people, the customs and to pinpoint where we were. He shunned me or gave clipped answers that delivered little insight about anything. Finally, I gave up. Probably for the best. Any conversation above that engine gatling, for those five hours, would have been even more grueling.

I fell into a reverie, the land reinforcing my journey, assuring me everything was going to plan, and to relax. But as the terrain became steeper, we were forced to go higher. My ears filled with pressure; I could see the fuel gauge dropping quickly. Ngowa gave it no mind. Not until we began to strafe a heavily forested ridge. The engine began to sputter. The fuel gauge plunged to zero. The plane gasped some more. We'd almost run out of fuel. With nowhere to land.

Ngowa leaned on the joystick. We began to fall. He wasn't the least concerned, his face invigorated and transfixed on the dense trees moving faster—and closer—below. I said nothing. *Where in hell did he think we were going to put down? No town or village in sight.*

We skimmed closer and closer to a sliver of remote high-forest ridgeback enveloped in shifting cloud cover.

"Hey!" I said.

The engine rattled and conceded. Abrupt silence. Empty.

I braced my arm against the tiny dashboard. "What's going on?!"

We continued to fall and glide, through wispy then hermetic clouds, blind to whatever lay below. Or to when we would impact it. Ngowa relaxed; a small smile—not his usual rigid one, something softer.

A momentary patch opened in the clouds, revealing a thin, barren strip of dirt. Ngowa's eyes locked onto the fast-coming strip, glancing occasionally at the trees on either side, which stood high and close—way too close. You could hardly call it an air strip. No markings except a small white flag at each end. And Ngowa flying without power as if he preferred our wings to his own feet. A craving for water gripped my throat. Ngowa stole a peek at me. At the end of the strip, the closely-packed trees peeled away—just enough to divulge a small wooden building.

"Hang on," said Ngowa. He took a second peek at me. "We will meet again in one form or another. Isn't that always the way?"

In that instant his eyes were on me, the left wing rolled and wobbled. The plane canted left, the wheels hit the earth too hard and unevenly. The struts were going to snap in half or fold. Either way, the impact of those struts in the ground would hurtle the plane over its nose. Our seats would be ripped out with us strapped in them. Thrown backward—our feet above us—as the plane hit the building or the forest.

Then Ngowa did the most terrifying thing of all: he took his hands off the joystick. He sat back, his palms on his thighs. He let the plane correct and land itself.

☽☽☽

The rotor grew still. I vibrated. Ngowa faced the nose of the plane. "Would you like to withdraw here?" he asked. "Nyanga, Zimbabwe."

Even though the cockpit smelled of fumes, I took in as much of its air as I could handle. "Okay. How do I get out of here?" I asked. My body quieted. I tried to make light of it. "Buses on the half-hour or hour?" I unbuckled my safety strap. Zimbabwe. *The woman at the hotel told me, "You cannot go through Zimbabwe."* Still, I was closer to Tanzania. I still had a little time.

"No, no buses, Ms. Cloonis." Ngowa checked the dials. A beaten tank truck pulled out of the forest and up to the rear of the left wing.

"I never told you my last name," I said.

"I am sure you did, Eunis. How else would I know it?"

"No, I didn't. I never mentioned it," I said.

"Well, then I must have seen it on something—like the tag on your backpack."

"Oh . . . I guess that's possible." I scanned the perimeter around me. "Is there a way out of here?"

"Hmm. I will ask someone to look into it for you. Might take a few days—possibly as long as a week—plus most of your Tanzanian currency, if they will accept it. Or if it isn't stolen from you, so be careful. And there will not be deluxe accommodations."

"You said I could get out here. We're in the mountains. I don't have a week." I put my hand on the door handle.

"And you can." Ngowa began to open his door.

"It's Zimbabwe," I repeated with irritation. I opened my door.

"I told you that from the start," he said. "But I think you should stay in the plane and come with me to Tanzania. More direct. Safer. It is a most beautiful country. The most beautiful in the world, I think. But, while you decide, go in the woods if you have to—you know for . . . release. We have another five hours ahead of us. Go over there," he pointed to the forest, "out of view, please."

WTF!

Except for the truck driver fueling our plane, no one in sight. The square windowless building appeared unmanned. I slipped out of the plane as Ngowa walked toward the tawny structure some forty yards away. His hand trailed over the straps of the thin leather pouch anchored to his back. The sun beat down through the clouds, but the temperature remained pleasant; seventy-five or so degrees, although humid; rain on its way. Within a few steps, the elevation squeezed my breath.

I reached the forest and began to relieve myself. The forest canopy, almost 200 feet above me, started pit-a-patting, a sprinkle. I looked over my shoulder. The door of the building opened just as Ngowa reached it. A Chinese man in bland head-to-toe khaki greeted him and welcomed him in.

The evergreen forest dripped with heavy dew, like a tropical rain forest, and my body commenced to drift from me, as it had in the Minnesota wetlands. The air sugary and delectable. I squatted there for quite a while, mesmerized by the forest's seductive murmurings.

A loud clank woke me from my trance. How long I'd reveled in it, I can't say. I looked to the plane, the truck driver had come round the back of his truck and—fueling the right wing—had me in his sights. I zipped up and returned quickly to the aircraft. The driver was Chinese.

I started burrowing through my backpack for my passport; *maybe I'd be better off turning around. But how? I'd call from Dar es Salaam.* Twice through, I gave up. Thankfully, my cell phone lay twisted in my jeans albeit without a signal and the charge low. The rain intensified, and while I welcomed the moisture, it obscured the plane's windshield, turning everything into mottled figures, and fogging my judgement.

Ngowa jumped into the cockpit. He brushed the rain off his hair and placed two thermoses—one gray, one orange— below his seat. "What have you decided?" he said to me. He made sure to secure his leather pouch against his back.

As cool as I could, I asked, "Did you take my passport?"

His eyes unwavering. . . "No, Eunis, I told you. Why would I do such a thing?" . . . Completely indifferent.

I retraced my steps. It came to me, "The man at the airstrip in Gaija!"

"No," Ngowa said as if talking to a child, "he never came

near you or your backpack as I recall. Perhaps you did leave it at the bank."

"But you said—"

"Perhaps I was mistaken." He inserted the key into the ignition. "But I do not have time to sort out your mistakes."

He really teed me off, but I kept it in check. "Can you call the bank, have the passport sent forward to our destination?"

"Perhaps when we land, if I can find a phone number. Are you coming with me or not?" His impatience unambiguous.

"I don't have much choice, do I?" I said.

"You always have choice." He turned the key, the engine barked, the propeller began to spin. "So?"

The plane began to taxi to the far end of the strip, where we'd first put down. I shrugged. *I guess Ngowa was my pilot. Would I be so lucky on my way back?* At the boundary of trees, Ngowa turned the plane around. My door swung open. The Chinese truck driver and an African man in a fluorescent green hoody grabbed hold of my arm and leg. The African man swung a small machete at my seat belt. Ngowa reached under his seat, pulled out a large pistol and shot a bullet into each man's temple. As they dropped away, Ngowa revved the engine. "Close your door," he yelled. And as I did, our plane rolled forward, only just gaining enough speed to lift us over the forest canopy—a foot or maybe two, through the cloud cover and into the blue sky.

)))

In the air, his mood shifted; I hung onto my seat. "Where in Tanzania are you headed?" he asked, as if nothing had happened.

"What?"

"Where and why in my beautiful country are you going?" According to the dashboard compass, we banked north and east. Shock still gripped my body. "You just shot two men."

"*Shida*, trouble. That's how it is here." His rigid smile resurfaced.

"Not in this day and age," I said.

"Oh, yes." He ran his hand over the joystick as if it had fur and needed consoling. "*Shida* is everywhere, no? Trouble everywhere." He followed the horizon, a man at peace. "Where do you hope to go in my country, and why?"

"Why did those men grab me?" I dwelled on the half-amputated seatbelt.

"I imagine you are worth something to them. Ransom, perhaps."

"Me!?"

"You have a certain charm." He gave me an almost-human smile. "Now come on, you are safe."

"I know but—"

"It's done." His tone now intolerant. "Do not bore me with what we both do not know." He gave a small tilt of his head *insisting* I agree. I fumbled, then acquiesced. I'd lost all leverage. He continued. "Don't make me ask these questions again. *Where? Why?*"

"I'm not sure where," I said. "I need to locate a young woman. She's in Tanzania. I hope."

"A U.S. citizen?"

"Jamaican," I said. "Elegant blue eyes. Effervescent corn-white hair. So beautiful, almost another species from the rest of us."

"Hmm. Like your hair," he said. "She is probably in Dar es Salaam. I cannot get there in this. And even the U.S. embassy there is only open for several hours twice a week. I have no idea of the Jamaican embassy's days or hours; I suspect fewer than the American."

"How far can you take me?" I had to be back to Silver Mist before Sheila and the crew. A week if they dawdled.

"Lichinga," he said.

"Where's that in Tanzania?"

"It is not. It is in northern Mozambique."

My body drained. "Back to Mozambique?"

He lay his palm on the top of the control panel. The rattle subsided. He lifted his hand and the cacophony returned. "She will only go five hours, and that is if I push her." He nudged down on the joystick and swung the plane further east.

"Then what?" I'd completely lost my coordinates—if I'd had any in the first place.

"Then I get out and take a train," he said. The plane leveled off. "Three days to Dar es Salaam."

"I don't have three extra days."

"And I do not have three days to give you. Or I would. Now sit back and contemplate what you will do after I let you off." He paused. "But I do hope you will get to see my country, its raw elegance, its lush forests . . ." His voice trailed off. He returned to his dials. He watched the contour of the land not far below. He shifted his back to me, the leather pouch taut against him. He'd committed to smothering another word of conversation.

Chapter 12

Tete Province, Cahora Bassa Dam, Mozambique

I guess we'd only been in the air a couple hours when another plane appeared above us. Tan, with a white logo I couldn't make out. Ngowa caught sight of it and swore—"*Mende wa kinyesi!*" At least it sounded *and looked* like he was cursing. His face more stonework than ever. Deep onyx. Impermeable. And pissed. That much Tanzanian I spoke. From the way his face contracted he couldn't decide if it were my fault or not.

"Mr. Ngowa?" I said.

His body stirred, he morphed less agile, denser, a creature more of rock than of bone. Strange, I know, even as I say it. He was alive, but somehow reformed, more patient. Breathing slowly. Very slowly. The sensation buried in my bones.

"Anything wrong," I asked.

"No." He gauged the tops of the mountains, his eyes darting from one small peak to another. He sighed. His jaw set like masonry. He scanned below. He banked; the other plane above banked with us. He contracted again. "*Scout amateur,*" he muttered.

"What?" I said.

"Never mind." He checked his dials, but more so the terrain; his eyes revering the land, as if about to embrace a relative. Asking for advice. He glanced above us. The tan plane still there, sitting on top of us. Its weight, bigger; tamping down on us. It hummed. We rattled. I'd willingly loaded myself into a thin corroding-metal bird, wind now blowing steadily through its copious decaying wounds. A long way from home.

Ngowa tilted the joystick ever so . . .

The plane above fairly laughed; it took to our ass with confidence. I viewed it as bullying. What had Mr. Ngowa done?

Ngowa jerked the plane harder this time. The plane tracking us didn't care; capable of—and intent on—either forcing a landing or crashing us.

"Mr. Ngowa?" We were an old bantam chased by a much stronger, more adroit raptor. Ngowa pushed our plane lower but not faster. It chattered. The other plane dropped behind and followed.

"Sir?" Afraid to touch him again.

Ngowa, emerged firmer. Nothing supple about him. As *dense* as I've ever seen a human. He took our plane still lower. Even in that rock-dense jaw, I recognized his rigid grin.

I craned over my shoulder. "We're being followed."

"Could be." His mouth moved!

"No!" I said. "This isn't safe, is it—what you're doing, I mean?"

"None of us . . ." his hand laced tighter around the joystick, ". . . rich or poor, young or old, smart or fool, know how it will end for us." He throttled the plane—it spluttered against the rough treatment.

"Love the homilies," I said and grabbed hold the seat. "But . . ."

We broke over a ridge slicing between rock formations 300 and 400 feet tall on either side. Below a wide river basin. "Geez!" I said, both in admiration of the landscape and in response to the drop of my stomach.

"The Zambezi," he said. He watched to see what the other plane would do. It settled further back but seemed undeterred. When we leveled off, we couldn't have been more than 150 feet above the river.

"Death follows me," I said, a reality check with myself and a warning to Ngowa. We were too damn close to the water. "So," I continued, "it's not like I don't appreciate fate and good intentions, but . . . people around me die."

"Obviously." He checked the other plane.

"You. Don't. Understand," I said. "You don't realize your own danger."

"Yes, I do," he said. "I just told you. It follows all of us."

"Fine. Is it so important that we run from that plane?"

"You want to be delivered, do you not?" He combed fingernails through his scalp.

"Not at the expense of my life," I said. "Or yours."

Seeing the river, still wide, but quickly narrowing, he said, "Too late." Then "Lose faith, you lose everything. Now quiet." His body softened.

I complained, "Don't I have anything to say?!"

"Not a thing, not quite yet."

"Yes, *quite yet!*"

"Here is the reality," Ngowa said. "On this plane I am pilot. Should you want to jump, even from this height and at the speed we're going, I would recommend not. However, since you are my guest, I will not stop you from whatever you feel you need to do."

Ten or so miles before us, a dam appeared. Beyond it the rocky topography closed in, got steeper, more crooked. Ngowa checked his dials.

What was there for me to say? "Look at this beauty all around us," I finally said. No response. "You really want to withdraw from this beauty forever? I don't."

"I must say," he continued as if I'd said nothing, "this is not what I had in mind, even if I survive."

"You!" *Get over it, Eunis.* My seat reverberated. I clung to it. "I'll take full responsibility for not having my passport," I said. "My fault completely. Let's just do this safely. I'll turn myself in. My stupid idea." My arms pumped, *enough, enough.*

He garbled something, his eyes steady on the dam, a goal line.

His tangled console of switches and gauges told me nothing. "Do we have a way to tell the other plane we'll meet with them? Ya know, like right away."

"Radio communication is not required in class G aircraft." Ngowa took hold of the amulet draped around his neck and kissed it. Without facing me, he said, "You have the power of death and life," he said. "What will it be?"

An educated man, and yet . . . "I don't know what superstitions run through your head, Mr. Ngowa, but please, let's turn around."

The dam drew closer.

"Mr. Ngowa?"

The violence ahead, where the water dropped off into rolling thunder, came too fast. Even in the cockpit, the sound of it, a deepening menace.

"Mr. Ngowa?" At once we were on top of it. "Mr. Ngowa!" Beyond the spill's millions of tons, the mass of water below suggested a thought. *You may die. It comes quickly, the end. Why not in water? Liquid. Rapturous.* My childhood fantasy.

"See the water below," said Ngowa, as if reading my mind. "Lots of it, yes? One of Africa's largest lakes, if I am not mistaken. Could you spare me, even if we go down?"

Our plane strafed the huge dam and its spillway.

"Mr. Ngowa!"

Foam roared from the dam's sluices, its tonnage only a few feet below us, all other sound canceled by its fury. The river's fingers leapt and caught our wheels and rocked us. The old bird's bones cried out. The right wing tottered. Ngowa held tight. We fluttered as if the old bird had been struck with an arrow. Ngowa strained at the stick, fighting the downdraft, battling the rolling wings. The end of flight. The turbulence and the rush of water ready to grab us again, rip us apart and drop us under its weight some 500 feet below. But the duel, brief. Ngowa knew before I or the plane. He lay back, then old bantam, too. I couldn't be sure.

He jockeyed us toward the craggy, constricting path of cliffs ahead. The old plane squawked less. The other plane fell back and lifted higher. I couldn't see it any longer. Away from the dam's spillage, Ngowa reduced our altitude over the river. If the plane over us could still see us, it wasn't about to follow us into the zig zag canyons ahead.

Ngowa flexed his body—the sinewy animal back, ready to face off the next assault. "You realize," he said, offering his first voluntary information and not concealing his disgust, "we are going towards the Indian Ocean, east and south . . . in the wrong direction."

Chapter 13

Zambezi River, Mozambique

The serpentine canyons descended to the easy-flowing Zambezi below. Ngowa tapped his fuel gauge, suddenly a font of information. "We spent most of our petrol for *kukwepa*, uselessly. Even if we could lift out of these canyons, we could not land, not up there." He pointed to harsh, uninhabited mountains. "The town of Songo is beyond us and south. In this region, no villages, no villagers."

My jaw remained locked from our plunge over the dam, I sputtered. "What are we even doing here? Who are we running from? And why?"

"We are no longer running from anyone," Ngowa said. "See," he raised his hand to the sky, "they are gone. Now we are more with the spirits."

"I asked a very straight question," I said, leaning into him. "This bullshit—I didn't sign up for it."

Ngowa stretched his neck. He regarded the canyons, solid walls of basalt, or some other white rock. "We go up and take our chances." He checked the gauge again. *"Uume wa zabibu!"*

"What does that mean?"

"Penis of a grapefruit."

"Okay . . . well . . ." I said through my teeth. ". . . I need food. Now." As if petulance would change his course. "Get us out of here and let me the hell off."

He put the plane's nose up and gave it power. "You are *buda*," he said, "and loathsome; you are the reason we are here in this bad luck. You are not doing your part." The plane jolted, gurgled, then wheezed throughout the cockpit. "Bad, bad luck. I do not think we can make it all the way up. This is my end."

I snapped, "*Your* end?! This really pisses me off!"

"Brace yourself," he said, his elegant skin now pallid. "Goodbye." He tugged at the stick; the plane didn't lift. We closed in on the palisades.

"Land it," I said. "Down there!"

He looked down and quivered. "I cannot swim."

"Well, I can," I said. "Put the motherfucker down in the water."

He pointed to the river below. "If I can, will you—?"

"Land it!"

"Good. Okay. Okay. Hold on." He began to manipulate the flaps, hoping—I suppose—to stall the plane in whatever air was still available to us. "Brace yourself." He gripped the joystick with his right hand. "Okay." His eyes closed momentarily. "*Nionyeshe*."

"What?" I said.

"I will count on you," he said. "Remember, you need me alive." We dropped.

I spotted something. A rawboned beach in the distance. I tucked the sunglasses in my top pocket, snapped it shut. Power transferred palpably between Ngowa and me. I looked around the cockpit—really around—for the first time. "No floatation vests?"

"Hold on." His voice shook. The nose went up, we went down tail first, hitting the water way too fast. I flashed on Roddy. *Never see him again.* The nose rocked forward and dipped hard into the river, almost ripping me out of my seat, the maimed belt compressing my stomach and chest, *ready to snap and fling me into the windshield?* We steamrolled forward. My stomach blistered. The cockpit submerged into the river. We bounced backward and out. Then dipped into the murky Zambezi again. "Get out," he yelled. "Unstrap yourself." He did. "*Mami Wata?*" His question somehow directed to me. "You are, are you not?" His eyes tucked in some deep insight. If I wasn't so shook-up, I'd have laughed.

"I'm Eunis," I underscored. "No myths right now. Let's keep our shit together."

He struggled to take hold of his amulet but gave up. "Do not forget about me. I got you here safely." Again laughable, considering. But the plane bobbed on its wings. The river sucked steadily on the fuselage—it let out a slow groan. I unfastened, I pushed on the door. It resisted. River bubbled up on us.

"Push hard," he said. "Thirty seconds I go down with the Hongdu."

I put my shoulder into the door. Water shot in. I jumped into the river.

"Do not forget about me," he yelled again, and jammed his shoulder against the door. It popped open. The river rushed around him. The two brightly colored thermos bottles he'd kept under his seat streamed out of the cockpit. As I swam away, his eyes, pleading. I drifted with the gentle current. The wings of the plane began to go under.

"Help!" He hung to the propeller. The plane willing to take him down.

"Let go," I screamed. "Just let go." I swam toward him. When I reached him, he wouldn't lift his hands off the prop. He pressed it to his body as if latched onto a bible. He swallowed water. "Now let go," I said, "I'm here."

He didn't.

"Mami Wata?" he asked again.

"Sure," I said. "Whatever works. Let go of the fucking plane."

He took a deep breath. He flung himself toward me. I grabbed his collar. "Let me do it."

"A siren, yes?" Ngowa babbled with relief. "I prayed it possible."

"Yes," I said. "I am." My arms strapped loosely around him. *How the hell did I get here?* "Float on your back. I'll guide us. The current is in our favor. Fifteen minutes we can land on that skinny beach. But don't fight me, or I'll let go."

He went limp. "Thank you, *Mami Wata*. I give myself to you."

"Right," I said. We drifted for a couple of minutes. Serene. The beach drew slowly closer. I drifted too, thinking about Chaz Keyes, and how right he was about life after TV. About how I'd probably run out of time, my short TV career over. And how it wasn't an end, not like Kyra's. And with that thought, a bad feeling overcame me. Something tugged at my foot. *A whirlpool? No, it grabbed.*

Ngowa screamed. "*Zambi!*"

"Zombie?" I paddled forward. "Oh geez, stop with the—"

"Shark." His voice echoed the canyon walls. "Get us out of here!"

"Don't be ridiculous," I said.

"Zambezi shark. Bull shark. Get us out of here!"

When I looked over him, I saw the fin. "What the fu—!"

He cried out, "*Mami Wata,* you can save me!" He kicked his legs, his arms flailed at the surface, as if he could drum the danger away with small slaps.

I felt another tug at my foot. I saw only one fin; *there could be more. Many more.* The orange thermos bobbed one stroke away. I managed to get to it easily. Ngowa fighting everything around him, including me. Above and below, the water wrenched at us, while he made things worse, less visible.

"Stop!" I swung Ngowa around.

He continued his panic. He yelled, "I will give you anything. Save me, as I would save you. We are allies."

I took hold of the thermos; still full of liquid, I hoped. The fin resurfaced and came at me. I lowered the thermos a foot under the water and held it there, the fin came on. I shoved the thermos into the shark's nose.

Except . . . I didn't get it square. When it turned, I knew it was coming back. And the others?

"Do you feel anything?" I said to Ngowa. He'd controlled his splashing a bit, but he kicked as vigorously two-three feet below, at the turbid darkness. I couldn't see anything—even if it was an eight-foot, 250-pound shark. Not until it was on me.

"Not now," he said, the panic now more vestigial.

"But you felt a tug?" I knew the answer.

"You felt it too." Acceptance in his voice. "If you are truly who you say you are, you will deliver us."

"I never said I was anybody. I'm a woman who wanted to get to Tanzania! That's all."

His body relaxed. He said, "I understand whose hands I am in now." He imagined some sort of tag team: between me and Great Spirit. I appreciated the affiliation, but still . . .

I re-checked the surface. "I think there's only one, a female. Let me know if you feel anything."

"*Yesu.* What do you think?" He began to mutter—no, he prayed. "*Mami Wata. Mami Wata. Mami Wata.*"

No fin emerged ahead of me, but the surface to my right rippled—against the current. The attack was on its way. I moved Ngowa closer to my left hip. I tightened around the thermos. I waited. "Mr. Ngowa," I said over my shoulder, but not too loud, "I hope your superstitions work."

"Do not deny us," he said.

The shark came a few feet from me. I separated from Ngowa, placed both hands on the thermos, and rammed that sucker into the shark's nose. Dead fucking on. The shark hit me with such force she pushed me a couple feet back, into Ngowa. But she got the brunt of it. Another attack from her or from an unseen buddy, however, and we were chum.

"*Mami Wata!*" Ngowa gasped. He started to sink.

I paddled to him. Before his head disappeared underwater, I had him. The current moved around us. Tranquil. My sense: not deep water. Maybe ten-fifteen feet. I reminded myself, *glide, it's just a morning in Minnesota.* I worked with the current, swimming toward the beach, maybe a half mile away. *Glide.*

I held tight to the orange thermos. I wondered, *what is my kinship to all this—the rain, the wind, the river, the sharks? The elements come more frequently.*

"Where are they?" Ngowa's horrors resurfacing. "The others?"

"Quiet." I ran my eyes over the surface. I hauled him along.

Chapter 14

Zambezi River, Mozambique

Within several hundred yards of the slender beach, occasional cuts in the ledges suggested a stairway out. Ngowa hung over me in a complete stupor or sleeping, hard to tell. The cliffs were steep and tricky, but now that Ngowa was having his beauty sleep, I figured we could make it. *After that?*

In the cliff's shadow, movement. My first thought, a beast. No, people! Three of them. As I got closer, one of them must have seen me, because she yelled something to the others and came toward me. The others followed in a hurry.

I dragged Ngowa onto the beach, I let the thermos drop with him. He lay there, eyes closed, breathing rather contentedly.

"*Er du okay?*" the blonde woman said. Then did a double-take of my face.

"We're fine," I folded over and puffed.

"You are American?" she asked, bending over me, then Ngowa.

"Tanzanian." I pointed to Ngowa. "I'm American."

"We are Danish. We too are in trouble." She motioned to the base of the cliffs. "My friend . . ."

Another female, thinner, taller, also in her late forties ran up to us. Her voice shrill. "*Er en af je ren læge?*"

The blonde put a hand on her tall friend's back and translated, "She's asking if either of you is a doctor."

"A doctor, yes?" said the tall woman, chance in her eyes.

"No," I said. "I'm sorry."

"My husband," said the tall woman. "He is dying."

The blonde woman jumped in. "Christel, we don't know if he's . . ."

Ngowa rolled over on the rocky sand and blinked at Christel. "What is his condition?"

My mouth gave way, startled at Ngowa's apparent recovery.

She knelt next to Ngowa. "Come see. A heart attack, I am sure." She pulled at his arms. Ngowa rose unsteadily. He removed her hands as if they'd sullied him. He dusted the sand off his leather pouch and let his hands rest there. It seemed to assure him. He shuffled with her toward the base of the cliff. I trekked after them, astonished at how quickly Ngowa had regained his equilibrium and uncertain what Ngowa thought he'd accomplish.

"I wanted Jann out of the sun, yes?" said Christel as we approached the crevice below the canyon wall. A bald man knelt holding the hand of the man on his back. "He's had others," said Christel. "I told him this would be too strenuous, but Jann always knows better."

"Shush, Christel," said Jann, his eyes closed tight and obviously in pain. "It is one of the few beaches." He gripped his free hand over his heart.

In the small crevice of rock surrounding us, frequencies began to possess me.

The bald man pointed to the almost invisible strata of natural steps in the canyon wall. "Jann collapsed even before we made it all the way down."

"Do you have medicines?" Ngowa looked around the group. "Of course not." He looked at me. "Come help, Eunis. Let us see what we can do."

My hands went up. "I'm no doctor. We could make things worse."

"But you have power." Ngowa motioned the group to give us room. Currents rippled through my body. The others oblivious to my kinesthesia.

"I'm Carsten," said the bald man. "Do what you can. Jann can't make it back up in this condition. It's more than five hundred meters, almost straight up. And we're still in the middle of nowhere."

"How did you get to *nowhere?*" asked Ngowa kneeling by Jann.

"Range Rover," said Carsten.

"Eunis," said Ngowa, "get the thermos."

"We gave him some water," said the blonde woman, "but I don't think enough. I'm Lisé. Thank you for helping. We came for the day but . . ."

"The thermos, please, Eunis." Determination returning to Ngowa's eyes.

I retrieved the orange thermos, by which time Ngowa and Carsten had Jann sitting up against the stone. Jann's eyes still closed, his hand still gripping his heart. By the look of him, a man in his late fifties but with a crew cut which advocated to be younger. His forehead beaded in sweat.

Christel looked down at her husband. "His body is without defense."

"Shush," Jann repeated. "I just need to rest." Pain drove through his body, he groaned.

Carsten looked at Ngowa and me; he swung his head as if to say, *this is much worse; he doesn't have much time.*

Ngowa started to unscrew the thermos. "I am afraid this could be a bit of a shock."

"He won't last, and we can't leave him here," said Carsten.

Christel nodded in agreement. "Anything that will help."

The crudely chiseled steps back to their vehicle were narrow; two people couldn't go up the rungs, not side-by-side. Carrying him would be impossible.

"It's special medicine," said Ngowa. "But it could kill him."

Christel went to stop the thermos in Ngowa's hand. "What do you mean?"

Ngowa pulled it back.

"No, Chrissie," said Jann, still without opening his eyes, "you must. This *is* an attack. The pain is . . ." His head dropped; his hand fell from his chest.

Something prompted me. "Let's get him in the water." The group stared at me as if I'd proposed a game of volleyball. "The water is a calming temperature. And it's the rhythm he needs."

"She's right," said Ngowa. "Help us get him over."

"Stop," said Christel. "He cannot consume medicine. Antibiotics have stripped him of defense."

"Mersa?" I said.

"Yes, mersa." Christel closed her eyes in despair.

"First World medicine." Ngowa tapped the thermos. "This is different."

My vibrations at full intensity. "Help us," I said to the group. The group looked at each other and, without saying a word, agreed. In synchrony, we lifted Jann and carried him to the beach shore. We could not take him too deep: sharks. But I couldn't tell them that. *Freyja be with us.*

I pulled Jann in with me, in three feet of water. Sharks have been known to come in that shallow. I nodded to Ngowa to proceed.

"You understand," he said turning to Christel, "this may kill him, or it may set him free from what is haunting him."

"Haunting?" said Carsten.

"Accursing," said Ngowa.

"What?!" said Carsten.

"Bedeviling him." Ngowa's irritability showed; he wasn't going any further with his explanations. Carsten looked at Christel. She looked wooly. "Let us begin," said Ngowa, unscrewing the thermos cap and beginning to pour a reddish-brown dirt into the cap.

"Wait," I said without thinking. "You should mix that with water. Have him drink it."

"No," said a younger man, a deep baritone of Asian descent. He hadn't yet spoken. "I have some knowledge of hydrology. This river likely has schistosomiasis—parasitic worms—typhoid fever, cholera, probably others."

Ngowa held the thermos cap above Jann's floating body. "There are parasites everywhere. Shall I continue?" Then looked at me. "Daughter?"

Daughter!? I called to the people on the shore. "Do you have any water left?"

"Very little," said Carsten. "But we could—"

"No," I said. "All of you, including Jann, will need it to climb back up. Let the river feed him. You'll have to trust the river." I held Jann in the river. Ngowa bent over him. The group on the shore looked on, people watching a baptism. "The water may heal him," I said to the group. "It's your call."

"I wouldn't," said the Asian man.

Everyone looked at Christel. She gulped and assented.

Ngowa dunked the cup into the Zambezi. I watched for sharks. He sprinkled a substantial amount of the dirt into the cup. The dirt turned to gruel. He mixed it with his finger. "I will give him a cup. It will be on him quickly," said Ngowa. "And it will be several hours that we will need to attend to him and reassure him. Perhaps a day. He may see things, but as I say, if it does not kill him, he will be fine."

"Stop saying that," said Lisé. "Christel is already a wreck." Lisé took hold of the cross around her neck to pray.

"I do not—as you say—make the rules." Ngowa's poor bedside manner revealed to the group, his unevenness ever more unnerving to me.

Chapter 15

Zambezi River, Mozambique

Jann floated on the Zambezi, scarcely breathing, eyes still shut. I held his shoulders and Ngowa fed him the cup of dirt porridge. "Daughter," he said again with subdued and uncharacteristic delight, "let us get him onto the shore and out of the sun." Which we did.

The group gathered around Jann. Ngowa stepped into the deep shelter of the cliff, perhaps afraid of the repercussions if Jann didn't awake. But the Dane began to rustle. I knelt next to him so he would not over-exert himself upon waking. His eyes fluttered open. He saw my freakish face, he screamed. He threw up a small amount of bile. He became disoriented. He wrapped his arms around himself as if chilled despite the 90° weather. He pitched back and forth mumbling indecipherably. Another heart attack?

"Jann, *min kære*," said Christel pushing me aside. "I'm here. I'm here."

Jann went silent. We watched him with sober anticipation, except the Asian man with the baritone. He fixed me with cynical eyes before standing and walking a few feet away.

Starting about twenty minutes after Jann ingested the "dirt," Jann began to speak. "I see you," he said, his eyes remained closed. He spoke in a broken English-Danish mix that Christel and Lisé alternated translating. "I see you watching, you insects surrounding me, who buzz around me, waiting for me to die, waiting for me to be the soil you eat." He spoke to his visions. "I see the eyes behind your eyes. Thousands of eyes. You see so much more than I. You are . . ." His body relaxed. "You are beyond me." A low hum parted his lips. He asked his phantasms, "How can I deal with my pain?" His eyes shot open, starring at the sky. He spoke in a second windswept voice, as if coming through the river's current, "Endure. Remove. Or reject. But do not pass your pain along to others. Do not let others carry it."

He turned to me, but with eyes of a blind man, looking *through* me. "Your glasses, please. The light is too much."

I handed him my sunglasses. He fumbled with them but slipped them on. Ngowa arrived beside us. "What do you see?" he said to Jann.

"I become soil," replied Jann. "Mantids devour me. I am taken into their visions."

"Yes," asked Ngowa. "And else what do you see?"

His body writhed. "I see hyena."

I tried to pull Ngowa off Jann, but he leaned into Jann and goaded him to continue his nightmare. "Yes, and of the battle?" asked Ngowa.

Jann fell silent.

"And the battle?" Ngowa ran his teeth together. "Jann, the battle?"

Jann's breath slowed to a steady wave-like rhythm. Seeing this, Ngowa's insistent questioning abated, his eyes cleared. His jaw loosened. A weight lifted from me.

I asked the group, "Do you have any food you could share with us?" We hadn't eaten since leaving for Zimbabwe.

"Yes, certainly," said Carsten. "Sorry." He went to various backpacks, pulled an apple and some trail mix, and returned. Ngowa and I quickly devoured the fruit and nuts.

"We will need to spend the night on this beach," said Ngowa to the group. "You will need to circulate a watch through the night."

"I'll watch Jann," said Christel.

"Not just him," said Ngowa. "But whatever might come from the cliffs or from the river. You must warn us."

Christel tensed as did the rest of the group, realizing perhaps for the first time, that Jann wasn't the only one in danger.

"I'll watch too," said Carsten.

"Good." Ngowa pointed at Jann. "We will see if he can climb tomorrow." Ngowa made for a spot under the crevice where the sand lacked stones. He curled up and went to sleep.

"I'm so sorry," said Lisé. "We didn't offer food. We have not asked how you and your father came to swim to us from the river."

I thought to correct her but didn't. "Our small plane went down," I gestured back toward the dam. "And we swam till this beach." I felt I could trust these people—more than Ngowa. But so much so fast, I decided to keep some things mine. I started to say *Ngowa*, then realized some had heard him call me *daughter*. "He still has his passport and papers, but I lost everything." *Maybe as father and daughter—even if I lacked the proper documents—my chances to reach Tanzania were improved.*

"Oh, that's awful," said Lisé. "Where were you headed?"

"Tanzania."

"You're in luck. When we get to the Rover, you will come with us to our quarters in Songo. You will be safe there. Then we fly to Dar es Salaam. Following that, Denmark; we should get Jann home."

☽☽☽

A small cool breeze woke me, the morning sun not yet breaching the hills above the beach. Christel and Carsten lay next to Jann, asleep. Lisé and The Baritone—probably Chinese—several yards apart. They began to rouse. I saw no sign of Ngowa . . . until I turned to the river. He stood there, a silhouette, starring at something. I looked closer. Halfway out of the water, blending with the ashen gray of the river and the dawn, sat a crocodile. Ten feet of him (or her) visible. It stared at Ngowa with mossy green eyes, exposing large, roller coaster, primordial teeth. Neither moved. I came silently to Ngowa. Without looking back to me, he raised his hand to signal not to come closer.

Nothing about the croc breathed, not a muscle. Its eyes, human-sized, rotated; locked fully on me. Crocs see a panorama far beyond our capacity for depth and clarity, day or night, above or below water. Yet, I saw not so much as a ripple of its muscle.

Its cave-like slits lingered on me, unblinking. Eyes sixty-five million years *older* than the dinosaurs, as if its extended time on the planet gave it some sort of ownership to which I should yield. Eyes still wide, it slipped inaudibly back into the river.

"It's a good sign," said Ngowa. "The spirits want you to see my magnificent homeland."

From behind us, Lisé's loud whispers started the group chattering. They hadn't seen a thing. Within minutes, the group had circled around Jann. He continued to descend in and out of coherence. He needed help to stand. He insisted he could make the climb back to the Range Rover, though multiple times he became overwhelmed.

Sensitive to his friend, Carsten said, "Our bodies . . . we are in the age of repairs. *Reparationsalder.* Let's wait."

Finally, with assistance, and frequently stopping for Jann to recalibrate himself, we made our way up the imprecise steps. Ngowa laid his palms on Jann's back which seemed to invoke Jann's voice. "The trees . . . " Jann said to no one in particular. "No new roots. It's genocide. No nutrients. Its intelligence wiped from us."

"Try not to speak," said Ngowa, a curious departure from his prodding of Jann the day before. "It will sap your energy. Just climb."

When we reached the Rover, Jann fell asleep in the back, crammed between me and Christel. She, too, fell asleep as we made our way over the rough earthen roads to Songo. Carsten at the wheel.

After an hour or so, Baritone Man, whose name turned out to be Martin, broke the undeclared exhaustion within the vehicle—a vague reprimand aimed at Mr. Ngowa. "Why were you flying over this area?"

Ngowa had been attentive to the road, though I sensed his mind idled somewhere else. I barged in; Ngowa's protection all I had. "Father wanted to show me the dam."

Martin clicked his tongue. "I'm surprised you weren't shot down." He returned to Ngowa. "What did you give Jann?"

"Dirt," said Ngowa. "I told you."

I'm not sure how, but I knew Ngowa was lying.

"Just dirt?" said Martin. In the light, his stubble showcased his churlishness and accentuated a nasty scar from his lower right lip to his chin.

"Loam," said Ngowa. "Sometimes that is all it takes."

"And you," Martin said pivoting back to me, "you were so sure of the water."

"I was," I said.

Martin pursed his lips. "Hmm." He paused. "You and your . . . *father* . . . came out of the water at just the right time."

The uneven road bounced us left and right. "Lucky for all of us," I said.

"Ditto," said Carsten. The group agreed.

Jann began to mumble, still hidden behind my dark glasses. "I said nothing," he said. As if he were bargaining with someone. We hit a malicious bump in the road, kicking us all in the chest. Jann whimpered.

Ngowa answered Martin. "Yes, *we came out of the water at just the right time.* 'Born again by the water and the spirit.' Is that not what you call it?"

Martin went silent, a scowl nested along his jawbone, obviously still dissatisfied.

Out of nowhere, thousands of finch-like birds capped in red and heather filled the sky. A wonder. They jabbered in diamond-bright cheeps. They dove as one and alighted on a good-sized watering hole; I'd say thirty yards in diameter, their thirst unaccountably also galvanizing in me. I knew better than to ask for anyone's water. The Range Rover wound its way over the deep troughs in the road and around the oasis—about five minutes. By the time we'd passed it, the birds had drunk the watering hole dry. They took flight as quickly as they'd come. They vanished.

Chapter 16

Zambezi River, Mozambique

"I do not trust this fellow, Martin." Ngowa opened the tent flap. I ducked and he ushered me into the small space. The tent, ripe canvas and bare except for two dilapidated cots and a whiz pot—an upgrade over the previous night. "I think he means you harm," said Ngowa. The accommodations were gonna be a bit too cozy for my taste.

"He's just surly," I said. "And you have to admit these are not people used to your ways."

"Or yours," said Ngowa.

"They're intelligent people," I said. "They care less about my ugliness. And with their invite to join them to Dar es Salaam I'd think you'd be happy. Together with your official papers and their support, I'll be able to get in. Won't I?"

"You do not see what is in front of you."

"Okay." I pointed to the two cots. "Which one do you want?"

Ngowa measured the difference from each cot to the tent flap. He threw his leather pouch to the bed on the right, the one closer to the opening. He flexed his body in his animalistic way. A cat, perhaps. Or something that sat and ran differently. Not a leopard or lion. He had a strange gait. "You'll do it my way," he said without looking at me. "What I am doing for you is unheard of. You go with that group, and you will be in prison. And not a very posh one. For a long time. And I will not stand up for you; it would bring disfavor upon me."

"You're shitting me," I said. "I saved your life."

"Thank you," he said, an imperious tone that made me want to slap him.

"I lost everything." I tapped my back pocket. "Except my phone, thank god."

"What?" Ngowa's left cheek twitched. "You still have that? Good, good for you. So, you have a god? You said, *thank god.*"

"Sure." I examined my feelings on the subject, mistrustfully, as if pulling a band aid off a wound. "Great Spirit," I said. "Or whatever you call it." I lowered myself onto my cot.

"Yes, good. Nevertheless, you are coming with me. And you will stay far away from Martin for these next few hours till they fly."

"I'll be fine," I said, "and I think I'll go with them."

Ngowa shook his head. "I cannot let you do that."

I stood. "I think I can do any damn thing I want."

"Yet you want to find someone's niece? Eunis, you will fail, and it will be *chungu*—painful. Maybe even fatal. But you will fail. And that man, Martin, he is out for you. You think you are strong . . ."

"I am."

"Well, not strong enough. There are things here that you say you do not comprehend, yet I am sure you do. But because you neglect your true place in the mix, you are afraid. To be sure, that may be wise. But you and I are allies . . ."

"You keep saying that," I said. "And if we're effin allies, you'll get me to Dar es Salaam."

"And I will, I will," he said motioning me to sit opposite him on our cots. "But you are in danger. Whatever you think of me, I am trying to warn you."

"Well," I said, "I'm going to get your sunglasses back from Jann and Christel, okay?"

"I need them back," he agreed. "Maybe I should come with you."

"Back off." I stepped past him to the tent's opening.

"Will you find your friend's niece? What is her name . . ?"

"Kyra. Kyra Nafasi."

" . . . Or will you both suffer badly?"

He was getting in my head. But I didn't hesitate at the tent's opening. "I'll be back," I said. Across from me, coming out of her tent, was Lisé who waved and smiled. "How are you two doing?" she asked.

"We're good. And you?"

"*Vi er gode.*" She laughed. "We are good. And Jann, too. Thank you so much. Both you and your father are very kind. Was he able to get you tickets?"

"I'm not sure," I said, surprising myself. "Anyhow, you are all friends?" I waved at their tents.

Lisé walked toward me. We both turned to the small hut that served as the campground office, a weathered sand brick structure. "Jann and Christel have been our best friends for fifteen years."

"You and Carsten?" I asked.

"Yah," Lisé said. "Not always easy, but we do pretty good."

"And Martin," I asked, "also a long-time friend?"

"No," she said. "We don't know him."

"What?"

Lisé explained, "He joined us just as we headed down the cliff. Pulled up in a tan Jeep. A driver dropped him off. He asked us if it was okay that he join us. We said, *of course*. I have no idea where he's going next. He hardly spoke on the way down. I thought it was kind of him to stay with us last night. He didn't have to. But maybe that was his plan, to sleep on the beach. Gorgeous spot."

"But he's Danish?"

"I don't know. Might be." She pointed to the approaching toilet, a cabinet with a bucket and a flap nominally covering the entrance, making it easy to see if anyone had already colonized the spot.

"Oh," I said as she stooped into the compartment and waved goodbye.

Around the corner, Martin lingered at the front of the structure.

"Hey," I said. "How are you?"

"I'm good, thank you." His surliness replaced with *that* look; I'd seen it many times; hungry for something, and I was part of the menu. So strange, how some men—and women— had found me so ugly that they found me irresistible. But that's the only way I could make sense of it after all these years. Truth, I enjoyed their bodies as much as they enjoyed mine, even the ones who turned out to be suicidal or killers.

"So," I asked, "is there any place here where I can charge my phone? I got a small jump in the Rover on the way here, but not enough."

"I don't know, not likely." He turned away from me. His jacket lifted in the breeze, just enough for me to see the handgun on his hip.

I went to Jann and Christel's tent. I called in, "Hello, it's Eunis. Would it be okay if I take back the sunglasses. They aren't mine. They're Ngowa's—my father's. I'm sorry but—"

Christel's arm poked out, admonishing. "Jann's sleeping. Don't wake him." Her arm retracted. I could hear her rummaging. Out came the sunglasses, with some annoyance, those hideous yellow striated sunglasses, but mine till I reached Dar es Salaam.

Chapter 17

Songo, Mozambique

I heard the Danes shuttling their backpacks to the Range Rover and again questioned my decision to stick with Ngowa. Time no longer an issue; I wasn't making it back in time to catch the crew. But he had the documents to get me to Dar es Salaam. He knew Tanzania. And whatever his other questionable attributes, he'd stuck by me when I'd done very little for him, except save his life. *Ruthie was counting on me.*

"Let us go," said Ngowa waving me out of the tent. "We will drive with them to the airport. They offered. We will not decline their generosity. You will continue to refer to me as *father*; it will help along the borders, you will see."

When we got to the Rover, Martin stood there too, next to a Jeep. "Come with me," he said. "It will be so much more comfortable. Less cramped."

"Thank you." Ngowa stepped into the Range Rover. He held out a hand for me. "But we will ride with Carsten and his group."

And so, we did, the cumulative stench of our bodies sufficient to make us want to stop breathing. Accordingly, none of us said much during the torturous ten miles of tropical scrub and rock—except Lisé who invited us to visit them in Denmark. She gave me her email. But much like with Freddie and Lewis, I knew I'd never see them again.

From Songo, we reached a paved route that took us over damaged highway to the tiny Chingozi airport. "Perhaps we should go with them after all?" I said to Ngowa. They waved goodbye and Martin drove up.

"No," said Ngowa. "They have a series of arduous flights *backwards* to Dar es Salaam. It will take them more than two days." He pulled me aside. "Come with me."

"I'm not in a hurry anymore."

"Perhaps, but I can get you into Tanzania. Can they say the same?"

We walked into and around a corner in the building. The tile walls smelled foul and had lost their sheen to layers of sticky kak. "You stay here, in this spot. You say nothing to no one." He moved to a small counter several yards away, rang the desk bell and waited. No one responded, he banged on the bell again. Finally, a man arrived smoking a cigarette. Based on his posture and the stricture of his lips, we'd obviously disturbed him from something more important. Ngowa pulled a passport from his leather pouch and pointed to me. The man studied me. Ngowa slipped something into the passport and then placed another document in front of him. The man nodded, put his cigarette on the lip of the counter, something he must have done quite often because, even from my vantage point, there were burn marks all along it. The man stamped several papers and returned them to Ngowa, who slipped them into his pouch and zipped it up.

The man disappeared only to return for his cigarette a few moments later. I never saw him again.

Ngowa returned to me and said, "We might as well sit. The plane will be here in a few hours. Do not leave this spot. Do you understand?"

"What if I need water or the bathroom?"

"Go behind the counter, there in the corner," he said.

"I can't do that."

"You must and you will if you want to find your Kyra. I will get you a bottle of water. Do not drink from the fountain. Do you understand? Sit on the floor."

I didn't hide my indignation. Ngowa couldn't care less. "Stay," he said. He left in search of bottled water.

When he returned with a couple of bottles, I thanked him. The bottle opened easily, too easily; I gave him a questioning look. "It's fine," he said. "But if you would rather wait till Tanzania, that is your prerogative." He drank from his bottle.

Thirst had followed me since camp; I quickly drank half the bottle. Within minutes nausea collapsed my belly and the room became unstable. I couldn't focus. I sank to the floor and closed my eyes.

"I will be back," I heard him say. "Do not move. Do not speak to anyone."

I couldn't even if I'd wanted to. Some time passed; I can't say how much. My phone rang. The sound intolerable, like icicles shattering around me. Without opening my eyes, I reached for it, just to stop its attack. I held it to my ear. "Yes?"

"Eunis? Is that you. Thank god. Are you alright? How's the shoot going?"

"Shoot?"

"Eunis, it's Roddy. I've been trying to reach you for days. How's it going?"

"Roddy?"

"Is it exciting? I was worried about you."

"You're in another universe," I said. "Why do you keep tormenting me?" I grabbed my stomach.

"Eunis? Eunis, are you okay?"

My breath came more rapidly. Bile rose through my chest and onto the floor.

"Eunis, it's me, Roddy."

I couldn't say another word. My belly completely knitted—a kinesthetic barricade: thinking way beyond my bandwidth. Sounds scrambled, words had no meaning.

"I guess you've heard the horrible news," he finally said. ". . . Eunis? . . . Eunis . . . your friend Chaz Keyes. . . I'm so sorry. His plane went down, all of them, in Brazil. But by now you've already heard."

My phone went dead.

☽☽☽

Sometime later, my eyes inoperative, my torso still erupting in spasms, the bite of metal filled the air. Wheeze after wheeze, choking me. Behemoth machinery blared; ponderous clanging—razor high notes—striking my bones, fracturing my temples, forcing me deeper. Everything around me, everywhere grinding me to dust. I purged. I dove deeper, as far from the surface and its pain as I could.

❭❭❭

I woke briefly, disoriented. Silhouettes moved. My eyes avoided the light. My head swiveled without movement. My stomach collapsed in on itself. Someone handed me water. I spiraled inward again, wrestling nausea and loss of place. Until I smelled freshly cut wood. An ambrosial lull. I wanted to open my eyes, but my eyes were lodged shut, less excruciating that way.

Chapter 18

Karatu, Tanzania

A man's voice boomed, "Born again of the water and the spirit." Laughter vaulted over the swell of reggae, then sank below the refrain. Swaying to the music, he said, "Alikiba. Had you heard of him before?"

"What?" I walked out of the nightmare, marginally aware of shapes. My body drained. Nails or rain pounding a metal roof. I covered my ears; stillness all that I craved.

A very black man in a very bright orange tunic and matching pants waited patiently for me; easygoing, without airs. A clean-cut beard framed his face, chin, and lips. A gentle smile. The regal stitching surrounding the neck and shoulders of his tunic, gorgeous. The man, too. "Had you heard his music in the United States?" the man asked again, his voice raspy, voice raised, so I could hear him over the downpour, the music, and the crowd in the room.

"No, no . . . No, I haven't," I said, unsure he heard me; I could barely hear myself. As if the rain wanted me out.

"Wonderful, no?" He leaned in with a comforting smile. A

gentleman. Hair close-cropped; rounded nose; that trimmed salt and pepper beard; great teeth. Eyes, sympathetic.

"Yes," I said tuning to the music rather than the roof. "Soothing." I really wanted quiet. I tried to clear my head. "Where am I?"

"Soothing, yes." He motioned to the room full of men. Men in their fifties. Some older still. All dressed finely in bright capes, paisley jackets, dashikis. A kaleidoscope. A woman or two, dressed as magnificently as the men. "In Swahili we say *kutuliza*. A smooth word in itself, no?" He beamed at the gathering. On second look, eyes so arresting, they could be dangerous.

"What? Yes," I said, all liquids disgorged from my body, and with it an urgency to run out into the rain for moisture. "Where am I?"

"Surely you see that it is a party," he said, again a gentleman, chill in his surroundings.

A gray-haired man with an equally gray close-cropped beard passed by and patted the attractive man's shoulder, then nodded to me, "Welcome." The dissonance and movement of the room too much to handle. And that pounding roof, the worst. I looked back to the handsome man. At least he was stationary. "How did I get here?" I asked.

"Mr. Ngowa brought you, obviously," said the man. "Quite a journey."

I searched for Ngowa; dizziness echoed back.

"You okay?" asked the man.

"Where's Mr. Ngowa? I want to see him."

"Oh, he will not be back. You are here now," said the man. Beef skewers were being passed around. Greens with peanuts, too. My stomach reeled. I thought I'd topple; the beautiful man placed a hand on my back and kept me upright. "Perhaps you should sit."

My legs wobbled, but I found them. "Where am I?"

A waiter came by with tall flutes of aquamarine drink. "Perhaps you would like one of those?" The gorgeous man pointed to the beverage on the tray. "No alcohol. This will settle your stomach," he said.

My lips so dry. "Yes, okay" I said. *I could try. Nothing left to evacuate.* The rain on the tin roof swelled. Hard and piercing at the same time. Excruciating.

He stopped the waiter. He lifted the drink from the coaster and handed it to me. (As if there was no cosmos but him and me. As if he didn't hear the rain at all. As if the roof wasn't about to be torn off.) The waiter lingered on my face, then realized—when the beautiful man found him still there—that he ought to depart.

"It is not Konyagi, I can assure you," the man in orange said. "No alcohol."

"Where am I? Dar es Salaam?"

He thought before speaking. "Karatu."

"Where's that?" I asked.

Surprise covered his face. "Tanzania. You do not think Mr. Ngowa would let you down?"

"What?" My body shook, crushed under the weight of the sound. I took a sip of the drink. Sweet and welcomed. "I need to get to Dar. Why am I at this party?" I was shouting.

"Well," he said exuding radiance, as if the volume of wet sound didn't exist for him, "it is for you."

"Me?!"

"A welcoming party. Mr. Ngowa told us of your difficult travels. *Ninafuraha kukutana na wewe,*" he bowed. "Nice to meet you. May your visit be easier now."

He took me by the elbow and walked me to the center of the room. His body rocked a bit, a slight limp. "Let me introduce you," he said, raising his arm above the crowd.

The crowd parted then circled around us. He spoke above the rain. "*Wanawake na wanaume.* Ladies and gentlemen . . . Let me introduce you to Eunis from the United States." Restrained applause followed. He whispered to me, "Go around and meet them personally."

"Well done." An aristocratic-looking woman with silver hair patted his back and smiled at me. The resplendent man in orange tipped his head and walked into the crowd.

Wait! I was rooted to the spot. He slowly disappeared. Gone. My green drink all that I knew. I downed it. The room wasn't small, yet it felt Times Square crowded. Maybe fifteen people. All looking at me. A much older man in a red, black, and turquoise wrap tottered up to me. His lack of teeth not appealing. He took my arm and squeezed my ass.

"Hey!" I pushed away.

"*Zawadi ya fisi,*" said the toothless man, this time with a leer.

"Away!" A lightly bronzed African man in a dashiki ushered the elder aside. Then apologized to me. "I am sorry for that. There are some who, despite their age, do not follow tradition. Would you like me to introduce you to some others?"

"No," I said. "I want to lay down. I want to see Mr. Ngowa."

"I will happily see you back to your room," he said. "But Mr. Ngowa is gone."

)))

The vehicle, a rather expensive SUV by the look and smell of the interior, kicked mud to either side of the road. We passed a scurrying chicken and a pair of large eyes on a sludge-surfing bicycle. I couldn't see much else in the rain and moonless night.

"I'm searching for a young woman, a college student," I said to the driver. "She'd begun classes some four months ago at the University of Manyara. About four hundred miles north of Dar es Salaam."

"A Christian school," he said, his eyes on the patch of headlight filtering the road into sheaths of crystals and black.

"Yes, Seventh Day Adventist," I said.

"I have heard of it. Only in passing. Is that your faith?"

"No." *Momma steeped us in Martin Luthor, biblical infallibility. I never once saw Momma open a Bible except to quote it as reprimand.* "But," I proceeded, "if I remember correctly, the key concept in Seventh Day is apocalyptic: The Second Coming is imminent."

"Well, as I say—"

"How near am I to that university? I need to find this young woman."

"Her name?" the driver asked.

"Kyra Nafasi. She's has albinism like me. Well, not like me. She's a pretty young woman."

"Do not do yourself disservice," he said, sizing me up for a moment. "You are young enough, you are healthy. You have power."

"Is it far?" I asked again.

He sighed as if I were burdening him. "I am not sure."

"But you've said you know the school."

"I know of it, that is all."

"Look," I said. "I believe she's in danger, this young woman. Maybe if I went to the school . . ."

He scratched at the steering wheel. "I am not familiar with that school or with her," he repeated.

I wiped at the window. All I could see was wet and black. "Well, where are we now? How far is Karatu from this college?"

He twinged at mention of the town. "I do not know," his voice descending into hostility. "Stop asking questions. I have no answers."

"Who were those people at the party?" I asked.

Even with the wipers going full blast, he battled the downpour. But he'd jerked, he'd heard me. I raised my voice. "Who were those people at the party? Why am I here?"

"You will understand more in the morning." His eyes on the road, but from the side, on me. "You are very lucky to have so many friends. So many well-connected friends—is that not what you say in your country?"

"I want to know now! Where am I? Who are you people?"

He sniffed, he sighed. "In the morning."

"No, I have a right to know now." He couldn't mistake my growing exasperation.

"Do not pester me." Veins in his head bulged. His fists clamped tighter around the wheel. "You will understand in the morning."

"I have a right to know now."

His lips compacted. His demeanor at this point heedless, completely estranged. He pulled up to a squalid set of mud brick buildings, climbed a small berm toward them, and began to turn off the engine. I swung open the door, jumped from the SUV and dove, on the run, into the deluge and the blackness.

Chapter 19

Karatu, Tanzania

Except for the nightfall, I had no idea of time. No idea how long it'd been since I'd seen Ngowa in Mozambique. No idea how long and how I'd traveled. How long had the party people taken care of me? Time a structure on which I could no longer rely. The concept of it lost. Without time's grid grounding me, the nausea resumed. Or maybe the tainted water's sickness lingered in my belly. At any rate, I'd lost it completely—that way of assembling and maneuvering through life—with time. Gone.

The *feel* of the huts on either side of me were my first indication that I'd entered a village. That and the incessant rain plunking on surfaces around me. I stopped to listen for the driver in the dashiki. His strained voice in the distance allowed me to catch my breath. My eyes acclimated. A few feet from me, a dim structure, about my height, separated from the night. A step closer and I could make out uneven corrugated panels cinched to a rudimentary lattice of branches or thick reeds. Tattered fabric nestled at its entrance.

Again, nausea.

*I remember Ngowa telling me to stay put. I remember drinking
. . . water, bottled water . . . beasts nested in my body.*

A cough and the stir of slumbering breaths kept me moving down the row of shacks.

The people at the party had been hospitable, despite the fact that I'd crossed illegally into Tanzania, without papers of any kind, without much cash. Had Ngowa introduced me to the group to protect me? Perhaps friends of Ngowa. Maybe Ngowa championing me while working to find Kyra for me. Or at least looking into leads.

My stomach moaned for anything more than water, though it continued to curdle. I had one set of clothes, dunked once for freshness in the Zambezi. I didn't speak Swahili or Bantu dialects. Phone gone. A paltry few Tanzanian shillings wedged in my pocket. Yet instinct had propelled me out of that SUV.

The rush of night air and the volley of rain added to my confusion, but it did move me along the strip of mud and tin huts, to an opening. Then down another corridor of ramshackle structures. Before long, another. And another. I could hardly take another step.

Dashiki Man had stopped calling or I was out of his range. Sopping wet and exhausted, I came upon a shed in a cluster within the cluster. I listened for a sleeping occupant. I heard nothing, I crept inside. I lay against the cool sheet metal wall and fell asleep.

☽☽☽

"*Zeru, zeru, ondoka! Ondoka!*"

My eyes jumped open. A long, needlelike wooden spear thrust at my heart, then thrust again. *"Ondoka!"* The leggy man reared up above me, yelling, crisis in his eyes. He raised the spear higher, then drove it closer. The tip pierced my shirt and breast.

"No, no," I said backing further into the rough wall. "I'll leave." I raised my hands. He plunged the spear into my left palm. "Shit! No! No harm. No harm." I scrambled to my feet. "I'll go." I pointed to the door flap.

He raised the spear once more, as if to skewer me with it. *"Ondoka!"*

I ran, my hand stinging, my heart racing. The rain had stopped but continued to drip from clogged roofs. I moved through a labyrinth, bumping, and sliding through sludge and past hovels. Villagers were already set up or setting up, inside and out. They gaped, some unmoved by my flight, as if they'd seen my wicked face before; others screeching, fleeing from me, children in arms, panic in their eyes.

Completely sapped, I reached a road carved from red dirt and less overloaded with muck. Oxen pulled carts weighed down with water drums. Men and women pulled livestock. Others balanced wooden poles and water jugs and woven baskets. I lowered my head, I followed them—boots caked in grunge—at a distance. When they turned onto a paved road with telephone poles along it, most of the travelers turned right. I followed. Eventually, the succession included trucks, vans, motorcycles, a bus! Lots of bicycles. The road sign said, "Karatu: 19 Km." I didn't have another twelve miles in me.

A hefty tricycle, enclosed and built to carry goods, slowed

several yards in front of me. A young woman hopped out, went to the back of her trike, and unloaded a large heavy sack which she flung on her back. She disappeared into a small roadside shop.

I crept up on the cargo bike and was met with a rich wave of coffee. The young woman had her back to me talking to the shopkeeper. I jumped in hoping her next stop would be closer to town. I buried under a few sacks.

☽☽☽

I sat silently sequestered in the back of her cargo bike surrounded by coffee beans, the smell staggering and delicious. About ninety minutes later the cargo bike stopped. I tried to push the sacks aside, but too late: she came around back, she stared at me. "*Unafanya nini kwenye kahawa yangu?*"

"I-I don't speak. I will go." I wrestled with the sacks to get out.

"What are you doing in my coffee?" she asked.

"I will go," I said.

"No, wait. You speak English."

"American, I'm sorry. I was tired."

"Where are you from?"

"New York." I popped out of her cargo bike. "I will go."

"Wait. I want to visit New York sometime," she said. A red headscarf, wrapped tightly, covered her hair. What remained of her tender face and ebony skin, was an elfin nose, full lips, and dark, steady eyes. "Where are you going?"

"The university," I said. "I'm sorry, I was just so tired."

"It's there, one block." She pointed.

"I'm sorry, thank you. I won't bother you." Then I thought to ask, "What does *zeru zeru ondoka* mean?"

She cleared her throat. "Ghost be gone. Why?"

"Nothing," I said.

"Could we talk sometime? Over fine coffee?" She tapped a sack at the back of her cargo trike.

"I don't expect to be here very long," I said.

"My name is Mariam. What is yours?"

"Eunis."

"Are you a student?"

"No," I said. "I'm looking for one."

"I pick up and deliver coffee to Fathom Roasters in Karatu. Their warehouse. Twice a week. Mondays and Wednesdays. Sometimes Thursdays instead. Usually around this time, eight in the morning."

"That's very kind. But I've gotta find this girl. . . Kyra Nafasi, she has albinism. Would you know her?"

"I don't, I'm sorry." She dallied. "Okay," she finally said. A disappointed smile faded. "I must make my delivery." She pedaled away.

A pristine white arch presided over the university's marble steps leading to the building's entrance. Students gathered around a street cart selling fresh baked goods. Craving *anything* solid, I purchased two small buns and finished the first in seconds. Students sat and stood everywhere, many with phones stuck to their ears. They spread up and down the steps of the university and onto the lush campus. They chatted, they laughed, they flirted. They wore dress shirts, t-shirts, slacks, blouses, skirts. No different than the students in the U.S.A., except they were all every shade of Black.

I entered the main building and found the administration offices. After asking for the Dean of Students, I was asked to wait. Fifteen minutes passed and a robust woman in a leather jacket rose over me and extended a hand. "I am Glory Baakari. Who do I have the pleasure of meeting?"

She led me into her office, thinking, I suppose that I was interested in becoming a late-blooming student. A photo of who I-assumed-to-be her husband and two children sat prominently on her desk. A small knife with a hand-carved hyena head lay to her left. I explained my mission.

"Yes, I remember her. A winsome young woman. Jamaican, am I right?" Mrs. Baarkari had an affable way about her.

"She's disappeared," I said. "Her family heard that she's been kidnapped . . . her hands cut off."

Mrs. Baakari shuddered. "Oh my, we just assumed she'd dropped out." Baakari held on to her desk.

"Her family didn't call?" I said.

"Not that I'm aware. I know we called them, left them messages. Never heard from them."

That was not what Ruthie and Anthony told me. "And you don't know where she went?"

Mrs. Baakari tried to process the images in her head, flinching at them. She corralled her ample head of hair then let it drop.

"There was a doctor," I said. "A Dr. Allen who supposedly took her in. But we cannot find him or her. Would you know anything about that?"

"I do not. But we had a Dr. Allen on faculty. He taught in our Humanities Department."

"He doesn't teach here anymore?"

"No, his wife died." Mrs. Baakari crossed herself. "A lovely woman, a terrible shock. The pain bent him over—as much spiritually as physically—from the way his face changed. Crushed inward. In sorrow . . . And if I must say, fear."

I leaned in. "Why would you say that?"

"I suppose because it was so sudden." Baakari's eyes sagged.

"How do you mean?"

"Aflatoxin shock," she said.

"What's that?"

"It's a mold. Kills thousands in Tanzania every year. I think he said it attacked her liver, her nervous system. But victims are usually less educated than Mrs. Allen. She knew better than to consume anything from an untrusted vendor. And Dr. Allen wasn't sick at all."

The bun I'd just scarfed! "What kind of food?"

"She must have ingested corn, nuts, rice, peanuts, something like that. Dried fruit. Even nutmeg or coffee. It came quick. Her face yellow the last I saw her."

"Jaundice?"

"Yes. It's a painful way to go: nausea, vomiting, excruciating seizures. Poor woman."

"How long ago?" I asked.

"About six weeks, two months." She thought about it. "Yes, about two months."

"And Dr. Allen left right after that?"

"Yes. And I haven't seen him since. No one has. I called. And both Mr. Charles and I visited his house, to offer him support. I knocked on the door. Several times. No answer."

"Could I have Dr. Allen's address?"

"I-I suppose. But be gentle with him if you find him. Tell him Glory is thinking of him and that I'd like to help. So would Mr. Charles." She paused. "But I think Dr. Allen's gone, left the area, poor man."

Chapter 20

Ngorongoro Conservation Area, Karatu, Tanzania

I hopped a small shuttle north, toward the massive Ngorongoro Conservation Area above Karatu. The shuttle serviced a luxury camping resort closed off to outsiders, a gated community. The doctor's house wasn't far away and not so grand—a modest two-story structure—but the setting equally spectacular. Except . . . tall grasses and shrubs had begun to take back his home. Several fruit trees looked forsaken. Despite the earlier rain, the air thick. A bit wary but still famished, I helped myself to what looked like several small mangos, bright orange with a thin skin. Found out they were called *himbi*. They didn't disappoint. Like an apricot but twice as sticky.

I knocked on Dr. Allen's door. No response. When more banging had no effect, I scouted around back. Something in the underbrush spooked me. I didn't move. After a few breaths, it disappeared. Or maybe it waited tactically.

I couldn't see in the side windows; they were draped closed with colorful cottons, gold, red and brown in geometric patterns. Anyway, the windows were too high, with barbed shrubs and three-inch pikes below, ready to impale me.

Around back, the jungle's creep even worse, thicker. It menaced the building. I heard something in the house; beefier than I'd heard in the shrubs. I climbed up a small set of stacked stone steps to the back door. I peeked in. More flamboyant cotton drapes blocked most of my view. But something inside moved in the late morning shadows. "Hello?" I called out.

I listened for it again. The rising heat of day had marshalled a long column of giant ants two inches or more in length, huge heads, marching out of the jungle past the base of a tree. They advanced soundlessly. Above on a limb, I caught a baboon watching me. A spider wasp began circling. Its stinger, the size of my thumb to knuckle. Its body would cover most of my palm. Like a small hairy bird. I'd been told by the shuttle driver they weren't aggressive but should not be aroused. As it orbited me, its drone the only sound I heard. I didn't swipe at it despite my fear. I trusted. "Hello!" I called again. "My name is Eunis Cloonis. I'm from . . . New York." *I guess that's where I'm from . . . now.* "I'm looking for a young woman who has disappeared."

From behind me at the bottom of the steps, a revolting, feral smell diverted my attention. "Geez!" An immense hyena—tan and spotted, eyes drawn back in attack—faced me. Its jaws wide, teeth yellow and jagged, drenched in saliva. I fell against the door; it bowed but did not give. My throat disabled; I was about to die. We stared into each other's eyes. It had the head of a super-sized pit bull, with a blunt slant muzzle. A thick neck. Shoulders higher than its hindquarters—almost four feet high. Another four or five in length. 200 pounds of muscle. And those fucking teeth! . . . It readied to spring at me in an odd half dog, half prehistoric way.

The door opened behind me; I fell backward into the house, onto the floor. The hyena came up a few steps. I heard the click of a gun. "*Pepo, ondoka!*"

The hyena dissolved—it must have leapt into the bush— with nothing but the sound of its muscle ripping its way through the forest.

Above me, a man in his late fifties, gaunt and impatient, holding a shotgun. "Get up," he said. "Then leave, while you can."

"Dr. Allen?"

"Be thankful . . . and leave," he said.

I caught my breath, lifted myself up. Still shaking.

"Go," he said. His upper half dressed traditionally in a muted dashiki, the bottom in professorial brown trousers, and black shoes.

I wound my arms around myself, trying to bottle the aftershocks. "I'm - I'm looking for Kyra Nafasi."

"I don't know where she is," said the doctor.

"But you took her in, didn't you?"

"You don't know what you're talking about." He pointed me into the sun. "Go."

I considered his recent heartbreak. "I heard about your wife. I'm so sorry. Glory Baakari at the school gave me your address. She's worried about you. She wants you to call. She and Mr. Charles are really worried."

The mention of their names pricked him, with the force of the spiny shrubs outside his window. "I have nothing to say to you or anyone. Leave me to mourn, now!" With more strength than I gave him credit for, he shoved me out the door and closed it.

Was the hyena waiting for me at the edge of the forest? The shuttle was a fifteen-minute walk away along a deserted road. Plus, whatever the wait might be. I knocked again. "I've come a long way. If you care about this young woman, Kyra, you'll at least tell me what you know." Still skittish, I peeked to my left, to my right.

Only the muted restlessness of the forest answered back.

"You can't be so cruel," I said, "that you wouldn't help her to safety?"

No reply.

I went around to the other side of the house, clawing my way through vegetation. The front door, covered in vines, impassable. I returned to the back door. The spider wasp also returned, circling me, closer and closer, until its outline coasted inches from my face. I froze. It landed on my cheek. I swung at it. Hellish electricity convulsed my body. I hit the ground; my flesh spasming as if in a bath invaded by an electric heater, stunning my entire body with voltage; my entire body constricting over and over again. I screamed, hoping to pass out. The doctor dragged me into the house and closed the door. I kept screaming.

"You fool with things you know nothing about," he said.

"I'm dying," I shrieked touching my cheek, already swollen to the size of a muffin.

"We are all dying," he said. "But this will not kill you. Painful, though."

"Shit, yes!" I tried to catch my breath. "Shit! It hurts!"

"And it will for several minutes," the doctor said. "It's a four on the Schmidt Index. Just lie there. I will get you some water. Don't touch!"

The pain circled my head and body. Round and round it went, shocking me without letting go. *Great Spirit, please . . .*

"Here," he said. "Drink this."

Each blow continued to shiver me. "I can't sit up."

"You can." He took me by the arms and propped me against a stiff couch. "Drink this." He handed me a bottle of water. "And then you will leave. Death follows you."

I had only so much time. "I won't die?"

"No. Not yet."

I took a sip of the water. "Listen, Doctor," I said between jolts, "I need to find Kyra. You took her in, didn't you?"

He closed his eyes.

"Didn't you? For god's sake, her hands were cut off." I convulsed again. "Shit, this fucking hurts!" I folded over myself.

"You've met the bone crusher."

I looked up at him. "The spider wasp," I said. "I know, I know. I was told not to."

"No." He chipped in a low, caustic laugh. "The spotted hyena, genus *Crocuta Crocuta: the bone crusher*. Neither cat nor dog with the wickedness of both. They come large and with a mass of thickness. Females, the larger and more aggressive, more dangerous; they've evolved with masculine traits and genitalia. Very smart. It's tracking you. Stay away from me. I want no part of it. Get out of my life and out of Tanzania. I don't want to be your next victim."

"I'll keep coming back," I croaked, with as much defiance as my wrung-out body could muster. Electricity convulsed me again.

"Not for long." He let his shoulders drop, accentuating the foreboding he carried in his face and eyes. "Please, please, please do as I say. Leave me alone and get out of the country."

"I was meant to be here," I said ". . . Somehow." *How quickly and turbulently I'd made it to his house.* "Is she alive?"

"I don't know. She was better when she left here—her arms, I mean. But . . ."

"But what?"

He shook his head. "You will never understand."

"You fixed her hands?"

"No. I'm not that kind of doctor. I bandaged her arms; I stopped the bleeding. Maybe I killed the infection."

"Who did this? And why?"

"You, of all people, don't understand *why?*" He paused. "She was albino."

All my grief and hers caved in on me. "They cut off her hands because she had albinism? Who? Who did this?"

"I really cannot help you." Both grief and dread still indelible in his eyes.

"Who?" I asked again. "Would they just take her hands, not the rest of her?"

"Many times. Please, if I tell you something that *may* help you find her—*if* she's still alive—you will leave?"

My body worn out. "Yes, I will. Of course."

"You will leave?" he asked again, offering a pact.

I nodded and took another sip of water.

"I don't know where she is," the doctor said. "Don't trust anyone. And if you speak of this, you will certainly cause my death as well as your own."

There was no denying he thought so. "Alright," I said.

His face surrendered to something inevitable. "Maybe it would not be so terrible . . . with Julieth gone." His deceased wife, I supposed. He hung his head and spoke to the floor. "There are gold mining towns in the Lake Zone. There might be something there."

"What do you mean *something?*" I said.

"I'm not sure."

I stood. "Who should I see there?"

He directed me to the back door. "The Geita Goldmine is one of the oldest and biggest. Trust no one." Again, with unlikely vigor, he directed me out, he closed the door behind me.

Chapter 21

Geita, Tanzania

On the fifteen-hour bus ride to the Geita Goldmine, I exhausted myself, compulsively wrestling with what the Japanese call "*kuebiko*," senseless acts of violence. How could people torture and kill others because they were genetically without color?

What's more, *Holy crap, what am I doing?* I was way in over my head searching for someone I knew almost nothing about. At most, I had a sliver of a lead (if in fact it had any credibility) and was nearing the end of my money. As usual, people on the bus stared at me. One woman even got off and argued for her money back when she saw me take my seat.

I no longer felt my education inoculated me from religious zealots, however absurd their mumbo jumbo. I'd waded into their mythologies without realizing how deep and still alive they could be. Facts no longer counted. And if quantity has any place in logic, then shit, I'd acquired a boatload in only a few weeks. Logically, I should've gotten out. I'd ventured unprepared into a completely foreign environment, and my exaggerated sense of self was showing. My growing uneasiness was not unreasonable. But what of my commitments—to Ruthie *and* myself? Empty gestures littered my life. As if grief gave me permission to follow my pride.

The Geita Goldmine sits about fifty miles south of Lake Victoria and about two and a half miles from the town of Geita. Even as the bus rumbled into the city center, it was clear that the corporation controlling the colossal mine also controlled the area and its people. The sparkle of lights from the huge processing plant illuminated the evening sky. Hundreds of those employed in extracting, processing, and transporting the gold—evidenced by their bright safety vests and corporate badges—moved in and out of the town despite it being the end of a normal workday. Our bus crept into Geita, through traffic almost as bad as Manhattan at commute time.

I'd started with $150 American, a wad of Tanzanian paper shillings. After bottles of water, food, and the bus rides, I was down to under a hundred. I needed to eat again, find a place to sleep and buy a phone.

A teenage boy bounded at me the minute I stepped off the bus. "Come, I have place for you to sleep." He pulled on my arm.

"No," I said. "Where's the police station?"

He let loose my arm. He trailed after me.

"Point me in the direction," I said. "And tell me where I can eat something without getting sick." My gut rumbled like a desk dragged across a floor. We passed a sign declaring: MUSHROOM RESTAURANT. "How bout there?" I said.

"My mother will cook," he said. "You can sleep there too. Cheap. Come."

"Okay. First, show me the police."

He agreed with a wave to follow him. We moved faster than the thick road traffic. I finally called to him to stop. "We've gone twenty minutes. I see no police station in sight."

He assured me. "Not far, ma'am."

Ma'am!

He motioned for me to continue. I considered turning around. "Not far, I promise," he said. He began to walk again. Sure enough, in another ten minutes we stood in front of the *"Polisi."*

"I wait here" he said, standing into the shadows. "Then you come for food with me."

I agreed and lumbered into the brightly lit station. Three men in khakis and berets smoked cigarettes. They looked at me—first shocked—then laughed. *"Mipira,"* the shortest one said, then asked, "What can we do for you, Miss?"

"I'm looking for a young girl with albinism, a college student. Blue eyes with a light, small birthmark on her upper right lip. Very beautiful. She was abducted. Her name is Kyra Nafasi. Someone cut off her hands."

The two other policemen chortled and rolled their eyes, suggesting my question was foolish. I gave them a dirty look. The short one continued, "I'm sorry, Miss, but there have been no recent abductions."

"Recent?"

He shrugged. "The last one was . . . almost a year ago." He turned to the other policemen for confirmation, which they supplied with indifference. Then continued, "But they chopped off one of *his* arms just above the elbow. I don't remember which one."

I grimaced. "This is a regular thing? Who is *they?*"

"No," he said stubbing out his cigarette, "I just told you it's been a year. What else can we do for you?"

I pushed again. "Who is they?"

"People who still believe." He reached for a bottle of water but didn't open it.

"Believe *what?*"

"That you people bring good luck. I've heard some miners believe they can make themselves invisible by ingesting *muti*, the potions made of albino body parts. But we've never caught one."

"Why is that?" I said. "That you've never caught these beasts?"

"I can't say." He twisted open the bottle cap and took a swig.

"But you can guess," I said.

He put the bottle back on the counter. He rubbed his fingers together. "Money. Now, is there anything else we can do for you?"

"Mmm, yes," said the tallest, finally speaking, "What can we do for you?" He reached for his belt buckle as if to undo it.

"Never mind," I said. "But tell me one more thing. When these albino hunters take people, do they always kill them and take all the parts?"

"Rarely."

I didn't know how to feel about that. I walked out.

"We go for food now, yes?" The teen boy stepped out of the shadows.

"Yes," I said. "Food."

He led me away from the city's bright lights, away from the traffic and the more affluent homes, onto scrabble dirt roads, past small outposts of murmuring people gathered around campfires. Donkeys brayed. I questioned my judgment. After almost an hour, we turned onto a smaller path and across a dirt bridge. Despite the halo of light from the Geita processing plant, I'd never be able to find my way back on my own.

"Watch your feet," the boy said as we approached a small campfire. An older woman and three men of various ages lifted their heads as we arrived.

"Mama," the boy said, urging two of the men to sit back down. "This woman needs food and sleep. She is willing to pay."

"Eunis," I said. "My name is Eunis. I'm from America."

His mother got up and walked beyond the campfire's glow. The boy seated me. The men stared. The woman returned with a bowl filled with a large mound of what looked like mashed potatoes and dark liquid. What it was, I had no idea.

"Eat," said the woman. "Twenty-five thousand shillings." She held out her hand.

I did a quick calculation. More than ten dollars. My abdomen cramped but . . . "Too much," I bluffed, pushing away the bowl.

The mother acted ready to take back the bowl. "*Ugali*," said the boy. "Delicious, you will see." He nodded at her. The old woman dropped a couple mushrooms in my bowl. Sweetening the haul, I suppose.

"Too much," I repeated.

"Okay," said the boy. "We will include your sleep."

The five of them waited patiently. They were asking too much, but they had so little. And I was famished. "Okay," I said. I picked up the bowl. "What is this?"

The mother answered. "*Ugali*." She dug her thumb into the large mound of white mash and used the mound as a scoop to pick up the surrounding juice. She handed it to me. "Eat," she said.

"You will see," said the boy. "Mushroom, too."

With mixed emotions, I took it from her. *Where had her hands been?* Nevertheless, it smelled savory and delicious. The mound had the consistency of polenta. The sauce some sort of greens and sour . . . milk. They watched me. I was so hungry. Within minutes, I'd left the bowl empty. The woman sat back and smiled. The men too.

The boy led me to an old mattress which, thankfully, I could not see in the dark. It smelled like dirt, sweat and garlic. He handed me a thin cloth with which to cover myself. It smelled worse. I fell asleep.

)))

At sunup the boy woke me. He handed me two fried buns, similar to those I'd purchased in Karatu. "You must go. I'll take you back. Eat while we walk."

My own sour smell ambushed me. "Will we be near water? A stream?"

"On the way," he said. "Come, before it is too light."

As we passed his mother's hut, photographs pinned to the entrance caught my eye. I stopped to see them. "Who are these men?" I asked.

"My brothers, my uncles," said the boy.

I pointed to one, a large man in a washed-out coral safety top, jeans, and hard hat with the goldmine logo. An enormous industrial wheel, twice his height and eight times his width overshadowed him. "Who is this?"

"My uncle Moses," said the boy. "He works in the mine. Drives that truck."

"What's his last name?"

"Charles. Now, let's go." We started walking.

"Charles?" I said.

"Yes, very common last name." He was tiring of my questions.

In the morning light, we retraced our steps from the night before. Small huts and deep crevices dotted the landscape. Occasionally, the land opened into muddy red pits with long wooden sluices. Workers already dug at the ground. Women toted heavy sacks on their shoulders. Seeing my interest, the boy said, "Artisanal mines. The government approves them. But nothing like Geita."

"Clean," I said. "Can I get clean?"

"You wait."

About a third of the way into town, he pointed me into a small thicket, hidden from the path. "Go there," he said. "Be quick or I leave you here."

Sure enough, beyond the thicket sat a small murky hole of water. Who knew what was in it, but I had little choice, everything stuck to me; I smelled awful. Still dressed in my camping pants and shirt, I dunked myself and hoped for the best.

When we reached the outskirts of Geita, the boy stopped.
"The money, please." He held out his hand. I paid him. "You
will go by yourself."

I tucked the rest of the bills back in my pocket. "Thank
you," I said. "What is your name?"

He'd already turned and was disappearing along the creek,
away from me.

Chapter 22

Geita Goldmine, Geita, Tanzania

No surprise, the guards told me I wasn't allowed in the Geita Goldmine. Safety reasons, they said. And, of course, the gold. Lots of it. Nothing to do but wait outside the gate till Moses Charles came out. With the mine operating twenty-four hours it might be a long wait. I settled in under a couple of shade trees.

From my view, the immense open pit mine dwarfed anything I'd ever seen. Probably two miles across in either direction; the Empire State Building could fit in it—from the top down, all one hundred and two floors! Thousands of tons of trucks, rock and earth moved along roads carved into the sides of the pit. Every once in a while, a shuttle brought workers in or out. The rumble of trucks and the smell of diesel somehow familiar, like I'd been there before.

I waited seven hours.

Even with the surge of workers leaving the shift, Moses Charles was easy to spot. His girth and broad smile perfectly matched his photo. His speed, however, measured by sundial;

he stopped to say hello to almost everyone or to chat with a guard.

I waited till the crowd thinned and he'd run out of chums. "Mr. Charles, Mr. Moses Charles?" I said.

Startled at first sight of me, he quickly relaxed and regained his smile. "I am."

A guard had us pegged. I steered Moses to the side. "I stayed with your nephew last night." I pointed south of town. "And with his mother—your sister? Others too. Brothers? Your photo hung outside the hut. I've come a long way . . ."

He cut me off. "What do you want?"

"Who hires here? A personnel director?"

He assumed I was looking for work in the mine. "What kind of job?"

"Office personnel, ya know, filing papers," I said. "Something like that." *The role of applicant. I liked that.*

"They're hiring no one. I've been here fifteen years. There isn't an opening." He began to walk.

"What's her name?" I asked. "The women who hires?"

Moses sized me up. "It's a *he*: Mulele Charles."

"Is he a relative?" I asked, hopeful.

"No."

"Can you mention that you know me?"

A great, brief laugh shuddered his frame. He cut it short. *I figured he appreciated my audacity.* "Even after fifteen years," he said, "I am nobody. Good luck."

I dusted myself off. I walked up to the security person standing to the right of the gate. "I'd like to see Mr. Charles, Mulele Charles," I said. "He's expecting me."

The guard's eyes lingered, heavy. My face hardly elicited a reaction—the first time in a long time that another being had seen past my face . . . or my body. I welcomed the disinterest.

He directed me around the building to a red door. Women and men streamed down the stairs as I fought to get up them, some pushing back. At the top, a woman was furiously clearing off her desk. Or at least organizing it the best she could. She peeked at me and, head down, addressed me. "Tonight, we have our own little Nyama Choma barbecue," she said as I walked up. "So I am going. We are closed." She waved me away.

"Is Mr. Charles still here?" I took a couple of steps back less she swing at me.

"Yes," she said, without swiping at me, but she gave me the eye. "But he has no appointments scheduled. So come on, you must go." She motioned for me to move on, this time with a little more anger . . . and a touch of disquiet.

"And," I said, "if his niece from America is sent away without him seeing her . . ." I paused. "That is a problem, isn't it?"

Her body retrenched. "His niece? No, listen, I must go. You too. No more tricks."

I sensed an advantage. But you never can be sure. "Uncle said he'd meet me around this time. His affairs completed." I looked down the hallway.

"Foolishness. Come back tomorrow." She thought about it. She frowned.

"What?" I asked.

She waved me off, but it was if she'd gagged on something.

"What!" I sniffed an opening.

She cleared her throat; she admitted, "He will not be in tomorrow. Or the rest of the week."

"That's why I'll wait," I said. "I can't miss him *this* trip. Not like last time." As soon as I said it, I knew I'd overplayed it.

She knew it too. "We have no job openings and I have been Mr. Charles' assistant for two years. I have never heard him mention a niece in America."

"I certainly would expect *not*," I said, rolling the dice. "He would find personal matters most inappropriate. Especially me."

Dinged with doubt, she soldiered on. "This is a big company, and we're not easily manipulated. *I* am not easily manipulated. And I have to go. Now. I'm already late."

"And I'll wait." I made myself welcome in the chair next to her desk.

She removed a bulky bag from beneath her desk. She looked at me. "What is your name?"

"Eunis Cloonis," I said.

"An odd name for a *mzungu*." She caught herself. "Sorry." She looked around; she had everything she needed. She checked the clock. "Okay, Miss Eunis. Better not be trouble or you be sure you will never have job here. I can see to that. If you are truly his niece, I apologize. But I do not believe you. And he may have you arrested." With that, she bustled off.

I moved down the hallway, reading placards, trying doors. All locked except a janitor's room and the last with Mulele Charles' name on it. I knocked; I didn't wait for an invitation.

"Can I help you?" he said looking up from his computer, the usual contortion on seeing my face.

"I'm searching for a miner that works for you." I advanced to his desk.

He stood up. A tall man but with an unsteady body. "Miss, you are impertinent. I can't share information about our employees. Who are you? You don't have an appointment. Did you not see Mrs. Simon at her desk? Please leave." He presented as prim, and his office—while not modern—reflected his desire for the same. Everything in its place. "I don't know how you got in here, but you'd best go. Now."

I held my ground. "The police said I should come see you."

"The police!" I had his attention.

"This miner of *yours* was one of a group that was said to encourage the taking of albino parts, *muti*."

He moved uneasily in his seat. "Are you with a civil rights group? If you are, make a formal request for information." He sat back down.

"The police said you'd give me his name. Shall I bring them and the press in?"

He stood up, hands indicating I should lower my voice. "He is gone, okay? We let him go. This is not our problem anymore. The man upstairs, he doesn't want this kind of publicity. We let the man go." He sat back down.

"When?"

"I can't be sure. Please leave. Or I will call security."

"I'll call the TV," I said. "Finding this man is important; dragging you into it is not."

Again, he lifted out his chair, this time coming around to usher me out of his office. "No. No. This is not an issue."

"When?" I repeated.

"Please go."

I parked myself.

"Okay," he said. "Then leave. It was after the last attacks. A year ago."

"His name?"

He barked back at me. "I don't recall." His nerves getting the better of him.

I moved to the door. "I'll get the police and the reporters. We need to find this man."

"Alright!" he said. "Jonas. Morgan Jonas. But he's gone."

"Where?"

"How would I know?" he said. "Haven't I said enough?"

"Shall I talk to your director?"

His head dropped. He sighed. "Please, do not do this. We don't condone witch doctor behavior. I assure you. We are supportive of your kind. Please. We've done what we can."

"Where did he go, this Morgan Jonas?"

"I heard a sawmill." He stole a look at me. "Lake Manyara."

Chapter 23

Karatu, Tanzania

Late afternoon light filtered through the tall grass, prompting several moments of melancholy. It drifted as quickly as it had come. *Head down*, I told myself. *Plod away*. But somewhere during that bus ride from Geita back to Karatu, I'd lost another measure of optimism. The humidity suffocated the pleasure of the rain. I seemed to be playing the land version of the children's water game Marco Polo, blindly jumping from one place to another, and now back. Kyra no closer. Kyra probably dead. I wanted to go home, wherever that might be now. *There is no home.*

It would require calling Roddy or Gordon for money and an airline ticket. More validation of failure. And for that, I needed to buy a phone, but no longer had enough money for one. Once back in New York I'd be out of a job. Sheila and her crew no doubt trashing me. *Who could blame them?* Damned if I was going back to Minnesota. My world had gotten even smaller than before I'd left New York.

At the university, I was told Mrs. Baakari was on vacation. "She's a very determined woman," said the secretary. "She wants more than this." The secretary indicated the scrimpy school offices. "She needs to take a break once in a while."

Next, Mariam, the young woman who delivered beans to the coffee company. She wouldn't arrive in Karatu for another two days. Dr. Allen, who had pleaded with me to leave him alone, might shoot me. But where else could I go?

So, I waited for the shuttle to the luxury campground. Not too long, just 143 fretful minutes, according to my obsessive and constant calculations. An obscurely depressed feeling followed me. Once the shuttle let me off, I found it was the last shuttle of the day. Even then, asking Dr. Allen seemed unwise and unfair. I didn't know what else to do.

The trees around Dr. Allen's had lost more of their fruit. Much of what remained struck me as diseased or attacked by voracious borers. The growth of the forest—I'd only been gone four days, after all—had tightened its grip on the grounds and his brick house. The front door not notably visible amidst the growth.

Around the back, I fought thick snag which had grown to my hips. As I passed through, it exploded in small swarms of black and brown jumpers, wings, and stingers. An occasional bite. (*Nothing* like the spider wasp, thank Great Spirit!) I moved cautiously, mindful of the sound in the underbrush I'd heard my first visit. The sun hung lower, too.

I stepped carefully over the stone steps to the back door; vines there as well, ready to trip me if I didn't treat them with respect. "Dr. Allen," I called out. I knocked on his door. "It's Eunis Cloonis. I'm sorry to come back. It wasn't my intention to ever bother you again."

No answer. Only the hum of the insects.

I called and knocked again. I tried the door handle, covered in thin tendrils that chewed at my fingers. The door gave way. I called into the house. "Dr. Allen?"

Drapes hung over every window, as before. In the gloom, the vibrant colors swallowed up. "Dr. Allen? It's Eunis. I have no excuse but I'm desperate. Only one night, I promise. Don't shoot. Please." I waited a second. "I'm not usually desperate. Really. I have no place to go. Dr. Allen?"

Sour air announced the room's abandonment. I relaxed and stopped yelling. I called one last time, *"Dr. Allen?"* I surveyed the living room. A small rodent crossed the floor. The room, very organized, except for a couple stacks of books, floor to six feet high, stuffed in two corners; the first thing you'd notice in such an orderly room. That and the simple cross hanging on the wall.

"Dr. Allen? I'm down here."

On the table, made of thick walnut and sitting firmly on more than a dozen spikey legs, sat an oil lamp and an open Bible. Between the Bible's spread pages, a furry king-sized spider struggled in a sticky web. The proprietor of the web off somewhere. Presumably, an even larger spider!

At arm's length, I carried the Bible to the back door, and with a dead frond scraped the trapped spider off it. I returned to the table. A sliver of the setting sun streamed into the living room, allowing me to read the open pages. I assumed the pencil-marked passages had been Dr. Allen's notations:

Corinthians 4:4

"Satan, who is the god of this world, has blinded the minds of those who don't believe. They are unable to see the glorious light of the Good News. They don't understand this message about the glory of Christ, who is the exact likeness of God."

Another page was flagged by a folded corner and a pencil line:

Ephesians 6:12

"For our struggle is not against flesh and blood, but against the rulers, against the authorities, against the powers of this dark world and against the spiritual forces of evil in the heavenly realms."

Alongside it he wrote "Mark 13:26," which I knew from Momma's rants to be the apocalyptic discourse, dividing man's present course and his full realization of God's kingdom—brought on by the apocalypse. Considering everything I'd seen people do to each other, I'd long ago concluded humans hadn't reached *full realization* yet. I wasn't too sure of how cleansing the apocalypse would be either.

Sunbeams poured down a tight stairway. The first step sturdy. But up the stairs headfirst into sticky cobwebs? Not the most inviting. Something crawled along my arm, something with many legs; I freaked, I screamed! My voice ricocheted around the house, a chorus of ghosts, knocking on every door.

I kept climbing. I wanted to see the light at the top; how it spread out. By then I knew Dr. Allen wasn't in the house; hadn't been—maybe since I'd seen him four days earlier.

The house had an odor. A familiar one. Like my late husband Harold's apartment where the bedclothes of death always left their scent. Or my brother's room where he lay dying. Musky. Each house and each room had its own measure. But if you dissected the air, it was always there. This house, I now realized, had that odor. A very thin blanket of it, but present.

The staircase opened into a small room with a couch and a tan afghan wrapped over it. Yellow curtains framed three large windows. An observatory. As I raised myself to see . . . Emerald forest laid out for miles. The breadth of it overpowering. It disappeared into an ancient volcanic crater more than ten miles across. It resurfaced in a lush rim for as far as I could see. The Ngorongoro Conservation Area.

Herds of African buffalo, gazelles and zebras grazed peacefully near and around Lake Magadi. I'd met at least one predator who awaited their inattention. Still, with all that life spread wide before me, I felt consoled and grateful. Its low hum entered my veins as if we were one. As if—if I looked closely enough—I could assay its DNA. Perhaps as part of mine. I felt . . . emboldened. *You've made progress.*

On the observatory's floor, sitting to the right of the couch, a full water bottle leaned against the couch leg, and next to it, a mahogany goblet. Empty. Also, several maps of the Ngorongoro. Life in this home must have been idyllic before . . . Before *what?* Before the musk.

After studying the maps, I went back down to find the kitchen. Small, with an undersized fridge. Quite a few knives hung from the wall, most with wooden handles roughly carved into animal heads: the head of an African water buffalo, a lion, elephant, and others. One hook was missing a knife. Tacked on to the side of the kitchen, I found an equally small bathroom, a shower, a toilet, no basin. I thought I might get slivers in my shoulders; it was that small. There, I almost missed a thin door. I slid it open. I discovered a compact workshop, the workbench lined with chisels. I surmised that Dr. Allen's hobby was whittling those animal knife handles.

Around the living room and ducking under the stairs, I located the bedroom. It provided a view *into* the forest, not above it. The bed was made. In the closet hung the usual basics of a man's wardrobe, including a sober black suit, easily attributed to a professor. Also, empty hangers. No sign of woman's attire.

Back in the kitchen, I found no coffee, no cola, no tea. No alcohol. Stimulants that would be taboo to a Seventh Day Adventist. The refrigerator boasted butter, a six-pack of bottled water, a dark juice, a bag of tuberous roots and bark, and a selection of unidentifiable fruits. I ate a piece of fruit—quite tasty—and poured myself a cup of the juice. I returned to the couch in the tiny observatory.

Night had fallen. I slid open the windows. The forest's cool called to me. First, a whistle and barking set against a low rhythmic grunting. Bestial. A chant. I listened—though I can't tell you for how long. I don't remember being happier, frequencies strumming through me at full strength, total harmony. My brother Lyle once quoted Maugham to me, "My spirit alone with the stars, seemed capable of any adventure."

But then came the vision.

Chapter 24

Ngorongoro Conservation Area, Karatu, Tanzania

Like a mirage, Momma appeared, skulking toward me carrying the misgivings of time. At first, I laughed. I told her to skedaddle. She pointed nicotine-stained fingers at me; I could smell her feculent breath. I held mine. The disillusionment in her pale blue eyes far more painful than the resentment that had been her hallmark, and that she'd leveled at me since I was a child. Whatever youth she'd once carried— the freckles, the flowing brown hair that had once made her desirable—had been overrun by life. Whatever battering she'd taken or embraced before me and since, I was helpless to defend her from any of it.

Her untilled hair crept gray over the brown. Her freckles no longer a distraction for the pain resident in her eyes. She was, again, telling me I was useless and helpless against the dark forces resident in me. A howl erupted from the forest and echoed across it. She disappeared, leaving only the deep indigo and starless sky. I breathed easier.

Downstairs, I found matches. I managed to light the lamp
on the table. The book stacks in the west corner of the room
formed a significant block of paper. (Probably 200 pounds or
more dead weight). It leaned away from me, up the corner
walls. It also tugged at me. I gave the room a 360 again: the
stack far and away the largest object in the room. For a moment
I thought the books breathed. I focused. Just a pile of books
and a few magazines stacked high and deep. But that stack of
books in the west corner kept fetching me, and what else was
there to do?

At the top of Dr. Allen's stack sat a well-bound book about
. . . hyenas. Clearly not a coincidence. Dr. Allen had saved my
ass. It hadn't been his first encounter with the beast. He wanted
no more. Still, I'd been led to that book. The covers of the other
three books topping the other three stacks. . . *all* about hyenas.
The one in hand I took to the table. I opened it. In short:

*The spotted hyena is the biggest of the hyenas. The
female larger and even more ferocious than the male.
Built for endurance. Great hunters, alone or in a clan.
They turn on a dime. They work well together, their
systems for hunting and defending very intelligent.
And brutal. They catch prey with their teeth rather
than their claws. They don't need to wait for their
prey to die, not with their extraordinary ability to eat
and digest bone, horns, hooves, hide and even teeth—
everything in just twenty-four hours. They have more
than thirty teeth that include conical premolars
designed specifically for cracking and crushing bone.*

The Bone Crusher. I dug at my scalp.

The highest density of hyenas in the world is in the Ngorongoro Conservation Area.

The lamp went out. With no lock on the back door, and the house pitch black, I pawed my way around the table and ran my hands over the walls, tracking down splinters and the bedroom.

☽☽☽

The next day I barricaded Dr. Allen's house. I moved the couch and an armchair against the backdoor and never bothered with the front; the jungle had effectively garroted that entrance. I spent most of my day in the observatory—as far from the backdoor as I could get—and afraid to eat anything but the fruit. To ground myself I looked at the maps of the crater and the surrounding areas. Much as I tried to stay centered on the maps, my head flooded with images of hyena. They'd come and go, then drift out over the Ngorongoro forest and its crater before melting into the clouds stretched across it.

I'd been in Africa five weeks.

I ran to meet the earliest shuttle back to Karatu, unsure if I'd be in time to reunite with Mariam, the young coffee bean woman. If not, then what? The entire way from the doctor's house, I glanced around, afraid of something amorphous. Nothing followed me, as far as I could tell. Still, I wasn't reassured. I shared a deep affinity with the Ngorongoro that I'd seldom found anywhere, except in my youth in the Minnesota wetlands. Yet I feared it too.

In Karatu, I made my way to Fathom Coffee Roasters. Around 8AM. No way to know if Mariam had already been and gone. I waited outside, in the back. Light pickup trucks pulled in and out, delivering and collecting. I stayed off to the side behind a row of tough-looking bushes; no reason to get her into trouble.

I didn't have to wait long. Mariam's vehicle dodged in between the larger trucks. She jumped out with purpose. She wasn't skinny, but she moved like a gazelle to the back of her cargo trike. She lifted a heavy sack onto each of her shoulders. I'm strong and I don't know how she did it. Then she went to the dock, said something to the guy directing logistics. He pointed to a spot. She walked over and gently laid the bags down. She went back to her trike and repeated the process three more times.

When done, she went back to the guy. He pointed inside. She came out with two bulky bags. Then another two. I rushed to her as she began to cycle away. "Mariam!"

At first, she didn't hear above the din, but my second call reached her. She slowed, then stopped. She saw me. She smiled. Her innocence intoxicating. "Hi," she said. "You came back." She tapped the seat next to her. I jumped in. The coffee's pleasure enveloped me, even stronger than before.

"I need help," I admitted.

Once again, she blessed me with her unguarded smile. "I will. And you will speak about New York."

"Deal," I said. I could tell from her expression, she didn't understand. "Whatever you want to know. I'm not an expert on New York. I'm not sure if anyone is."

She held my gaze as if handling delicate china. Affectionately. "You like coffee?" she asked.

I looked to see if we were being watched. "I do, but maybe we should do so in private."

"We can do that. My youngest brother has a small stand not far from here. We can sit in the back."

"I'm sorry to ask," I said, my fears growing, getting the best of me. "But I need help buying a cheap phone. I don't have much money left."

She laid a hand on my mine, the calm in her eyes also in her touch. "My brother can do that, too. Let's see if he's at work or at the boxing ring, working out."

I sat back. She pedaled south to the outskirts of town. We came to a short row of free-standing shops all emblazoned wall-to-wall with advertising. We stopped in front of one with an umbrella, a picnic table and a Pepsi sign hanging above it:

"Raymond Shop"

"Oh," she said, seeing two men at the table look at me with dread. "Privacy, we will go around back." She turned the cargo bike toward the rear of the shop and steered to it. In the exposed back, her brother Raymond waved to her. Upon seeing me, his face grew dark. He came to unload one of the sacks into his shop.

"Sister," he said and gave her a hug. "Who is this?"

"She's my friend Eunis, from New York." Mariam pinning a badge on both of us.

"New York," he said, also with a hint of admiration but still uneasy.

"Yes," said Mariam. She proceeded to dispense coffee for each of us while explaining I needed a "cheap" phone.

"How cheap?" he asked.

Mariam looked at me.

I counted my remaining shillings. "Forty-thousand," I said putting the bills on one of the two small chairs he had in the back. I got a dismissive shake in return.

"You're joking," he said. He wrestled the bag of coffee beans into the corner.

"Can you do anything for her?" asked Mariam.

He picked up the bills and stuffed them in his pocket. "I'll see what I can do."

"Thank you." I wanted to ask *how quickly*, but that seemed inapt given my low bid. I did add, "I'll need to call New York. Soon."

"I will see what I can do," he repeated. He went back to work at the front counter of his establishment. The two men who had been seated at the picnic table in front, bellied up to the counter—no doubt with questions about me.

Mariam and I sat sipping our coffees, as robust as their smell had promised. She explained that Raymond was the youngest after her, and I determined that despite her baby face, she was in her mid-twenties. Raymond worked three jobs, as did she. One of his jobs involved gathering beans, one dispensing them in his small shop, and one working in the sawmill as an apprentice. She harvested and delivered beans, she painted buildings, when such work became available.

"There are few jobs, though we are lucky to have the coffee plantations and the sawmill," she said.

"I'm in trouble," I blurted. "I don't want my danger to become yours."

She stopped drinking her coffee and set it on the ground. "Tell me about New York."

"No, you don't understand," I said.

"You're albino," she said. "I understand. You're looking for a young girl."

"She's not much younger than you. I think she's been murdered. I know she's been tortured."

"For her body parts."

"Yes," I said. "And there are people who know I'm looking for her."

"Oh." Mariam's innocence erased. "Oh."

Chapter 25

Karatu and the sawmill, Mto wa Mbu Village, Tanzania

Mariam and I sat and talked about Karatu and New York City—mostly New York City—for an hour. I learned a few Swahili words from her. Her brother Raymond returned with a cloth sack. It appeared to have been rolled in black sludge. "Here," he said shoving it at me and glancing around in the same way I'd done leaving Dr. Allen's house. "This is the best I could do. And you are lucky for it. You did not get it from me."

Mariam seemed taken by surprise.

"Do not give me that look," Raymond said to her. "She is your friend, that is all." He walked back into his shop.

The sack contained a cell phone, almost as grungy as the sack. A brand I've never heard of. I excused myself from Mariam and tramped into the dry grass behind the row of shops. Who to call, Gordon or Roddy? I couldn't keep asking Roddy for favors, though his voice would soothe me.

I called the Weather One offices hoping to reach Gordon.

After three attempts, I got through to the station's main number which pitched me to general voice mail. I was more or less eight hours ahead of New York: the office closed. *What should I say in the allotted 20 seconds?* I got the obligatory beep, I sputtered; just long enough for the call to disconnect.

It took me a moment to remember Roddy's number; there I could leave a personal message, even if he didn't pick up. "Roddy, it's me. Eunis." *What to say?* "I'm in Tanzania, in the Lake Zone. Karatu. I-I got separated from my crew. I'm looking for Ruthie's niece. I-I . . . I've run out of money. I lost my passport." The phone went dead. "Roddy?" I looked at the phone. Dead. I pressed buttons, I pounded on it. Dead. *Shit!*

I cut back through the tall grass, morning giving way to mid-day. Despite the rising heat, Mariam had wrapped herself in a rich *khanga* of muted colors.

"What's the matter?" she asked as I passed on my way to Raymond.

Even before I'd reached him, I knew his answer. "Sorry to bother you, Raymond," I said, "is there a charger for the phone?"

His head sagged further down, scribbling a list on the counter. And it was going to stay that way; *down*. He stopped scribbling. "It's old," he said and went back to his work.

Mariam took my hand. She directed me to her cargo bike and into it. Raymond called out to her, "The first Yellow Sac of the season."

"What does that mean?" I asked.

"Nothing, it's a spider," said Mariam.

"And?"

"They're trouble, they hurt."

"He means me," I said.

She swept away the inference. "I think you should go home. Go back to New York."

"No, I can't."

She began to pedal. "This is very dangerous, what you are doing. Wise is knowing what to overlook."

"I can't overlook this," I said. "I need to find a man at the sawmill. Morgan Jonas."

"What does he do there?"

"I don't know. He used to be a miner in Geita."

"Very dangerous." She reproached me as if I were ten.

"I'm beginning to get the picture," I said. "Anyhow, I can't leave now, even if I wanted to. I've lost my passport, my identification. And now . . . the money's all gone."

"I can lend you," she said.

"No! You won't. I got myself into this. Let me off. You don't even know me." I started to slip out of the trike.

She reached over and pulled me back into my seat. "I know you. You will invite me to New York. It will be worth it for both of us." Her face unexpectedly mature, though still crisply bound in rose red to show off her youth. The *khanga* of dark greens, browns and yellows cascaded off her shoulders like a goddess.

Since I'd laid eyes on her, I'd been trying to explain to myself *how* she was captivating? How *so* beautiful? Now I knew. Her beauty reflected her compassion; it sat steady in her eyes. She was wise. And gentle. "It will be worth it for both of us," she repeated.

"Not if we're dead," I reminded her. And in a way I was only talking about her, as my death might be unavoidable and perhaps not that important anymore. *Strange as I thought it.*

"It is inevitable, one way or the other." She smiled without actually smiling. "But I am no warrior; I just want to help."

One way or the other, the recurring acceptance of our destiny, though most of us deny it. "Death seems to be a mantra here," I said.

"What is *mantra*?"

"A prayer, sometimes a phrase of faith."

"I would think so," she said. "What else can we count on?" She waited till I faced her properly. "Now, where shall we go?"

I raised my hands. "Hey, no, I can't let you do that. You're not going anywhere. Your life is good here. Sunshine, water . . . coffee!"

"We know we're going to die," she said. "Still, we do not expect it. Who will I be if I do not help?"

"I'm no one."

"We're all *no one*." She waved to both sides of the road, the bustle of town thinning out. "I'm someone by helping you."

"Fu—no, I'll be okay."

"You will be butchered."

Butchered struck a chord.

"Your friend, the one whose niece was kidnapped and tortured . . ."

"It's not your responsibility," I said.

"Her name?"

Shit. "Ruthie. So what?"

"Yes, Ruthie. She's counting on you. And you love her."

Mariam looked at me like Roddy would, like we'd known each other too long to trifle in lies.

"This isn't your fight," I repeated.

She kept cycling. "It has gone on too long, this witchcraft. Not good for any of us."

"And you're gonna end it by getting yourself killed?"

"I am not going to die," she said. "I'm just going to help you determine if Kyra's alive or dead. Maybe that will punch sense into you . . . I want to see the Statue of Liberty. I want New York pizza."

We passed the turn off to Lake Manyara. "Hey," I said, "I need to get to the sawmill."

"Of course. But Lake Manyara is less than twelve feet deep even in the rainiest season—which this is not. And it's salty. It's only mud flats now. There's no sawmill there." She pointed ahead. "You can trust me."

We passed the village of Mto wa Mbu. Pronounced *mita wanbu.* "It translates to 'Mosquito River,'" Mariam said. "Tent camps and tourist lodges up there. Fruit markets. Lots of bananas. Not many mosquitos, actually."

"Let me off, I'll walk the rest of the way."

"It's another twelve kilometers," she said. She pulled the trike to the side of the road. "What will it be?"

Eight miles! Who was I kidding? Who was I to refuse help? I needed a tether to reality if I was going to help anybody. I disarmed. "Okay, okay. Thank you, I could use some help; people out here hunt albinos."

She looked at me and back to the road. "That's right." She began biking again. Within a few miles, a scattering of small shops on bikes dotted the roadside. Unfamiliar smells wafted past me, and with each I felt an unaccountable heaviness added to my body, as if being sucked into a vacuum. Maybe it was Mariam's simple acknowledgment of the terrors to come, paired with images of her being slaughtered, that reset me. "I know what I said, Mariam, but *no*. It can't happen. I won't let you put yourself in harm's way. Let me off."

"Just hold on," she said.

With that, the smell of freshly sawn wood sweetened the air, a hilltop forest rose above us. The woodland's appendages spread out like the legs of a scarab beetle, approximately ten miles across at its widest point. Green like I've never seen. We slowed. At the base of the 7,000-foot forest, a tapestry of emerald braids spiraled down on us. Each braid maintaining its own texture. Juniper, conifer, yellowwood. Beneath the trees, close-knit shrubs, and wildflowers.

She took in its grandeur. "It's said that from above, you can see the faces of men and women, birds and beasts embroidered, all in Lake Selela's canopy."

"Spectacular," I said. The force pulling at me even more inescapable and yet Mariam seemed not to notice. "But," I said clutching the bike lest I be yanked from it, "now I'll say goodbye."

"You see that?" She pointed ahead to a huge, gated sawmill. "Raymond apprentices there. And recently, Raymond has established a cart right there." She pointed across the road to a bike cart and a pudgy young man. "That's Celvin. He works every day for Raymond. And you would call this . . ." she pointed to the cart on wheels marked RAYMOND COFFEE.

". . . . a 'prime location.' Wouldn't you? I need to drop beans for Raymond's cart."

"Did you hear me?" I said. The wind slackened. She slowed the cargo bike to a stop in front of Raymond's bike café. "I can't let you do this."

She jumped out of her cargo bike, lifted a bag of beans, and plopped it onto the loading platform of Raymond's café on wheels. Two large coffee urns and paper cups balanced the weight in front of the cart. Celvin barely acknowledged her, preoccupied with the music from a small—and exceptionally tinny—transistor radio.

"Goodbye," I said. "We won't be able to see each other again. Thank you for everything. I'm going into the sawmill, see if I can find Morgan Jonas."

Before I'd swiveled out of my seat, Mariam sprinted across the road. A massive truck carrying a huge load of sawn planks turned out of the sawmill separating us. She called to me, "You will draw too much attention." Then louder, "I'll return soon. Stay with my vehicle."

The truck of timber let off a brittle, ear-splitting warning to get out of the way.

"No! Hey!" I yelled at Mariam. She ducked behind the truck. She made it out of the way. I pulled back; a few vendors had already directed their attention to me. The truck with its load of boards, blocked my view of all but Mariam's legs as she headed for the front gate. I waited for the truck to pass. As it cleared, she'd begun mesmerizing a guard; he would have carried her in had she asked. He nodded. She held up her fingers to me like *it won't be long*.

I laid back; Mariam was right, I drew attention. Always had: the gift of frightfulness. Hordes of workers strolled in and out of the sawmill, some stopping at Raymond's café on wheels, others stopping at the various coffee and food vendors lined along the road. I kept my head down.

After a bit, I couldn't help myself; the breeze returned, wrapping me in the smell of fresh baked goods, calling me, raising my head, dragging me into the aromas. I stood in front of a vendor, lightheaded, a buzz throughout my body. I guess I was really hungry.

"What can I get you?" he asked, waving his hand across his wares. "One of these," he raised a muffin, lifting my eyes. Beyond the muffin, in the crowd leaving the sawmill, a large woman, curiously distinctive.

Still rippling with the wind, I left the vendor without a word, absorbed with the woman, and not knowing why. Closer, I did a double take. Standing a few yards away was the hefty Chinese woman I'd encountered in the rural Mozambican bank—chastised by Ngowa for shorting me money. She ambled toward a doughnut stand, and with her an older, well-dressed Chinese man in a western-style suit. I couldn't recall her name. As I got closer to them, the vendor said, "Welcome back, Mr. Hsu, Ms. Zhou." The vendor genuflected; comic given his matchstick frame.

Ms. Zhou turned to Mr. Hsu. "Let me buy this for you." Hsu eagerly surveyed the fried breads. *Mr. Hsu*; Ngowa had mentioned that name in the bank. With it, Ms. Zhou had snapped to attention and had restored the money she owed me.

I came up to them. "Ms. Zhou," I said, "Do you remember

me?" I figured I'm hard to forget. "We met at the rural bank in southern Mozambique. I was changing dollars to—"

"I do not! Go away." She gawked, thunderstruck, then petrified.

I tried to calm her. "Mr. Ngowa came in with me, remember? About a month ago."

At the mention of Ngowa's name, Hsu's face iced up. "*Lai,*" she said to Hsu. He gave me one last glance and they both walked quickly away, Hsu brandishing his fist at her. They went back through the sawmill gate. The guard, too, bowed to them. He obviously knew them. The lanky vendor glared at me. I'd screwed up his sale.

Mariam stood by Raymond's coffee cart searching the line of vendors for me. "That was weird," I said as I approached her.

"Let's get out of here," she said. She waved goodbye to Celvin, and we were off, heading back into town.

"How'd you get in? I asked.

"I told him I was looking for my brother. With that guard I could have said anything."

"I noticed. Did you find Morgan Jonas?"

"No, but I got the feeling asking about him was not smart."

"He's an albino hunter. Or was," I admitted.

She closed her eyes for a second. "In our village we had a man who advocated for albino rights. They cut off his genitals and arms. They left him in the street to die."

"But the police?" I said.

"Forget the police. More than a hundred people in the region have been arrested for crimes against albinos, but no one has even been taken to court. Policemen defend attackers and destroy evidence. You really have to get out of here. The hunters, they're savages, sometimes helped by the victim's own family. Husbands setting up their wives, mothers their own children. Girls are being raped because of a belief they offer a cure for AIDS. They dismember children while they're still alive."

I held my chest. "Oh, my god."

"You have got to get out. They even believe witchcraft ritual is more powerful if victims scream during amputation." Her eyes welled with tears. "Now do you understand why you must leave?"

"What happened in there?" I pointed to the sawmill and for the first time noticed the razor wire along its rampart.

She admitted, "I was told to realize how short life can be."

"By whom?"

She placed both hands over her mouth. "It was passed on to me."

"How?"

"Asides and intentional jarring." She shrank. Her paranoia affirmed mine. "No more of this. Doesn't matter. *You* go away. Please," she said. "We should both leave this alone."

"Racist barbarians. If Kyra's still alive, I've gotta find her. And if I do—those bastards—I'll get them, at least one of them."

"And," she said placing her hand on mine, "if they get you?"

Chapter 26

Karatu, Tanzania

Mariam went on. "You're determined to die because of racists? What about the racists in your country?"

"Don't try to talk me out of this. It's not happening," I said.

"Your racists, they're white." She laced her fingers together, bent them inside out to me, a defiant gesture that pricked me. "But our racists are Black, so you do something about it." She puffed. "Do it in your own country."

"Wrong tactic, Mariam. I know what you're trying to do. I'm way past turnaround. I can't look away any longer. Besides . . . racists—like thugs, fruits, and politicians—come in all colors. You know that. Look at me, you're not going to convince me. I don't know how all this came on me. It doesn't matter anymore. It doesn't even seem real half the time, like tradewinds dumped me here."

"It is real," Mariam sighed.

"Give it up, because I'm not going to."

)))

Until I could articulate a plan for what Mariam called my "death wish," Mariam insisted I stay with her in the family settlement. It included her, Raymond, her mother, and her three older brothers. We squabbled all the way to the cluster of small buildings that lay miles outside Karatu. But I didn't jump out.

By the time we arrived, we'd agreed on some ground rules. We agreed that I should stay, incognito, inside her hut with her mother until sundown. She also made clear that her brothers should not know that I was there. Safer for everyone.

The three mud brick and thatched huts, an outlier of a small village, were bound together with roots and sticks. A tiny concrete latrine being the only other structure. This made Mariam's family one of the more prosperous in the area.

We arrived with everyone away, including her mother, who picked coffee beans at a local plantation. Mariam pointed at the largest of the buildings where two of her brothers lived. It was no more than twelve-foot square. She said it had the biggest kitchen so the family could eat together at least once a week. "We used to have dinner together every night when father was alive. Now we all have to pull the weight."

The hut she shared with her mother—propped up with irregular five-foot poles—forced us to squat inside. A bed on posts rose a foot above the dirt floor to accommodate her mother. Mariam slept on the floor on a thin mattress. A tabular stone in the center served as the dining table with pots scattered around it, and a small campfire at its end for cooking. Two small stools and several plastic buckets filled out the room.

"You must be tired." She implied I should lay down on her mattress.

"I need to find Kyra," I said. But my body sank to the dusty mattress. I closed my eyes. I hadn't realized how tired I'd become.

Even in the humidity, the warmth of Mariam's body against my mine grounded me. "Resting will help you make smarter decisions," she said. She held my hand in hers.

I opened my eyes. Her cool unflappability only inches away. I touched her face. She touched mine. Her eyes, hickory, so empathic. Her lips, as always, sanguine and smiling, abundant. I lost my head, I touched her lips, then kissed them. So soft. *What am I doing!?* She held my face in her hands and returned my kiss.

)))

We made love for an hour or so, an easefulness I'd been needing for too long—since my time with Roddy in Minnesota, if I was honest. I fell asleep. When I awoke, Mariam had disappeared. She'd left me a jug of water; I knew better than to drink it. Despite my gritty throat, I'd learned *bottled water only*. But she *had* left me more relaxed and ready to sort things out.

Why were Ms. Zhou and Mr. Hsu at the giant sawmill? Why did Ms. Zhou pretend she didn't know me? Why did they both bolt when I mentioned Ngowa's name?

Could I find Morgan Jonas, the miner and albino bounty hunter from Geita at the sawmill? If I did, did he have any connection to Kyra? Would he tell me? Would he turn on me and hunt me down? Who could tell me if Morgan Jonas really worked there? The mill must have employed more than a thousand people. I'd need to speak to someone at the top, someone who had access to employee records. Why would he or she give me that information?

I wasn't keen to return to Dr. Allen's house, whether or not he might be there. He'd been clear he wanted nothing more to do with me; he was terrified of something, he had nothing more to say. How about Mrs. Baakari at the university? Would she be back from vacation? Even if she was, what more could she tell me? Would she let me use her phone, for a long-distance call?

Having a phone made sense, even borrowing one. But Raymond and the other brothers were the only ones in the family who had them. Raymond's reluctance had already been made evident. The other brothers couldn't know of my existence. So, at least for the time being, no phone.

I'd added plenty of questions with no answers. I'd gotten in pretty deep, and that surprised me—I hadn't been aware of the transition.

All of this made Mariam's hut even more stifling. I poked my head out of it. No one was around. I needed a walk to flex my legs and clear my head. No more than half a mile from Mariam's family settlement, I had the sensation I was being followed. When I turned around, no one in sight; probably all off working. *The first signs of paranoia, great.*

Up the dirt road, a little girl played with her dog. He stood taller than her, slim, completely white with large pointy ears and a tongue lavishing the girl's ears. She responded with gleeful shrieks and giggles. I stepped out of the side brush and waved to the girl; she waved back. I approached slowly. Just watching them was therapeutic. All that joy, all that love.

"You, *mzimu*, you give me finger." A chubby boy, at most

twelve, appeared in front of me, holding out a machete. "You do it for me and I help you with your business. I am not afraid."

The little girl turned and ran, her dog bounding after her.

"No," I said, like an adult teaching a child and brushing him off. "I am not giving up my finger. I use it."

He looked to his right. He'd been joined by other children, most of them younger. Six of them. They circled me.

"Do not make me prove," he said. He swung the machete up and down like a hatchet. If he'd thrown it, it would have cut me three-four inches deep somewhere.

"*Ipate*," said one of the girls egging him on. "Get it."

This was ridiculous. "Listen, forget your stories. I'm human just like you . . ." I swiveled to his cheerleader, " and you!" She jumped back. "Want *your* finger cut off?"

She lifted her left hand. Her fourth finger was already missing.

"I will too," said the next oldest boy, a face already scared by lance and unhappiness. He took a step toward me.

"Who else has a sharp object?" I asked.

"*Ipate*," Lanced Boy said to Machete Boy.

I kicked him in the nuts so hard he couldn't make a sound, except the thud of his body to the ground. He went into a fetal position; the circle opened a bit.

"*Endelea*," I said. "Go on." I waved them away. The machete came at my shoulder; I ducked, feeling the wind of it pass by.

A boy from behind set his teeth in my thigh. I tore him from me and tossed him three feet away. "Fuckers!" The group gathered around him while the Lanced Boy continued to writhe on the ground. I looked for Machete Boy; he was running away, the machete in hand slicing the air in front of him.

"Fuck," I said and glared at the children. "*Endelea*, go on."
I walked away. *WTF!*

))))

Back at Mariam's, making sure no one followed me, I laid down
on the mat. For the first time—so close to the ground—I felt
pursuit, as if I were being tracked, again. I understood it in some
carnal way. After New York, you'd think I'd be a little savvier.
I'd been stalked there, too, by beasts older but as deluded as
these children. There it felt random, maybe because of the
concrete, though just as pernicious, just as primal: to control.
In Tanzania it *drummed,* deep rooted in the soil, inescapable—
to hold power—where so few had it. Survival of the fittest.

I still had no idea what to do. As bait, maybe I'd find Kyra,
that was one shitty idea. Then what? I bent in circles on the
floor of that claustrophobic hut, doing my best to loosen my
body. Whatever that pulse was pumping from the ground, I
had to tune in to it, too, if just to keep a *feel* for my hunters.

Getting practical again, I had to track down Morgan
Jonas. After that, I told myself, there'd be some lead, maybe
a connection directly to Kyra? That meant going back to the
sawmill, finding someone who oversaw the employee records.
Someone high enough who might be responsive to my search.
Near or at the top of the sawmill food chain. They'd be
educated, less likely to freak at my appearance, hopefully more
compassionate. I'd had luck at the Geita mine. That was my
rationale.

))))

Mariam explained my presence to her mother. Her mother turned her humped back on me. But she didn't argue with Mariam.

I jumped into the rear of Mariam's cargo bike and hunkered down. She cycled safely out of her small village. "Okay," she said glancing at me in the back. "You'll look for more information," she said. "But more discreetly this time."

She signaled to come sit next to her. It didn't seem wise, flouting The Bait like that. As usual, she persisted. She stopped the bike. Her voice rose. "Sit with me."

"What? No," I said. "People want to hunt me down."

Her voice climbed again, making more of a spectacle than if I quietly agreed. "You're not important yet," she said. So, I sat up front, across from her.

I kept my head tilted away from the road's shoulder and from the people walking and cycling along it. Mariam's offhand nature came across as weird, and contradictory. "What if we've been followed?" I said.

Eyes firmly on the road, she proclaimed, "No, not from my village."

I thought to tell her about the children not far from her home. She was in many ways as uneducated about the dangers of the albino myths as I. Or, she was setting me up.

More questions poured from her about New York City, the U.S., how we barbecue, Howard Zinn (!) and horror films. I learned of a few Tanzanian ceremonies and added to my Swahili.

Karatu hustled with commerce. A city of over 30,000. Once you are in the center, everything moves, and I am—as

Mariam had asserted—a small part of the noise. But as one heads away from it, on the outskirts, one can feel the drive of the city wane and the land take over. People and animals shoot off in every direction, into a patchwork of roads, trails, and footpaths. There, I was more noticeable.

The sawmill area lacked the density of town, though not the sparsity of the more remote outskirts. The sound that came out of the mill, however, had a far heavier heartbeat than the city. We pulled up to Raymond's café on wheels. Celvin nodded but made no attempt to talk to me, once again absorbed by music from the local radio station.

"I have to find a way in," I said to Mariam.

She shook her head. "You won't get in. You'll draw attention."

"I have to, and I will. It's the only lead I've got."

She lifted a sack of beans off her vehicle and laid it on Raymond's stand. "You need to get off and wait for me here," she said. "I'll only be a short time." She gestured at the sawmill gate. "I have a delivery inside. Stay here and talk to Celvin. Please get off." When I hesitated, her irritation was clear. "*Endelea*," she said. "Go on. I have to go to the CEO's office. I'll ask his secretary if she's heard anything. She likes me. I'll be vague."

"It's not your problem."

"Get off," she commanded. She cycled off.

Celvin spun away from me. I walked over to the twiglike vendor who had served Mr. Hsu and Ms. Zhou. "Oh, you again," he said, rubbing his hands on a towel, preparing for a fight. "You want to scare off all my customers?"

"I just need to know about Mr. Hsu and Ms. Zhou."

"If I were an informer, I wouldn't be here every morning and night, I'd be buried. They like my breads. Why don't you buy some? I lost my last sale to them because of you."

"How often are they here?"

"If I were you, I would not hang around." His voice trifling but with a panicky undertone. He wanted me far from his cart.

"So?" My hands on my hips. "I can hang out."

"*Mzuka.*" He spit on the ground. "Mr. Hsu, at least once a month. She comes along occasionally. Now out of here, ghost woman. Let the living do business."

"A man named Ngowa, have you met him?"

"I meet many people. That name means nothing." His teeth clenched. He spit *at me*. It caught my arm. I withdrew to Raymond's cart, the smell of his gob triggering queasiness.

When Mariam returned, I asked about her delivery inside the mill. She told me that once a week she "provided" a sack of beans to the executive offices. "That's how Raymond got his apprenticeship. Free beans. That's how things are done here. Nothing's truly free. Raymond's smart."

"What did you find out?" I asked.

"Nothing. Let's get out of here."

I questioned again. "His secretary hadn't heard of Morgan Jonas?"

"No."

"What's her name, the secretary?"

"Forget it," said Mariam.

"Her name?"

Mariam bristled. "I have to work with these people."

"I just want a name."

"Flaviana Jioni. You are happy now? What good is this?" We mounted her vehicle. She began wheeling back into town.

"How much do those sacks weigh when full?" I asked.

"About sixty kilos; a little over a hundred thirty pounds. Why?"

"Fantastic!" I leaned over, wrapped my arms around her, and kissed her on the mouth. She drew a fist and hit me so hard I had to catch myself on the trike's frame or I would have toppled out of the vehicle.

Chapter 27

The sawmill, Mto wa Mbu Village, Tanzania

"What the hell! Why'd you hit me?" Stunned, I rubbed my arm, then remembered the vendor had spit on the same spot.

Mariam faced me, eyes hysterical. "You dare kiss me in public! Tanzanian women go to prison for that kind of kiss—for life. What's wrong with you?"

"Oh, no," I said. "I'm sorry. I never—"

"Not in public, ever!" she said. "Why would you do that?"

"Because of you," I said. "And your hypnotic bags of coffee beans."

"Huh?" She still fumed, still checking the vicinity if anyone had seen.

)))

When I explained my plan, Mariam thought I was nuts, and she fought me on the idea. But every day for ten days, as I lost a pound or two, I slipped into a sack, and she filled coffee beans around me. Eventually, my weight plus the beans came in right around 132 pounds. I waited for the Chinese to arrive. Because of their attire, I figured they, too, were headed to the executive offices. Maybe I could kill two birds with one stone, if the birds didn't turn out to be deadly cassowary.

Mr. Hsu finally arrived. Mariam tried again to talk me out of the scheme. I refused to back down; she wheeled me into the executive offices, into the conference room and the closet where the beans were kept. She told Flaviana Jioni, the secretary, "We are giving you an extra bag this week." It was that simple. All I had to do was breathe slowly and not move, at least until the office closed in the evening.

The room remained quiet for a couple hours until the conference door opened and clicked shut. "Mr. Hsu," a man with a gravelly voice said. "We welcome you as usual." I couldn't see either one of them. Chairs squeaked as the men sat.

"Mr. Charles," said Hsu acknowledging the courtesy. "I trust you are well."

"Yes, thank you. And you?" said Mr. Charles.

Hsu answered, "I see that the last shipment is being delayed. Beijing is not happy."

"The border has become ever more delicate, as you might imagine. I assure you, you will have your timber in the next two weeks."

"Two weeks!"

"We are doing the best we can."

The room fell silent, the tension between the two men palpable.

Mr. Charles tried to untangle the knot. "And how is everything else?"

"Not so good." Mr. Hsu's irritability still conspicuous. "There was a young woman, an albino, asking about Ngowa. Do you know who she is?"

"I think I do," said Mr. Charles.

"You think!?"

Mr. Charles spoke calmly. "I assure you we will take care of this matter."

"And Ngowa?" asked Hsu.

"He's on other business right now."

"*Muti* business, Mr. Charles?" Hsu's displeasure unabated.

"No, no. Nothing like that," said Mr. Charles. "That's a dirty business."

"Well," said Hsu, "see that this is taken care of immediately. You have much at stake."

Mr. Charles did not beg from the fight. "As does your country." A pause. "But as I say, we will take care of it."

"And," said Hsu, "if anyone connected to this witchcraft business is hanging around your mill, I suggest you extricate him or her now. Do not complicate our commerce with such . . ."

". . . Antiquated beliefs?" offered Charles.

". . . Barbaric traditions. You get my point?" A chair scrapped back from the table.

"Mr. Hsu," said Charles, "the trucks will move across the border in two weeks, you have my word."

))))

After steeping in the coffee for another four hours, the office quieted down. A welcome moment: I desperately had to pee.

I cut myself out of the bag, took a leak in a plant, and went searching for the employee files—specifically Morgan Jonas'. Every file cabinet and every drawer locked with nothing but numbers ascribed to them. Nothing that provided a clue as to what the files held. I gave up.

Even at that hour, the sound of the mill thumped the night. But the office hallways were vacant and sparsely illuminated. Every twenty feet, a single bulb guided me till I reached the first set of stairs, then the next. On the ground floor, under another single bulb, a night watchman hunched over his desk, asleep. *Shit.*

With caution, I moved toward him. He was a rotund man, arms the size of a recently fed boa constrictor. As I passed, his hand quavered above a handgun. At the door, the wooden floor groaned. He woke. He tried to make sense of his vision. "Wha . . . stop!" He pulled the gun from his hip. He wobbled, pointing it at me. He stood up. He was short and missing his left hand.

"Don't shoot, please."

His gun hand shook. "*Zeru zeru.*"

"No," I said. "I'm no ghost. I'm just like you."

"No!"

"Yes. Please, what's your name?"

He squirmed. He brooded over something. "They call me Kasoro," he said bitterly.

"So, Kasoro . . ."

"That's not my name," he snapped.

"You just said—"

"I said that's what they call me. My parents named me Jamil." He steadied.

"So, Jamil . . ."

"It means handsome." He added a sarcastic laugh.

"That's very nice. So what is *kasoro*?"

"In your language, *defective*." He raised his club arm. "This is all I'm good for now, killing *zeru zeru* like you. You shouldn't be here."

"I'm flesh and bones, like you. You must know that. I have a genetic disorder, albinism. I was born with it; it strips me of pigmentation. How did you lose your hand and forearm?"

"Stop talking." He fixed the pistol on me. He took aim.

"How?"

"I was born with it."

"'Congenital amputation;' your parents' DNA or maybe some toxin or drug your mother was around or ingested while you were in her belly. We are the same."

"No."

"It's not your fault."

"This means nothing now. What are you doing on sawmill property?"

"I'm trying to find information about a young girl, a young girl with albinism. And for that, someone cut off her hands. You've heard of such things, I know. Please put down the gun."

"You shouldn't be here." He waggled the revolver at me.

"She may still be alive."

He paused. "Even after her hands . . .?"

"It doesn't need to be a death. You and I—"

"You shouldn't have come here, stealing in the night."

"I'm not here to hurt anyone. I stole nothing. I hoped for information. But I can leave now. You see I have nothing on me. I've taken nothing."

He pondered his options. "You broke in."

"No, I was escorted in." Stretching the truth a bit. "I just stayed late."

His head drooped; he took aim. "You're going to run. I'm going to shoot. I'm a very good shot, even with this one hand. But I'm going to miss. Do not come again."

I fled into the night. The shot rang out. My body unwound. I spotted Mariam waiting for me. Before I reached her, two large logging trucks, both fully loaded with logs, pulled *into* the sawmill.

"You are okay?" she asked. "I heard gunfire."

"I'm fine, let's get out of here."

She began to motor into the night.

"That's strange," I said.

"What?"

"Those two trucks, they entered the sawmill *with* logs." I turned once more to see the second truck roll in and the gate close.

"So?"

"Shouldn't the rough logs be coming from the lake then leaving the mill sawn?"

"I've seen it before," she said. "Never thought much about it. What happened inside?"

I explained what I'd heard between Mr. Hsu and Mr. Charles. "I'm not surprised," She said. "There have been rumors for years. Wealthy Tanzanians are often linked to *muti* medicine. Even government officials in this county are said to be consulting with witch doctors."

"You told me Tanzanians are among the most educated in Africa."

"No, we have better *access* than many African countries, but we have so many religions and ethnic groups. We speak a hundred different languages. We're not well educated. All sorts of traditions survive."

"But you and Raymond . . .?" I said.

"My father insisted we take every opportunity. I just *sound* educated." She canned the subject. "If a politician needs to win an election, they consult a witch doctor. Your body parts are said to bring good luck. If a politician is called out for supporting witchcraft, they blame the fishermen. Maybe they're scapegoats. But some fishermen are known to weave albino hair into their nets to increase their catch."

I struggled to make sense of what she was saying. "What about the timber they talked about?"

Mariam shrugged. "I know nothing about that." The swoosh and rattle of the bike blended with the night. We slipped into our own thoughts; we didn't exchange another word the rest of the way to her hut, and to sleep.

〉〉〉

Just before sunrise the next morning, and despite Mariam's recriminations, Mariam dropped me off; I stationed across from the sawmill gate behind a row of hedges. I can't say exactly what I hoped to achieve. Call it intuition. I just knew that Mr. Charles knew Ngowa, and he knew about *muti* killings. Maybe I could identify Charles as he came to work. Probably a fancy car. If so, perhaps he could lead me to Morgan Jonas. Or better yet, to Kyra.

As I waited, two more trucks fully loaded with logs *entered* the mill. Not much other activity.

The morning air tranquillized me; I must have dozed off. I can't say for how long, but I was awakened by blue and red flares flooding my eyelids. Several police vehicles arrived—no sirens—followed by an ambulance. The sun hadn't fully risen. People started to gather. The gate opened and most of the police vehicles drove in. The gate closed. I took a chance, I stepped next to one of the officers who waited outside. He didn't even look at me. "Go away," he said. "Police business."

"What's happening?" I asked.

About to physically push back, he stopped. He looked me up and down, like a side of beef. He was one of those. "I told you," he said, "police business." He couldn't keep his eyes off my body. I guess for him my face didn't exist.

The few gawkers were paying attention to the police vehicles. I casually undid the second button of my shirt. "It seems so exciting," I said.

"Not exciting," he said. "Just another accident in the mill. Clumsy workers." He peeked at my cleavage. I smiled at him.

The cop expanded *his* chest. "You would think workers would be more careful around a multi-rip. They're working with seven-hundred-millimeter blades. But they're not the smartest blokes."

"Oh," I said, showing great deference. "What happened?"

He made a roaring sound and looped his finger in the air. "Got chewed *down*. Not much left of him, poor bastard. We should meet you and I, after my shift. I could tell you more about my work. I have stories."

"That sounds awful—the millworker, I mean." An ambulance siren shrieked. The sawmill's titanic doors cranked opened. "Who was it?" I said. The police vehicles started their engines. They began lining up behind the ambulance. "You must be strong to handle such horrible things." I flipped my hair to the side and showed the officer more adoring attention.

"Just a man," he said. "Just a foolish man." He tilted his head upward and sniffed.

"Did he have a name?"

"Don't know."

"Can you find out?"

A very short policeman walked out the gate. My Big Policeman tapped him on the shoulder. "What was the name of the bloke who scattered?"

The short cop looked at me. He kept his distaste in check. "Morgan something. Jonas. Morgan Jonas." He eyed the big cop and shook his head then walked away.

"Yes. Jonas," said the big cop. "Morgan Jonas."

Chapter 28

Karatu, Tanzania

Mariam lit two lamps, turned over one of the buckets and sat me on it. "My mother will not be here tonight," she said.

"Oh?" Her mother hadn't said a single word to me the ten days I'd slept there. Occasionally, she'd sit across but wouldn't raise her head to confront my appearance. Most of the time, she turned away, laid down on her bed, and went to sleep. "She seemed a bit withdrawn with me at first," I said, "but—"

"—One hundred ninety-eight million shillings. That's what you are worth." The equanimity in Mariam's eyes had given way to unrest. "In U.S. dollars, that is eighty-five thousand. A bounty. Raymond just heard. He asked me if I had seen you recently. Even my brother! My mother cannot stay here. I cannot be seen with you. Any of us could be slaughtered. I am so sorry, but this is out of control."

"A bounty?" I asked.

"You must leave." Weight bent her over. "I am so sorry."

I stood up. "No, no. I understand. I'll go right now." I pointed to the night.

"Where will you go?" she asked.

I closed my eyes. I hadn't a clue. "I'll be fine. I'll keep low from now on."

"You will need to be invisible," she said. "Will you take money? It isn't much." She reached into a woven basket tucked under a self on the dirt floor.

"Your money can't help," I said. "But thank you. Thank you for everything."

She handed me the bills. "An early payment on New York." She labored for a smile.

I accepted them with a bow and shoved them in my pocket. "Where are the witch doctors?" I said. "They're the only ones who might have direct information about Kyra."

"And you're worth a fortune to them. That is *wazimu* . . . madness. By now Kyra is probably dead. Save yourself."

"Not until I'm sure."

Reluctantly, she said, "There is one around here."

"Is he a strong man?"

"You mean physically strong? No, our Babu is old. But he is wicked, his power is dark. Find your way out of Karatu, Eunis. There may be enough there for the bus." She gestured to the money in my pocket. "Maybe in Dar Es Salaam you can find your way home. It should be safer there. Still, be careful."

"Where can I find him?"

"No," she said. "No."

"So," I said, "You want me asking around for this Babu?"

She kneaded her forehead. "Please do not do this."

"Okay," I said. "Goodbye." I went to kiss her.

She drew in. "Eunis, please."

"Where?" I repeated.

She chewed her lip, I was steadfast. She relented. "After the bus station about eight kilometers, go south past the Catholic Church. Keep going past the old cemetery, two miles, maybe more. The land will slope down. You will come to a wash. A place where two dry beds converge. If there is water—and with more coming rains it is quite possible—it should still be passable. You can wade through. In the middle of the two dry beds, you will see a shack. Babu lives there. With the dogs."

"I love dogs," I said.

"Maybe," she said. "But not these dogs." She thought for a moment. "It's wild out there. And with the antelopes and errant zebras, hyenas." She handed me a bottled water.

"I'll be fine," I said.

She straightened up. She caressed my cheek. Finding courage, she said, "When you make it back to New York, you will contact me at Raymond's, okay? I will come, you will show me New York."

"I will, I promise." I kissed her and passed into the night.

☽☽☽

From her village, where I knew the road, the dark held and protected me. Clouds camouflaged the stars. I kept a steady pace and blew past quite a few people, even those going in my direction. The sustained movement quieted my mind. I made it to the bus station in a little under two hours. Another twenty minutes and I caught the road south; paved and well-maintained until it turned to dirt and narrowed. In the limited moonlight, dangerously uneven. Another fringe of Karatu for which I had no coordinates, my first real sense that I was, again, on my own. And impermanent.

In the distance, a hacking sound bit into the quiet; similar to a braying donkey. *Per Mariam*, most likely a zebra. As if in recognition, a different call followed; it could have been the halloo of a band of didgeridoos or large croaking frogs or a predator in pursuit. I found all of it indiscernible. I tried to sense its size, its rhythm, its roots.

In genetics, we start with the "twisted ladder," the double helix; we build from there. In school, when I finally dropped my trepidation with DNA, I began to decode it. Here? Where to start, what to build from? The language of the land being so foreign? In Minnesota I was a part of nature. I had no fear. Surviving Tanzanian nature, I'd needed to tame the butterflies in my bones.

A gust of air emptied all sound. Again, *no coordinates*. A warning? For whom? From what? Or just mating calls? In my life, I'd found those just as dangerous. *Skip the weather in your head; trust the physical.*

Vapory shades came and went; that's about all I could see. I imagined far more and far worse. *Failing Premonitions 101.* Evening had cooled the land yet sweat beaded my forehead. My body all at once rigid. Misgiving tugged at my neck and back. I admit—despite my previous inner lectures—I considered turning around. The night felt sinister. Behind me a mile, or two, or three—I could no longer measure distance—the scattered housing had disappeared. I had the sensation of being alone. Yet I knew I wasn't.

The land had a way of parsing energy like that. It could be comforting, as it had in my Minnesota wetlands. Karatu's magnificence spread over hundreds and hundreds of miles, as far as I could see: a serene balance of rolling grasslands, shimmery flora, and solitary baobab trees. But along the impassable ground and in the brambly forests, where shadows threatened, I'd learned it could be savage. And now, no light.

Still, my relationship to the land had become more malleable since my arrival. Tanzania's terrain and moisture worked on my musculature, straining my body. But in a good way. Logic, evaluation, and human speech meant less here. As if survival depended on my animal instincts rather than my human rationale. More and more, I felt lost between the two energies. As if the energies were competing, appropriating them at will and reshaping them, at my discomfort. One thing I did know, human or animal, I was prey. Even that, as I say, had become familiar. Though not palliative.

A cold droplet struck my neck. Several more signaled rain. Without my usual instinct for such things, and in only seconds, the storm emerged with vengeance. I'd been led astray by reasoning. I'd been thinking too much. Needle-like droplets pelted my face and chest. I love water but this, this was wrathful. If shelter was nearby, I had no idea what or where it was. So, I squatted right there in the road. The road quickly turned to goop, then a small stream moistening my privates. Only seconds more, it flowed *over* my feet. I *had* to move. Where?

I couldn't abandon the road, as improvised as it was. Once off it, I'd be lost till the downpour stopped and the morning came. Even then, I might never find my way back. I hunched against it. The road dropped away; more water cascaded over my ankles and legs. The yawl of it matched the rain's barrage, so loud that yelling wouldn't have pierced it, not even six feet away. The flood pushed from behind, bulldozing me to land in Babu's front yard.

The small river objected to my feet in its path. *Let go*, it said. *Meet your destiny.* It knocked me down and sent me sliding over the hill, on my ass and back; enough water so the scrapes, at first, were minimal. But as the rain slackened and the swell ebbed, the road began to claw at me. When the trough of water could no longer hold my weight, my body caught on rocks, and my back ripped along them. Within seconds, the rain and its voice stopped, as if Great Spirit itself insisted on it and took hold of my fate.

In the distance, a pinpoint of light flickered in the mist.

Chapter 29
_____

The remote fringes, Karatu, Tanzania

A t first light, silent shapes gathered around me. Low to the
ground, patient like hyenas. They didn't move. *Waiting to
unleash their attack?* I scarcely breathed. After several minutes of
standoff, I got the courage to reach out; a cool stone. Another a
few feet away, rock and masonry. The sun snuck over the ridge
behind me, my eyes acclimated. The structures appeared to be
dog houses, some with towers, others where the towers had
broken off. Tombs. Very old and long abandoned.

The crypts spread out in disorder, overgrown and
decomposing, for about forty yards. Overnight, I'd curled into
a fetal position just a few feet from one of them. No wonder
my whole body ached. Had I known I'd parked in a graveyard,
I could have slipped inside one of the tiny burial chambers for
protection. Instead, against the stabbing rain and a complete
absence of light, I'd tried to stay awake.

If this was the cemetery Mariam had cited, I had another
couple miles or more to where the two dry riverbeds converged,
where Babu the witch doctor lived. Possibly the pinhole of light
I'd seen the night before.

A sip of water and I flexed my rheumatic parts. The road now a thin, overgrown path. Slimy. It meandered past me a few yards away, then down a slope. Morning sun hung on the dew, clinging to the grass, pearls at my feet. I got back on the trail. Ready. Sort of.

I'd dropped down another thousand feet in elevation when the shack came into view. Just as Mariam had described. A pack of large black and dark brown dogs came from behind the hut barking, as if they'd seen or smelled me, even though they were well below me, a quarter mile away. I stepped to the far side of a giant clump of miscanthus grass for cover and hoped the dogs would lose interest. When I peeked from the grass's woody plumes, a skinny old man—a stake of black ink against the tawny landscape—stood looking up the hill in my direction. Though he couldn't possibly see me, he waved for me to come down.

I didn't budge. After a few minutes he turned and went inside, calling the dogs with him. I sat behind the tall grass. The day heated up; the insects took over. I quarreled with my options, and as I did, I felt less and less a part of the geography, more and more a potential target on it. I looked down. On my ankle, as if sent by the witch doctor himself, crawled a tiger orange and black centipede with fluorescent blue legs and long bright orange antennae. Four inches in length. No question, poisonous.

I jumped, shrieked, kicked it off; landed on my ass, unsure of where the centipede had fallen. Helter-skelter off the ground, I slapped at my clothes.

Down below, Babu stood watching. The riverbeds surrounding him and his shack purled with small streams from the night's rain. Now, clothed waist down in pelt and rags, shells or bones wrapping his legs and ankles, Babu might have looked like an animal from a greater distance. Nothing but the wild spread out beyond him and his hut. What else but wild would be there? I hadn't seen a visitor since I'd arrived at the overlook. And where would they come from besides the path I'd traveled?

Babu tossed his head, raised his arms above it; he couldn't comprehend my pretense of invisibility. He went back inside the house. Even from my vantage point, I had at least four or five inches on him. I had the strength to knock him down and escape if I needed to. Rationale.

A gazelle came out of the thicket, separated from its herd, and sipped from the shallow river. Alone, like me.

That's water's trance: it lures us, we gather around it. It brings us life. Predators have only to wait for us there. Mesmerized by it, we're targets. Drawn to our death. I imagined the witch doctor opening the door and setting the dogs on the gazelle. It didn't happen.

Instead, I consumed my time with arguments for confronting the witch doctor or turning back. Guilt had a heavy hand on the scale. My head amounted to a battleground, with warring objections from each side—until the stalemate was worse than the choice. Anyhow, I really didn't have much to look forward to if I went back . . . except more regret.

I made my way down the path. The gazelle took off. I called out to the witch doctor. The dogs began their deep mournful barking but remained behind his closed door.

At the bottom, I called again, stiffening my resolve. Again, no response. I crossed the stream, the water inches topping my ankles. I called once more. Had he slipped away? Had I imagined him? The door swung open, the dogs came snarling out and circled me. "*Subiri!*" Babu yelled at the dogs. They gnashed their teeth. He snapped at them, "*Tena!*" They quieted. "*Karibu*," he said and folded in a small bow. "Welcome." He had put on a dark *kofia*, a traditional brimless hat that sat jauntily on his shriveled walnut head. His lips were thin, like paper. His eyes—large burnt orange and bosky green marbles—did not match his face. On his right-hand thumb and pinky, he had attached two small white feathers; he had polydactyly DNA: six (!) fingers on each hand. He motioned for me to come into his hut.

"I'll stay out here, if you don't mind," I said. *What could I learn—or lose—by going inside?* The dogs looked like mastiffs—large black muzzles and blocky heads, each easily 150 to 175 pounds of muscle.

"You come for something," he said. "A long way."

"I'm looking for a young woman, a young albino woman. A student. Very pretty. Abducted and tortured several months ago in this region. I want to take her home. She alive?"

"You think I know thas woman?"

"Yes?"

The dogs strained against some invisible force, prepared to attack at the witch doctor's command. Again, he held up his hand restraining them. "Important to you?"

"She is." It was if the ground shifted, but it was my trembling.

"How important?" He lowered his hand escalating my fear.

"Please hold your dogs back," I said. Like I had any say in the matter.

"But you love dogs," he said. His paper-thin lips slack, mocking me. "You had one, you were young, yes?"

How could he possibly know about my little Nemo? Maybe all young American girls are thought to have dolls and puppies. "Yes."

"Sad how your little dog found its end," he said, reopening the wound, as if I'd whispered my whole perverse history in his ear.

"How do you know that?" I asked.

He laughed. "Babu here a long time." After a moment he said, "What you give in return for the young girl?"

"She's alive?"

"Tha pretty one," he said. "Kyra Nafasi. Yes, she alive. Maybe not much longer."

I jerked toward him. "I want to see her." The dogs showed teeth. I laid back.

"Not much to bargain with," Babu said.

"What do you want? I just want to get her home to her family. Surely you—"

He held up his hand, the six-fingered maestro readying his hounds for attack. I went silent; he reigned over me too. "Thas only one thing, I want," the witch doctor said. "Only one."

Hopeful, I asked, "And that is?"

"You."

Chapter 30

The remote fringes, Karatu, Tanzania

"What does that mean?" I asked the witch doctor, although I had a pretty good idea of the answer. I prepared for him to try to take me right there.

Babu set his palms skyward. "You fight tha spirits in you. I find young albino woman; I let her go; you offer yourself in trade." He made no movement toward me.

"You don't have her?"

"I know where. I have thrown the bones; thas best for everyone."

Quite the comedian. "Everyone!?"

He nodded. "My client agrees. Wants you no marks, no damage."

Too valuable to debase, that was a new one. "What client?"

"Tha Hyena. Powerful person . . . you say 'ambitious.' I say hungry. You bring thas person much success. Younger woman—Kyra—could not; not like you." His expression tinged with esteem. *I seemed to find favor in all the wrong places.*

"Is this *Hyena* Mr. Ngowa?" I asked.

He looked perplexed. "Ngowa? Know no one by thas name. No, Hyena is leader. Best client. Hungry. Not person to fool. You understand?"

"What's his name?"

He waved his finger at me not to ask such questions. "Never said it a man." He tilted his head. "So, you ready to save girl?"

The prospect of placing myself in Babu's hands terrified me. But I was pretty sure I could overpower him once Kyra proved to be safe. "How do I know you would honor such a trade? How would I guarantee she was safe?"

"Aah," he said seeing that I might be open to the opportunity. "She be released to someone you trust. You able to check for certain her release. And I tell you, there is other person looking for you—not my client. Thas person finds you, you *and* tha young woman will not like end."

"What other person?" I asked.

"Don't know. Only know thas someone scenting you. You very prized."

"I don't believe you."

"Thas up to you. I am not *mwongo*—liar. So . . .?"

"What will you do with me?" I asked.

"You strong *muti* medicine. You *Mami Wata* and more. Know you know it. You already dead and cannot die. But young albino friend, Kyra, she maybe not so lucky."

"I want to see Kyra."

He drew snot and spewed it to the ground. "Why you bargain; have already told you conditions?"

"If you want a deal, I have to see her."

He thought about it. He shook his head. "You are *buda*, I know."

"But valuable," I said. *Funny how life found me a way.*

"More work for me," argued Babu, signaling a weak spot in his sovereignty. "You make deal as I say."

"Not if you want me in one piece, alive, *no marks.*"

"*Buda!*"

"That's the deal," I said, a bluff without fallback.

))))

"I'm Kyra," she said head down to the camera. She lifted it; a gaze so frayed it took the breath out of me. Her face gaunt. She dropped her head. But even in that instant, with dead eyes, she looked almost . . . angelic. The eyes, purple with blue geodes, framed by new snow skin, a childlike nose, and white-pink lips—a pale, delicate mole on her upper right lip. Straight, effervescent hair. Innocent, except for the eyes, her spirit, undone, leeching life.

She closed her eyes. "Why are you doing this?," she said to the floor, head lolling. "I came to study for my ancestors. Are you my ancestors?" Her head rolled.

"You be quiet," said the voice behind the camera. "Look up."

"*Masoko*, a marketing campaign for you," laughed another.

"Shut up." This time a woman's voice.

Kyra's eyes opened, filled with tears. "Why?"

"Stand up so they can see all of you," said the voice behind the camera.

Kyra steeled herself, looked directly into the camera. "Today for me, tomorrow for you."

"She makes joke," said the man behind the camera.

She didn't budge. "Let me go," she said. "Please."

The video went black. Babu tucked the phone under his sash.

"When was this taken?" I said.

"She's alive," Babu said, the dogs hovering around us. "Now you go." He turned to them. "*Fungua.*" He waved to them to open the circle and allow me to pass back up the hill. "By tomorrow thas time, if you not here or if other person already taken you, our agreement be . . ." He raised his fist skyward and opened it, "*Vumbi*. . . dust." And with that, he fairly waltzed away from me, the demented conductor. I expected him to wait at the door for applause. He reentered his shack.

I waffled, then inched my way past the dogs, who followed me with cold eyes. I didn't look back.

)))

By the time I'd returned to the graveyard, I'd already run different scenarios through my head—none of which I liked. I wondered why the witch doctor let me go. Perhaps knowing I would put up a fight and that his dogs would rip me apart; he didn't want to mangle the merchandise. I was "prized."

His tip that more than one person was tracking me, crowded my already overflowing brain. I had no idea if it were true. Was Ngowa still pursuing me? Tanzanian border control? Or Martin, the man on the Zambezi River, the one who kept trying to entice us to travel with him?

I knew I couldn't return to Mariam's compound without bringing horrors upon her family. Still, the atrocities awaiting me and/or Kyra left me numb, indecisive. Who was The

Hyena who treasured such dark possessions, and wielded such depraved power?

If I decided to make the swap, I felt sure I could trust Mrs. Baakari at the university. She'd confirm Kyra's release and ensure Kyra's safe return to the U.S. I arrived at the university ready to check my intuition about Mrs. Baakari, perhaps talk to Mr. Charles. Mrs. Baakari had said Mr. Charles showed concern for Dr. Allen. Had Dr. Allen returned?

Mrs. Baakari welcomed me into her office, eager to hear about Kyra, but also oddly cool. "Have you found her?" she asked. "I've worried about her ever since you told me about what happened." *Baakari's disingenuousness about Kyra didn't match the woman or her position at the school. But she was all I had.*

"No," I said, "unfortunately not. But I've been told Kyra's alive."

"Oh, that's wonderful news." Mrs. Baakari clasped her hands together. "Who? Where?"

She's all you have. "I don't know," I said. "I don't even know if Kyra's really alive. But if she is, and I can secure her release. . ."

"Yes?"

". . .Would you be willing to ensure that she returns safely to the U.S.?"

"Of course. Anything I can do. Anything. Should we call the police?"

The police. They seemed to be a cleaning mechanism, a kind of tidying up, not only for The Hyena, but any number of albino hunters. They might even be a scouting and procuring resource. I imagined revenue passing hands. "No, I don't think that's a good idea," I said. "Let me find out more information."

"Eunis," she said, so frigid her bite surprised me. "I have checked on you. You were a murder suspect in Minnesota. Twice."

I stammered. I tore at my roots. "Cleared, I was cleared. What has this to do with—?"

"Who are you?" she said and grabbed my wrist.

"I'm a friend of Kyra's family. I told you. I want to help her. Let go."

Baakari sucked in, she waited for me. She twisted my wrist.

"Why don't you call her family?" I said. "Go ahead, do it right now. And while you're at it, let me speak to them."

"Perhaps I will," Baakari said. She let go my wrist.

"Why not now?" I argued. "Let's settle this once and for all."

"We're eight hours ahead. And I'll want to talk to the family in private. I'm curious how you know these people who have Kyra."

"Just let me deliver Kyra to you. I haven't much time. It's all better for you and the school's reputation."

Mrs. Baakari sifted through her thoughts. She leaned forward, she placed her palms firmly on her desk and before I knew it, looked. . . borderline . . . civil. "Well, I'm sure the university would even pay for her airfare back, if you can deliver her, the poor girl."

"Really? Thank you." I wanted to believe.

"Then we are done," she said, standing.

I debated before going on. "Have you heard of a man or a woman who goes by the name The Hyena?"

She leveled me, eyes stony. "No. What an awful name. Nasty animals. You don't want to sleep outside when they're around. They take off your face first."

It might have been a threat. I noticed her desk. "Didn't you have a small knife, the handle carved as a hyena head?"

"Yes," she said holding my eyes. "A gift from Dr. Allen. Why?"

"Has Dr. Allen returned?"

She loosened up. "Sadly, no. No one's heard from him. I asked Mr. Charles. He hadn't heard anything either."

"I'd like to speak to Mr. Charles," I said.

"Kadiri? I'm not sure he would be open to talking to you."

"What can it hurt?"

"How can I be sure of you? I wouldn't be a reference for you."

"No, of course not. But if Kyra's welfare is of real concern . . ."

"Hmm. Let me see if he's available." Something seesawed across her face; balancing—I imagined—a strategic choice. She continued, "Although he's rarely here except for the Trustee Committee meetings, once a month." She offered me a bottle of water. She picked up the phone and dialed another office. "Johanna, is Mr. Charles here today?" Mrs. Baakari glanced at me. "No," Mrs. Baakari responded, "KC—Kadiri Charles." She held her hand over the phone and whispered to me, "We have two Mr. Charles here." She took her hand off the phone. "Hmm, yes, I'm not surprised. Thank you."

Baakari hung up the phone. "No, he's probably at the sawmill or in Geita at the mine. He's a busy man." She glanced at her calendar. "I have appointments."

"Kadiri Charles, that's his name?"

She nodded. "Some people call him KC, mostly behind his back—a little too informal for us in here. You'll have to take care of this on your own." She began to sit.

"What kind of man—?"

She huffed. "Charming. If he'll see you, if you can catch up to him. He's always on the move. Man has the speed and skill of the hare. Although I doubt he has any more information about Dr. Allen than I do. But I'm no reference, you understand. Keep my name out of it."

"What does KC—Kadiri Charles do at the mill?"

"He's Chief Executive Officer, I believe. Why?"

"Nothing." I rose from my chair.

"Eunis," she pulled open the top drawer of her desk and placed the hyena blade in her hand, "you can count on me *if* you find Kyra. Otherwise, I want nothing to do with you."

"Would it be possible to use your phone?"

"No." Then added, "God is offended by the smoke of man-made fires." Before I could decipher her meaning, she lay the hyena blade down and trapped my hand in both of hers. She walked me out of her office. "*If* you see Mr. Charles he is not to believe you and I are friends." She added, "I can make life unpleasant for you."

Chapter 31

The remote fringes, Karatu, Tanzania

Apparently, sawmill CEO, Kadiri Charles knew I'd been inquiring about Mr. Ngowa. Or maybe some other albino woman had been asking around. Who knew what Ngowa was up to? Nevertheless, bounty hunter Morgan Jonas had come to a swift and grisly end suspiciously soon after Mr. Hsu had demanded the sawmill be divested of such witchcraft. From what I heard in that conference room, Hsu believed it might endanger their sketchy timber enterprise.

Although the cast of ominous players had multiplied, I still thought I had the strength to handle the witch doctor. In most ways, he seemed less of a worry than his dogs. Or Kadiri Charles. Or the anonymous person Babu alleged also stalked me. As for his other threats, I brushed off the witch doctor's superstitious nonsense. Except . . . what if Babu had disciples in addition to his patrons? What if I couldn't get the better of him? What if he was able to hand me over to The Hyena?

I'd made a promise to Ruthie but now it smacked of lunacy. And futility. No matter how I wrestled with the idea of saving Kyra, I couldn't shake the prospect of myself being tortured.

Still, without me, Kyra's remaining days—if she was indeed alive—would be agony, a slow death. Time and possibilities waning; I was her only hope. After all my grandiose ideas and proclamations, was there really any avenger in me?

"Okay, Babu," I said to the witch doctor, "I'll make the trade when I'm sure the young woman is free and safe."

Stepping from his porch, he appeared pleased but not surprised. "Promised," he said. He stretched his arms over his head as if he was about to resurrect his grandmaster role, a role which still seemed incompatible with his physical make-up and primitive dress of feathers and bones. The dogs surrounded him. I did my best to breathe.

Then his demeanor—even his body language—became . . . this may sound strange . . . more like his dogs. As if he were even more a part of their pack.

The dogs breathing intensified. His did too. A sound far in the brush raised the dogs' heads to the sky, sniffing. Babu followed in unison. He wiped away slaver. Along with his dogs, he became excitable, as if his next incarnation would be even more brutish.

In bare, restless tones he set forth his rules for our engagement: A one-time pre-paid cell phone would be delivered to a public but hidden place in Karatu. I'd be informed. If I used the phone inappropriately, he would know. I was to tell no one of the covenant. This included Mrs. Baakari who could simply be alerted that Kyra would be released, but not who was involved or why.

Once I heard back from Mrs. Baakari at the university, I would surrender to Babu at his shack; no police or other backup support from anyone. He would deny everything, and he had *important clients.* He reminded me that, were I to break the agreement in any way, he would see that I was abducted, that Kyra *and* Mrs. Baakari would be dismembered, and that I'd be forced to watch. He didn't say what might happen to me after that. He did say that anyone else who might come forward with claims of his involvement would be dealt with in the same way; "*kulipiza kisasi,*" he said. I took it to mean retribution. "Remember," he said, "Hyena powerful in its world. Me in mine, too." He waved at his surroundings. "You be sure, Babu age and simple way not weakness. Time *Mami Wata* surrender body, find other."

The whole time he spoke, I schemed for an escape that wouldn't imperil Mrs. Baakari following Kyra's safe departure from Tanzania. None immediately came. And how would I deal with Babu's five monstrous dogs? It reminded me of the first time as a child I dove into a lake, unsure what was below the surface, yet blindly willing. It made no sense.

"Okay," I said to him—no logical solution supporting such a conclusion. I just knew I had to try. Since childhood, my life had been a series of terrors . . . but also a charmed one, in which I'd always escaped. With my grotesque face, all sorts of people had spoken of dark spirits, had anointed me part of that coven. In spite of that brainwashing, the only spirit I'd taken to heart was The Great Spirit, in the way the Original People understand it. A love of nature, a respect for it. Being part of it. That spirit had always been benevolent with me. Given no clear direction, by compass or otherwise, I trusted some escape plan would come. If it didn't, I'd had a good life. I'd go back into the earth. I'd always wondered about my worth; here I could prove it. Then I looked at those fucking dogs as they looked up at me, and I drew back into panic.

The witch doctor said I would receive a message where I would find the phone. He didn't say *how* that message would be delivered. He would call when Kyra had been freed. I'd then call Mrs. Baakari for confirmation that Kyra was safe and in the air, headed to LaGuardia or JFK. Once that had been established, I had twenty-four hours to present myself to the witch doctor or I'd be hunted down along with Mrs. Baakari.

☽☽☽

I hunkered in the graveyard above the two riverbeds and Babu's shack. I ran a reconnaissance of the small broken tombs for one large enough to house me for the night. I'd keep watch on the old man. Thanks to Mariam's financial contribution, I ate fry bread and a small serving of cold *wali wa nazi*, rice mixed with coconut milk that I'd gathered in Karatu. Except for those few hours in town, I'd kept an eye on the witch doctor's every move as he circulated around his shack. I watched how he managed his dogs. They were very attentive to him, but also to their territory. Several times one of the pack would get up and walk around the perimeter in front of the house. Another would circle in the opposite direction walking the perimeter behind the house, which I couldn't see. I waited for a sign directing me to the cell phone. The incongruity of the situation—both primitive and oddly connected to technology—jangled me. Not exactly a pain, or anything sharp. More a discordant *pressure*, the land expelling the human. A very weird sensation. It could have been the *wali wa nazi*. It could have been the first twinges of my approaching suffering, the knowledge that my body might soon not be mine. And the physical taking off it; my kamikaze choice.

I pulled a loose brick from a tumbledown tomb. I crawled to one nearby. It appeared large enough for me to sit up in, to house me for the night. I swatted cobwebs, I brushed aside thistles—a large bat flew at me. I tumbled from the opening.

I sat thinking, *what the hell are you afraid of . . .?* Especially after all the shit I'd gone through to get there, and with what awaited me. *Stay practical. Avoid the sun and blend into the vault's cover.*

When I prodded them, the tomb walls didn't give way. I pushed harder. Sturdy, considering they were probably 800 years old. I eyeballed the crypt's stonework, then the ground for carnival-colored centipedes. I declared *Tomb de Eunis* to be my home away from home, away from home, away from home . . .

Surveilling the witch doctor's domain uncovered nothing extraordinary; just an old man wading into the tall weeds around his hut, picking something out of them, smoking and talking to his dogs. He could have been a Black Mister Rogers without the cardigan. He wandered into one of the riverbeds, still flowing with ankle deep water. He splashed playfully with two of the dogs. I thought they'd knock him over, they got so rough. The others sat on the shore and watched. A disturbingly bucolic scene given what I knew about the man and his clientele. He returned to his porch. For about a half hour . . .

The dogs—all five of them—sat up. Their heads turned to the southernmost boundary, growling. In seconds, all were on their feet. Their bodies vibrating. One of them began to howl, pain itself. The old man stepped out from the porch, lifted his nose to the wind, and yelled "*Ndani!* In!" The dogs high-tailed it into the house. He closed the rickety door.

The bushes to the west began to swing back and forth—not in rhythm with the slight northeast breeze. Two paths tunneled through the tall scrub toward the shack. Fast. First a gazelle, then two hyenas, broke into the open. The hunt. The hyenas sprinted over the first riverbed making a grisly, guttural sound from hell, an unequivocal assurance of death. As if they were already tearing at flesh and bone. One caught up to the gazelle, tore it down to its knees. Both hyenas began ripping it apart.

Their gnarr amounted to a macabre celebration of death echoing triumphantly over the fields. The eyes of the gazelle gyrated. The larger and darker of the hyenas lifted its head for a moment, glancing up the hill, in my direction.

Chapter 32

The remote fringes, Karatu, Tanzania

The sun began setting. The hyenas dragged what remained of the gazelle's corpse into the brush. They disappeared as quickly as they'd arrived; my shoulders knotted again. The witch doctor came out of his shack holding a small pouch. He spread a woven mat on the dirt. He closed his eyes. I got the idea he was muttering. His eyes jumped open. He threw objects onto the mat. He surveyed them, touched them, kissed a few, and closed his eyes again. This went on for more than an hour before he disappeared into the falling light. Night settled in.

I ate my last piece of fry bread. Clouds obscured the stars. I worried about The Bone Crushers. Would they come up the hill? I found a fallen tombstone, hauled it across the opening of Tomb de Eunis, pinned my legs against it, and sealed myself in the pocket-sized burial chamber. I fought the fatigue. I curled up. I laid my head on the dirt *Soil is not dirt, remember. Dirt is dead. Soil is alive with microbes.* They offered a jungle fragrance. Moist, rich. My head came to rest on top of a small cool pillow of microbes. Just beyond me, staring back, two light-colored mycelia. Mushrooms. Not red, not poisonous . . . I guessed. They glowed in the descending light. Edible? I mean, fry breads are great, but if you don't mix in some living matter . . . it saps your energy till it's toast. *Humor,* I thought, *a tool for my survival.* And I sure did need to reset. *They'll nourish me or kill me.* I was *that* hungry. What the hell, I chewed them, I swallowed. I embraced that cozy death chamber. I relinquished control. I let go, I let go, I let go.

NEMO! Nemo of my first illusions; my pup, my first love. He bonded me in love when no one else did. He limped into the ramshackle shed behind Momma's farmhouse. He laid his head in my five-year-old lap. "I thought you were dead," I said without speaking.

Nemo met my eyes. He replied, also without speaking "You loved me. You found me in your bones. Why change now? There're other dogs, too. Stay open."

"Where have you been . . .?"

Mist enveloped him . . .

"Nemo?"

A lanky figure stood in front of Momma's sand-colored barn. Brightly lit by the fading western sky, he was more outline than man. His shadow draped long against the dirt giving him the impression of being taller than he was. His right foot tapped gently, close to his guitar case. My brother, Lyle. A feline smirk. Lost to kidney cancer. The wind came up fast—blew open a door. I jumped. "Come whatever happens now," he sang to me, "ain't it nice to know that dreams still come true?"

☽☽☽

The next day, true to his word, Babu or someone working with him, released Kyra. Left blindfolded at the university steps, according to Mrs. Baakari, Kyra murmured, sometimes incoherently, undeniably traumatized. But the only obvious physical damage, the horrific removal of her hands. Mrs. Baakari hadn't wanted to press the poor girl about her abductors or what else she'd been subjected to. She put Kyra to bed; let her rest for her plane ride back to New York the next day. The university assigned a school staffer to accompany Kyra back, I suppose to protect their reputation. I asked Mrs. Baakari if someone would stand guard in front of Kyra's room while she slept, just in case. Despite my concerns for and about Mrs. Baakari, she insisted she would do so herself.

The following afternoon, Glory Baakari confirmed that Kyra and the staffer had been put on the plane to New York and that Ruthie's family had been notified. Success!

My relief evaporated in short order. My time had come. I still searched for ways out. I couldn't sacrifice Mrs. Baakari and her family to my recklessness, I knew that. Running was out of the question. Could I kill the witch doctor? I wasn't sure I could, even if I could overpower him. And what about the dogs? If I were to eradicate Babu, the Hyena would surely track me down; he or she would probably find Glory Baakari too. And the unknown person chasing me? Who? Why? What did this person plan to do with me? An eddy of unanswerable questions and choices.

One bright spot: I'd found a chink in the witch doctor's armor: the hyenas. His dogs, too, lost all their fight when hyena roamed their area. I understood; the foul, feral smell of the beast at Dr. Allen's was still with me. The memory blighted my body, messed with my mind. An enemy I never imagined in my life. And *then* the worst would come.

I recalled Dr. Allen shaking his head; he'd let optimism drain away, no longer willing to fight whatever it was. But his surrender had been recent, so perhaps even more demoralizing. Whatever the passage of time, he couldn't reckon hyena's evil. "Hyenas," *he said,* "carry virulent strains of rabies, but never suffer from any of the symptoms."

On my way down the path to Babu's shack, my body fought me, every step. *This is madness.* The closer I got to his shack, the more disoriented I became. My body deadened. Everything blurred. His shack became a wash of saturating colors. I was in the Minnesota woods, Roddy embracing me. The air sweet. The air thick with moisture . . .

But the dogs came out barking, then circled me. Babu sauntered out of his shanty. With what appeared to be graciousness, he waved me in. To my end.

It was as if I'd unloosed his inherently cruel and imperious temperament, his victory within taste. It made me realize how badly I'd misjudged him. This frightened me more than anything. Against preposterous odds, I reasoned with myself, *it may kill me, but at least I'll know I purposely stepped into it. I chose this.*

Babu motioned for me to sit with him on a dark animal hide littered with ceramic pots, feathers, bones, and woven baskets. From the ceiling hung more than a dozen full skeletons of large dogs or midsized primates—I couldn't be sure—strung together on a chord. Some of the baskets overflowed with herbs and stems. Others with brown and red dirt, not unlike that which Mr. Ngowa had given to Jann, the Dane on the Zambezi beach. A large Christian cross lay against the wall.

Babu recognized the confusion on my face. "Yes," he said, "Christians and Muslims, too, trust my connection to spirit world."

When I'd first encountered Babu, he wore a few pelts around his waist, and bones around his legs. Now he'd adorned himself with furs and hides around his shoulders, colorful beads and skeleta around his neck and head, topped with a jolly *kofia* of yellows, greens, and blacks. Quite festive. He smiled. "We drink." He poured two goblets of dark liquid from a carafe and handed me one.

"I don't think so," I said. He'd left the dogs outside. *This might be my only chance to take him.* Outside, the dogs would tear me to shreds.

"Come." He jabbed the goblet toward me. "I drink too. You prefer, you have other." He motioned to the other goblet.

"Babu," I said. "Kill me, if that's what you have in mind." Death seemed preferable to torture.

His face pulled back, affronted. "Oh, no. I heal. Give people fluids, special hemp. Thas special ratings. Special ratings each of thas." He waved his hand around the room. "Soak in water, melt down. They drink, they cured. You, too." Again, he handed me the goblet. He saw my resistance. He put the goblet down and handed me his. "Many demon devils; problems. Thirty years, more, I cure." He breathed deeply and with great pride. "You too."

"Let me go, please." I motioned to the cross. "You're a Christian."

Quite cheery—and through broken teeth—he said, "No, I am welcome all. Christians have arch angels and Angel Gabriel.

We have ancestors. Christians call them demons." His voice dropped down a measure. It reflected the callousness that appeared in his eyes. "Your demons, our angels; our link to god."

"I'm not a Christian," I said, *still ashamed of my own sticky history and seeing The Bible raised to demonize others.* I glanced out Babu's window. The bright land beyond . . . alive, where everything in Babu's shack lay dark and dead. I said, "I have the same religion as that miscanthus up the ridge." In saying it, I knew it was true. *Was his religion so very much different?* Still . . . . he was planning on butchering me.

Babu said, "And thas why you and I must speak before tha ceremonies."

"*Ceremonies?* You mean my dismemberment?"

"You a special gift. We all understand." He bent, offering a small salaam.

"So . . ." I said, "you honor me and then you cut me to pieces? . . . Perhaps alive. And, by the way, who the fuck are '*we*?'"

Babu rocked his body back and forth, as if discussing a picnic by the sea. "All thas become clear. So now," he picked up his goblet and again handed it to me, "we drink, we find our other selves."

The conversation civil. So far. I wasn't sliced into—yet. "Okay, what is it?" I nodded at the goblet.

"Iboga," he said. "Root bark. Help bring common mind."

That made me laugh.

He continued. "Medicinal and ritual origins. Even give to babies."

"Sacrifices," I said.

"Spiritual passage."

A whiff of the bitter concoction drew me backward.

"Like coffee plant," he said. "You like coffee?"

"If I drink this, I'll get ataxia."

He looked confused. "Don't know thas."

"I won't be able to move," I said. "Muscles will go in different directions; east-west-north-south, all at the same time. Dry mouth, maybe nausea."

"Yes," he said.

"And then my mind will wander."

"Yes," he agreed. "Maybe meet ancestors. Bring common mind."

"Thanks." A short recoil of my head signaling I'd declined. "I may have already experienced this before. None of it can be lovelier the second time around."

"What you learn?" he asked.

"I don't remember. I remember that I didn't want to do it again."

"You not forget these." He picked up and shook the iboga roots, his hand loose around them. "We be there together. We make common sense."

I stretched, thinking about kicking him in the face and taking on his dogs.

"You see," he said placing the goblet in my hand and drinking from his own.

Would he be unfazed by the iboga, and I helpless?

"You *Mami Wata*, yes? he said. "You cross into thas places many times."

Out front, one of his dogs started growling and another snarling. Their weight and power outsized the shack. Babu called to the dogs, "*Tayari?*" They quieted down.

"What does that mean?" I asked. " '*Those places?*'"

"Ready," he said. "They are ready." *The dogs.*

Drinking the iboga suddenly made the most sense.

Chapter 33

The remote fringes, Karatu, Tanzania

I drank the iboga, the taste even more disagreeable now that I knew what it was. Babu polished his off with the relish of a milk shake. He held my hands in his leathered palms and tipped my goblet dry, making sure I finished the whole thing. He lay down on the hide staring at the cosmos of bones hanging above us on the ceiling. I battled against the elixir, but nausea came quickly. I succumbed to the floor.

"*Pumua,*" he said, as my head settled into the hide. "We different. True. You water, me soil. Both half-light in distant kingdoms. We different thas others. We *wahamaji*—you say 'nomads.' We along same unending road."

"Parallel." The word spilled out of me. I didn't know why or how.

"Hmm, *sambamba,*" he said, interpreting the relationship. "Yes." He went silent for some time; I'd lost all sense of it. "You not first of us I meet," he said. "But you my first *Mami Wata.*"

A voice arrived from my throat. "You think I'm a mermaid."

His words surrounded me. "You know, you always know. Since little."

I dove deep into one of my Minnesota lakes. I fought the iboga. "Childish," I said. "Just a good swimmer. Loved swimming."

Slightly above a whisper, he asked, "Swim in ocean?"

"No," I drifted. "Rivers, lakes, lagoons." *My refuge.*

"Under water, your hiding place."

Nausea yanked my gut. I drew a big breath hoping to challenge it. I let it out.

I surfaced in water, my arms pumping through waves and across them. The river's current all muscle. Shoreline rocks poked unevenly from the mud. No place to land. My native domain unexpectedly wrathful. Get to shore. *My world, the blood and bones of my legs ready for accommodation, my arms possessed. I'm part of this.*

The current grabbed at me, hell-bent to drag me under and knock me downstream. For a moment—underwater—not by my own accord. Not hiding. You're testing me?

The river and I strained against each other. I launched at it. It swiped at me like we'd never met. I got low and thrust at it again. It rolled me back. Really? *I hammered my legs. I live here!*

It flung me back and under. One charge after another, its earthly power greater than mine. I fought for answers . . . only to be forced to physically give in, just so I could think.

"I'm not surrendering," *I told the current,* "I'm calculating." *The volume and undertow grew. Temporal strength my only asset. My soul space had disavowed me. I didn't want to believe.*

Great spumes heaved from below the horizon, a signal that a series of drops in the river weren't far off. Get to shore. *The river churned, thousands and thousands of cubic feet per second. My sanctuary turned unholy? Why?* If not this world, where?

I punched and stroked and swallowed it. I fought the welling; I fought it all the way to shore.

I laid on a patch of soil, warm against the mud, breath returning, my legs dangling in the current, accepting the flood's mastery—which I'd never challenged in the first place. And yes, it still rolled in my ears, so loud I could barely make out the voices coming from it. The air moist, dripping; it must have just rained. Hard. The air, the water, the loam—all of it fit me. My world.

From upstream, a larger wall of water retaliates, thundering toward me, overtaking me.

☽☽☽

Babu rustled.

I found him sitting crossed legged. "Sit outside with me," he said, eyes half closed and focused on some distant point.

I laid back down, ready to retch.

"I help," he said. He lifted me as if he was my age and twice as strong.

I struggled to stand, then tumbled my way to the door, sure I would puke his home. He deposited me on the front grounds just before the first eruption, a chunky chowder splattering my legs. There were several, for however long I sat in my own puddle, eyes closed. He too from the sound of it, but me way ahead in the standings.

The sun moved. I could tell, it warmed my back.

"Drink," he said. My eyes fought the light, but I took the water. The earth below, warm and breathing, comforted me. I wanted nothing but rest. I didn't worry about The Hyena or Babu's plan. I was beyond suffering and regret. I didn't miss my body. I was nature. Nor separate from Babu. Or The Hyena. Death, a part of me.

A crow screeched. It seemed to invite Babu to reach into my mind and pull my thoughts from his mouth. "Can you kill?" he asked.

I'd seen more than one dead body, more than one dead face, in my thirty-nine years. From the depths of my guilt, all my dead appeared—one intertwined face. "Why do you want to know?" An answer I was no longer sure of myself.

"Best for me to know," he said, a jaunty tone I'd never heard him use before.

I snorted; it echoed through my head. "It best for *me* to know," I said.

He grunted. "Then we walk."

I forced my eyes open. The sun had moved again. I just sat. My fingers ran through the powdered dirt, wishing it was soil; soon I'd be a contribution to one of them. I hoped soil. I closed my eyes.

"You are *buda*, aren't you?" he asked. "You have evil eye. Can become hyena too?"

Ngowa's story of the man in Los Angeles came to me: *The evil eye, its curses rooted in envy.* "I do not envy you," I said to Babu.

"You don't answer my question." Then Babu shouted something to his dogs. I hadn't heard them or thought of them the whole time—off in a different world. He went on. "Can you be hyena?"

The vivid spectre and stench of hyena revisited me. Right away I understood. "You're afraid of me?"

He scoffed. "Just discovering your instincts. *Muti* is not pepper and salt."

"But you say I'm *Mami Wata*." My voice disconnected, still emanating from another entity.

"Yes."

"And *Mami Wata*, she's valuable to you. *I'm* valuable to you. Like all mermaids I can bring you great physical pleasure, pleasure you've never before experienced. Or will ever again in your many lifetimes. I can heal," I said. "I could bring you great treasures. I don't have to be destroyed."

"Yes, like me a healer, and like me *mnyongaji*, an executioner. Traditions do not lie. You can provide all thas things . . ."

I envisioned myself swimming effortlessly. Babu and I were homies, we could work together.

". . . But you cursed by gods—look at your face," he said. "Nature marked you. You carry desires and fears. You be jealous. You be hungry. Bleached like dead grass; you never die. In body you only bring death. You so hungry. You . . .you *zeru zeru*. You vapor."

Words began to reside in my body. "Babu, I do not understand. Long ago, you saw the valuable parts in me. You appreciate me. Let's work this together, as you say."

"Don't know thas."

"You value me," I said.

He admitted, "An albino *Mami Wata* . . . I never heard of before. I'm honored. Your qualities perfect for many my clients. They want to know what they getting. You make me stronger and very rich."

"But not dismembered or dead." I pictured myself free, diving under the water's surface.

"Would you sell loaf of bread when you could sell many slices?" he said. "When you could mix essences to make most benefit?"

))))

I vaguely remember being led to the enclosure. I remember laying down.

"Ssh," he said.

When the iboga finally wore off, I smelled wood. No longer in water or on dirt or soil, I was caged in a box.

Chapter 34

The remote fringes, Karatu, Tanzania

B abu's box had a small hole on the side, large enough to poke my head through. It scraped back my ears—in and out—every time I scavenged for air, till they bled. I surmised that my ears weren't worth much. Through that opening he handed me water once a day, just enough to keep me alive. The seasonal rains had stopped abruptly after my night in the graveyard, almost two weeks, and the heat had climbed into the nineties, unseasonable with unforgiving humidity. I sweated day and night. I slept in my own piss and drank it when I could. Judging from the odor baked into the wood, I wasn't the first to have been incarcerated there.

Kicking at the slats once or twice, I knew I would eventually splinter my tibias, so I stopped. Every kink in my body was tender, inflamed and threshed from my hunched positions. On several of the planks I recognized the stamp of the Selela sawmill. Through the planks, I watched Babu's dogs snap at each other in ways I hadn't seen before. The witch doctor threw meat on the ground as he had previously, but too often he was forced to separate the dogs when feeding. The riverbeds had dried to sand, and he divvied what water he had carefully so even the dogs looked to be leaner and prostrated by the heat.

What and where he'd gotten the meat, I feared to imagine.

Around the third week, I pleaded with Babu. Surprised at what I pleaded *for*, he waited above, arms crossed. My lips cracked and bleeding, and only with difficulty, I mustered the words. "Before I die . . ." I croaked and took a breath.

"You already vapor," he said. "Do not try, you convince me of nothing." He handed me my daily cup of water.

It took so much energy just to speak. "Babu, Babu, you're clearly masterful at the *muti*." I sipped the precious water. I reminded myself to come back to the water. "May I see your backroom just once to understand how you will use me?"

"You think you trick me; I not afraid," he said. Still, vanity unfurled, luminous in his eyes, his chest rose.

I clung to the slats. "I was educated as a scientist, and yet you have learned so much more than I. I'm too weak to overpower you, you must realize that?" I said. And truly, would I ever be able to straighten up again?

"*Mami Wata* is also trickster," he said.

I panted. "You must see who I am without water, without food."

He massaged his hands, the old master thirsting for the adulation he deserved.

"Just once," I said.

He thought for a moment. "I suppose. But understand, thas heat and humidity . . . my dogs very irritable. Cannot afford to lose you to them, so no quick movements."

"Quick movements?" I wheezed. "I'm barely capable of walking. You need to assist me."

He pulled a key from his pocket and unlocked the box. He helped lift me out of it, my legs gave way, I fell over. He caught me. The sun roasted my arms; I covered my eyes from the glare. Babu led me to his hut. Every step my unused muscles seized up, spasmed in pain.

"You want go back in box?" he said.

"No," I said, "I want to learn before I leave this body. You are a master."

His grip strengthened. "Good."

Inside, the shade no more merciful, the air clammy—full of the old man's swelter—and unrelenting as we cut through to the back room. There, laid out on a rough wooden bench and hung above it, an array of large and small bones, herbs, tree and root barks, animal skins, furs, claws, eyeballs, and powders. Also, three crude rusted saws, several stacked granite pestles alongside mortars, and a row of various-sized glass jars, some filled with liquids and others, indistinguishable parts.

Even my years studying with the taxidermist did not prime me for this. "These are your medicines?" I clung to the workbench.

"Some of them," he said proudly, and repeated, "*Muti* is not pepper and salt."

"That empty jar there," I said, "what's usually in that?"

"*Uboho*, bone marrow."

"Oh . . ."

His head lolled, casually quantifying me, as if he hoped his manner could persuade me it was all in my best interest.

"And what will you use of me?"

"Almost all. But I wait for The Hyena's instructions." He drew his thumb over a saw on the bench top.

I steadied against the counter. "Hyena makes *muti* medicine too?"

"The Hyena?" Babu mocked. "No. My client depends on me."

"Then why wait?" I said.

"My client maybe want sex with you first."

No more unimaginable than anything else I'd heard or seen. "With me?" I said, finally accepting I was no more than a slab of delicacies to him.

"You young enough." He ran his tongue over his lips. "You body beautiful. Perfect, really. Not surprising for a *Mami Wata*. If my client has sex diseases, you cure them."

I jeered.

"Well," Babu shrugged, "you believe what you believe. But even as old as Babu be, if I not bound to my client, I would take you before . . ." He dismissed the remaining thought. "Well known, sex with *zeru zeru* cures many things, not just desire."

"That's gratifying," I said. I pointed to the far end of his workbench. "What's that?"

He turned to see what I was referring to, an oily, yellowish substance in a squat, square jar. While he did, I copped a small handful of iboga bark and slid it into my back pocket.

"Thas?" He admired the viscous liquid. "Thas rare. You keen eye. Hyena fluid. From ass, anal glands. Mark territories with it. Very useful to my client."

"And you will include that with my organs and body parts?"

"After my client finished with you, and after I separate and sanctify your pieces, yes. Now thas enough. Back to you castle," he chuckled. "Not be long now. I hear from client soon. Maybe you meet my client; Hyena may want to put eyes on you."

"Your client will see my face and be disgusted," I said.

"I imagine opposite. My client understand your potency."

Frequencies began vibrating through my body. I nearly crumpled to the floor, before Babu caught me. "It will rain soon," I said.

"Yes, certainly, long overdue. April and May rainiest months and still no rain for weeks. It time for rain."

"It will be a lot of rain," I said. "You should let me go." I drew the rain closer; a wish perhaps, but that's what it felt like.

"I have seen rain before." Babu uninterested in my chatter when he had the stage.

"You will regret holding me," I said.

"Will I?" He smiled. "You not so powerful now. I think heat and lack of water weaken *Mami Wata*. You wish for rain, but you cannot bring it. You be happy, think how you live on in powerful Hyena. You meant for me . . . and for my client. You come all thas way from Minnesota, to create *muti* medicine."

"From New York," I said, ruing the day I left Minnesota, regretting listening to Gordon and his rosy persuasions. Lamenting the day I joined the Weather One crew, and the day I pledged myself to Ruthie and her niece. *How long would the pain last?*

I went limp; Babu would have none of it. He grabbed me, and as he did, I swiped red bark from his workbench. He dragged me back to the box, threw me onto the rim, then rolled me into it, and latched the top closed. "You'll be sorry," I threatened; the little bravado I had left. "You'll see my power soon enough." Even to me the words held little hope. I was going through the Kubler-Ross stages, beyond bargaining, beyond depressed, and halfway to acceptance. "You'll be sorry," I repeated.

"Look very forward to you showing these powers," he said with a smirk. "Maybe you tempt me to raise my price."

Chapter 35

The remote fringes, Karatu, Tanzania

D ogs. They don't take shelter from my face. They acclimate to my smell and touch. I treat them as partners. We get along. They speak to those who listen. My little Nemo was spot on. Why forsake my relationship with dogs now?

I filled my cup with urine and called the dogs, hoping to curry favor with them. The dogs came around, I hurled my urine to the ground. They sniffed it, one even licked it. They quickly lost interest. It was a start.

Then, contorting into position, I chewed on the red bark I'd swiped from Babu's workbench, pretty sure that it was purple willow—from my college studies a natural aspirin alternative that might ease my body pain. If it wasn't and it killed me, so be it. Better than the alternative.

A few days later, the heat still uncompromising, the dogs started whining incessantly. Along the rim of the hillside, a group of townspeople began to congregate. By evening a crowd of perhaps forty people had settled above us. That brought the witch doctor out of his shack. He yelled at them to go away; only a few responded. He threatened to sic the dogs on them.

Several of them hollered back that they wanted to see *Mami Wata*. "You have *Mami Wata* prisoner," they said. *Where'd they get that information?* "Everything is dry, *iliyonyauka*, we have no rain. You have *Mami Wata*."

"She's not here," Babu called to them. "Go away or I send the dogs."

Instead of leaving, another fifty or so joined them in the next few hours, circling the hillside, appearing to camp there. Later that night, without a sliver of moon, the witch doctor came stealthily to the box and handed me my daily cup of water; an unusual time, as if he hoped neither one of us would be seen by the assemblage. I spent the rest of the night crushing and re-crushing the stolen iboga bark between my palms, until my hands oozed blood from its splints, and the bark resembled dirt.

The next morning, the crowd had grown anew, the unwieldy heat enflaming their restlessness. Babu warned them again, but several in the assembly raised machetes as if to challenge the dogs. They called once more to see *Mami Wata*.

With what little strength I had left, I poked my head out of the box. At least two in the group saw me and pointed, bringing some attention to me. Word spread along the rim. As it did, the sky went black. Everyone, including the witch doctor, looked skyward. A huge flock of dark, diminutive birds, hundreds of thousands of them, braided in a massive black ribbon of flight—an aerial ballet hurled from the Ngorongoro cauldron itself, an eruption—dancing in the wind. I'd heard of this; what ornithologists call a murmuration.

As one, the birds swept across the sky metamorphosing form and blotting out the sun. The wings found each other, boiling collectively in the blink of an eye, emerging coalesced as figures: a salmon fluid in its stream, an octopus flexing all arms at us, and finally, a cloud; the birds mimicking pouring rain. No mistaking the formations, their precision ethereal *and* eerily aboriginal, as if related by blood. Calming. The birds controlled our eyes to the sky—all of us harbored in its canopy; minute after minute after minute until I was exhilarated and once more exhausted. Certain I'd been watching for hours, I regained my sense of time, and realized it had lasted no more than five minutes. Then, the birds as one, comprised an ebony spear, launched and disappeared.

The calls to see *Mami Wata* rose to a chant, challenging the witch doctor. He held his ground, as did the crowd. Their attendance, a blessing, even if it only forestalled my eventuality. *Eventuality* being fundamental to the land.

The sky, at once so blue and now free of the birds, transported me to my childhood, under the stairwell, where I sat reading the waterlogged encyclopedias, my window to the world. *Murmurations*. From the book to the sky, I wondered where and if they would come, this miracle of flight. I stood for days, eyes to the sky, waiting. For which I was mocked. The little I *did* learn and remember about murmurations, leafing through those encyclopedias: the birds share information about predators, and with that they find safe nesting places. I had the sense I was no longer alone.

Babu banged on the box. "Who did you tell?" he hissed.

I fumbled for words.

"Who?!" He struck again with even more force but kept his back to the box as if he were conversing with the heat.

"No one, I told you. No one. Who could I tell?"

"Now I will remove your friend Mrs. Baakari. I warned you."

"No, I swear, I've told no one," I repeated. "She knows nothing. Someone would have come to rescue me weeks ago if I had."

"Then," he broke his form and sneered down at me, "why these people have gathered here?"

"You see my power," I said. "Even the birds want me free."

"*Ng'ombe.* Bullshit." He slapped the box and walked away.

The crowd moved closer. Babu stood out front, he moved with two of the dogs on either side, circling the shack, hurling invectives at the crowd. He called the dogs to attention. The gallery pulled up. "Let us see *Mami Wata* and we will leave," yelled one of the crowd. "Free her and we will have rain." The crowd cheered support.

"*Panya!* Rodents! She's not here," Babu called back. "You and your families will pay price for thas. Don't dare threaten me. Come no closer." He raised his hand, his six fingers spread widely apart. On cue, the dogs formed a circle around his shack, each of them snarling and snapping at the people along the slope. "Shall I release them?" the witch doctor shouted. The people retreated, but only a few yards. Babu shook his fists at them and swore "*panya!*" again then pointed to a number of them. "You! You with the ugly son. You will pay the price. You! You with the wife who weaves now in brown and red. Make way for the strong one; you will pay the price." He did this five times. He withdrew to his shelter.

I mixed the pulverized iboga bark into my cup of water and drank it; likely my last chance to escape on any level. It didn't take long before the nausea rode up my chest. I thrust my head out the hole and heaved to the ground what was left in me. I fell back into the box, almost forgetting to call the dogs.

☽☽☽

I woke to a distorted chorus moaning *"Mami Wata! Mami Wata!"* It bowled across the vale in taffy-like waves. The hillside undulated with giant ants and trees. Deformed people swayed in time to the elegy. It grew louder and louder. The dogs lashed out at them, baying as if a great cataclysm was about to implode upon the ravine, just as the witch doctor had warned.

The dogs ran in odd patterns, snapping at the crowd, jowls slobbering. One rammed his huge body hard against my box, presumably to break in and devour me. The final stages of the apocalypse. One dog, tongue distended and dragging, lay panting on the ground, eyes remote and orbiting. I struggled to make sense of the vision. I'd had a plan . . . but I couldn't disentangle my thoughts. Whatever my purpose had been, it had vanished.

The witch doctor stood waving his arms. They bent like rubber. His six fingers had grown longer. He yelled at the crowd. It bellowed back, *"Mami Wata! Mami Wata!"* They pointed at the dogs. Babu went to one of his beasts. He tried to raise it off the ground, it remained limp, too heavy for the old man. Another of his canines trundled in a continuous Möbius loop, over and over again, hanging its head and howling. Babu went to it and attempted to lead it back to his shed. It paid him no mind.

A moment of clarity, like the Fallstreak Hole opening the sky over Kingdom Lake: the dogs were responding as I'd hoped. As most dogs would, they'd consumed my vomit and were experiencing the iboga.

The anthem continued. "*Mami Wata! Mami Wata!*"

I slumped back into the box. Babu hung over me, obstructing my few slivers of sunlight. "What have you done to my guardians?" he said.

I roamed two worlds without a single voice. I told myself to choose words from either one, *just speak.* "I warned you, Babu," I said, my voice separated from my body.

His voice oscillated. "I should kill you now."

Once more, my words came from an uncharted place. "But for these people and your client, you cannot." The vibrations began, the frequencies filling my body. "Now," I said, "now, I will bring rain." And I had no doubt about it. "Release me and run."

He smashed his fist against the box. "You underestimate Babu's power."

"And you, mine." Lightning turned the landscape white. Thunder cracked across the dell. People on the hillside cried out and began to disperse. *Taking with them my last chance for rescue?* The trees yielded to the wind; they appeared resigned to be torn from their roots and spread over the valley.

"Go!" Babu yelled at the scattering crowd. "I warned you. Go! Go! Run!" He looked back at me in the box. Lightning bleached his face. He oozed arrogance; he radiated ridicule. He raised his arms to the hard pouring rain and turned in a circle welcoming it, triumphant. Another flash of lightning and concussion of thunder. Most of the remaining crowd disassembled. Babu called his dogs to the front of his shack and signaled them to go inside. One by one, still glazed and tottering, they responded to his command. He waved at me, smug and self-congratulatory; he joined his dogs and closed the door. The rain came harder; the very sound of it hitting his roof, my box, and the ground, almost matched the wind, until the outrage of both forced me to cover my ears.

Water cascaded through the top of the box and began streaming into the bottom. The river coming alive! My legs quickly covered with muck then water. It reached my hips and flowed with more urgency. It raised me up in the spare space. My nose rubbed raw against the top pressing for air. Before long I'd be trapped in the box, underwater with no escape. I thrashed at the walls, but as before only my legs suffered. I was about to drown, a prisoner in my own element.

The storm became more ferocious, the wind and rain gaining. My ears filled with river; the river brimming its banks. Another swell and I jammed against the far side of the box. The box lifted, throwing me on end. It surged off the ground and began moving with the current. The river closed over me; I swallowed it. My childhood mermaid fantasies ironic as the box lifted again, tumbled, and slalomed with the current, then torpedoed and shattered against what I assumed to be the witch doctor's shanty. All pain replaced with more.

I surfaced in water, my arms pumping through waves and across them. The river's current all muscle. Shoreline rocks poked unevenly from the mud. No place to land.

Babu's shack rose from its foundation—both branches of the river now one, reaching his roof line—and tearing it into tortuous objects before completely uprooting it and sending its mangled members downstream, voices of man and dogs buried in the torrent's howl.

Get to shore.

The current grabbed at me, hell-bent to drag me under and knock me downstream. And then, as if we had no affiliation, it did.

I strained against the channel. I launched at it. Thrust at it again. It rolled me back. My legs fought. It flung me forward and under. Despite one charge after another, the river's power greater than mine.

The volume and undertow grew. Great spumes heaved from below the horizon, a signal that a series of drops in the river weren't far off. *Get to shore.* The river churned. *If not this world, where?*

I punched and stroked and swallowed it. Still no sign of kinship or charity from the river. It slammed and funneled me where it wanted. A branch slapped hard across my head. I latched onto it and hoped it hadn't lost its mooring. It bowed but held. Hand-over-hand I grappled my way to shore.

))))

I lay on a patch of soil, my breath catching. The current yanked at my legs as if it still wanted me, still howling. The air moist. The air, the water, the loam—*did it all still fit me?*

From upstream, a still larger chute of water caterwauled toward me.

"Let's get you out of here," yelled Mariam. She pulled me from the shore and up the hillside.

Chapter 36

The remote fringes, Karatu, Tanzania

"It was you," I said. Mariam sat me to rest in the graveyard. The rain letting up, but still plonking the ground, the tombs, and us.

"It was, *what?*" she said. She squeezed rain off her head and shoulders.

I was still catching my breath. She squinted.

"You," I said, "you started the rumor in town about *Mami Wata*. To expose the witch doctor. To set me free."

"No." She shook her head. "I heard it from Celvin at the coffee cart. The story buzzed around the entrance to the sawmill. All the vendors talked about it. My brother heard it, too. You see, the people believe in such things; perhaps not such a bad thing, after all."

"If you didn't, who?" *Mrs. Baakari didn't know about the witch doctor or my connection to him. At least I didn't think so.*

Mariam brushed water from her forehead. "Anyway, you're safe. Your friend's niece . . ." She placed a sympathetic hand on me. ". . . taken with Babu, by the flood? They can't have survived that. I'm sorry."

"No, no. Kyra? She's out of danger in New York. Safe with family. Duck in here," I said. "Let's get out of the rain."

"A crypt?" she asked.

"Yes, Tomb de Eunis. Whenever I'm here, looking over the serene valley and river, I always stay here. I do wish they had a pool and buffet." I held out my arm. "Please, you first."

"Huh? Really? Okay. . ." She brightened. She kneeled, reached inside, and out of the darkness pulled a small bundle of brown paper and twine. She tucked the bundle under her arm.

"What's this?"

"You will see," she said. "I tossed it here on the way down." She ducked into the tomb. There she found a spot in the corner where the psylocibin had grown and was already coming back to life. She began to squat on it.

"Mariam, how bout you take this corner?" I said.

"Is that superstition? From you?" She dropped her head, eyes following me.

"Not superstition."

"Sure, okay, it's your place." She found her seat.

I took mine.

"Wonderful," she said, draping her arms over her knees, a wide grin filling her face. "You go home now." She bent closer and kissed the top of my head. "I'll visit you in New York. The worst is over. Now take this and go." She placed the small bundle in my lap. "It might help."

"What is this?"

Mariam pulled it from my lap and tore it open. She held up what she could, given the low, low ceiling. A spectacular yellow and green cotton *khanga* decorated with leaves. "Mariam, this will draw more attention to me," I said.

"No, you're more *asili*—more native Tanzanian—this way. It should help you move around less noticeably. To get out of Karatu. But," she warned, "you're still *zeru zeru* to many. And now you're aware of the folklore."

"Racist tales," I said.

"Yes. But knowing that doesn't make you immune. Just go home."

The storm had soaked and revived me. The purple willow I'd ingested had eased the strikes on my back and shoulders, though much of my confinement still had hold of my body. I ran my finger along my forehead where the branch had nailed me. I considered Mariam's advice. New York sounded uncharacteristically restful. Although without money and a passport . . . Then I envisioned Momma, waiting at the end of the driveway; hands across her chest, "welcoming" me back, ever more secure in her beliefs and ready, again, to lock shackles around me for good, as someone *other* and useless. I crawled to the chamber's opening and looked at the last falling rain.

If there was a tide rising against me, it wasn't an ocean or a river, it was my past. "Empty victories," I said, looking beyond Mariam to the flooding river below. "I'm not through here. I want to come back someday, but not as quarry."

"Maybe, someday," admitted Mariam. "But not now."

"Yes, now. I'm not gonna be a prize pulled from a box or a defenseless victim, not anymore."

Mariam jeered. She looked at me as if I were foreign to her. "What's wrong with you!? What are you trying to prove? You wish for death? Get out of here. I thought you were smart."

I spit rain away. "Well, I've made it this far."

"Eunis, leave Tanzania. Don't push it. Your mother is not here. We'll have a good time in New York. Kyra's free. You are, too."

"I have albinism, a genetic condition. Like blue fucking eyes, brittle bones, and six fingers. I'm not diseased. I'm not infectious. . . I'm not a ghost! Not a duppy, not a white walker with fangs.

"Of course not."

"I'm not a good luck charm!" I began to stand up; the world tilted. The iboga still whispering to me. "Shit!" I said. Mariam caught me. She settled me onto the grass and mud mush. "I'm not a hapless monster who will go down easy."

"Of course not."

I grabbed my hair. "Where do these fucking myths come from?"

"You've got your stories, we've got ours." Her eyes tranquil.

"Yours are so fucking primitive," I said. "So primeval."

"Yes," Mariam said. "The Maasi have this belief, '*It takes a day to destroy a house; to build a new house takes months, sometimes years. If we abandon our way of life to construct a new one, it will take thousands of years.*'" Mariam went on, "I'm not sure what to make of *your* stories, Eunis; the stories of your country." She popped her head out of the tomb and around the graveyard as if she was checking in with the souls of that community. She sat back down and said, "But I think I understand enough about you to trust *you. Our stories* . . . Our Tanzanian stories? We haven't figured which ones to keep and which ones to let pass. I haven't, have you yours?"

"Shit," I said, with nothing better to add.

"Just go back to The States."

"No," I said calmly. "I'm gonna track down the mother-fucking Hyena."

She closed her eyes to make sure she'd heard me. "The Hyena?"

"Yeah, the person who paid for me to be delivered. Babu was only the retailer, fulfilling a customer order. The Hyena is a connoisseur, he likes his *muti* . . . I'm just another resource to her—or him—like everything else, I guess. Power and bones, something he or she is apparently intent to control and exploit and savor. If I walk away The Hyena will do it again. And I'll feel like . . ."

"What? You're fine as you are."

"No, this is for me. This Hyena embodies the worst of our species, the truly damaged, and obviously greeds for the spirit world—I know that sounds crazy coming from me: *The Spirit World*. But Hyena wants it all, the material and the sacred."

"No, it doesn't sound crazy, not at all."

"Drop me by the sawmill," I said.

"Why?"

"I like the fried breads there."

Walking back to town, Mariam bit her lip. She muttered indistinctly. Reluctantly, she dropped me at the sawmill gate, along with two sacks of coffee beans for Raymond's café on wheels. "I hope you'll reconsider," she said. "I can't do any more. I just can't."

"I won't," I said. "And I understand. Thanks for everything."

She batted the seat in frustration. She hugged me and turned quickly away, rubbing her eyes. She pedaled off.

)))

What I'd do once I'd found The Hyena, I had no idea. But tracking that monster—instead of being the one pursued— gave me a certain satisfaction.

Cloaked in my new *khanga*, I waited for Mr. Hsu to show up at the sawmill's front gate, where I might be able to question him as to what he knew about the albino abductions. I did so, low key, out of site, away from the loquacious Celvin. I traded fry bread for a pair of used sunglasses. One week passed. Then another. I watched the forest grow around and consume an abandoned bicycle. I drank gallons of coffee, gearing up for the eventual commotion I was bound to create. Afternoons and evenings I pissed the coffee out. Quite a few jam-packed trucks left the facility. But about twice a week, always late at night, two more trucks would ramble *in* stacked with logs. I moved from one location in the village of Mto wa Mbu to the next, stealing food when I could. Until I'd pissed away three weeks. Then, instead of Mr. Hsu showing up at the front gate, there stood Martin, the Asian man Ngowa and I had met along the Zambezi with the group of Danes.

He stepped out of a tan Jeep, the same tan I'd seen on the airplane that had chased Mr. Ngowa and me over the Cahora Bassa Dam in Mozambique. The same tan as the Jeep in which Martin had ridden back to the Chingozi Airport, where I lost time, sick or drugged. Both?

"This man, Martin," Ngowa had warned, "he means you harm." Maybe Martin was the anonymous man the witch doctor said was following my trail. But so far from Mozambique? Still, he represented the only action in almost a month of tedium. I decided to follow him.

He wandered up to the mill door that was guarded twenty-four hours. The sentry asked for something. Martin pulled a paper from his pocket and when frisked, gave up his revolver without pushback. The security guard waved him through. It appeared Martin was a known quantity and had easy access to the inside of the mill. *Part of the mill's security force or Kadiri Charles' personal hired gun?*

A half-hour later, he exited, and his revolver was returned. He went to his Jeep, made a short phone call, and prepared to pull away.

I confronted him. "Martin, do you remember me? Along the Zambezi?"

He startled. "You and Mr. Ngowa, I remember. You think it's wise to show yourself around here?"

"Why not?" I said, perhaps a little too ballsy.

"I'd think you'd be more covert." He assessed me.

I tugged at my *khanga*. "Too flashy?"

"No, no. It's beautiful. You look good in it. At least it's something you can take legally across the border."

He must have known I'd entered Tanzania without proper documentation. But how? I skirted his inference. "Martin, you seem to think you know me. You work here?" I pointed to the sawmill.

"If you don't know, it's none of your business." He began to get into the 4x4.

"What's *your* last name?" I asked.

"Yang," he snapped. "Does that help?"

"What brings you to Karatu, Martin Yang? Something here at the sawmill?"

"Probably the same as you." He looked to be decrypting me. "Your friend Mr. Ngowa, he's around on this trip?"

"What is it you think I do?"

He laughed. "Out here, you're safe. You're just another tourist. Or whatever you call yourself." He waved at the sawmill. "But we'll track you down. Your time will come." He tapped the hood of his Jeep and got into it. "We'll meet again, you can be sure."

The initials stenciled on his vehicle were mud-spattered and impossible to read. He wheeled past the sawmill gate and headed south into the countryside.

The gate opened. I jumped out of the way of a pickup in a hurry to go down the same road.

Chapter 37

The sawmill, Mto wa Mbu Village, Tanzania

I hung around the sawmill hoping Mr. Hsu or Martin would return. Sun and heat had replaced the rain. About the time a few vendors started taking their afternoon siestas, I wandered over to Raymond's café on wheels. As usual, I found Celvin riveted to his squawky radio, avoiding me. His body juddered—rather comedically—to jaunty *zeze* violin music. An announcer broke in:

> "Noted wildlife conservationist, Martin Yang was found dead this morning a mile south of the Endabash Airfield. Yang's vehicle apparently overturned at high-speed avoiding a buffalo. The celebrated fourteen-year WWA activist was quote, 'a powerful force taking on the illegal timber traffickers who are decimating Tanzania's forests.' His work also focused on improving East Africa's forest cover and fighting climate change effects. According to posts from the WWA dating back

to 2015, the pillage of Tanzania's greatest resource has deprived Tanzania of more than four million hectares of timber (almost ten million acres) and well over twenty million dollars in revenue annually. The widespread illegal cross-border logging and smuggling between Mozambique and Tanzania is said to go primarily to mainland China, where the country's insatiable demand for timber is driving the unsustainable logging and timber smuggling. And it is flourishing at an alarming pace. In east, central, and west Africa, criminal groups are thought to make more money from selling illegal wood products—up to twenty billion dollars annually—than through street-level drug-dealing. Illegal logging destroys the forests that nearly eighty percent of the world's known terrestrial plant and animal species rely on to live. The Taiwanese-born Yang is survived by his wife Anya and their two children, ten and eight."

Wow. Martin Yang's death stunned me. He wasn't what Ngowa had inferred at all. Martin Yang might have been someone I revered had I really known him. Ngowa made him a villain. Why? It wasn't farfetched: Ngowa had something to do with Martin's death. *Ngowa, The Hyena after all?* Would Martin have had intel on The Hyena? My guts turned; was I somehow complicit in Martin's death? Was I hurting innocent people with my Hyena vendetta? Every time I thought I was on firm ground, the terrain changed. *Was that the message I should heed?*

So, I found a spot in the tall roasting grass behind

Raymond's Café on wheels. I let my back laze on the earth, the sawmill and the insects quarreling for my ears. My mind, as usual, fighting to be heard above the din—guilt-tripping me. *Not now. Breathe.* I slowed. I pressed into the soil . . . I waited for calm . . . *I am not suicidal . . . but I gotta find The Hyena . . . don't I?* The sun's amber warmed my eyelids. A luxurious spot.

You can leave.

The tall grass, toasty but still green, and tempting. *I know.*

The sawmill screeched. I brushed an insect from my cheek. I released old air.

Go.

The insects' buzz diffused the mill's metallic squeals. New, sweet air and I was . . . afloat. *Do I leave what must be done to someone else?*

Who or what would that be?

What if I'm wrong about this? It's not my culture. The land, perhaps, but I've been wrong before. What am I missing? What harm could I cause?

The sawmill roared louder, the high-pitched whine of massive teeth a fundamental condition of its being. In unison, the insects chirred and defended kinship; they tried to convince me that everything was as it should be.

Through the grass, tangled in weeks of growing thicket, lay the bike, lodged next to an unmanned food cart. No one had claimed it. I tore away the weeds; I stole it. I'm not proud of it. A rationalized theft. I vowed to return the bike. The guilt remained.

I pedaled to where Martin Yang had crashed his vehicle. It'd already been hauled away. The cops long gone. The dead buffalo lingered, bloated, and gathering flies. With the bovine baking in the sun like that, I wouldn't be communing with it too long.

Two women, both in western attire, stood away surveying the scene. In my bright *khanga,* I "looked native" (just as Mariam had hoped). The women paid me no mind until I started inspecting the buffalo—as if I knew anything about buffalos, as if I wanted to marinate in its fetor. "What is your interest in this animal? Is it yours?" asked the muscular of the two women, her tone straightaway belligerent. "*Mnyama wako?*" asked the other woman, Asian.

"No," I said. "I speak English. Not mine." Everything about that poor buffalo screamed *you want nothing to do with me.* Almost a ton of it; he wasn't a picky eater. Only the flies exulted in its rank misfortune. I pushed away from it. "Just wondered . . . Whose is it?"

"Why are you poking around?" The tall Asian woman wore a tan World Wildlife Association tee-shirt, a locket around her neck. The bitterness on her tongue hard to miss.

"Just interested," I said. I walked around; the buffalo showed no sign of being slammed by a vehicle. The "U" shaped horns, five feet across, fused together over its head, didn't look damaged. The beast spread out eight or nine feet. Maybe the Jeep took the worst of it. But in the heat, the buffalo's DNA was decomposing rapidly.

"It's not yours . . . the animal?" the Asian women asked again.

"No," I repeated.

The Asian woman cast a brief look at her colleague who

joined us. Written unmistakably across both their faces: you are unwanted *and* possibly objectionable.

"I knew him . . ." I said hoping to curry a modicum of favor. ". . . Martin Yang. I knew him."

Their faces flattened. "You knew Martin? How?" asked the Asian woman.

"I met him on the Zambezi River, in Mozambique." I counted the missing days. "About four months ago." *Geez, that long.*

The two women shared a moment of recognition. The Asian woman said, "You were in that junker, the one that crashed just beyond the Cahora Basa Dam. You and a man."

"Mr. Ngowa, yes. Do you know him?" I asked.

"No." Hostility rooted in the Asian woman's eyes. "And you dare show your face here? Now?"

Her partner held her back; I separated a few feet. "I had nothing to do with this." *Did I?*

The Asian women threw off her friend. "You rape the land of your own people; you murder for profits. And you have 'nothing to do with *this*?'" She grunted. She strode toward me. This time her brawny friend tugged on her pretty good. "We're going to catch you," she said. "All of you."

"You've got me wrong," I said.

"Bullshit!" The Asian woman beat her chest.

"I'm American. I'm trying to track down a man or woman. A monster. It brutalized a young woman. Now the monster is hunting me."

"Monsters!" she laughed. "You are going to try to voodoo us out of this? We're gonna get you. We'll hunt *you* to the ends of the earth."

I bristled. She hoped to provoke me. My first instinct was to leap on her and take her down. "You're fucking with the wrong person," I said. "I'm being tracked and inventoried to be sold for parts—because of my lack of color, a genetic disorder from *your norm*. And *you're* coming after *me?* Give me a break."

The powerfully built woman said, "Let's get out of here." She motioned her Asian colleague toward the tan WWA van.

"No! You wait!" I said, beast in my bones. "Tell me something, anything, about a Mr. Hsu or the CEO at the sawmill, Kadiri Charles?"

They stopped in their tracks. The Asian woman asked, "You know those men?"

"I know of them. I know they're somehow involved. Maybe they lead me to the killer called The Hyena—uses humans with albinism as a drug." The two women lingered, indecisive. "And, hey," I continued, "I'm next. So seriously, any information about Hsu or Charles, you give it to me. It's my turn. And my friggin' life depends on it."

The Asian woman took a few threatening steps toward me. "You expect us to believe that?"

"Do you know Kadiri Charles? Or Mr. Hsu? Or a woman named Zhou?" I repeated, readying for their slightest aggression.

"Do you know who I am?" the Asian woman asked.

"No, how would I know? From the start, you and your friend have been so hospitable. Surprised you haven't asked me over for tea yet. Assuming the worst of me? Because I'm albino?"

"I'm Martine Yang," she said.

"Yang?" *Lots of Yangs in the world.* "You related to Martin?"

"Was. Martin was my brother." The Asian woman grabbed the locket around her neck, tucked her head, then lifted it, a dogged look covering the sorrow. "Martin/Martine, our parents had a poor sense of humor. So do I."

"I'm sorry, sorry for your loss." But if she thought she could bully me, she was mistaken. Maybe five months before, but not now. "Why would I tell you about Hsu or the others if I was part of their group?" I said. "Listen, I need to track down The Hyena before I'm tracked down myself. Ya know, The *Muti* Queen. I'm sure you're acquainted with *muti* medicine. I rate high on the Tanzanian supplement surveys. I'm all the rage, powdered up and ingested, only the last painful indignity. Medicine murder; has a nice ring to it, huh?"

Martine bobbed her head in acknowledgement. That's as far as it went.

"I need your help," I said. "I won't mess with what you do. I'm no environmentalist, I just need you to tell me about Kadiri Charles and Hsu? *Anything* about the albino trade."

"Don't tell her anything," said the muscled woman.

"You want blood on your hands?" I asked. "It looks like there's more coming."

The two women, between looks, speculated over my trustworthiness.

"Don't fuck around," I said. "Just tell me what you know."

Chapter 38

Outskirts of Mto wa Mbu Village, Tanzania

"I'll tell you what," said Martine Yang. "You tell us what you know and if we believe what you say, we'll share our information."

"I don't care if you believe me or not, my life depends on this." I stared them down.

They waited unperturbed.

"Fine." I grit my teeth, I described everything I'd heard between Kadiri Charles and Mr. Hsu in the conference room. I told them of the reactions I'd had from Hsu and Zhou when I confronted them at the sawmill gate. My mention of the timber delay crossing the Mozambique border seemed to assure Martine of my sincerity. Her colleague, not so much.

"What about this Ngowa fellow?" asked Martine. "My brother had your plane in his sights. He said it was a Chinese Hongdu N-5, an antiquated agricultural plane. More than thirty years old. Used for crop dusting. A low-flying, under-the-radar plane to manage the logistics of your thievery. Counter technology, counter intuitive. Why else fly such a plane over such a long distance?"

"All I know," I said, "is that Ngowa's Tanzanian. Well educated. He offered me a ride and I took it. I needed it. I know nothing more about his involvement."

"Hmm. Why'd you need it, the plane ride?" asked Martine.

"I thought I was smarter than I am. Shit, I don't have time. Look," I said, "a young albino girl was abducted."

The bull-necked woman. Interjected, "And you just swooped in to save her?"

"Well," I considered the narrative, "yeah. Yeah, and I did."

"But you're still here," said the bigger woman, clearly disbelieving. "Why?"

"Do you or do you not have information for me?"

Martine mulled this over, said something low to the muscular woman, then confirmed that they believed Kadiri Charles, Hsu and Zhou were all involved in the illegal timber trade. But they couldn't prove it. "If we could catch either Charles or Hsu, we'd put a serious dent in the profiteering and the devastation of Tanzanian wood. Perhaps there's someone above Charles here in Tanzania; don't know. But Beijing seems to have a lot of confidence in both Hsu and Charles."

"I'd be willing to testify to what I heard," I said.

"No." Martine's colleague crimped her lips. "Too flimsy."

"On more thing," I said. "Your brother went into the sawmill shortly before his death. I talked to him briefly when he came out. He thought I was one of them. He drove away. I think a pickup truck followed him, but I can't be sure of that."

Martine blinked at the steaming buffalo. More flies and now maggots had begun chewing on the carcass. A loud and unsavory gas extruded from the buffalo. I turned away and recognized pain well up in Martine, reality setting in again, wilting her body. Having lost my brother, I understood. She took a second before speaking. "Martin must have been getting close to something."

Her colleague corralled Martine and gave her a hug.

"No, Corrin!" barked Martine. Corrin withdrew.

"What do you know about albino hunters in the region?" I asked. "Anything about Kadiri Charles being involved? Have you ever heard of The Hyena?"

Both women offered a cold shoulder. "I'm sorry," said Corrin giving Martine a chance to breathe, "we don't know any more than you do. That's not our focus. Never heard of The Hyena. But it's unwise to go after those people. They're everywhere, and I wouldn't trust the police."

"Could I count on you in a pinch?" I asked.

Martine snapped into place. "No, probably not . . . unless it was connected to the illegal timber trade. The WWA has to be very careful where we step and who we step on."

"It's very complicated," added Corrin. "Sorry."

》》》

"I'm here to see Mr. Charles," I said.

Flaviana Jioni, Kadiri Charles' secretary, was a woman in her late forties, a head like an anvil and shoulders to match. She wore a low-cut dress. Her outfit out of place, but probably welcomed by the staff males; quite conspicuous where propriety was usually the Tanzanian rule.

"I'll tell you what . . ." she said, surprising me, as if pleased to see me and ready to set up a meeting.

Two other workers entered the room; Jioni appeared to reappraise the situation. She pinched her oversized mouth (and negligible lips) in annoyance. She wasn't particularly attractive in the first place. Not that I, of all people, should pass judgment. She leaned over her desk plaque, the size of a giant Toblerone, to move me back. She raised her voice. And with obvious impatience said, "*Nê.*"

Unnerved by her change in manner, I locked onto my hair for courage. So only she could hear I said, "Ms. Jioni, I'm an acquaintance of Erevu Ngowa and I know what's going on across the Mozambique border. Tell Mr. Charles that. I'd like to see him—immediately."

"Well," she sniffed and said loudly so the others in the room could hear, "between your face and your rude manner, you're quite a calling card." Her lips parted; she didn't hide her sense of superiority. "He's not here. He's away."

"I'll wait." I looked for a chair. There weren't any. I found that odd.

"I'll call security," said the secretary. "Because he won't be back for . . . a long time. Days, weeks. Who knows?"

"I'd think you would. And I don't think you understand," I said. Again, I lowered my voice. "I'm willing to trade information with Mr. Charles. I'm trying to find someone, and I think Mr. Charles can help. And I—"

Ms. Jioni threw up her hands. "Mr. Charles doesn't make trades."

"The hell he doesn't," I whispered, glancing to see if the other workers were watching. They were. "He's got his fingers in everything around here."

"Not with you," she said pressing a button on her phone and speaking into her headset. "James, can you and Benno come up here? Bring your handcuffs."

❯❯❯

Well, I was still alive.

Nevertheless, scaling the sawmill hierarchy like that was unreasoned . . . and inept, though I wondered how I could have misread Ms. Jioni's initial eagerness. Nevertheless, there had to be a way. The best thing about the encounter, it might undo the repetition of being chased; it held some small relief. I hoped there'd be fallout from my visit. Perhaps rooting prey from the underbrush. Ha! Still chased, *less* victim.

In the meantime, I hoped Mrs. Baakari at the university could offer some insight into Kadiri Charles. I'd have to tread softly, of course. I didn't want her implicated in my search. It weighed on me; I'd already imposed on her. And she clearly had no use for me. But who else did I know had access to the man?

I followed her from the university. The evening sky inky, cobalt blue. The air a tad cooler than the days, now parched for rain. Streetlamps stood not-quite 90° every fifteen yards. In between, the dark spills blessed the street with safe harbors. "Mrs. Baakari," I said as quietly and gently as I could—she bolted several steps away. I ambled into the light.

"My god!" she said. "You scared the . . . What are you doing here?" She turned around and around on the street as if I'd brought a posse.

"It's just me. I didn't mean to scare you." July's chill riffled through my *khanga* and raised goosebumps. "Can I walk with you?"

A truck rumbled by. She twitched, she looked over her shoulder.

"I'm sorry to bother you," I said coming to her side.

She started forward. I caught up to her. She slowed. "What do you want? Kyra's gone. I did my part. Why do you hang around?" If you need to talk to me again, schedule an office meeting. Don't meet me here like some criminal." She moved aside as another couple passed. She turned to watch them.

I jumped ahead of her. She started again. "I'll call the police," she said searching for her cell phone.

I walked backwards attempting to reason with her. "I need to meet Mr. Charles. It's important."

An enormous sigh and she finally stood still. "I know very little about you," she said. Then, caught between a whisper and scream, "What I do know I find unsavory."

"I'm sorry."

"You think the world is your idea. Now you want more information about Mr. Charles. I can't do that. We're not like that here."

"You're aware of what happened to Kyra. You saw it, the brutality. Well, I'm next, *muti* medicine." I ran my hand down my body. "All of me. You get it? I know things about Mr. Charles, but I'm willing to trade information with him. No strings attached."

"You assume I know more than you do about Mr. Charles. He sits on our Trustee Committee, that's all. And now that Kyra's safe, what do you care? You should be out of this country." Her fright caught in my stomach.

I said, "Mr. Charles is very well respected, apparently."

"He has money." Baakari's mouth cramped. "But surely not an albino hunter? Kyra's safe—"

"Right, we've established that. But today it's me. Tomorrow someone else. Can you keep turning your head?"

"Kadiri does a lot for the community."

I quoted her. "'But surely not an albino hunter.'"

"Yes. No. No. . . . I just don't understand why you're focusing on him. Or bothering me."

"I'm not interested in money." I dodged her question. "This is just a transfer of information. Mr. Charles and me. And without it, I'm probably dead."

"Go to the police," she said.

"Ha."

"Then you should probably leave the country."

"Dead," I repeated. "You and I both know what that means—*limb by limb. Tongue. Blood. Bone.*"

"Stop!" she said.

"I'm scared, okay? Someone's out to get me. Mr. Charles can help me, I'm sure. I don't want you involved. Really. No one ever has to know. *He* doesn't need to know. But Mr. Charles would want this information."

"Just leave the country."

"I won't."

"Then don't expect support." She jeered.

"I'm close to something, I know it."

She ebbed. "I can help pay part of your flight, but it will take some time."

"I'm not leaving." She *couldn't* understand.

"This is not my place," Baakari said. "I really can't help. I'm sorry." She started walking again. "Leave here."

I called to her, "When is the next Trustee Committee meeting?"

Again, an enormous sigh and over her shoulder, "Next Wednesday."

))))

I had four days to skulk around the sweltering graveyard, stewing in my own horror stories, worrying if The Hyena and the other stalker would track me down. Or I could be proactive, gleaning background on Kadiri Charles prior to the Trustee meeting—assuming I could get in. As usual, I had to do it carefully, under the radar.

The university library seemed to be a good place to start since Charles was obviously a man of some repute in the region. His credentials, accomplishments and photos would be archived there, and perhaps useful to my meeting with him. I knew he'd be antagonistic.

No more than fifteen minutes after requesting one article after another on the man, it became clear that someone, or perhaps more than one, was as interested in researching the man as I was. Or was interested in making sure I couldn't: articles missing, photos torn out.

There were awards of course. High praise. A man who'd risen from very little. A heroic man, once attacked by a hyena and he'd valiantly fought it off. But no photos except one of his wife, quite beautiful, smiling and wearing yellow striated dark glasses, which according to the article she'd designed herself for sale to the public. The same dark glasses Ngowa had given me and were now lost.

Finally, amidst the library stacks, while researching another photo-less article that Mr. Charles wrote on advances in timber technology, a man passed so closely behind me that his body rubbed mine. I wheeled around. There stood a toothless old man, dressed in a traditional white *kanzu* robe, ogling me, his face familiar. "*Zawadi ya fisi*," he said and leered—in a flash I recognized the lech who'd grabbed my ass at the welcoming party when I'd first arrived in Karatu.

"Go away! Don't you dare touch me again!" My voice too loud in the library.

Unmoved, he continued lasciviously dissecting my body. "*Nitakuwa mchanga tena.*" Again, he reached for me. I evaded him.

Shit. What do I do now? Don't make a scene.

He grappled for something inside his robe around his neck. He pulled out a small wooden necklace, resembling an eye. Similar to Ngowa's amulet. "Do you know Ngowa?" I asked.

The old man waved the talisman at me as if he was invincible with it.

"Ngowa?" I repeated. 'Do you know Mr. Ngowa?"

"*Ya fisi*," he repeated. Then in strained English, "Hyena."

I drew back. "You're The Hyena?"

He nodded and pointed at me, then padded away, out of the aisle.

"Wait," I said. I turned the corner after him and into the open library hall. I grabbed his arm. The library crowd faced me with loathing. "Who the hell are you?" I said to the old man.

A larger, younger man, perhaps a student, stepped in front of me and knocked my hand away. "No," he said. "You leave him alone. We respect our elders."

Chapter 39

Karatu, Tanzania

"That's her!" The young man from the library pointed at me. "She's the one."

Two police officers took hold of my arms, pulled them roughly behind me, and manacled me in handcuffs. "What's going on?" I said.

They snuck a look at each other. "You're coming with us," said the taller.

Without explanation, they drove me to the police station and locked me in a cell. "Why am I being held?"

"Just shut your mouth, no *shida*," was all I got from the jailer.

"*Shida?* Trouble? What trouble?" I said. The jailer turned his back on me and went into another room.

Surely the episode with the toothless man hadn't prompted my incarceration. Nevertheless, caged again. I considered asking for Mrs. Baakari or Mariam, but that could very well have put them at risk. Maybe Martine Yang? Anyway, the police isolated me; no phone call, not even another prisoner with whom to interact.

A couple hours later, another cop slid water into my cell. "Why am I being held?" I asked.

"Dunno, but you pissed off someone. You people should stay out of town."

"I'm an American citizen." *How was I going to prove that?* "You can't hold me for nothing."

He laughed. "You're special, I'm sure. A special *zeru zeru*." He smiled. "But not my problem." He started to leave.

"Wait! Who complained about me?" I asked.

"I told you, it's not my business." He tapped on the crossbars of my pen.

"Whose business is it?"

"Why humiliate yourself?" He shook his head. "Just stay in the dark away from normal people."

I spent the rest of the day pacing the cage. Late in the evening, the jailer came to my cell and unlocked it. "You are free to go," he said.

"Damn right," I said. "I didn't do anything."

"Just get your *buda* face out of here," he said, "and be thankful someone paid to have you released."

"Who?" *Ngowa? Mrs. Baakari? Mariam?* How would any of them know I was jailed? "Who paid?"

He wouldn't say another word and shoved me into the late night, too late to wander back to the cemetery. The air sweet, dry, but untroubled . . .

Two burly men came out of the shadows, one in front, one behind. *Shiiiit!* For a fraction of a second, I detected an amulet swinging around one of their necks. "What do you want?"

"You come with us," said the guy in front. The guy behind prepared to attack.

Scanning for an escape, I said casually, "Where would we go?" As if a party might be our next stop.

"A party," said the front man sardonically.

Made me think maybe I'd engaged his mind. Weird. In so many ways. "I haven't found parties here much fun," I said.

"You come with us."

"You work for Hyena?" I tensed; they froze, prepared to fight. Darkness tightened around the three of us, a small world, little elbow room. Again, the glint of the amulet, a quartz eye. "You know I have great power," I said looking at each of them; the light too dim except to recognize the men's bulk and the gleam of the talisman. "Why do you think they send you to take me? You've heard the talk; I am special."

"You come with us. No bullshit."

"They sent you, but will you prosper or bleed from it? Money isn't everything. *You know*. You both know."

"Fairytale bullshit," said the guy in front. "We are not idiots."

The guy behind grunted, supportive rather than agreeing with his friend, leaving his options open. I turned on him. He fell back. "*Zeru zeru!*" The guy in front moored himself.

"You will look at this face," I said, stepping into the spindly beam of moonlight.

Behind me, the guy said, "*Hebu tumchukue, Benno*. We take her."

"Benno!" I said, stopping them both, "you're the guy that works for Kadiri Charles and Flaviana Jioni at the sawmill offices."

"Take her!" yelled Benno. The back guy stood fast; Benno hesitated.

"No, because you're right to be afraid. No money can protect you from the night. Not these people, not even The Hyena. They want my strength; they hope to take my parts. I die laughing. I have all the power. I live forever." *My hoodoo running out. Great Spirit?*

A cloud unwrapped the moon, homing in on a decaying log . . . a foot beyond my attackers' thick boots. In its hollow, a nebulous glow. They followed my head; they saw it too. I stumbled then regained footing, surprising the men and myself.

Below me, in the log's hollow, the faint orb. The men gave ground. I reached in; my imagined horrors overcome by my lack of alternatives. I pulled the diaphanous particles out of the log; it agitated: a hatching ground of spiders. Thousands of sacs. Still glowing, as if rhythm itself. If they were Yellow Sac or Brown Recluse spiders, they would destroy my insides, would burst the red blood cells in my eyes, could even kill me. I hoped for something non-venomous. And something dramatic for the thugs.

I guessed. "Benno, you have a family. Do you let them play with spiders?"

"Benno, come on." His accomplice took a step toward me.

"Hold on." Benno held up his hand. "What do you know about my family?"

"Watch," I said. "One of you will die, the other will live with spiders spilling from your mouth every day for the rest of your lives." I gave Great Spirit a nod and lifting the emerging spiders to my mouth, I swallowed the entire nest.

"*Kichaa*, she is crazy," said Benno.

I stood erect, as if I'd eaten cotton candy. It kinda felt like that but for the taste. I prayed to Great Spirit. I let my palms lay out, like tentacles, loose. "You think Hyena is more powerful than I? Look again at my face, my skin. You have never seen such a face but in your nightmares. Your ancestors don't lie. *Buda* will transform into hyena. I will crush your bones. And there are many ways." I gave them the eye. "Who dies now in *maumivu*, eaten away, *kuliwa mbali,* slowly as on an ant hill? . . . Whose belly will fill with venom and spit spiders for eternity?" I jumped at them. Benno stood his ground, the other guy faced him, desperate for permission to retreat. When Benno gave him none, he took tail and ran anyway. Benno loomed bigger than I'd thought. *Push it.* I widened my eyes till I heard my ears crack. "Your family will pay the price," I said.

"Bullshit!"

I lunged at him. He stumbled backward. My mouth tickled. My jaw opened and three small spiders crawled out of it. He began to run. I knocked them off my chin. I watched him flee; rare satisfaction bubbled in me. Or was it the nest coming alive? A melodic trill I'd never heard, lifted from my throat.

)))

Funny the things you'll do when faced with torture and dismemberment. One of my sister's best friends in Minnesota was in Dismemberment Insurance. I'd had my chance, but no policy now. I waited for more spiders to erupt. I waited for my stomach to collapse. I biked to Raymond's coffee shop and curled up behind it, wrestling with the past and the future. I ended up with nothing, not even a bellyached. I fell asleep wrapped in empty burlap coffee sacks; cloaked in the ripe smell of my body.

)))

"What are you doing here?" Raymond pulled me off the ground. "Did my sister tell you you could do this?"

"Mariam had nothing to do with this. I'll go. I just needed—"

"You better go! And don't come back. Two men came looking for you yesterday." Raymond scanned the surrounding area, obviously unsettled. "You can't be around here."

"Two?"

"One then another, hours apart. One Tanzanian, one *mzungu* or *rangi mbili*; a white or a two color, I couldn't tell. You're not welcome here anymore."

"Can you describe them?"

"Big."

"Did they leave names?" I asked.

"Don't be ridiculous." He shoved me away from the coffee stand.

"Hey!" I wriggled free. "They said nothing at all?"

"Well, nothing from the Tanzanian. But yeah, the Two Color, he said to tell you Roddy was looking for you."

Roddy!

Raymond continued, "I told him I hadn't seen you. I don't know how he thought I would, and I didn't want to find out. You are *buda* to everyone. My sister, my family . . . Just leave."

I pressed him. "Where did he say he was staying?"

"Go, now," he said. I yawned in defiance. His eyes draped and iced over; he wanted me out of sight. "I just told you. Now you go or I'll call the police."

"Where?" I said again. "He must have said where I could

meet him."

"By the lake. He said meet him the west side, near the docks. After dark. I imagine he's figured out that you cause death wherever you go. We all have enemies. Perhaps he's here to borrow an arm or a leg." Raymond pulled his cell phone from his pocket. "I'm calling the police. You're bad luck. And you smell like oxen dung."

I biked to the sawmill, the first light at my back, relieved . . . Roddy tonight! At one point I almost lost my balance, hitting a trough of Black Cotton: a clay-like soil that shrinks hard without moisture, but swells to a supremely hellish-type of quicksand when it rains. Very Jekyll and Hyde, if soil can have such a thing. Anyway, I didn't land on my ass. I sailed on.

At the mill, morning light reflected off the top of its ramparts; made it look almost missionary. Except for the barbed wire. I inhaled the morning, a combination of dust-blown wildebeest—they'd started their migration—and the expiring sweetness of flame vine. (No amount of the plant could help *my* skin.) I knelt behind a hedge of purple willow. Hidden, I had an unobstructed view of the gate and of the growing list of partygoers to my funeral who seemed to swarm around there.

I'd only just seated in the dry grass when Kadiri Charles' secretary, Ms. Jioni, advanced out of the gate. She came directly to the hedge. She spoke to me as if I was in clear sight. "Mr. Charles hopes that you appreciate his intervention."

I didn't move, pretending invisibility.

The secretary peered down at me through the hedge. "Did you hear what I said?"

I stood up and brushed off, self-consciousness deflating me head to toe. "And what would that be, *his intervention*?"

"No need to hide from me," she said. Even standing she had a couple inches on me. "Mr. Charles just wanted to be sure that you were safe."

"How did you know I was here?"

"Mr. Charles would like to meet with you. To discuss a trade of mutually beneficial information."

It took me a moment to confirm what I'd heard. "He would?"

"Privately, of course. It must be discreet."

I turned in several directions to see if anyone had come near. "And how can I be certain it will be safe for me?"

"Mr. Charles said you can suggest a location. Tonight."

Tonight! "Well, I . . .Okay." *Where would that be? Near Roddy. Near water.* "The main dock on Lake Selela. Where the mill timbers accumulate." *Open enough.*

"After dark," she said. "When there's no activity. Ten PM."

"Thank you."

"We'll see," she said.

⟩⟩⟩

I arrived early, hoping to find Roddy first. The thunk, thunk, thunk of logs ramming the dock, like someone trying to get out of a locked trunk. "Roddy?" I called. The wind smothered my voice, it jacked up the nip in the air; it mounted ocean-like whitecaps across the lake. The dock's single lamppost rocked unsteadily. Ghosts of light skipped across the decking. I waited. No Roddy.

Shortly after the agreed time, the contour of a man appeared at the dock's entrance. I'd seen no car deposit him. "Roddy?"

The man appeared alone and moved slowly toward me. It wasn't until he arrived under the lamppost that the frenzied light offered a glimpse of his face. Mr. Hsu.

"I was expecting Mr. Charles," I said. "That was our agreement."

"Well, he couldn't be here. And besides, you want to deal with me. Mr. Charles seems to have a disposition to your kind, to help you out, an indulgence I have little patience for. I run a business."

"I want specific information from Mr. Charles." I tried to move around Mr. Hsu and caught my ankle on a dock cleat.

Mr. Hsu stepped in front of me. "Yes, and we want specific information from you."

"Okay, well, then you know who The Hyena is?"

Mr. Hsu scratched his neck. "You will tell me first about your encounter with the women from the WWA. What do they know?"

"That's not how it works." I feigned departure.

Hsu wasn't a big man, but again he blocked my path. "It is how it works for me," he said.

"Who is The Hyena?" A spasm of wind rolled the deck. Both of us almost lost our footing.

Hsu grappled for the dock and stability, his face a shade greener. He regained footing and composed himself. "So. You have no information for me?"

"Who's The Hyena?" I repeated.

He shook his head. "You are foolish. If I knew who you speak of, I would tell you. I have never heard of this person. You and I do not travel in the same circles." He appeared candid. "Now tell me about the environmental crusaders and what they know."

"It doesn't seem like a fair trade," I said.

"Very well." He looked beyond me. "Bo, let us help the lady remember."

From behind, large arms wrapped around me, lifted me up. Where he'd come from, I have no idea. He was strong. He smelled of cardamom. "Get off me!" I kicked my leg back; my strength must have surprised him because he loosened his grip and staggered, though still had hold on me. I bowled backwards against him. We both went over the dock's edge. The conk of his head as it struck the log sickened me. His arms fell away. I struggled to reclaim my feet as the log began to roll.

I leapt for the dock. Got a grip. "Now you tell me," Hsu said. He ground his heel into my outstretch fingers.

"Sonuvabitch," I yelled and grabbed his ankle with my free hand. He tugged back. "Fuck no!" I said, and yanked hard on his leg. He fell awkwardly on the rocking deck. I dragged him to the edge, barely maintaining my own balance on the rolling logs. He kicked with his free leg and hit me square in the nose. The crackle of bone I'll never forget. *The Bone Crusher.* "Are you The Hyena?" I screamed, pain shooting through my forehead. He kicked again, thankfully missing me. I hauled him onto the bucking cluster of logs. The scud and swell of the lake opened a trench of water between the wooden rounds. I dove under as the logs slammed together and Hsu wailed, his hand dangling below the surface. The lake breached again, and Hsu plunged into it. He gasped. He reached for the surface. The timbers closed above him, sealing him under the lake's skin. I tried to snatch him; his arm pinned between logs. I yanked at his legs; my air depleted; there was no give. I had to resurface or drown. Above, only slivers of the dock's lamp light eked through the battery of warring logs. Trapped again. Beyond the muted wind, a rare rain began pattering the lumber above and—with a more distinct plonking—a small patch of open lake became visible. I swam to it, my lungs ready to rupture. I sprang to the surface about thirty yards from the dock.

Chapter 40

Selela Lake, Mto wa Mbu Village, Tanzania

"Keep moving." The cop waived the crowd on as the rescue team pulled the body out of Lake Selela. Despite the cop's best effort, the morning assemblage lingered. Buggies, tuk-tuks, a tan Jeep, and a small bus of tourists, jammed to a near standstill. Yells came from beyond the bottleneck far up the road. It wasn't Hsu's body, *that* I could see, even from a distance, the body too big. *Hsu's goon? Roddy? Please, no! I couldn't let myself think that.* They put the body on a large gurney, wrapped it up, and loaded it into an ambulance.

The night before, once out of the lake, I hadn't been able to find Hsu. I hadn't seen him swim free of the logs. To be honest, I hadn't waited around too long. I assumed he'd drowned; they'd find his remains later. I was touching all sorts of nerves, more than I'd intended. Anyway, the dip in the lake improved my body odor. I'd climbed up from the lake, along a ravine. In a hollow above the mill and midway between the village, I'd found an abandoned goat shed. I'd slept there.

The crowd around the lake thinned a bit. It struck me that the *other* man tracking me could've been Hsu's strong arm. But by no means had I caught sight of his face in the dark as he tackled me. Maybe *he* was The Hyena. Or Hsu. I doubted it. Didn't look like Benno. And where was Roddy? My stomach reminded me that maybe the spiders hadn't yet hatched. *I couldn't let myself think that.*

Hsu *had* said, *'Mr. Charles seems to have a disposition to your kind, to help you out.'* And hadn't Mr. Charles (or someone he employed) dispatched the bounty hunter, Morgan Jonas, just as Hsu had directed? Not that I could waltz into Mr. Charles' office. But maybe I'd inferred the worst about the man given that he was decidedly a crooked businessman and an environmental looter, possibly a killer. Either way, it didn't say much for his character. But he could help me locate The Hyena.

"You have anything to do with this?" Martine Yang and her chiseled buddy Corrin stood on either side of me.

They'd caught me off balance. "W-Why would you say that?"

Corrin pressed, "Did you?" More and more she reminded me of an attack animal under restraint.

I said, "Well, to quote Twain, 'I didn't attend, but I approve of it.'" I thought to qualify it. "Assuming it's Hsu or his sidekick. They attacked me."

"And we know that how?" said Martine.

"You here to judge me?" I asked.

"That's not the only reason," said Corrin.

Shit, I thought, *you have to trust someone.* I told them what happened. "Mr. Charles reneged on his agreement to meet me. But I didn't kill Mr. Hsu."

"Don't tell us anymore," Martine said. "Better that we don't know details."

"Really," I said, "I didn't—"

"Don't!" Corrin raised her hand.

"Okay," I took a breath. "But I'm no closer to tracking down The Hyena. The only person who might be able to offer a lead would be Kadiri Charles, he knows everything and everyone around here. Help me meet him. Or assume I'll be hunted down."

"And you don't know him?" asked Martine. "Mr. Charles?"

"You've got to trust me," I said.

"No, we don't," said Corrin. "Why else would Hsu want you dead? . . . Unless you knew too much, and he knew you'd talked to us."

"He just wanted information," I said.

Corrin smirked. "So do we. Did he say anything to you . . . about the movement of wood? Those involved?"

Martine piped in. "How can we be sure you aren't part of their operation?"

My hands went up in disbelief. "Do I look like an international timber dealer?"

"I don't know *what* you look like," said Corrin, her face no more genial than the first time I'd met her.

"Corrin!" Martine gave her a *cool it down* expression. "Look," Martine said turning to me, "things are very tense right now."

"Tell me about it," I said.

"And," continued Martine, "we have to be very careful what we say and to whom. We don't know you. We don't know if this Hyena stunt is some sort of misdirection on your part. You obviously got into Tanzania under suspicious circumstances. Let's see your passport."

Without mine would they take me into custody? "I don't carry it with me."

"Right," scoffed Corrin. As the ambulance pulled away, I caught a glimpse of Glory Baakari in the crowd. *On her way to work?*

Martine shuffled her feet, ready to move on. "Give us information that we can use and maybe we'll have something to trade."

"If I'm not diced into *muti* medicine first." I said.

"Is that even true?" said Corrin.

"Oh fuck!" My fists clenched. "Can or can't you help me meet Charles?"

"Tell you what," said Martine, "there's a Trustee Meeting happening—"

"I already know about that," I said. "I'd planned on going to it. But after what happened with Hsu, a public meeting's only gonna scare Charles. He won't talk to me in public. He's already passed the hatchet once. I'd rather meet him somewhere safe—for both of us, alone. Maybe *you* could set up a meeting . . ."

Corrin balked. "What!? You're really out of your mind."

"Hold on," said Martine. "He knows we're on to him, but he keeps up appearances. Like he's trying to help us get to the real thieves. He's always a step ahead. Might even be someone inside the WWA helping him."

"What if," I said, "you started a rumor that I know too

much about the WWA operation, and that I'm already leaking information; you're planning to get me out of the country before I wreck your plans? Charles would want to get me one-on-one before I was extradited."

"Complete madness." Corrin sought agreement from Martine, but Martine was deep in thought.

"If it will get me in the door, I could get you information, too," I said. *The role of bait, once again.*

Martine clutched at her locket. "Risky."

"It's a mistake," said Corrin. "We can't trust her."

I jumped in. "You want to find Martin's killer?"

Martine held the locket tighter.

"There isn't anything I know about the WWA plans that he doesn't already know," I said. "There's no downside for you."

"Might take a couple of days to set up," said Martine. "No matter what happens, we'll never acknowledge you."

Corrin snorted. "This is a bad idea."

$$\rangle\rangle\rangle$$

Martine said she or Corrin would leave a note in the abandoned goat shed when they could confirm the rumor had made its way to Kadiri Charles—a couple days, at least. The morning still sweet, I decided to stay out, carefully, wrapped in a scarf like a devout Muslim woman. Though temperatures hovered agreeably in the low 70's, it remained uncomfortably dry, at least for me. More rain had been expected, but none came. Dirt roads had become powder and the grasses withered. My mouth had grown pasty, and my insides chafed, half-starved for moisture. Thirst being all the proof I needed that water is primal. But the lack of rain didn't seem to bother the locals—in fact, if anything, it seemed to animate them. More of them out and about. They had faith.

I had to duck and weave a bit as I cycled to the north end of the lake, away from the sawmill, to immerse myself and gather my thoughts. I'd found out that Selela is Maasai for "clean water." I felt modestly encouraged. And maybe I'd connect with Roddy there.

No sooner had I removed my *niqab* and relaxed my legs, luxuriating in the lake, than a knife pressed my throat and nicked it. "I'm going to cut it now, be done with you, *buda*." I knew the man's voice.

I tried to turn around. The first slice of his blade, like cool wire tickling my throat. "Hyena?" I said.

"Don't move," the man insisted. He clamped my shoulder with his free hand. "I asked you to leave my family alone and now Mariam has been attacked," he said. "More people asking for you."

"Mariam?!" I said.

"Don't turn around." He tightened the blade against my throat.

"Raymond!"

"She could have killed Mariam," he said.

"Are you gonna kill me?"

He loosened his grip.

I turned to face him. "What are you talking about?"

Raymond scrapped the knife under my chin. He leaned on a small pile of clothes by his side. "Last night. A woman. She beat Mariam, looking for you. Get out of Karatu. Leave us alone."

"Is she okay?"

"No, she's not okay. She has bruises over her whole body, her face is cut, her eye."

I'd done it again, my ego. I motioned for him to lower the dagger. "Please." He did not. "Who was this woman?"

"A woman, I don't know. Strong, Mariam said. She couldn't see much of her. But the woman wanted you. She knew my sister was connected to you."

"Celvin told someone?" I said.

"Celvin couldn't hurt his back carrying his brains. Do not blame Celvin. You are the evil eye. People keep coming for you."

"People?"

"Just get out of here or I'll come back. I'll do what must be done."

"I'm being scavenged for parts," I said.

"Not my family's problem." Raymond brought the steel to his side. "You may be important to Mariam, but you mean nothing to me. If I see your wicked face again, I'll . . ." He got to his feet. "And stop wearing her *khanga*, you draw more attention to her." He pointed at the jeans and a t-shirt he'd brought on the ground. "Burn the *khanga*. Don't wear it again."

"Tell Mariam I'm so sorry."

Raymond pointed the knife at me. "Last time." He backed up the path, his eyes still menacing and locked on me. "Leave Karatu."

A man was coming down the shoreline, quickly, but with a pronounced limp. He'd seen Raymond waving his knife. Raymond saw the man, turned, and sprinted up the bank.

The man rushed up to me. "Are you okay?" Black. Handsome. From the welcoming party! The man in the bright orange tunic and matching pants. "You!" he said. "Are you okay?"

I touched my finger to my neck, only a little blood. "I'm fine."

"I'll go after him."

"No. Leave him," I said.

"You know him?"

"It's nothing."

"But you know him?"

"No, no I think he just wanted my *khanga*."

"In daylight?" He clucked; he found it implausible. "He wanted something more. He saw you dangling in the lake; he became envious of the water." A real charmer.

"What's your name?" I said, still mesmerized by his timing and elegant symmetry.

He took one last look for Raymond; Raymond was gone. "Kadiri," he said. "Kadiri Charles." He held out his hand to shake. "Remember me?"

I thought, *if I touch him, I'll never let go.* "I've been trying to meet you for weeks," I said.

"Me?" he laughed. Then thought about it. "Yes, probably. I'm sorry. Too busy, too many layers to get through."

Having again noticed his limp, I asked, "Are you alright?"

"A hyena at my leg." Kadiri brushed away the history. "Long ago. I was lucky. How have you been since the party? A number of us were worried when you left so quickly. Then disappeared."

Did he know I'd jumped out of the SUV? He must have, though gave no indication that he did. "I'm trying to leave Tanzania," I said. "But first I have to find someone."

"So soon? That's a shame. I imagine it has to do with your albinism. But I can help." He sat on the slope.

I remained standing. "Have you heard of The Hyena?"

He didn't blink. "Spotted or striped?" He tapped the ground to join him.

I didn't move. "A man or woman. Looking for *muti*."

"Better to have the name Hitler," he chuckled. "No, not in my circles. But I'm aware such people exist. How can I help you? I have money. I could arrange something. I guess this country hasn't been very hospitable to you. I gathered that would be the case, which is why some of us put the party together. To let you know everyone is welcome here. You just have to be careful. That's one of the things I was hoping to tell you before you . . ."

". . . Disappeared," I said.

"Yes."

"What happened to Mr. Ngowa?" I asked.

"What do you mean? He works for me, the tropo antennas. I keep him busy."

I squatted and planted myself face-to-face with Mr. Charles. "I need to talk to him again."

"Good luck." He smiled. "It often takes *me* weeks to find him. I guess he could say the same about me." Charles threw a pebble in the lake.

"You know I know about your timber dealings with the Chinese," I said, tempting fate. "You were supposed to meet me to trade information. Mr. Hsu met me instead. Why?"

"Ah, yes. Mr. Hsu. He's gone missing."

I measured for any sign in Charles' face. "He's probably dead. Drowned," I said. "Why didn't you come?"

"Dead? I wasn't aware of any meeting, or I would have come. But it's common knowledge that we deal with the Chinese. We have lots of foreign clients."

"I doubt everyone is informed about the tons of timber slipping illegally through Mozambique."

He sighed. "I run an honest business. Is it profitable? Yes, of course. Relatively small compared to others, and all very legal. What information could you possibly have for me?"

"I need to find The Hyena," I said.

"Why is this person so important?"

I finally sat. "He or she is a killer."

"Leave that to the police," he said, no trace of cynicism or mockery. "What do you think you know about my dealings with the Chinese? And who else have you spoken to about this? I have a reputation."

"Not without information about The Hyena," I said.

"You're a businesswoman at heart." He chuckled. A couple strolled toward us. "So, if I could, somehow, locate such information?"

"You can" I said. "Then I'll tell you what I know."

He offered a hand and lifted me off the ground. "I'll see what I can do. Where shall I find you?"

"I'll find you," I said.

Chapter 41

Mto wa Mbu Village, Tanzania

The streets of Mto wa Mbu bustled. They always bustled. A happy babble—humans taking on the color of birds and the sounds of nourished beasts. No jostling. An easy flow and a rhythm spiked with coconut drums. A hub, the fruit vendors with their red, green, and yellow bananas, lots of bananas. The carvers with their polished wood bowls; the weavers, the painters, the cooks of *matoke* stew. A melting pot of about hundred and twenty tribes—a lustrous fusion of languages. But my mind was still on Mariam and how my presence in this paradise had almost killed her.

I slowed as a tribe of Maasai twined past me and through the streets. Adolescent boys. "What is this?" I asked a man dressed in crimson wrap, sunshine lemon shorts, and a San Francisco Giants baseball cap.

"*Enkipaata,*" he said. He chopped his hands together. "Circumcision. These young men. It is over. They have just finished. The new age set." He turned back to watch the young men.

A man's hand settled on my back. I went to rip it off. "It's a tragedy when we can't grow old with the people we love," he said.

I turned. "Roddy!"

He threw his arms around me, and me around him. "Thank god," he said. "Oh, geez, thank god."

"Oh, Roddy!" I looked up at him, our mouths fastened on each other's. Neither of us would let go. Finally, still holding him tight so his smell couldn't escape, I said, "How did you find me?"

"I didn't," he said. "You found me." He pointed up the hill. "Tent camp. I figured I'd come all the way to Tanzania why stay in anything else . . . God, are you okay?"

A squall of tears burst from me, triggered, I guess, by gratitude. I couldn't stop. I couldn't let go of him.

"Ssh, shh. It's okay. It's over now," he said. "I've been looking for more than a month. I'd almost given up. Oh, geez." He held me tighter.

☽ ☽ ☽

We laid down in Roddy's tent. We fell asleep in each other's arms. A deep sleep.

When I woke, it was midafternoon. He wasn't there.

"I'm working on it, stay close and low," his note read.

I popped my head outside the tent. A few campers wandered around, but no Roddy. I searched for a while, surprised he hadn't roused me. His rented 4x4 gone, but he'd unloaded my bike. The one I still needed to return.

Nevertheless, and inexplicably, I was blessed with

comforts: Roddy, in a jungle in a sleeping bag; I laughed at the extravagance. Safe, I could sleep. I could cast off the exhaustion. And just as remarkably, I was blessed with not one, but two paths, to Kadiri Charles: A meeting at the sawmill offices prompted by Martine's planted rumor. (Perhaps a note from her or Corrin already awaited me at the goat shed.) And . . . assuming I really could approach Kadiri on my terms, as he'd proposed, I was assured of leads to The Hyena.

If meeting Kadiri away from his offices, I needed to suss out a safe location to my liking. And I needed to learn more about the man, his schedule, his movements. I needed to be prepared. I was sure he knew—or could find—information on The Hyena. Maybe I could add information for Martine and Corrin.

But first, given those blessings, I needed to cut anchor. Roddy's pen laid next to his notepaper. I began to write:

> *Dear Momma,*
>
> *I'm so very lucky in my life, and I wanted you to know that you've been a part of that. I'm grateful to you. You made me stronger. Whether by design or providence, you led me to nature and to be resourceful on my own. Thank you.*
>
> *I'm aware now how few blessings you've been given in your life, and how I must have been an extra burden. With Lyle now gone and Carly off with her friends and busy with her life, I'm glad I was able to restore the farmhouse for you. But I also know, it's not enough. I've experienced a life-changing adventure and now that it is almost over and I've survived it, I want to share it with you. When I return from Africa—yes, I'm in Africa—I will. You need*

to know that I love you and will do what I can to make
your life easier.

--Eunis

I stuck the note in my pocket, I biked down to the mill. I figured twenty minutes. Scout around a little. Then head back, find Roddy. Maybe have a real meal. Then check the shed after dark.

The lack of rain had furrowed the dirt path into crisscrossing cordons of cement-like mud. Some 6-8" deep. They grabbed at the bike, rattling, and wobbling me. As usual, my legs held up under the pummeling. Halfway there, I took a sharp turn, and fists raged down on me, wild shrieks exploded in my ears. I face-planted off the bike. Mariam on me, beastlike.

"What? Mariam!"

She chewed into my shoulder.

"What the fu—! Stop! What's the matter with you?" I tried to get up. She wrestled me to the ground. She went for my face and eyes. I kicked her hard. She grunted; she fell back. She sprang to her feet and charged again.

"What—???"

"I'll kill you," she said. "I'll tear you to ribbons. Chew up your bones. Shit them out. This is how you repay my family? I will listen to my ancestors. You are *buda*, you're evil. You bring pain. You bring grief. You bring death." She tore at my hair.

"Stop! Let go my hair! What're you talking about?" I bashed her arm, to no avail.

"I'll kill you," she screamed. "I'll be The Hyena for this kill." With great pride she exposed her teeth. She hurtled forward.

I bent to shoulder her blow, my one good shoulder. "What have I done, damn it? Get the fuck off me."

She gnawed deep into my skin. "You killed my brother."

"What?! Raymond?"

"Raymond." She put her knee in my back and tried to crack it in half.

That's the last I remember.

⟩⟩⟩

Tied in a corner, my wrists abraded from rope, Mariam squatted opposite me, head down. The air swollen with dust, the wooden structure tick-ticking from drouth. The roof low and failing. A dwindling scroll of chicken wire lay to my right bound in spider ravel. An old hen house? "What happened?" I asked.

She lifted her head. "You killed him."

"Mariam, I'm so sorry. But I didn't—"

"Just stop!" she said. Hate, only one of many contortions on her face. "You probably didn't physically drag him away. You probably didn't drown him. Maybe you weren't even there . . ."

"Mariam!"

". . . But your *buda* eye: it as our ancestors say. You caused it. I am a fool." She threw a weak fistful of dirt at me. It landed short but its powder spiraled forward, gagging me. "I should kill you . . ." she said, heaving and beginning to cry.

"Mariam."

". . . But I'll let the real Hyena do his or her job. Every rip of its teeth will have my blessing."

She stood up. She wiped away the tears.

"But you're okay?" I said.

She cut me loose. "The damage is inside."

She stood me up. She growled as if she were about to tear into my other shoulder. "You can't outdistance the wisdom of my ancestors. Run, you devil, run. Until The Hyena brings you down."

I broke for my bike and got the hell out.

☽☽☽

There hadn't been so much as a scratch on Mariam's face. No cuts or bruises that I could see. Raymond said she'd been attacked. Why? Why had Raymond been targeted, other than because of me? . . . More contrition to tote around. But it was Mariam's pain that really took hold of me—in my head, in my body, so I ached. *Raymond.* Leaving a hole in the souls of her whole family and a woman I loved. *What am I doing?*

I rode back to camp, my shoulder burning, my poor decisions smoldering. Hunting The Hyena had just spread more of my dark stamp over a new set of innocent people. Time to stop my lethal narcissism.

I dropped the bike by the tent. I opened the flap . . .

"Ah, *Mami Wata* returns." Erevu Ngowa sat square legged, dressed as he always did; impeccable, almost business, almost casual. As ever, the congealed grin, his trademark. As if nothing had happened since I'd last seen him.

"What the effin' hell are you doing here? How'd you find me? Where've you been! Where's Roddy?"

Ngowa held up his hand. "All is as it should be. Come, sit."

"You're fucking kidding me. You left me at a party in the middle of nowhere! For money? Who the hell are you? You're part of the hunt?"

He patted the ground again. His rigid smile up at me. "Do you remember," he said, "the crocodile?"

"What the hell are you talking about now! Get down to earth!"

"The Zambezi," he said. "You remember that morning?"

"I don't know, probably. Where the hell have you been?"

"The crocodile," he repeated, "you remember it?"

The memory came up—not in my head—but through my feet, legs, butt and back. "Yeah. On the beach. Early morning. No one else up. You raised your hand to slow me."

Ngowa leaned forward to amend me. "No, to respect the conversation I was in."

"You and the crocodile?" *Well, shit. This ought to be good.* "Really?"

"Oh yes. Those who don't believe in *mamba* will never hear her." He paused, gentler in the face than I'd ever seen him.

"So what?" My impatience growing. "Why'd you come back? Because the witch doctor's clinic is no longer in operation? You need a new retail outlet."

He went on, "Crocodile works below and above the water line. She is dangerous. Strong amongst the slippery rockweed and grasses. Patient. All must be aware—she strikes quickly from the depths. She plucks the most ferocious from the shore." He patted the ground; my shoulder throbbed, I relented.

"Do you understand?" Ngowa said. "Even the most feared creatures cannot be unprepared for crocodile, for what is below the surface, from which we all come."

"No, I don't understand," I said. "Not at all. You're The Hyena, right?"

His lips drew in. "Do you believe we're allies?"

My mouth dropped open. "Are you freakin' kidding me! Allies?"

"We are," he said.

"So, you service me, I'll service you? You fly me here. And in my service to you, I don't come back alive. Nor in one piece. What a deal. All for the local apothecary."

"You are wrong about my intentions."

"What will I bring?" I said. "In U.S. dollars please, not Tanzanian shillings; I can't convert such large numbers. Just checking my worth on the open market. Not that it's likely to raise my self-esteem."

"It is too late, now," Ngowa said. "But it was always meant to be."

The beating sun added to the canvas stink. "Meant to be?" I said. "I'm not meant to be here."

"Yet that is the exact opposite of what you said in transport. "You *wanted* to be here. It was important that you be here. You were here for a family, someone you love. Anyway, you should realize, money is not a factor . . . for me."

"Comforting. What *is* a factor? And why should I believe you?"

"Do you honestly think I would harm you?" His tone so fatherly, so stern, not at all inspiring; a man dragging two worlds with him, unable to speak one clear language. Then he added, "Tonight, we travel."

"We?" I started to get up. "No, no. You're not moving me. You've got a shitty track record. Get the *F* out of here."

"'Let everything happen to you, beauty, and terror. Just keep going. No feeling is final.'"

"Another of your homilies?" I asked, directing him out of the tent.

"Rilke," he said. He motioned for me to sit back down. I stood. He carried on, "If we are about to be stopped and questioned, I'll let you off before going on."

"What?"

"Safer for both of us," he said.

"Why?"

"Safer for both of us."

"Where? Where do you think *we're* going?"

"Just up there." He pointed over our heads, to the northwest. "The Cradle of Humankind. Just outside the cauldron's shadow. Quite a special place."

"Where's Roddy? I'm not going anywhere without my friend." I waited for another ambiguity.

Resignation crossed his face. He said, "Yes, I'm afraid that is another matter."

Chapter 42

Ngorongoro Conservation Area, Karatu, Tanzania

"Where's Roddy?" I asked again. "What've you done with him?"

Ngowa slowed the four-wheel to allow a donkey wagon to cut across our path.

We'd made it smoothly past the Lodoare Gate into the Ngorongoro Conservation Area, up along the volcano's rim, past the thinning tourist vans and caravans. Past roads branching off to posh glamping experiences overlooking the Ngorongoro Crater. Even at sundown, the sightseers, and small strings of Maasai on foot, buzzed everywhere along the northwest ledge. Once we were outside the Ngorongoro, a few miles from the eastern entrance to Serengeti National Park, the paved road ended, and most other traffic disappeared.

Ngowa had told me to stop asking questions because "I have few answers and those I will share with you when we get there. Otherwise, look at the beautiful flora or wrestle by yourself in your head."

"What have you done with him?"

"I have done nothing," he finally answered. The open 4x4 bumped along, squealing metal, and coughing with each thump of the road. Ngowa's wrists stuttered in sync with the steering wheel, trying to control the dry, washboard and deep ruts below us. "But," he admitted, "your friend, he is in trouble."

"Alive?"

"I believe so," he said. "He will be used as bait."

"For me?"

"Of course," he said.

Every step got me deeper. "What the hell is going on?"

He spread his hands on the wheel as if to say, *it is too much to explain.*

"Why am I following you?" I said. "I should get out now."

"Because you care for Roddy. He is your responsibility. Because—whether you admit it or not—this is your birthright, your accountability, your domain before the water evaporated. . ."

"Oh, geez."

". . . Long ago, you aligned with it. For someone as special as you, I suspect this will happen more than once in your body if this body survives. But even after that."

"Terrific," I said, no longer willing to untangle his mythologies. "Survive The Hyena?"

"Perhaps," Ngowa said. "Perhaps."

"Who is he?"

"I do not know." He pulled the four-wheel to a stop, enveloping us in dust.

"Well, you know *something*," I said, adrenalin pumping.

"To the left," he pointed, "is the Olduvai Gorge. The Paleoanthropologists Louis and Mary Leakey made their world-altering discoveries there. You know, about early human evolution."

"Why here?" I said. "Where's Roddy?"

"Keep in mind," he continued, "that unearthing the very first human remains began as a trial excavation—an ancient bog where animals had been trapped. 'Nature's slaughterhouse,' they called it. See the two large concrete skulls? You will be on the other side, away from the gorge, another split in the earth at the base of a very deep, deep funnel where incalculable water drained millions, thousands of years ago. There are several bogs around here. You can thank me for that."

"More riddles," I said. "If you're truly an ally, why won't you help me save Roddy? Give me some answers."

"I am. But I cannot save your friend, or you," Ngowa said. "You are *Mami Wata*. You have the power. I bring you here to save Roddy. That should be enough. Please get out." He pointed up the road. "You are going there, another thousand yards or so on the right. Go on."

I slipped out of the vehicle, unsure what else to do. "Give me a hint," I said.

"Careful," he said, "in this light it is easy to miss. Dusk can play tricks. Behind that deep row of junipers and African redwood, a trench begins sharply downward into the forest and into the Olbalbal Depression. Probably two thousand or more feet, just outside the base of the cauldron and the Conservation Area."

"Give me a gun," I said.

"I don't carry one. And I doubt it would be of much help. I am quite sure your friend Roddy will be down there, and I am hopeful you will both be back." He jammed the four-wheel in reverse, spun it around. He leaned out. "May we meet again, on reliable soil. May there forever be reliable soil. Thank you."

"What?" I said as he drove off.

After walking up and down the road, measuring my steps, swatting away the occasional tsetse fly, I found a small opening and a dry stream bed carved into the hillside. It led steeply down, over rocks, between thick thistle shrubs, over decomposing trees, and away from the Ngorongoro highlands. Not a path but a vertical obstacle course.

I found out the hard way—falling, sliding, and rolling—that each step had to be secured before moving on. Sizeable welts and lacerations along my arms and legs confirmed my initiation. I worried about baboons and spiders and things I couldn't see.

The temperature dropped precipitously with each fifty yards I descended, until despite working a sweat, an unpleasant chill followed me. At least the cold had driven off the tsetse flies. Navigating the almost lightless evergreen forest, the yellowwoods, the seven-foot palm-like succulents, and the mean thistle shrub, I was distracted from what awaited me below. My eyes adjusted.

The forest became even more overgrown, adding a moist mixture of uncooperative ferns, vines, and mosses. Until an engine purred, at first barely audible. I continued down the dried watercourse, the hum ever closer. Then it stopped.

As quietly as I could, I edged through the teeming vegetation in the direction of the extinguished sound.

"Eunis, please join us," said the voice. A man's voice. A familiar voice.

I didn't move. Stifling my breath only made my heart beat faster.

"You did not come all this way only to retreat back up that ravine," he said.

That voice. I combed through my hair then tugged on it trying to place it. I did my damnedest to slow my breath.

"Come down," he said. "We will turn on our parking lights. Follow them. Your friend Roddy is here, waiting for you."

Two small amber dots appeared yards away and below me through the foliage. Another thirty yards at most.

"Get out of here!" yelled Roddy. Followed by a sickening snap and a muffled groan. *His head bouncing off metal?*

"I'm coming," I said, sliding down several more yards. Within seconds I stood in the dim light. I adjusted to being center stage, I spotted my audience. Three figures, all gray gauze in the twilight, sat or stood in the open 4x4. "That's better," said the man. He stepped into the vehicle's light.

"Kadiri!" I said. "It was you all along."

He smiled. "Believe what you want. Are you ready to trade?"

"How do I know," I said, "that you'll free Roddy and let him return to the states?"

"You do not. But a deal is a deal. Do you have a better one?"

"No," moaned Roddy. "No."

"Let me see him," I said.

Kadiri flicked on a halogen flashlight and swung it to the Jeep Rubicon. Ms. Jioni lifted Roddy's slumped head. His face badly bruised. Next to her, a figure in a white Klan-like hood, two eyes cut out. Charles panned the light back on me. "Come with us and I'll free him," he said.

"You have me here," I said. The half-light didn't offer an escape route. "Let him go. You know I can't make it out of here."

Kadiri dosed the flashlight.

"Kadiri . . .?" I braced for his attack. Instead, a minute passed. A muffled discussion in the 4x4. The flashlight came back on.

"Okay," he said. He nodded at his secretary, "Flaviana," indicating she should remove Roddy's blindfold. "See, we'll make it sportier." Flaviana untied Roddy and shoved him out of the 4x4.

"Thank you, Ms. Jioni," Kadiri said. Both he and Flaviana had dressed in khaki camouflage fit for the savannah, a little out of place in the lowlands, especially this lowland of greens. I'd misjudged her frame; she was considerably bigger and more muscular than I'd given her credit. He more feline, probably quicker.

Roddy stumbled over the deep black ruts toward me.

"And now," said Kadiri in theatrical tones, "you shall have your hunt."

Under his breath Roddy said, "Run." And we both began to sprint away, tripping on crest after crest of baked black cotton soil.

Kadiri yelled after us, mocking, "We appreciate your backbone." He jumped into the four-wheel Rubicon, started the ignition, and drove toward us.

"We should split up," I said to Roddy. "They only really want me."

"Not happening," Roddy said. I hadn't noticed before, but he was badly favoring his left leg; could hardly stand up on it.

"I have no idea where we are," I said.

"Then let's get behind them." Roddy pulled me to the left and we waited for their vehicle to pass. "You should go on without me."

"Yeah. Right." I gave him my good shoulder to lean on. He took a deep breath. We made our way back to the base of the creek bed. From that angle the ravine looked even steeper than on my way down. "Are you well enough," I asked, "to climb up to the highland? It's perpendicular."

Before he could answer, the Rubicon's headlights had turned around and were headed for us.

Chapter 43

Lowlands, outside Ngorongoro Conservation Area

We squatted in the underbrush. I whispered to Roddy, "When they drove you in . . .?"

He interrupted with strangled breath, scarcely audible, "They had me blindfolded. I have no idea where we are."

"There's gotta be some sort of road or . . ."

Several yards away, high hysterical laughter soared over the jungle, almost human. Tops of plants rocked from side to side then disappeared; the four-wheeler uprooted everything as it bore down on us.

"Hyena's dominion," called Kadiri, heralding a sovereign. "Hyena hunts this land as royalty, unchallenged." His words ricocheted and promptly died. He waited for us to make a sound. We barely breathed. "Give yourself up, it's the code of the land; your friend can go free. We are home here, you are not."

"C'mon," said Roddy grabbing my hand.

"No, maybe he's right," I said.

Roddy yanked again. "They'll butcher us both, whatever we do."

"Eunis?" Kadiri shut off the four-wheeler. Even with the winch protecting its grill, the four-wheel Rubicon had been contained by the knotted vegetation. He turned off the lights. "You may wander but eventually you will need to sleep. We enjoy the pursuit. We enjoy the take down. But let your friend go free. He doesn't need to suffer. Let us make this work for everybody."

I wanted to taunt him. "*So powerful you need a manmade Jeep to track us down? Then come get us.*" But my pride would only ensure a speedier carnage.

From the little I could see, the territory in front of us promised uncompromising jungle forest. But it also suggested level ground. The land behind us guaranteed Kadiri, his secretary and the hooded man. To the left and right, mostly unscalable escarpments. "Come on," I said to Roddy. "Maybe nightfall will save us." Knowing full well that dusk and dawn are hyena's most rapacious time.

We headed into the somber light, and with it, the slightest mist. Roddy couldn't stand up for more than three/four feet before giving in to pain and gravity. Under his breath he said, "Do you know *anything* about this area?"

"What's your level of pain?" I asked.

"No, we don't have time for that." Roddy stood, wincing. I moved forward; branches and fronds slapped as he followed. "Anything about this area?" he asked again. "Where are we?"

We heard Kadiri's pack move.

We crept ahead. "Well, I've seen maps," I said.

"Maps?"

What did Dr. Allen's maps show me? "Unfortunately," I said, "we're outside and north of the crater. We're outside the Ngorongoro Conservation Area entirely. We're on the periphery of the maps I saw."

"Then forward." Roddy's chest rose and fell as though a millstone draped his neck and would topple him any minute; he hurt pretty bad.

Moving toward us through the maze of foliage came The Hyena and his clan, not more than twenty yards behind us. Roddy and I froze. Nightmarish bellows ripped the air, dropping both of us to our knees. A rasping, beastly call from hell. No longer hysterical but now feverishly stalking flesh and bone. Its howl climbed my spine as if it were already upon Roddy and severing him. It would mutilate and devour us, even as we watched ourselves being consumed.

Horror-struck, Roddy asked, "What's that?"

"Never mind." I said. "Come on." We crawled, head down, stopping every few feet, to listen. When Kadiri and his pack moved, which was most of the time, we moved too, staying low. When they stopped to listen, we stopped. "There might be something," I said. "But in this light . . ." Rich loam filled my nose. Actinomycetes; from my college studies, bacteria—harmless, productive, or deadly.

"Anything," Roddy said. "Any fucking thing. Let's do it. We can't just sit here."

Over the years, despite my attempts to disengage from him in the city, I'd always leaned on Roddy. But here, now, it was my turn for him to lean on me. "Okay," I said. "I could be wrong, but something Ngowa said when he dropped me off . . ."

"Ngowa?" Roddy put his palm to the ground steadying himself. "He's back? And . . .?"

"Let's go straight," I said. "No promises. All I got is a couple days looking over maps at Dr. Allen's. But I think if we keep in this direction, just watching that last light catching the headlands, we'll be ready to go up hill—even a yard or two—if we have to. And we might."

Roddy whispered back, "I don't understand."

"Listen," I said, "we might be able to take those three."

"What did Ngowa say?"

"Did you hear me?" I said. "We can take them. I suspect Kadiri's secretary won't be much of a fighter, so it will be the two of us on Kadiri and the hooded man."

"Yeah, who the hell is the hooded man? He didn't say a word the whole time he was in the vehicle with me."

A machete hacked through the vegetation. I put my finger to my lips. We held our breath. Peering through the thicket only offered more foliage, little else. Except . . . I picked up discord in the air. Perhaps an acrimonious word or two between the three hunters. I wasn't sure. And then nothing. They'd moved further away.

I shrugged. "The hooded man? Another mercenary? The Hyena's type. Or maybe *The* Hyena, so untamed that they need to keep him hooded. Like they do with predacious hawks."

"You mean," whispered Roddy, "like some freak in a carnival sideshow?"

Kadiri's retinue moved closer again. "Anyway, we don't have a choice," I said.

"Okay," Roddy said. "Where from here?"

"If I'm correct," I looked at the lower and upper canopies, "we're approximately . . . I'd say maybe . . . somewhere beyond us . . ."

"Eunis!" Roddy motioned for me to spill it out.

"Aaah . . . possibly. . ." I said. ". . . a mile, two miles, maybe 200 yards—fuck if I know—there might be some wetlands. Maybe." *The kind of environment I grew up in in Minnesota, sort of.* "There aren't many around here."

"What's *not so* good about this direction?" Roddy said.

He knows me too well. "I didn't say that." *Eyes ahead.*

"It was in your voice."

I glanced at him. "Just keep moving," I said. "We'll know when we get there."

He caught me on the arm. "Where?"

"If you feel the earth suck at your feet, stop. Let me know. Might be time to find higher ground. If we can. But until then, we need to keep—"

The creature's howl rolled over us again and died unnaturally in the distance, as if swallowed by the land itself. We couldn't be too far from the canyon's end. From there, everything shot straight up. Our last stand closing in. "Just remember what I said."

Roddy nodded.

What had Ngowa said? *There are bogs around. . .* That, and he wished for *reliable soil.* Desperate for ideas, I was falling back on Ngowa's dubious logistics and his Tanzanian mysticism, as if they made any practical sense. Nevertheless, onward.

The Hyena and his group advanced behind us, possibly a

bit slower and further from us than before. But if my hunch was right, we were running out of controllable space.

"Squishy," said Roddy a foot or two ahead of me.

"Already? Shit."

"Really tacky," he said. "Almost pulled my boot off."

"Don't move. Listen." I took hold of his arm. I closed my eyes to tune in. "No hippos, no elephants. No herons. Not even crickets. No sound at all."

"Yeah?"

"This is it; we can't go any farther."

"I don't mind getting my boots dirty," he said. "I'd rather live."

"Roddy! Don't freakin' move."

"Okay, okay."

I said, "You're going to go left and curl back from here, back to where Kadiri dropped you off."

"I'm not leaving you."

"You're not," I motioned him to calm down. "I'm gonna go right and curl back too. This is it, Rod. Really." I paused. *Might be the last time I ever see him again.* "I'm sorry. For everything. I never should have involved you. Sometimes I'm so . . ."

"I wouldn't be anywhere else." He dropped his head. "Well, maybe . . ."

"Okay," I said, "From here, don't worry about what you hear. Trust me. Now go."

"But . . ."

"Do you trust me?"

"Of course."

"Then start moving, but only backward from here," I said.

Roddy checked me again. I nodded. He limped into the jungle, bent and stumbling. Just before disappearing, he lifted his hand above his head and waved back, *goodbye.* My heart collapsed on itself, wistful, with no time to languish in it.

In his condition, I didn't know how far Roddy could make it. Or how quietly. Which meant I had to do something. *Something quick!* I knelt on the damp ground, hoping to steady my breath. My legs more mine since escaping The Box, maybe even better. The sky fell gently; the mist soothing, as if I was cocooned from risk, and even Roddy would be safe if I willed it.

It had no connection to reality. But somehow, I was safer there than any other place since Land of the Mist. In that imagined cover, I could stop and consider: *Hyena's hunting technique?* Take down at high speed. Savagely. Without hesitation. *Its greatest weakness . . .?*

What had brought me here to this lethal spot of fertile mud? I'd led myself here, now with nowhere to go. Hubris. Same as The Hyena.

I listened. The jungle still, perhaps soothed as I, because of the mist. Comforting. To stay in the silence, hyenas hear everything . . .

The thwack of machete came through the jungle . . . and murmurs. Kadiri and his hunters not as quiet as they'd been; not being careful; self-possessed, arrogant. *Adapt.* I dug my hands into the wet soil and rubbed it over my face and body. I laid out on the ground and slithered forward. Along the edge of the expanding swamp, I discovered small ramps of earth, squishy but as yet still capable of supporting some weight. I settled beneath one, immersed in ooze.

Let The Hyena smell blood. "Okay," I yelled to Kadiri and his ghouls, "c'mon, take me. But only me. And if I can find a way to kill myself first, go fuck yourselves. I'll just be dead meat." I inched back into the coppice. I waited.

A light rain began to patter on the leaves, the first rainfall in weeks. Silken droplets showered me in the fading light. Good fortune. The swamp sighed.

Kadiri's Rubicon came to life. The engine whined and jerked forward, headlamps on full beam, crashing faster, more committed, through thick foliage; occasionally thrown back or tangled. But the scent of me ruled Hyena. The Jeep picked up speed. *This is it,* I thought.

"Here!" I yelled. The 4x4 wheeled toward me, half a football field away. If I survived this, could I separate the clan? And if so who and how? I wasn't too worried about Flaviana. Didn't know anything about hooded man. But I did know Kadiri.

"Kadiri," I shouted, "Get off your damn mechanical horse and run with me. Did ya hear me? . . . Maybe The Hyena is not swift as natural hyenas. Maybe not as quick. Not as smart."

"Let me off," I heard Flaviana say, perhaps feeling over her head in the morbid chase. The 4x4 slowed briefly then sped up, coming dead on.

When it was no more than ten yards in front of me, I grabbed hold of the muddy ground, and called, "Here!"

The Rubicon swerved, hit the small grade of earth above me, and catapulted out of the jungle, ten-twelve feet in the air. With its last roar, it sailed thirty feet into the swamp and immediately began sinking. Kadiri stood at the wheel, his head twisting side-to-side. "Flaviana," he called. "I need help."

Despite his newfound vulnerability and emerging panic, equanimity saturated the swamp; rain plunking the fronds, the soggy ground. All cushioned and collected. Then a cavernous *glug*, as the black cotton began in earnest to swallow the 4x4.

"Flaviana?"

The mud now up to the 4x4's doors.

"I believe she's left the building." I yelled. I didn't have to yell—the space so congenial—but I did anyway; I still had work to do on my newborn pride.

"What?" Kadiri searched for my face in the dripping, swirling fog, the realm a deep indigo. But Kadiri knew even before I said it. . .

"Olbalbal Swamp," I yelled again, drawing his attention. "Year round, deep, wet black cotton soil. It never dries completely here, never shrinks to solid. It doesn't let go."

"Fuck you," he said, and called out, in several directions, "Flaviana!"

The Jeep continued to sink. The rain picked up. The black soil—intimate with moisture—expanded, losing its structure, losing all strength. Even more fatal.

Kadiri was fast vanishing, and just now fully *decoding* it. "Eunis, listen. I need help—Fuck, come on Flaviana!"

"I can't help you," I said. *And I was truly sorry that I couldn't.* "I have no way to reach you without going down myself, which I'm not about to do."

"I'll die.

"I'm sorry." I said. The 4x4 burrowed deeper, the quicksand crawling over the door handles. Kadiri slid frantically from one side of the Jeep to the other, scavenging for a way out, only making things worse. *Tragic. . . and mortal.* He started to say something. The Jeep went sideways. He fell out alongside. Then, with no more warning than the steam hiss from the 4x4's engine, the swamp fed on them, leaving only ghosts on the surface. Water rings rolled briefly out. Nothing more.

Where was the hooded man? Where was Flaviana?

The rain cranked up. The swamp engorged, took on more water, creeping toward me on shore. I backed up and kept my eyes on it.

"Hey," said Flaviana walking through the wet blades, calling through the night. "Follow me. You're safe now." She was, at most, fifteen yards away, but couldn't see me.

She meant *to drier ground*, more familiar, safer for her.

"We can get out of here now," she called again. I could hear her brushing the fronds, turning one direction, then another, combing for any movement. The slightest sound and she'd be on me, but as the rain continued to fall, the swamp continued to encroach on me.

"Eunis?"

The longer I laid still, the better chance Roddy had of escaping. But my choices for death had narrowed: Flaviana or the swamp. The swamp, free of pride, simply *was*; a life form collaborating with Gaia, without malice. But not without peril. The hooded man? Flaviana? Rudiments of nature, but not collaborative. I felt better off with the swamp, but only stood a chance with the humans.

Wrapped in the shoreline mud, I found a deep sense of peace as I waited for Flaviana to find a direction. My bed of soil, all soil, the amalgam of roots, fins, wings, horns, and bodies—our bodies; millennia's compost. From which springs new roots, new fins, new wings, new bodies, and longings that even science cannot quantify. . .

Thank you Great Spirit.

"Eunis, you cannot hide from me." I heard Flaviana drop to all fours. I tore at the mudflats' closest earthbound stems, and pulling up a root ball, threw it into the bog worming at my shoulder.

She came at the sound—I imagined hair raised, eyes tapered, jaws open—and leapt over me to the torn bundle of roots.

The bog, like the crocodile, sucked on her. "*Hapana!*"

I rolled to solid ground.

"I'm not finished with you," she said, struggling in the mire.

"One of the things I never understood," I said rubbing the mud from my face, "was why Kadiri would choose this ground, so unfamiliar to a hunting hyena. One of the few places. I know hyenas are smart animals."

Her tone all at once conciliatory. "I just follow what Mr. Charles says. I am not *that*." Something about her eyes, a kind of movement I hadn't noticed before; not entirely unlike mine, moving left/right/left. Still scouting, but now faster in fear. "Help me."

"I can't."

She said, "I think Mr. Ngowa convinced Mr. Charles that this was the best place to meet, far away from the crowds, or anybody, really. I thought it was a poor choice. Get me a branch, something to hold on to."

I shook my head.

"Eunis, you *buda*." She growled.

I turned to the sky. The rain bathed my face. "Thank you," I said.

"I am timeless," she howled. And was gone.

Chapter 44

Lowlands, outside Ngorongoro Conservation Area

After calling in loud whispers, I found Roddy halfway to the clearing, safe but shivering, and still wobbly. We moved cautiously back to where we'd met The Hyena and Kadiri. Or was the hooded man also a hyena? Had Flaviana merely disarmed me?

The jungle forest began to breathe again, a screech from a nightjar, a hoot from an owl. At the opening where I'd first met Kadiri and Flaviana, the hooded man brawled with the ground, grunting in bursts of fury. His legs banded with cord. I motioned for Roddy to step quietly as we approached him. From both sides, we dropped on him clamping his shoulders down. I peeled off his hood. Erevu Ngowa looked up at me relieved, a patch of duct tape sealing his mouth.

We untied his hands and lifted him to his feet. He caught his breath. "I knew you could do this," he said. His face suddenly fraught again, he asked, "Are they gone?"

"Yes," I nodded, "in the swamp."

Ngowa relaxed. "You see," he said, "let go or be dragged? You see that now?"

Still furious with him I asked, "Why didn't you tell me The Hyena was Flaviana?"

"I never thought it was, and I was not sure about Kadiri either. I *did* know Kadiri was looting our forests. That was my focus," he said.

"You delivered me to him."

"I knew you would be a magnet. I am sorry. But you were the only one up to the task, the only one capable of rectifying the situation quietly and without retribution." He stretched his body in that cat-like way he had. "But when you escaped the welcoming party, you put Kadiri in a very difficult situation. His reputation with the other partygoers—for whom you were a showcase as evidence of his power—was in jeopardy. More particularly, your escape held grave danger for him with The Hyena, Flaviana."

"That must have been why she was at first thrilled to have me in her office, alone. But when the other workers arrived, she knew to make a spectacle of throwing me out."

"You are charmed."

"And what do you mean," I said, "'the only one up to the task?'"

"If I had defied Kadiri in any way, he would have cut me in half and buried me, even if he wasn't The Hyena. What good would that do? He wielded so much power. People were terrified of him."

"Great, and I could have died in the witch doctor's box or on his table."

"I was watching you. I did what I could. Who do you think started the rumor in town about *Mami Wata?* Who do you think convinced Kadiri to meet you in the wetlands?"

"I'm supposed to thank you? My friend's brother was drowned," I said.

"Your female friend complicated things, but her brother brought that upon himself when he threatened you. Kadiri saw him. It was up to Kadiri to bring you to The Hyena alive, in one piece. By now you know how valuable you are—but to all of us in different ways."

Questions kept multiplying. "The calls from Kyra's family? Mrs. Baakari said she never received any. She's part of the operation?"

"Not that I am aware. But knowing Flaviana and Kadiri, I would assume they had the switchboard route all such calls to them, where, of course, they died." Ngowa regrouped. "But do you see now how it all makes sense; every hyena is subordinate to the largest, cruelest female in the clan. Flaviana had all the power, Kadiri served at her pleasure, her pawn. And," Ngowa said cheerily, "there is an old proverb: 'After the game, the queen and the pawn go into the same box.'"

"Why me?" I said.

"Word about you traveled quickly," said Ngowa, "even before you crossed into Mozambique. Only *Mami Wata* could save our forests."

"I didn't save anyone but Kyra," I said.

Roddy piped in, "And me. You saved me."

"My country is indebted to you." Ngowa bowed. "You gutted a portion of the illegal Chinese wood export. Kadiri and

Hsu will not be easily replaced. Distrust is heightened. And," he continued, "did you notice that more wood came out of that mill than seemed logical for the adjoining forest?"

"You know, I did," I said.

"Because that mill is a distribution point for a number of other rogue traders. That network is at least disabled for a while. You have done Tanzania a great service." He bowed again. "But now you must rest. If you attempt walking out of here tonight, you will surely get lost and possibly attacked. Possibly by hyena. Rest on that rock over there so your heads are not easily reached. Wrap yourselves around each other to fight off the cold and make yourselves look bigger."

"And what about you?" Roddy said.

"I am used to the cold. I will be right over there, on that rock." He pointed a few feet away. "And then I must vanish. As you know now, Flaviana knew I knew too much and had already dictated I was to die. But I love my country. I have no intention of leaving. As long as I am not connected to Kadiri or Flaviana's disappearance, I will be able to resurface at some point. Now sleep. We all must get some rest."

When we woke, Ngowa was gone.

)))

"It says here," Roddy read from his tablet, "The hyena's only real predator is the crocodile. When venturing near rivers, hyena is surprised from below."

"Yeah, I know."

The plane dropped a foot and with it my stomach. He took my hand. "We'll be fine," he said. "But I've got to warn you. When your friend Gordon at the station told your boss, Charlie whatshisname . . ."

"Grissom," I said.

"Yeah, him. When he heard you were safe and what you'd done, he thought it was a great piece of PR for Weather One. Just imagine," Roddy arced his hands above our heads, cinematically, a banner headline, "lost correspondent—"

"—Now I'm a correspondent?"

Roddy continued, "Weather One's lost correspondent is a hero."

"Oh, geez." I had to laugh. I was no hero, just a woman who'd learned to trust my intuition, my strength, in nature.

"They'll be a shitload of reporters waiting for you at JFK."

The thought of a crowd of reporters scared me. I said, "Why me? I don't know how I did it." *No, I thought, you'll deal with it.* But then I didn't really know what awaited me.

Deep in their roots,
All flowers keep their light.
—Theodore Roethke

About Author
PG LENGSFELDER

As with any journey, life has offered me more twists and turns than I could have imagined. At seven, sure I was destined to be a fireman or a forest ranger, my parents gave me a toy printing press. I thought, *I'll put out a neighborhood newspaper.* With a circulation of ten—at five cents a copy—I was hooked: I had readers. I've been writing ever since.

I began as a copywriter in a major New York advertising agency and co-authored the best-selling nonfiction book *FILTHY RICH* (Ten Speed Press). My first two novels *BEAUTIFUL TO THE BONE* and *OUR SONG, MEMENTO MORI* (Woodsmoke Publishing) met with critical acclaim, which told me I was on the right path. And, really, writing is my drug of choice.

I've written songs, I've written for numerous publications, my stories have been heard on National Public Radio and seen on CNN, Discovery Channel, and other national television. I've written and produced documentaries on AIDS, the environment, the NFL's Oakland Raiders, and Bud Nathan's bathroom remodel (no kidding).

Among my writing awards are a regional TV Emmy (plus four nominations), the 2021 Best Thriller Book Finalist award (BestThrillers.com), Frontier Tales Reader's Choice Short Story Award.

I'm a member of the Mystery Writers of America and Rocky Mountain Fiction Writers. I believe that there are many things that can't be seen, but that are real. When I can get away from my keyboard, there's nothing better than being in nature.

ACKNOWLEDGEMENTS

So much of this book is factual, and without the help of the following people I'd have been over my head. The knowledge and assistance of award-winning on-air meteorologist, **Erin Yost** (KPAX-TV, Missoula, MT) was incalculable. **Dr. Kay Holekamp**, Behavioral Ecologist at the Michigan State University Department of Integrated Biology, has a lot more first-hand experience with hyenas than I do, and offered solid information I couldn't have found anywhere else. Likewise, my friend **Deb Bloomfield** has had personal experience with ball lightning, twice! My nephew, **John Wilson**, originally from South Africa, offered valuable insights, and **Ms. Ikponwosa "I.K." Ero,** Director, Human Rights Advocacy at Under the Same Sun (a non-profit organization) ensured that my information about albinism and the Tanzanian albinism community was accurate. Finally, and as usual, I am indebted to my editor, **Peter Gelfan**, who kept me from tripping on my words. To all these folks, I am profoundly grateful for their time and expertise.

HOW YOU CAN HELP

If you found the issues in this book as disturbing as I, there are ways you can help. Here are just a few organizations to whom you can go for more information and to donate:

UNDER THE SAME SUN
https://www.underthesamesun.com/

MAASI WILDERNESS CONSERVATION TRUST
http://maasaiwilderness.org/maasai/

MAASI ASSOCIATION
http://www.maasai-association.org/ceremonies

NGORONGORO DISTRICT COUNCIL
https://udahiliportal.com/nafasi-za-kazi-ngorongoro/

Lightning Source UK Ltd.
Milton Keynes UK
UKHW010707090223
416681UK00007B/1639